Look and See Me

Opposites Attract: Book 1

Look and See Me... 1

Acknowledgements.. 2

Chapter 1 Green Eyes 3

Chapter 2 The Boldin's.. 13

Chapter 3 The Boys 31

Chapter 4 Transition 62

Chapter 5 Squad.. 76

Chapter 6 Unnecessary Stress... 103

Chapter 7 The Block! 127

Chapter 8 First Date.. 153

Chapter 9 Kickback 206

Chapter 10 Out of the Loop.. 234

Chapter 11 Feeling You... 284

Chapter 12 Protect 327

Chapter 13 It's Not You 345

Chapter 14 Gangsta' Party.. 356

Chapter 15 Weight... 380

Chapter 16 Anxiety... 411

Chapter 17 Be Mine... 455

Chapter 18 Lady Scrap 478

Chapter 19 This Shit Ain't Over! 499

Acknowledgements

To my twins, Imir and Imani. You two are my motivations. The day that you two were born, mommy's life changed for the better. Always remember to complete the task. Even if your passion changes, complete the task and move forward. I love you two with all my heart! You will always be #MyForeverLoves

To my mother, Tottie Wilson. You said, "Just do it!" So, I did it! Thank you for being my listening ear and my shoulder to lean on when I needed it the most. You have been "Mother of the Year," every year! Thank you for loving me unconditionally and being right there by my side with all the stages that I have been through in my life. Like I always say, "In my eyes, you are a true goddess!" And I cannot wait to give you everything that you dream of to show you how blessed and grateful that I am to have you as my mother. I love you!

To my auntie, Treshawn Wade... (Yes, you made it to my dedications) You believed in me the most. This passion started off as just a hobby and my therapy. I just wanted to step into my own world for a moment while I dealt with life. I'll never forget when I finally let you read my book and you called me back screaming! All I can hear right now is, "Tete, you're an author! You're a real author!" Just from the tone in your voice, I could see the smile on your face and ever since then you have been going "hard in the paint" for me!

2

You have truly left a mark in my heart for your love and support! Thank you!

To the rest of my family and friends, I love you so much and I thank you for all the love and support that you have shown me, and please know that there are more books and acknowledgements to come. A lot of you have been heavy on my mind and my heart! I will be shouting out a lot of you soon. Right now, just step into my world and grow with me on this journey! I love you all!

Chapter 1 Green Eyes

Scrap

I sat on the edge of the hill in Ladera Heights looking down on the bright city of Los Angeles, California.

My big homie, Ice, lived in this neighborhood, and anytime I just needed to get my mind right, this is where I came. Shit, this was the only place that I felt at peace!

I would take one of my brothers' cars and drive thirty minutes from the LBC just to sit on this hill and spend hours looking down at the busy city, thinking about my life and the shit that I had been through.

I start school tomorrow at Long Beach Jordan High

School.

I had been on *lock* for two whole years. I spent a year and a half in *juvie,* and then got put on house arrest for the remainder of my time.

My freshman year at Woodrow Wilson High School, I got caught up with a bag of *coke* in my locker. I knew it was a wrap when I saw the K9s. I was fucked.

While I was on house arrest, my older brothers cashed out so that I could be homeschooled and didn't have to be held back again.

Because of our situation and not having anywhere to live when I was younger, I was already held back one year, and they didn't want that shit to happen again.

When I was locked up in "juvie," the niggas that didn't know me on the streets thought I was just a little *pretty boy*.

They had the game fucked up. All they could see was this mixed breed with green eyes and long hair that I kept pulled back in a ponytail. I didn't like braids, and I honestly didn't want to cut my shit.

I was getting into fights every day. Once the word got out on who I was, and who my brothers were, niggas started calming the fuck down and staying out of my way.

At first, I didn't get why my brothers wanted me homeschooled. These niggas were so determined to make me finish school, but I just wanted to *trap*. That was all that I knew. That was all that *we* knew!

I felt like they just wanted it to be different for *me*. They've been in and out of jail since they were kids. They made sure that I learned from their mistakes, so I was slick with my every move. It was the first time that I ever got caught with anything.

But that one slip-up wasn't stopping shit! I was already a part of this game. We all had to be a part of this life, or none of us would have survived on the streets. We needed protection, because our parents couldn't give it to us.

This was the type of shit that was on my mind all the time, how my brothers and I got into the game and how it was all that we lived by since my dad left.

I was five years old when he left. I'm seventeen now and I'm doing more shit than your average teenager.

My brothers and I are known on the streets of Long Beach—them Gaither boys—the family that's gang affiliated, and doing bigger things than your average dope boys.

I'm from the set known as Shottas, and I'm *crippin'* proudly.

When we were out there in the streets and didn't have a place to lay our heads, our big homies stepped up.

My brothers tried not to expose me to the shit that they were doin', but because I was always around, they couldn't keep it from me either. By the time that I turned nine, I already knew everything that I needed to know about the *game* from just observing. It had become a part of my life.

At that age, I learned how to hold a gun, how to put the safety on and load that bitch up.

The only reason why they taught me was because for years they had me stay home with my mom and my twin brothers while they were runnin' the streets.

My mom was always drunk, so I had to stay home with them so that, if anything happened, I could call my brothers and, if they couldn't get to us right away, then I already knew how to *merk* the first ma'fucka that walked through those doors.

I watched my brothers and my big homies as they ran the blocks, bustin' *knocks* (drug addicts) and throwing bitches on the *blade*, seeing niggas on the wrong side, the *ops,* and having shootouts in broad daylight.

When I finally got *put on*, I was eleven. I was a natural at trappin', and all I did was observe.

I came up on my first *hoe bitch* when I turned fourteen. She was a naïve ass little bitch. She kept mistaking me for a pretty boy, too, and then she found out how much of a *gangsta* I really was.

Mia . . . I fucked with Mia hard because she was willing to do anything for my ass.

When we first started rockin', she wasn't as irritating as she was now, but this "game" will change you.

The money, the tricks . . . the obsession . . .

The more that she rocked with the team, she started thinkin' that she ran shit, getting beside herself. She had a personality filled with envy.

She didn't like bitches getting too close to me, even the ones that she would put on herself. She started spazzing out over the smallest shit, and I felt like I was checking the bitch every five seconds just to keep her in her place.

If anyone knew me though, they knew that I didn't give a fuck about a bitch unless it was about my money. So, all the extra shit that she was doing to get my attention didn't mean shit to me.

She was still just another bitch, and I was still "*that nigga*" so I could easily pull another young hoe on my own.

In this generation, it wasn't hard to find a little "thot" that was willing to sell that pussy.

Shit, in this year, 2018, bitches treat that shit like it was a fashion statement. All of them hoes are for the streets! You see them on social media showing the world what they got and how they got it. No shame, no respect for themselves, nor their bodies. So, I treated them the same way that they treated themselves.

I tried to keep my bitches discreet, but once again, jealousy is a true bitch, and with jealousy comes more problems.

I couldn't stand an insecure-ass bitch that couldn't keep their feelings and emotions to their selves, especially when it was only supposed to be business . . .

It was a cold, misty night. Huey and his two escorts were leaving the bar, laughing and joking, while the two women held on to each of his arms, leaning into him. He said his farewells to the security guard at the front entrance as all three of them walked to his car.

He opened the passenger front and back door for the ladies as they both stepped in, and they showed an impressed expression on their face.

"Look at you, being a gentlemen and shit!" The escort with a short blonde wig and red-laced dress said as she stepped into the front passenger seat.

9

She was a smooth cocoa brown with these long, extended eyelashes and rusted burgundy color lipstick painted on her lips.

"Right!" the second one said, following along.

The second escort wore a baby-blue leather skirt with a white crop top, and she had jet black straight hair that you can tell was a wig as well, a lace front that was glued on to her scalp with her false baby hairs swirling and slicked down.

Her complexion was much darker than the first escorts, and you could see the beauty underneath all the makeup batted on her face used to disguise her identity.

"Well, you know I try!" Huey said, smiling as he placed his hand on his chest.

Huey was in his mid-forties. He dressed like your average sugar daddy with the collared shirt buttoned halfway down, and his permed hair slicked back. It was obvious that he was trying to grow his beard out because of his rugged sideburns that were still struggling to connect and all you could see were the little beads of hair around his cheeks.

He closed the doors for them and walked around to the

driver's side of his car. He opened the door, got in and pulled

his phone out.

As his phone automatically connected to the Bluetooth

to his car, he played, "I Wanna Sex You Up" by Color Me

Badd.

The escorts' eyes widened in excitement, and they

danced in their seats while they sang along to the song. Huey

pulled out of the parking space and drove off.

They continued to dance to the beat while the bass

vibrated the empty streets of Long Beach. They drove down

Artesia Way, at three o'clock in the morning, and came to a red

light. They continued to sing and laugh in their drunken state

waiting for the red light to turn green and be on their way.

There was then a blue and white Falcon automatic

sport bike with blue LED lights shining inside of the wheel that

pulled up in the lane beside them.

You could hear the loud roar of the motorcycle, but

Huey and the escorts paid no attention as they continued to

dance and sing their hearts out to the next song that played.

11

The guy on the bike wore a white and blue Scorpion Exo Air motorcycle helmet with a white and black "Pro Mesh motorcycle jacket.

As Huey finally noticed the guy on the bike, he looked up with this smile turning into a grimace as he observed the man next to him. Because he had his helmet on, Huey could not make out who the man was.

The man pulled his arm up as Huey was now staring at the barrel of a 9mm (about 0.35 in) Uzi Pro submachine pistol.

His eyes widened, and before he could react, the man squeezed the trigger as he let out all twenty rounds, spraying Huey's vehicle up with nonstop bullets piercing through the side of the doors and the windows.

Once the clip was empty, the man on the motorcycle raced off as the light turned green, leaving Huey and the two escorts there, lifeless with bullets piercing all through the car and their bodies. Blood painted the windows, the steering wheel and the seats . . .

Chapter 2 The Boldin's

Janeeva

"Janeeva, get out the shower!"

I placed my head under the spigot, enjoying the feel of the hot drops hitting my head as I wet my long thick hair.

"Janeeva, get out of the shower! You gon' make us late for school!"

That's my brother, Trevor. He gets on my last nerve, but I love him to death.

My name is Janeeva, and today is my first day as a junior. I'm not particularly excited about it. I'll be more excited when I finally graduate andleave behind all the obnoxious-ass high school kids I'm stuck with for one more year.

I'm not much of a *people person,* and I'm honestly not that popular.

I'm the type of kid who likes to keep to herself and is very anti-social. I freeze up like a dumbass whenever I realize that someone is speaking to me outside of class discussions or anything similar. I only have one best friend that I talk to, and that's about it.

I'm not big on keeping up with the latest trends, so my everyday outfits usually consist of a t-shirt, loose jeans, and a pair of sneakers. I prefer to keep things simple, and because my hair is so thick, and I hate dealing with it, I usually throw it up into a messy bun and be on my way.

Although my best friend is bothered by my simple style, I'm comfortable with it. I feel too anxious when I think someone is staring at me too hard, and I hate attention.

Every now and then, I experience anxiety attacks, but fortunately, it's been a while since my last one.

On a positive note, I'm highly intelligent, your typical "4.0" student! However, I'm not the only prodigy in my family.

Trevor banged his heavy hand on the door once again. I rolled my eyes in irritation and sighed. I wrapped the towel around me and opened the door.

There I was, standing directly in front of him with this huge smile on my face.

"The bathroom is all yours!" I said, taunting him.

I had my own bathroom. Well, we all did, but they were being renovated so we had to use the guest bathroom. I promise I hated it, but I couldn't do much about it.

As I walked to my room, Trevor stood in front of the door glaring at me.

He took all that time glaring and got stopped in the moment by my little sister, Maimi, who ran into the bathroom before he could even step in.

She quickly closed the door behind her. I guffawed at how slick she was about it. He grabbed the doorknob so that she couldn't lock it, but it was too late. It was already locked! "Maimi! I'm gon' beat yo little ass! Get out the

bathroom!" he yelled.

"You have to wait! I have to boo-boo!" she yelled back.

Trevor went and stood on top of the stairs and yelled out my mother's name.

"Mama, come get yo daughter!"

My mother stuck her head out of her bedroom door and yelled out, "Janeeva La'shae Boldin, get out of the shower now!"

I laughed. It's always me! "I'm not in the shower! That's Maimi doing all my dirty work!" I yelled back with a smile on my face.

I was so proud of my sister!

Trevor had finally gotten into the bathroom, having to smell Maimi's stinky ass. I laughed harder hearing him curse.

"Shit, Maimi! What did you *eat*?"

He's a year and a couple of months older than me. He was a senior this year. Most would call him a true prodigy as well.

However, he is still the complete opposite of me. He's not only a high achiever in every sport imaginable but also immensely popular. Girls adore him, and most boys can't stand him. He's also the captain and quarterback of the varsity football team. He sounds annoying already, right?

I must admit that he is a very handsome young man. These thirsty-ass females just can't resist his tall and masculine

16

frame, fair brown skin, and light-brown eyes. He's what most would consider a "pretty boy" with his natural silky curls, which he keeps trimmed and lined-up.

He has always had his own swag, from going to the barber every two weeks to rocking the latest trends. He's one of those guys.

And once again, these thirsty-ass females can't get enough of him! They'll sit on the sideline and blow kisses to him like elephants sucking on peanuts. In my opinion, he gets too much credit, but I'm not going to act like a hater.

Despite our differences, he and I have a close relationship. He often tries to get me to come out of my shell and be more social. He thinks that I would enjoy high school more if I were to make new friends aside from the "one" that I already have.

I was okay with my one friend though and the truth is, I'm just not interested in all of that. I'm content with my simple life.

I walked downstairs into the kitchen.

When I walked in, Maimi was at the table eating a bowl of Trix cereal. "Hi, Jay!" she said, with cereal stuffed in her mouth, blowing up her cheeks. I sat down at the table and poured some Lucky Charms into my bowl.

"Hey, Maimi," I responded.

I looked over at my dad while he leaned against the kitchen counter and read his newspaper.

My dad was a laidback type of man. He worked a lot, so we barely saw him, but when he was around, he was always chill.

When he did get a day off, he would try to spend some time with us. I was normally the one who ended up bonding with him, though.

Trevor was always on the move, and Maimi was too much of a busy body for my dad.

Most of his days off consisted of me and him watching our favorite shows and movies all day. I enjoyed it. I was the *true* daddy's girl in the pack, so I found any reason to spend some time with him. I didn't have shit else to do anyway.

As much as he works, it surprised me that he has not been in pain lately.

He got into a bad motorcycle accident when Trevor and I were little and he was supposed to be paralyzed, but as he always says, "By the grace of God, he allowed me to walk and continue my normal life."

It took a good year of physical therapy, but he did it. He still limps sometimes when he walks and needs a good rest, but aside from that, he's perfectly fine. He worked hard and did all the physical therapy he was supposed to do to get back to his normal self.

I remember seeing him start off in a wheelchair for a couple of months, and then he went to a cane, and then eventually he didn't need either one of them at all.

Those were tough times, especially for my mom trying to take care of us and him. But she's always been a soldier, so it didn't break her.

My mom walked into the kitchen with her nursing uniform and supplies. She was rushing. She grabbed her keys off the counter, kissed my dad that was leaning against the counter reading his newspaper, walked over to me and kissed me on my forehead. "Enjoy your day at school, baby."

"I will," I responded.

My mom walked to the staircase, stood on the first step and yelled up to Trevor. "Trevor, if I get a call from the school telling me that you were late, boy we gon' have some problems!"

"It's the first day of school! Everybody late on the first day of school, Mama!" he yelled back down.

As she grabbed Maimi's backpack and put it on her back, she yelled back up to him, sending her simple but most powerful threat, *"Try me!"* and started walking toward the door.

After my mom left, Trevor came running down the stairs. I wasn't shocked to see him in his Oteil denim fitted jeans with his white and blue collard West Louis brand designer polo shirt on, always *flyy*.

I knew that I was staring at *Mr. Cool Guy* way too hard because he looked up, cut his eyes at me and said under his breath, "Boo, nigga!" I glared at him and rolled my eyes.

20

I looked down at my phone, and my best friend, Lia, was texting me. She was trying to figure out what time I was going to be at school. As I looked up to ask Trevor what time we were leaving, he said it. "You ready?" he asked as he started walking toward the door. I nodded my head and got up. We headed out the door and said bye to my dad.

We live only four blocks away from the school, but Trevor gets frustrated looking for a parking spot, so we choose to walk instead of using his car.

As we walked through the parking lot to the front entrance of the school, one of the students was coming in on a blue and white motorcycle with his music playing.

His music was so loud that it filled the whole parking lot, and some of the students danced around us as "I Can't Lose" by Iamsu played.

You could obviously tell that the student was a male, but because he had his blue and white helmet on, I couldn't see his face to see if I knew him. I didn't know any of Trevor's friends who drove a motorcycle, so I took it that I didn't. I looked at my brother because he was the only one not dancing.

He cut his eyes at the student on the motorcycle and pressed his lips together.

"C'mon," he said as he kept walking to the front entrance of the school.

"You know that guy?" I asked. He sighed.

"Yeah," he responded.

As we walked up to the school, I wasn't surprised to see all the people crowded around the front entrance when we got there. There were so many people around me that I tried my hardest to stay close to Trevor.

However, once we got through the metal detectors, he was already parting from me as he was pulled away by some of his teammates and friends. I sighed as I looked around, searching for my best friend Lia.

I walked quietly through the halls as all the students around me were yelling and screaming and reuniting with their friends from last year. As I looked around for her, she was still nowhere in sight. I was standing around a crowd of people that I knew by faces but never associated with. There were a couple of *fresh* faces too. Some were transfer students from other schools, and most were freshmen just getting out of junior high.

As I searched for her, I heard Trevor's name being called, and I was relieved, not by the familiar voice, but knowing that he was somewhere close. When I followed the voice, I spotted him and his girlfriend, Talawny.

I turned around to see her approaching him and wrapping her arms around his neck. Among the many females that mess around with him and are on my dislike list, Talawny belongs in the "hate" category, which is a fucked-up situation given that she is his "main."

They've been dating for at least three months, and Talawny is a little Latina chick who is also stunningly beautiful but sadly, the hoe of the century. It's baffling how someone could be so gorgeous and let it all go to waste.

She has the shape of a plus-size model, with a very thick chest, hips that spread out, and a small, tight waist. Her naturally dark, curly brown hair is dyed a flaming hot red with blond streaks in the front. The bitch looked like Ariel from the Little Mermaids.

Before dating my brother, she was with a different guy at school every other week, and she had a reputation for being promiscuous. However, that's not why I disliked her so much.

The beginning of my first year, she caught herself trying to tease the wrong bitch, and even though I can hold my own, my best friend stepped in to let her know that I wasn't the one.

"So, are you like . . . gay? You dress like a lil boy," Talawny said as I sat at the lunch table, minding my business. I cut my eyes at her and didn't say anything at all.

"You better be careful. She may just try to fuck you, looking too hard," one of her friends said, following along behind her. They both laughed.

"Come on now, Talawny . . . even if she were gay, you and I both know that she wouldn't want that worn out pussy of yours. I mean, half of the student body has already run through that shit! What she gon' do with it?" my best friend retorted as she stood from the table, placing her hand on her hip with a smirk on her face.

I smiled as I remained quiet, and the students that were in hearing-distance laughed at her comeback.

Since that incident, they have been talking shit to each other every other day. We all knew that her scary ass couldn't fight, so she knows when to humble herself when the arguments and threats started getting a little too heated for her. She's all *bark and no bite.*

I didn't get what my brother saw in her aside from the fact that she was beautiful. I felt like she was only with him because she knew how he was getting the extra money from the things he did on the streets.

Even though he was a multi-athlete and kept a grade point average above a "3.0", he had this whole other life that I only knew bits and parts of. It wasn't until I had to help him that I even discovered that he did these other things.

I don't know much about what he does because he barely lets me in when it comes to it, but one thing that I do know is that he keeps a gun with him most of the time, and the only reason why I know that is because I had to hold it for him a couple of times in the middle of getting pulled over by the cops.

Other than that, I don't know anything about his other life, and I promised that I would never say anything to our parents about it. It's the one thing that he just doesn't share with me. I knew that's how he was getting the extra money though.

Talawny massaged her tongue with his as he gripped on to her ass. *Ewe*. When they finally stopped, my brother smiled at her. He was as nasty as her.

I stared at them for a moment as I went into deep thought. I never even kissed a boy before. It seemed like everyone that went to this school was already having sex, and I was probably the only virgin left. Well, that's what it felt like.

"Janeeva!" I smiled hard, hearing the familiar voice. I turned around to see my best friend running toward me. Lia Shante' Moore! She has been my best friend ever since private school in kindergarten at Children R Us in East Compton. It was crazy how we met though.

I had a bad bladder problem, so of course there were a lot of accidents, and one day, three of the boys in my class just kept messing with me, so Lia stepped in and defended me. We didn't know each other well enough for her to be fighting for me, but she did. Even though we were both sent home that day, we have been inseparable ever since.

"Man! I've been looking all over this damn school for you!" she said, relieved.

"I've been looking for you too!"

"Damn, Lia," Rashad said, coming behind her as he admired her from her feet on up.

Rashad was one of our old classmates from last year. He rubbed his finger down Lia's arm, and Lia smacked his hand away from her. "Don't touch me!" she retorted.

"My bad. I just wanted to let you know that I'm happy to see yo sexy ass again."

"Do you have anywhere else to be besides right here fuckin' with me?" she said, rolling her eyes.

"Damn." He flinched. "I see you still a *bitch*," he spat, walking away.

Lia didn't flinch at the word. I think she was used to being called a bitch by now. I shrugged as she looked at me.

"Dumbass boy . . ." she said in disgust.

"I thought you liked Rashad?" I asked.
"Not like that!" I shrugged again.

Lia confuses me sometimes. She was gorgeous. She was also immensely popular.

Like Trevor, she kept up with the latest trends. Her thick-ass shoulder-length hair stayed *slayed* in unique styles every other week, and boys loved her little coke-bottle shape with her smooth cocoa-butter skin and mahogany-brown almond eyes, and she was into all the cosmetics and beauty tips that went along with it.

She knows that she's *that bitch* even though she is mean as hell!

When it came to boys, she barely gave them the time of day. She dawgs every one of them that comes her way.

I do know that she has this fascination with older boys, like seniors or the ones that are just getting out of high school, but other than that, her ass will dawg you trying to shoot your shot!

"Did you get your schedule?" she asked.

"Yeah, but I don't like my electives."

Lia held her hand out. "Let me see it."

I pulled my neatly folded schedule out of my pocket, and she pulled out her crumpled-up schedule from her purse. She unscrambled her paper and put mine and hers together. She went over both, seeing what classes we had together.

"You only have two classes with me," she said, disappointed. "Well, I'm TA in the office first period. Maybe I can try to convince them to change your schedule." I grabbed my paper out of her hands.

"No. I'm cool. I like my schedule. It has everything I wanted to do aside from drama."

"*Drama*? That's the best class!" Lia blurted out.

"Yeah, I know. Drama is supposed to be fun!" I said sarcastically, rolling my eyes. "Well, I don't get up in front of a whole bunch of people and act. I'm not the type to embarrass myself."

"Don't worry, sis. You'll be just fine." I smiled at her because she always tried to make me feel better when I was not so sure about something.

"I have to get to class," I said, folding my schedule up and putting it in my pocket.

"Okay, see you at lunch." I hugged her, and we went our separate ways.

Chapter 3 The Boys

Janeeva

I walked into my first class, which was drama. When I walked in, I knew that I would be the first one there because the bell hadn't even rung yet. I usually sat in the front, but the chairs were put out to form a circle. The front was the middle. My teacher looked at me and smiled.

"Hi, how are you? Come in and have a seat. We will begin when everyone else gets in." I smiled at her as she turned around to write something on the board, and I walked to the seat all the way across the room.

As I walked to my seat, I felt my binder slipping out of my hand because I was trying to hold all three of my notebooks plus my jacket at once. I tried to hurry before I lost my grip on everything, but I was too late.

It all slipped from under my arms and fell to the ground. I cursed under my breath. I took my backpack off my shoulder so I could pick up my binder and my notebook. As people walked in and they saw me picking my stuff up, no one offered to help. *Fuckers* . . . I cursed in my head.

As I tried to get back up and I placed the strap to my backpack on my shoulders, it slid right back off, down my arm, bringing everything I had in my hand back down to the ground once again.

As people walked past me, they laughed. *This cannot be happening to me!* I got on my knees and piled my stuff on top of each other one by one on the floor.

Then I saw two hands reach down for my binder. I looked up, and when I caught his eyes, I froze. I was literally stuck in my place. I didn't know what to say or how to react. The first thing that caught my attention was his eyes. They were so beautiful . . . They were green. His complexion was an almond brown, and his hair was pulled back into a ponytail, puffed out, with a fresh line-up. Even in the ponytail, his hair dropped past his shoulders.

He had the custom bottom diamond, white-gold grill in his mouth with fangs on it. The grill was blinging as he held his mouth open slightly. I was curious about how many carats he had. I knew a little about diamonds because of my uncle. I was thinking 18k? Maybe 24k? Maybe it was a gift. The grill had to be expensive.

I didn't realize that I was so stuck until his eyes scrunched up from the smile that he had surfaced and the bottom grill in his mouth blinged even more. I snapped out of it and blinked. He spoke in this sweet but deep, raspy, voice.

"Ma' bad. I was just tryin' to help," he said, picking my binder up off the floor. I stood as he did but could not stop staring at him. I was so mesmerized by his eyes.

After a moment, I studied the rest of his body and noticed the blue and white motorcycle jacket he had on. He was the student in the parking lot.

I then brought my eyes on the white and blue football jersey under the jacket that read, "Panthers." It was the exact same jersey that my brother had; so, he played on the varsity team as well. He also had on the white and royal blue with black around the soles Air Jordan 13 Hyper Royal shoes on his feet that went good with his jersey.

"Hey, Daddy . . ." a soft voice said behind him. He looked back and smiled hard when he saw the high-yellow girl standing there. *Daddy?* I questioned myself.

I examined the girl from her head down to her feet as well. She was gorgeous and, from what it looked like, grown! She had long black glossy hair. I assumed that she had a couple of extensions in her hair, but it blended so good with her own that I knew my best friend would want to know where she got it from!

She had these pretty almond eyes, and her eyelashes were amazingly long, with her blue eyeshadow that stood out perfectly. Her lip gloss was popping too, making her lips look thick and luscious. Shit, I was feeling like a lesbian, but that wasn't all!

Her body was banging! She had this small tight-ass waist with these ball-park hips! Her legs looked like she ran track, and I was sure you could sit a cup of water on her ass without it tipping over. Her breasts sat up perfectly in her tight white blouse that hugged her small waist, and her royal blue leggings were so skin-tight that you could see every detail of her perfectly toned hips, thighs and legs. She was curved in all the right places, and what made her body look even better were the 6" suede black stilettos that she was rocking! I honestly didn't get the stilettos though! Who the hell would wear high-heel shoes to fucking school?

"What's good, Ma?" he greeted, placing his hand on her hip and appraising her as I did.

"What happened yesterday? I was calling you all day!" she asked. I was shocked by her accent. I didn't know why I was so shocked. She looked like a little mixed breed. She had to be Puerto Rican or somewhere in that category. Dominican, maybe? Her accent was deep, and then I really started thinking that I was gay as hell because it was sexy too!

Before the boy answered her, he looked at me. I looked back at him and was stuck again as the blinged-out bottom diamond grill shined in his mouth, bringing out his pretty-ass green eyes even more.

"You want yo binder?" he asked, becoming impatient with my nosy ass.

Once his attention was back on me, I realized how nosy I was truly being. I looked down, embarrassed that I was still standing there, and I snatched my binder out of his hands and turned away. I was so ashamed. I heard the girl giggling behind me.

"You're welcome!" he said, sarcastically.

Embarrassing! I didn't even say thank you, but I couldn't find the nerve to turn back around and say it.

I hurried to my seat and sat there, still embarrassed. I threw my head down in shame, but I looked back up when I heard the teacher speak.

She introduced herself, but as she walked around the middle of the circle looking at her students and passed the boy with the green eyes, my attention was back on him. All I really heard her say was that her name was Mrs. Joyce.

I watched him and the high-yellow girl from across the room. It looked like they were in a deep conversation and did not want anyone else to hear them. I kept seeing his eyes flicker back and forth to make sure that no one else was listening. He would show a slight grin every now and then as he spoke to her, but the conversation still looked serious. He was slouched down in his chair, and she sat straight up with her legs crossed over the other.

The whole period, I watched them, and I felt like I was envying the girl sitting next to the gorgeous boy with the beautiful green eyes. It was weird. I fantasized about that girl being me that he was touching and talking to. I didn't snap out of it until she snapped her head up at Mrs. Joyce.

"Here!" she responded as Mrs. Joyce read off her attendance sheet.

"Gah . . . leni . . . Uh?" Mrs. Joyce repeated, trying to make sure that she was pronouncing her name right.

"*Hah . . . l*eni. Uh . . . the G is silent," the girl corrected. "Friends call me Lovely," she finished with that deep accent that she had.

"Lovely?" Mrs. Joyce nodded her head in admiration. "I like that! And what grade are you in?" she asked.

"I'm a junior," Lovely responded.

There were sophomores and juniors in this class, and some were even freshmen. It was crazy how you could tell the freshmen from the sophomores and juniors.

All they saw was a whole new world and a whole new environment with kids that were older than them. Lia and her friends were running all over this school the first year here, excited to finally be in high school.

"Well, nice to meet you, Lovely. Do you think that your pants are appropriate for school?" Mrs. Joyce asked. Well, this conversation took a turn. I was wondering the same thing though.

"There's no skin showing," she retorted, displaying the irritation all in her tone. I could tell that Lovely thought this conversation was too long for her liking.

"Well, if you don't mind, I would appreciate seeing you in something a little more appropriate tomorrow, something that won't have these young men breaking their necks to see?" she asked. Lovely smiled.

"Yes, ma'am!" she responded.

"Thank you!" Mrs. Joyce responded back.

I must have missed the teacher calling the boy's name when I was daydreaming, because I never heard him answer her. When the bell rang, he and the girl got up from their seats and walked out the door.

You would think that she was his girlfriend, but even with them walking next to each other, there was no type of intimacy. I was so confused about where they stood with each other. I followed them down the hallway, not realizing exactly what I was doing. They stopped and talked for another moment after he slipped her a piece of paper.

Once he slipped the piece of paper to her, she reached up, whispered something in his ear and slipped him a small stack of money that was rolled up in a rubber band.

My eyes lit up! She did it so smoothly that only a nosyass person that was watching them like a hawk would notice. She walked away as he turned around and walked right into the bathroom. I snapped out of it once they were both out of my sight.

I was embarrassed once again when I realized what my nosy ass was doing. *What the fuck is wrong with me?*

39

I turned around quickly, ducking my head, hoping that no one was watching me. When I realized that I was going the wrong way to my class, I had to turn back around to go the right way.

My next class was chemistry. I got there right before the bell rang.

I walked in, but I wasn't the first person like I was usually. Everyone else was already seated in their seats.

I took a seat in the front of the class, took all my stuff out and set it neatly out on my desk as I waited quietly for the teacher's instructions.

As I waited, the boy with the green eyes walked in. He was starting to become a distraction to my fucking learning environment. My teacher walked into the room and spoke. I was trying my hardest to pay attention through the whole damn hour.

Lunch came around, and I sat at a table with Lia as we talked. She was telling me about how much fun she was having with her old and new group of friends. While she talked, I stared across the room at the boy with the green eyes.

"Jay are you listening to me?" she asked. I could hear the frustration in her voice. I turned to her, confused.

"What?" I asked.

"What's wrong with you? You just died on me for a second." I looked back at the boy with the green eyes, and right when I did, Lovely walked into their group and everyone greeted her.

She took her spot next to him and posted with everyone else, while he talked to the boy that was standing on the other side of him. I sighed and then looked at Lia. I still had to know his name and his status with the girl if Lia knew anything.

"Lia, who's that boy over there?" I asked, still staring at him. She followed my gaze but didn't know who I was looking at.

"Which one?" she asked, looking between the boy with the green eyes and the chunky one.

"The one with the pretty eyes . . ." I responded. Lia looked at me skeptically and then smiled.

"His name is Scrap."

"Scrap?" I asked.

"Yeah, it's his street name. I've seen him around outside of school a couple of times. They said that he went to Wilson, and something happened, so now he's here."

"Well, it looks like he didn't have a tough time making friends his first day at a new school," I responded.

"Actually, most of them in that group have known him for years. Two of them are his best friends."

Well, she gave me more information than I needed, but I was grateful for it. I have never seen the chunky boy either and he didn't look like a freshman.

"What's his real name?" I asked.

"Brian Gaither! The one that all girls favor!" she crooned. "They say he's the finest junior at this school . . ." She finished that part as if she doubted it. I believed what everyone else was saying. I tried to keep my *cool* so that she wouldn't see my excitement.

"He *is* kind of cute," I said, agreeing with her sources. She rolled her eyes.

"Whatever you say Jay. It's what's on the inside that counts, not how fine people think his ass is," she said, rolling her eyes and then glaring at him.

"I take it that you don't like him too much?" I asked.

She sucked her teeth in irritation. I could tell that she was thinking about something that happened earlier.

"He asked me to write him a pass for class, and when I told him that I couldn't just write him a pass unless he had a note, he got an attitude with me, and some other bitch wrote it up for him," she said disgusted. "What was even more pathetic is that he put on this little charm, and she was practically drooling over him."

Listening to Lia was hilarious. Her face expression, her hand gestures, everything about her was just hilarious.

"That's why I can't stand these damn pretty boys. They believe that every bitch is supposed to praise them, especially the fucking mixed breeds." I smiled, trying not to laugh.

"What is he mixed with anyway?" I asked.

"Black . . . and some type of French or Spanish or some shit like that. I don't remember," she said, shaking her head, confused on which one. "I think the French creole. My girl Skittles was telling me some shit. I thought creole was a fucking language, but I guess it's more than that," she finished. I rolled my eyes from her ignorance.

"Yeah, you may want to do your research on creole ancestry. It'll be a good history project," I said. She laughed.

"I'll leave that up to you because I really don't care. Anyways, the lil *fucker* thinks he's better than everyone else." I laughed and shook my head.

"Whatever you say, Lia, and his race has nothing to do with it."

"You know these girls love those mutts! Long hair, random-ass pretty eyes, and with the perfect almond skin complexion. That's just how shallow females these days are," she said, shrugging. "And boys go along with it. Besides, all he likes are those girls who dress like strippers," she finished.

I knew that she was referring the stripper part to Lovely. I giggled. "Then he must love you!" I joked. Lia did a fake laugh and gave me the finger.

44

"You're not funny." I laughed harder.

"So, who is the girl standing next to him?" I finally asked.

"Who? Lovely? I don't know that girl like that. One of my girls introduced us. She's quiet. She doesn't say much, but she's been clinging on to that nigga all day. I don't know who or what she is to him though. He doesn't reject her when she is all up under him, but he doesn't show any affection toward her either. So, I don't know what the fuck they got goin' on." I was so happy that I wasn't the only one who was lost.

I wanted to tell her about the stack of money she slid him earlier, but I was too zoned off to really care.

I sat there thinking, while Lia continued to talk. I looked at her because, as curious as I was, I wanted to know if every time I looked in the mirror if I saw the same thing that everyone else saw.

"Lia, am I pretty?" I asked.

She looked at me and said with her mouth full of food, "You're gorgeous!" She forcefully swallowed her food so that she could finish her sentence and looked at my outfit with a disgusted look. "You just dress like a lil boy . . . And I wish you would let me *slay* your hair just once so that I can show you how to rock some shit!"

"Oh! Now, you gon' get at me like Talawny ass did?" I asked, laughing.

"First of all, don't compare me to that bitch! It's all *love* over here!" she said, throwing her hands up. "And even though that bitch can fight me, she wasn't lying. Let's just say that you dress like a cute-ass stud," she joked. I laughed harder and slapped her on her shoulder for the friendly insult. She smiled and flipped her hair back.

"You kinda dress like Trevor in a way. But, of course, big bruh flyy as hell. You basic." I flinched at her bluntness. "T-shirt and some jeans. Your jeans aren't baggy, but with that ass that nobody knows about, you shouldn't have the extra space in them ma'fuckas." I rolled my eyes as I continued to listen to her. If I didn't already know her personality, she would have me fucked up.

"Well, since you claim you know so much about how to dress, then help me out!" I asked, getting right to the point. Lia almost choked on her fries when the words came out of my mouth.

"You're asking me?" she said, unsure if she heard me correctly. "The girl that you think is always too exposed to come and hook you up?"

I always loved the clothes that she wore but she loved showing a little too much skin for my liking.

I thought about whether I really wanted to go through with this change and after being in my thoughts for a long moment, I answered her question. "Yeah, I want to see what a change feels like." She looked at me for a good moment and then smiled.

"You know what I think, Jay?"

I rolled my eyes and took a deep breath, because I had a feeling about what she was going to say next. "What do you think, Lia?"

"I think you're trying to impress Scrap." I knew it was coming.

47

"Actually, Ms. Know-It-All, I'm doing this for myself. It's just to see what a change feels like," I lied. "It's a new school year. Why not?" I asked, shrugging. She stared at me for a long moment and then sighed, nodding her head.

"Okay. I'll be at your house at four. That will give you some time to do whatever you do. If you're not there, then I'm out!"

I was grinning so hard that I felt as if my teeth were going to fall out, not that I didn't know that she was going to say yes. I knew that she would, but I was so excited to see how this would turn out! I was ecstatic!

"Thank you, sis!" I crooned. I got up and wrapped my arms around her neck and hugged her tight.

Lia and I had the last two classes together, so we walked shoulder to shoulder through the hallway. As we walked through the hallways, she spotted some of her friends and walked into their group.

My heart dropped when I saw Scrap leaning against the locker with a couple of his friends as well, talking to them. I stood there silently behind her as she talked to them.

As she talked, I saw one of the boys across the hallway toss his football as the chunky boy that was with Scrap earlier tried to catch it. He stumbled right into the group, accidentally bumping Lia straight into the locker.

"Oh shit! My bad, Ma!" he said, trying to help her.

Lia pushed him off her. "What the fuck?" she yelled, checking her arm as she rubbed it.

"Damn! I said I was sorry!"

"Why are you throwing a damn football around in this small-ass hallway anyway?" she complained.

"Ooouh . . . Lil Attitude, he said that he was sorry," Scrap said as he stepped beside the chunky boy with a smirk on his face. "Yo Twinkie, I'on like how she gettin' at you, loc," he said, now taunting Lia with this sexy-ass smile and his bottom grill blinging.

I knew now that the chunky boy's name was Twinkie. All these weird-ass nicknames!

"I told her ass that I was sorry!" Twinkie said, shrugging as he smiled as well.

"Whatever," she responded, throwing her hands up to dismiss them.

She was pissed. To me it wasn't that serious, but Lia probably took it in a different way.

"What up, bruh!" I heard another masculine voice yell as he walked up to Scrap and Twinkie.

He jumped on them, and they both laughed. They started teaming up on the boy as Lia and I watched. When the boy finally gave up and told them to stop playing, they greeted him in a more proper way.

"Nigga, where the fuck you been all day?" Twinkie questioned, throwing up his hands. He shook his head.

"Shit, you know how it be at home, cuz. It was just a lot goin' on this mornin'."

"You good though, right?" Scrap asked in a more serious tone, looking at the boy with a concerned look. The boy gave him a half shrug and twisted his lips up.

"It is what it is," he responded.

Scrap sighed and shook his head. I could tell that he knew more about the story, but it was none of my business. I was just being the nosy person that I am.

As the boy came out of his deep thought and greeted everybody else in the group, his eyes flickered upon Lia. "Goddamn!" he said as he stepped closer to her.

He stared at her for a moment and then balled his fist up into his hand as he licked his lips, admiring her from her feet on up.

Lia crossed her arms over her torso as she watched him. I could tell that she was ready to give him the proper disrespectful ass *Lia Welcome*. I also realized that her attitude turned him on even more.

"So, do yo fine ass have a name?" he asked, licking his lips.

He was cute as hell and tall. He looked like he was at least 6'4", with this smooth dark-brown skin and brown almond eyes.

He had the two-strand twist with his sides shaved off and lined up. He wore the same varsity football jersey as

Trevor and Scrap. You could tell based off his actions and Lia's attitude that he wasn't afraid of rejection. I'm pretty sure that, deep down inside, that was turning her ass on, too, but she would never admit that.

Lia looked at him in disgust. She didn't even bother to answer his question. She just turned away. However, the boy wasn't giving up. I believe that he knew what "cold shoulder" meant, but from the looks of it, he didn't take cold shoulders too well.

"Why you look at me like that?" he asked, following her every move. "Like I'm gon' bite you? I was just trying to figure out what ch'yo name is, ma," he asked.

"That's the way you try to get a name?" she asked as she faced him again. "Staring up and down at a female like she a piece of meat?" she finished. He laughed.

"Okay, I apologize . . . But I honestly couldn't help myself." He shrugged with this sneaky-ass smirk on his face. "You a lil *baddie*," he finished.

She rolled her eyes and looked at me. "Let's go before we're late." We started walking off, and he grabbed her hand.

"Damn! No thank you! No nothin'? You just gon' give me the cold shoulder and walk off!" he said, still smiling.

"I wouldn't even trip off of her lil stuck-up ass, loc," Scrap said, looking at Lia from the side of his eye. I could tell that he wasn't feeling her.

"Stuck up?" she snapped, looking at Scrap. "Boy, please! I'm far from that!" she said, defending herself.

"Then what's the whole attitude for?" he asked shrugging, not understanding. "You just got at both of ma' niggas sideways for no real reason," he finished, glaring at her.

"First of all! Why are you sticking up for the two niggas standing right in front of me?" she retorted, smiling.

He raised his eyebrows a little impressed with Lia's feisty ass. I just stood there, invisible from them, not saying a word at all. The whole scene was entertaining.

"Because he over here tryin' to *shoot his shot* and give you a compliment, and you bein' ruder than you say he's bein'!" Scrap clapped back.

"It's good, bruh!" the boy said as he slapped the back of his hand on Scrap's chest while he kept his eyes on Lia. "You know that feisty shit turns me on . . ." He showed this seductive smile on his face. "I already gotta nickname for her. *Ms. Attitude.*"

She rolled her eyes. "My name is Lia," she corrected, shaking her head and trying not to smile. She was giving in.

"Damn! I had to nickname yo ass to get a response out of you?" he asked, laughing. "I'm Luther. Friends call me SixPacc," he said, introducing himself. She flinched at the stupid-ass name they chose to give him.

"Who the fuck named you SixPacc?" she asked, rolling her eyes. "It better not have been yo homeboys," she finished. He laughed.

"No nigga gave me that name," he responded, rolling his eyes and smiling. "And maybe if we get to know each other better, I'll show you why I got the name," he said, stepping closer to her. She laughed.

"Boy, bye!" She moved him out of her way. He smiled harder.

"You goin' to the scrimmage tonight, Ms. Attitude?" Scrap asked before we could walk off. "You should come watch ya boy play and bring a friend. Actually . . . bring a couple of them ma'fuckas." He displayed this sneaky-ass smirk. She rolled her eyes.

"I was going but not for y'all, and don't you have a girl?" she asked.

Scrap twisted his lips up. "What makes you think that I got a girl?"

"Because she's been with you all day. Lovely?" she reminded him.

Scrap threw his head down and chuckled. SixPacc and Twinkie did a silent chuckle as well.

"Naw, that ain't my girl, and we ain't talking about Lovely right now. We're talking about you coming to see us play."

"Like I said, I was going, but not for you."

"Oh! Then you must have been going for me," SixPacc responded as he traced his finger down her arm.

"You wish!" she said, pushing his hand away.

"Are you forgetting about me?" I finally spoke. I figured she had forgotten about my makeover.

"Oh! I'm sorry, Jay. I forgot . . ."

Something clicked in my head that I didn't think about before. *Scrap is playing tonight*. Of course, he would be at the game, and now that I knew that Lovely wasn't his girl . . .

"Do you think you can come by my house right after school?" I asked.

"I can, but I don't want to," she admitted.

"Come on, Li! Then we can go to the scrimmage." Lia scrunched her face up.

"Janeeva, you don't even like football. Yo mama be havin' to drag you out the house just to come see your own brother play!" she reminded me.

I looked over at Scrap as he and Twinkie started slapboxing each other in the hallway as they laughed. Lia followed my gaze and smiled at me.

"I knew you liked him," she said, catching me redhanded. I blushed. "Okay," she agreed. "Right after school," she warned.

"Thank you! Thank you! I love you!" I said in a low excited voice. I hugged her tightly. She turned back around facing them.

"Now we're holding secrets?" Scrap asked with that same sneaky-ass grin on his face.

"Don't worry about what we got goin' on. Mind ya' business," she retorted.

Scrap looked at me for the first time all fucking day! I mean the butterflies in my stomach were going crazy!

"You're in my drama and chemistry class," he said to me.

I was melting at the fact that he even knew! However, I had to shy away from the feeling, trying not to smile too hard. I nodded my head. He smiled at me and then looked back at Lia. "Well! Ms. Attitude, if you come tonight, maybe you'll get lucky with my nigga right here. Matter of fact, maybe with all of us," he said, boldly. Lia's face turned red.

57

"Nigga, I get lucky every day, and that's because I don't waste my time on sorry-ass clowns like you!" she retorted.

"If you'll stop bein' a lil *bitch*, then maybe one day you'll get to know a nigga like me. Be careful, though, because I'm rare . . ." he said, still taunting her. The "bitch" word always throws me off, but like always, it didn't bother her.

"I'm good," she responded, rejecting the offer. She was getting weary talking to them.

"Come on, Jay. We have a class to attend." She grabbed me by my arm and dragged me all the way to class.

It seemed like Scrap and his friends were following right behind us. I walked into the classroom and grabbed a seat. Lia stopped right in front of the doorway and put both of her hands in front of the entrance.

"Are you following us?" They looked back as if she was talking to someone else. "I'm talking to y'all!" she said as her voice rose with a more immature attitude.

"No, this is actually the class we have to attend right now!" Twinkie mimicked her.

"Yeah, so excuse me! We're about to be late and I want

the seat in the back where I see ass and thighs," Scrap finished.

"That's pathetic and so disrespectful."

"We're really not like this, but you're fun to fuck with," SixPacc retorted, smiling at her.

One of the girls that sat in the back with blonde braids in her hair dropped something on the ground, and she bent down. The shape of her ass was perfect. I even managed to glance for about four seconds. She tried to keep her skirt down as she picked up whatever she had dropped. SixPacc immediately looked up and smiled harder.

"Goddamn! I see booty, so excuse me!" he crooned.

He moved Lia's hand out of his way, and all three of them walked past her.

They went all the way to the back where the girl was sitting and talked with her and her friends.

Lia grabbed a seat by me. When she sat down, she looked back at SixPacc. He was back there introducing himself to the girls and laughing.

When he noticed Lia staring at him, he smiled at her, but she just rolled her eyes and turned around in her seat.

When she realized that she was in the dead center of the room, she ducked down in her seat and looked at me. "Damn, Jay!" she complained.

I rolled my eyes and shook my head. "You can always move if you want," I offered. That shut her ass up. She wasn't going to sit by herself and look all lonely in front of him.

"No . . . I'm good," she responded.

She looked back again, hoping that this time when SixPacc looked up, she would be able to smile back. He didn't look up this time though. The teacher walked in and introduced himself right away.

"Good morning, class! I need everyone to get a piece of paper and a pen or pencil out to write down some notes!"

Not to be mean, but he looks dead on that actor that played in the movie *Freeway*. What was that man's name? Bob! That's who he looks like! He wrote his name on the board, *Mr. Vansteinburg.*

"Mr. Van-steen-burg is my name, not Van-stine-berg or

Van-stain-burg. It's Van-*steen*-burg," he said sarcastically.

"We should have a lot of fun this semester. I have a lot planned for you guys, and I'm not one of the boring teachers. I'm the cool guy! I like to make the assignments and homeworks fun, but . . . if you take advantage, I will and I'm willing to do so! I will make your time here a living hell! This is high school! It isn't middle school anymore. We're looking for kids that we know can act like mature young ladies and gentlemen!" Everyone in the back started laughing. Mr. Vansteinburg looked back.

"Is there something you guys would like to share with the class?" he asked. Scrap and everyone else that he was talking to looked up at Mr. Vansteinburg.

"No, sir. Not at all!" Twinkie responded.

"Then I need you to pay attention and turn around in your seat," he instructed.

They all turned around in their seats and faced the front. Scrap was the only one that didn't move. Even though his desk was already facing the front, he remained slouched down in his seat with this smirk on his face as he looked at the rest of them giving Mr. Vansteinburg their full attention.

You could tell that he just didn't care, and for some weird-ass reason, I couldn't think of shit else but how sexy his ass was.

Chapter 4 Transition

Janeeva

Once the bell rang, Lia and I walked to the front of the school and waited for Trevor. We would have just walked to the house, but I still didn't have a key. When we finally spotted him in the crowd, coming out of the school, he was walking out with Talawny. I sighed. I couldn't help but think that he could do better.

They walked over to us, and instead of saying his goodbyes and walking the fuck off, he stood there choking on her tongue. I was really on an important mission, and even though we were only four blocks away from the house, he was wasting every second of my time that he spent with her.

"Trevor, let's go," I said, calmly, trying to control my temper. He acted as if he didn't hear me. He had me fucked up. "Trevor!" I yelled, impatiently. They both looked at me. I could see the irritation all on his face. "Let's . . . go," I demanded so that he could see how serious I was. "Patience, Mami . . . What? You don't have any respect for your brother's boundaries?" Talawny retorted, looking at me.

"Whoa, whoa! Be cool, man!" he said.

"I was just saying . . ." she responded, shrugging her shoulders with this nonchalant look on her face.

"But that's still my sister, babe, and that's between me and her, not you."

"Fuck it," I said, done with the whole conversation. "Give me your key!" I demanded.

"Jay, just wait!" he snapped, getting irritated with me.

"I have shit to do!"

"Go ahead, babe. I have things to do anyway," she said, cutting her eyes at me and then rolling them. When she walked away, he glared at me and shook his head. I crossed my arms over my torso and glared back.

"Walk," he demanded, pointing his finger in the direction we were walking. I turned around and walked with Lia right beside me and my brother on my heel. I knew he was about to curse me out once we got home.

We were almost to the house, and he talked his shit the whole walk. After he talked his shit, he begged me to try to get along with the bitch. I guess he couldn't wait until we got home for this bullshit. After I promised him that I would try and *only* try, he nudged me on my shoulder. "Thanks." Once we got home, Trevor let us know the plan.

"Aye, if you going to the scrimmage, then hurry up and get dressed. I'm leaving in an hour and a half." He ran upstairs, and I looked at Lia. She smiled.

"You ready to do this?" she asked.

"Yep!" I replied, nodding my head.

"Let's do this then!" she said as we both ran up the stairs into my room.

When we got to my room, we shut the door and locked it. Lia pulled out a little carry-around makeup kit. "I am about to make a whole new you!" she said, smiling.

She made me hop in the shower first and wash my face good before she started.

When I got out the shower, she did a quick wash and blow-dried my hair. My hair looked a hot mess when she cut that blow-dryer on. I could tell that she was getting frustrated because it was so thick, so she decided to press it out with the pressing combs that I had under my sink afterwards. She had gotten them for me for Christmas, but I never felt the need to use them. I honestly thought her ass was trying to be funny when she gave them to me.

She wouldn't let me look in the mirror yet, and while she was looking for something cute and sexy to put on me, I tried to sneak in the bathroom a couple of times, forgetting that the shit was being renovated and I didn't have a fucking mirror. What the hell was my mama trying to do in here anyway?

Lia thanked God that she was so forgetful because most of her clothes were in my closet for all the times that she had spent the night. She pulled out a black "BEBE" tank top that looked too small for her, and she tossed it to me. I looked at her like she was out of her mind.

"Are you serious?" I asked.

"Dead serious," she said, smiling.

I didn't know what else she was looking for, but she was searching all of my drawers and under my bed. "Have you seen my red shorts that I wore like two weeks ago?" she asked. I nodded my head.

"Yeah, they were in my dirty clothes hamper. My mom washed all that stuff yesterday."

"That's even better! They're clean!" she crooned. My jaw dropped as I listened to her.

She raced down the stairs to the laundry room and came back up in a matter of minutes with the red shorts in her hands. She tossed them to me.

"Awe, c'mon!" I said, not wanting to go through with this anymore.

"Aye! I'm the stylist here, and you will do as you are told!" she said with a big smile on her face. I sighed and did as

I was told.

It was the end of the summer still, and it was hot as hell! So, the black tank top and the red shorts were "okay" to wear. I just wished the tank top came down a little more on my stomach because I felt so exposed with my navel showing.

After I slipped on the tank top and the shorts, she opened her makeup kit and ordered me to sit in the chair that she stole from the kitchen.

She brushed and dabbed makeup all over my face. Not a lot I must say. It sure didn't feel like it was a lot.

"You don't need a lot of makeup on your face because you're naturally beautiful. If you were looking like some of the girls at our school, I would tell you that you needed more, but you don't," she said giving me fashion tips.

Awe, that was sweet . . . But she was just talking about how *beauty is within* earlier, so I just laughed to myself and let her continue. I knew that she was serious about her little tips, because after tonight, she wanted me to continue with the look that I haven't seen yet.

"The bags under your eyes are hideous though." *Okay, now I'm insulted.* "Don't worry; I can fix that," she said, dabbing a little more of the powder foundation under my eyes.

I slipped on some low-cut socks and a pair of my Jordan shoes that had never been worn. My dad got them for me over the summer.

When Lia was through with me, I felt more worn out than anything, but I felt as if it was worth it. I was impressed that she fixed me up so quickly. We used the whole hour and a half wisely. Lia stared at me with a big smile on her face.

"I'm jealous," she said.

"Can I see now?" I asked, becoming impatient. I was so anxious to see if she really did hook me up or if she was just saying that to be funny.

She moved out of the way so that I could open my door and run to the guest bathroom.

When I entered the bathroom and looked in the mirror, my eyes got wide! I didn't see myself in it.

My long thick tangled hair was now straight and flowing down my back. I was scared at first when I felt her cutting my hair in the front, but when I saw the China bangs falling over my forehead, I fell in love. I didn't even know my hair was this long.

The eye shadow, mascara and eyeliner stood out my creamy light-brown almond eyes, making them glow and seem lighter than what they were before, and the bangs brought more attention to them as well. The red eyeshadow also matched my outfit.

I chuckled and then gently put my hands over my mouth in shock. I looked at Lia as she still had a big smile on her face. I knew she felt good. I looked like an Indian doll.

As I forcefully pulled my eyes from my face in the mirror, I appraised the rest of my body and the outfit that she picked out for me. I didn't feel out of place or abnormal. I felt good!

Well, aside from my stomach being out. As much as I thought that the black BEBE tank top and the red shorts were not going to work or even match, they went perfect with my makeup and my shoes. I was shocked!

"Lia . . ." I choked, trying to figure out the words that I was trying to say.

"I know, I know . . . I am a pro!" she said. I shook my head, still shocked.

"Thank you," I said, appreciative. "I didn't think it would work out, but you did an amazing job with me," I crooned.

"Anytime, sis." She walked over to me, and I hugged her tight.

I know it's weird, but I never felt so good in my life. *I feel . . . beautiful!* I went from geek of the month to the sexiest junior of the year.

"My best friend is a baddie! Go, best friend, that's my best friend!" Lia crooned. "And I told you that your body is bangin'! Look at them hips!" she sang out. I laughed.

I honestly always thought that I was a little thicker than an average teenager and it made me self-conscious, but right now, I felt like my body filled out perfectly. I also used to wonder why people went crazy over Trevor's creamy lightbrown eyes, but now that I was looking at my own, I was going crazy!

I walked downstairs, and Lia was right behind me with a big smile on her face. I knew that she was feeling good about her work. As we approached the kitchen, I heard Trevor yelling our names from upstairs.

"C'mon! I gotta go!" he yelled, coming down the stairs, thinking that we were still in my room.

The time was going on four forty, and his game started at five thirty. He was already running late. Right now, junior varsity should be warming up. Trevor yelled out our names again.

"Stop yelling," I said, coming out of the kitchen.

He turned around, and the moment that his eyes caught mine, they grew wide. He stared at me, from head to toe, until the look registered in his head.

"Janeeva?" he asked, like it wasn't me. I rolled my eyes.

"Trevor?" I said, sarcastically.

"What the fuck you got on?" he growled. I flinched at his hostility.

"I wanted to dress cute tonight."

He was shocked by my response. If anyone knew me, it would be my brother, and he knew that this style wasn't me. It was time for a change though, and it was already growing on me. He shook his head.

"What made you want to dress like this?" he asked. I shrugged.

"Just an experiment. We're doing a survey on what looks our friends like best on me," I said, sarcastically.

"What friends?"

I cut my eyes at him because I knew that he was trying to be funny. Lia threw her hands on my shoulder and pushed me to the door before Trevor tried to make me go upstairs and change.

"My friends! That will soon be hers!" she said, smiling. "Now, while you're asking all these questions," she said, looking at her phone, "you're already late! Are you going to waste your time on what Janeeva have on or have your coach yell at you?" she finished. God, I loved her!

He thought about it and shook his head. He couldn't stop staring at me, and the expression on his face was very homicidal. I think the look was toward Lia though. He walked out the door, and we followed right behind him. He stopped on the porch and looked at my outfit again.

"Go put on a jacket. You don't need them niggas looking at you, especially any of them on my team," he demanded.

I did as I was told, because for the first time, he was making me feel a little uncomfortable with the looks that he was giving me. I ran upstairs to get a jacket, but as I looked through my closet, there was no jacket that went with my outfit.

I looked all through my closet, pulling my clothes apart from the others so that I could see what else I had. Then I spotted the cute black half BEBE jacket that Lia got me for my birthday. She had a thing for BEBE designer clothes. They were expensive though. I pulled it out and slid it on. I thought I

73

was never going to wear this jacket! It wasn't cute to me at first. As I went to the guest bathroom and looked in the mirror, I couldn't doubt it now because it went perfect with the outfit.

I ran back down the stairs, and Trevor looked at me like, *How the hell is that changing anything?* He didn't say it, but he shook his head in a way meaning it. Lia looked at me and appraised the half jacket. She smiled.

"Hey! I got that jacket for you!" she said, smiling harder. "High-five!" she crooned. Trevor couldn't say anything. I knew what he was thinking though.

He walked out the house and mumbled, "This is going to be a long-ass night."

We got into the car and drove off.

When we got there, I didn't even have time to get out the car as Trevor started lecturing me and giving me instructions on where to meet him after his game.

Now, before this change, he didn't even care where I met him. I would have to bring it to his attention so my ass wouldn't get left. Now, he wanted to give me orders.

I know why he's doing this. People weren't interested in me when I was dressed like a little tomboy so he knew that I wouldn't get into any kind of trouble, but now . . . now is *now*!

Now is the time to see what a change feels like . . .

Chapter 5 Squad

Janeeva

"Are you done?" I asked, impatiently. I was tired of hearing his voice at this point.

"Jay, this whole look that you got goin' on right now is about to bring a lot of attention to you, and it's not something that you're used to," he pressed. "I just want to know that you're going to be okay."

I thought about what he was saying and took a deep breath. *He knows how I am when too much attention is on me. My anxiety.* Lia nodded her head in agreement. I guess she never thought about that part.

"Look, I can do this. I'll be okay. Okay?" I responded. He sighed.

"Just be careful. I don't want to have to fuck nobody up."

"Man, can we just go? You're late anyway! You better go and let me be!" I begged.

At this point, I just felt like I had taken enough therapy sessions to try to control any anxiety attack tonight. Trevor looked at the time on his phone. "Meet me right here," he warned.

"Okay!" I said, now anxious for him to go away.

He walked the opposite way to the entrance. I guess he was going around to where the locker rooms were. Lia looked at me and smiled.

"Are you ready, Hot Mama?" she said. I smiled and nodded.

I will admit—I was too nervous. When we got to the gate, people were already staring at me, and I had to try not to make eye contact with them. I kept my eyes either on Lia or on the ground the whole time.

As we entered the stadium, we walked up the steps, and the whole way up, I kept my eyes on the steps to make sure that I wouldn't fall. I didn't even bother to look at Lia while I walked. As I walked, I thought about what people would think of me and my new look. Finally, the football field came into sight as we reached the last step.

"Let's go, Jordan!" someone yelled out from behind me.

I turned around, and the crowd of people in the stands had me struggling to breathe right. My mouth dropped looking at all the people. Fear overtook me, and I started to panic. Lia grabbed my hand for a moment. She knew how I was around too many people.

"Jay, you're good . . . Chill . . ." I took a deep gulp.

As I stood there in my own little world for a moment, Lia pulled me by my arm and up the next set of steps.

There were a lot of people in the stands for it only to be a scrimmage.

"C'mon!" she said, now dragging me.
I walked slowly behind her with my eyes on the steps, trying not to look back up at the crowd. As we walked, I heard the voices of two girls screaming Lia's name.

"Lia! Up here!" they yelled.

Lia looked up, and I just looked at her, trying not to drag my attention on the crowd. She waved her arms in the air, letting them know that we were coming.

They were at the very top, and as hard as it was to not look up, I couldn't help but look at the girls who were calling her name. As I did so, my eyes fell on the crowd.

"C'mon!" she repeated, grabbing me by my arm while my eyes were pleading for her to understand how scared I was.

"Jay, they're not going to bite yo ass!" She pressed her lips together with her head tilted like I was over-exaggerating. "I didn't fix you up for nothing!" she said, putting her hand on her hips. I sighed.

"Give me a break, Lia," I complained.
"I will, but right now you will cooperate! Now c'mon!" she said, grabbing my arm and dragging me up the steps.

I was so relieved when we got to our seats. We sat down, and there were about twenty other females around us. I was probably being a little dramatic, but it was a lot of them. They were deep in the stands.

I didn't know Lia was so popular until now. I knew that she was popular but not this popular.

The first one that I noticed was Lovely. She was sitting above me as she texted and talked to the girl next to her.

"Lia, you haven't introduced us to your friend," I heard a feminine voice say behind me. I turned around to see a cute yellow girl with freckles, looking down at me. "She can be so rude!"

I giggled, as I sat quietly.

I knew the freckled girl by just seeing her around school. I never knew her name. I knew most of the girls sitting around by their faces. There would only be a handful that I knew by names.

"I don't have to introduce her; you know her," Lia said, smiling.

"We know her?" the girl sitting next to the yellow freckled girl said.

"I don't know her," another one sitting next to Lovely responded.

The girl sitting next to Lovely was pretty, smooth, dark chocolate, and her hair was slicked back into two scraps. She sucked on a tootsie roll sucker with her legs crossed. "And even if I did know her, I would've been tried to get up in that," the girl said, giving me this seductive-ass look. She was too bold for me . . .

Lia laughed. "Skittles why are you the only lesbo that can't keep your thoughts to yourself?" she asked. She smiled and then shrugged. "Y'all seem pretty desperate to know who she is." Lia taunted.

"Why can't she introduce herself? Shit! We been sitting here talking to you like she deaf!" the freckled girl said. She held her hand out to me and introduced herself.

"I'm Freckles," she greeted me, smiling and shaking my hand.

"And I'm Dimples," the girl next to her said, smiling at me.

"Skittles," the lesbian introduced, smiling at me as well while she licked her lips. "I'm pretty sure you already know why they call me that." Freckles and Dimples guffawed.

"You just nasty!" Dimples laughed.

"I know," Skittles responded, shrugging her shoulders and smiling. "And this is Lovely," she introduced, moving out of the way so that Lovely could be seen.

She was so quiet because she was texting nonstop. When she heard her name, she looked at me. "Hi," she said dully and went back to texting.

"Don't worry about her. She's handling business right now," Skittles said, brushing Lovely's bitchy-ass attitude off.

"So, what's your name?" Dimples asked.

"Janeeva," I responded, giving them a half smile.

Dimples was a little chubby in the face, and her features were beautiful. The chubbiness was adorable on her.

"Now how do we know you?" Skittles asked. Lia looked at them in disbelief.

"Omigod! Y'all still don't know who she is? Her brother plays for varsity! You guys talk about him every day! *Oh, he's so fine! He this; he that!*" She mimicked them. Freckles looked at Dimples and flipped her hair back.

"Girl, we do a lotta dat!" she said, laughing.

"Real shit!" Dimples agreed and gave Freckles a highfive.

"Talawny's boyfriend!" Lia yelled out, becoming impatient.

"Who? Trevor?" Dimples asked.
Freckles' eyes widened from just hearing his name.

"Quarterback! Oooouh! That's my *huuusband!*" Freckles crooned, looking at Dimples.

"But his girlfriend is a lil *thot*," Dimples said. *Thot*? I questioned myself, not understanding what she meant by that.

"Yep! The biggest hoe that you know. You know that bitch get on my last nerve," Freckles agreed.

I looked at them with this big Kool-Aid-ass smile on my face. I knew that I wasn't the only one that couldn't stand that bitch.

"Man, you remember when that dumb-ass bitch—" Freckles cut Dimples off as she looked at me.

"Wait, wait, wait!" she said, catching on. "You the same girl that was wearing those worn-out jeans and big ass tshirt earlier, huh?" she asked. I was a little insulted about my jeans.

I saw Lovely pull away from her phone and look at me from the corner of her eyes. I knew that she remembered me from earlier now.

I pressed my lips together and nodded my head. They all screamed.

"Damn! Who hooked you up like this?" Dimples asked as she swept her hand through my straight hair. I pointed at Lia, and she looked at them smiling.

After they complimented me on how good I looked, they praised Lia.

Varsity was now starting. After they did their little school chant onto the field, they started stretching. I saw Trevor from a distance. You can't really tell who they are with their helmets on, but since I knew his number, which he calls the *Lucky 7*, I knew exactly who he was.

I leaned over Lia and whispered in her ear. "Which one is Scrap?" I asked.

"Four."

I watched number four as he ran across the field. I was so entranced by him that he was the only one who had my attention.

"I see you staring at number four pretty hard there," Freckles said, smiling ear to ear as she watched me.

I snapped my head up at her and blushed.

How did she even know which one I was looking at? Maybe because he was the only one running to the end of the field while his players threw the ball to him. My head was turning wherever he went.

"Did Lia tell you who he is already?" she asked as she and Dimples smiled.

I looked over at Lovely, but she was too occupied to really pay attention to our conversation because she was still texting. I nodded my head.

Lia looked at me, and I knew what the look meant. She wanted to tell them about my little crush. I sighed and rolled my eyes.

She gave me those pleading eyes to spill the "*tea*," and as I thought for a moment, I felt like it wouldn't hurt sharing my little secret. I nodded my head.

She smiled, and then Freckles and Dimples brought their heads down to her so that she could speak in a lower voice and tell them what was up. After she told them, Freckles nodded her head as she smiled harder.

"So that's who the new look is for, huh?" she asked. "Oh girl! I got 'chu!" I could hear the excitement all in her tone. "Now who I know in these ma'fuckin' stands that's gon' go back and run they mouth!" she said, looking around. I was confused.

She scanned the crowd, and when she finally found her prey, she got up and went down the steps to another group and started a conversation with a boy that I didn't know.

As they talked and laughed, she looked up at me and my heart dropped. The boy did the same, and as he stared at me, I saw the smile surface across his face.

She came back up and sat back down. Dimples smiled hard, as did Lia.

"Now let's see how long it takes to get the word back to *Mr. Number Four*," she said.

"Did you tell him that I was crushing on Scrap?" I asked in a whisper with these wide eyes.

"Don't trip, Ma. We got 'chu! You didn't get all dolledup for nothin'!" she said, flipping her hair back. I looked at Lia as I panicked.

"Chill!" she said, chuckling at my reaction. "It's going to be okay!"

Twinkie

"Twinkie!"

I heard someone yell my name from the stands. I looked around and didn't know where my name was being called. Then I spotted Freckles and the rest of her little squad in the stands.

She really doesn't know the thangs that I would do to her fine ass! It doesn't make any sense to look that damn good!

I searched out her crowd to see if I saw any new faces, and I was a little taken aback when I saw one unfamiliar face.

Who the fuck is that?

"Yo, Twinkie!" I heard someone call my name again. I turned around to see my *loc*. Ryan approached me with two of the other homies.

"Wassup, loc?" he crooned.

"What's good," I responded as I turned my head back to the girl that was sitting next to Lia. As Ryan started talking, I stopped him. "Yo . . . You see the girl up there sitting next to Lia?" I asked. He looked up.

"Yeah, yeah, yeah! That's Quarterback's sister!" he responded. *Quarterback's sister*? I didn't even know he had a sister.

As I stared at her talking to Lia, I thought about the girl that was with her earlier.

I noticed her when Scrap said something to her about classes. She was cute in the face, but she was dressed like a nigga. Her hair was a little fucked up earlier too.

Is that the same girl? It couldn't be! Damn! That can't be the same girl... No way! The girl I was looking at right now was not the same person that I saw earlier.

"Yo . . . Word is that she gotta lil crush on Scrap. I was up there earlier and overheard Freckles saying some shit about it," Ryan said, spilling the "tea."

"What a surprise!" I responded, sarcastically.

There wasn't a female that I didn't know that wasn't on my homie's nuts. I'm not hating though. But these bitches were always *thirstin'* for his ass.

"Yeah, man, he betta' get her fine ass!"

I wasn't really paying attention to anything that he was saying. He knew that I was about to run back and tell him, but he was on the field right now, so I had to wait until the game was over.

For the first time, I wasn't into the game like I usually was. I was just ready to run my mouth and make sure Scrap hopped on that ass before someone else got to the girl.

89

Once the game ended, people started leaving the stadium, and I walked to the locker rooms where Scrap and SixPacc were.

"Well, y'all did well tonight . . . Y'all need to toughin' up a lil bit moe', but y'all did good, and we got time before our first game. We gon' have a long practice tomorrow so y'all betta' be ready. Unda'stand?"

"Yes, sir!" the team shouted out. The coach shook his head, not satisfied with their strident.

"Naw, I said UNDA'STAND?" His voice rose with aggression.

"Yes, sir!" they shouted.

"Aight then! Get outta he'yea," he said, finally, dismissing them.

"Trevuh!" Coach called out before Quarterback could leave.

"Yes, sir!" he responded.

"Let me talk to you." Quarterback walked to the back, right behind Coach, into his office.

Scrap and SixPacc walked toward me as they saw me standing near the exit to the locker room. They looked drained.

"Look tired. Y'all need a pillow?" I teased.

"Yeah, can we use yo stomach as a cushion?" SixPacc retorted. We walked out, and I got right on the subject with the ole' girl.

"Aye, cuz! You remember ole' girl that was with Ms. Attitude earlier?" I asked Scrap.

He thought about it as he zoned off. "Naw . . ." he responded.

"Man! You know who I'm talking about!" I pressed. "When we were messing with her after lunch and there was a girl with her . . . She had on some jeans and a big-ass t-shirt," I said, trying to explain. He thought about it again.

"Yeah . . . I was watching her . . . She was kind of cute. She dresses like a nigga, but them ma'fuckin' eyes . . ." he crooned, smiling.

They were both tired as hell. I could tell from the way that they were dragging their feet on the concrete.

"Well word is . . . she wants you, nigga!"

I felt a sting on the back of my neck as SixPacc swung his hand, open handed, and slapped me.

"What the fuck was that for, cuz?" I yelled, ready to beat his ass.

He gave me this nonchalant look and pressed his lips together.

"All these lil *thirst buckets* trying to get at this nigga, and you think one lil girl makes a difference?" Scrap laughed, finishing SixPacc's sentence.

"And I swore that girl was gay, cuz!" he said, laughing harder. "Naw, nigga, I'm G," he said, brushing me off.

I laughed, too, but I was laughing for a whole different reason. I knew that he was going to want to talk to her once he saw her, and if he didn't, then I know she'll go for a little big boned.

"Okay, we'll see if you'll still be saying that in a minute," I responded.

"Oh, really?" I could see in his eyes that he was ready for a bet.

"Yup!" I was too sure about this one.

"Aight then, nigga! Put ya' money where ya' mouth is!" he responded, going right into it.

This nigga loved trying to prove somebody wrong.

I dug in my pockets and pulled out a twenty-dollar bill. Scrap looked at it like it was nothing. Of course, it was nothing to him the way he and his brothers get money. He made a deal with me.

"I tell you what . . . Is the ole' girl here right now?" he asked.

I smiled. "Yeah, she here. Well, I hope she's still here," I said forgetting about how everyone cleared out of the stadium but Lia's crew.

"Aight. Point her out to me, and if I think different of her, then the next time we go to Red Lobster, it's on me!"

I took that bet. Knowing me, I love some food, especially some food I don't have to pay for! SixPacc looked over Scrap's shoulder.

93

"Aye! If Twinkie win, you gotta pay for my food, too."

He nodded his head.

"Deal." We walked to the other side of the stadium.

"Yo . . . where Lovely at?" I asked Scrap.

"On her way to my money," he responded. "She just texted me and told me she left right after the game," he said, looking down at his phone. I nodded my head.

Good, because I didn't want that bitch ruining anything!

Lovely was his *"new bitch."* She sexy as hell but dumb as hell! However, the bitch knew how to run up a bag, and she's loyal as fuck! When it comes to Scrap's order's, the bitch jumps with no hesitation.

His *bottom* bitch, Mia, didn't like that too much. She always on some other shit though, and he truly didn't give a fuck about how she felt.

We finally got to the spot where the girls were sitting, and when they saw us, they instantly greeted us.

"Hey, boys!" Freckles crooned, looking down at us, smiling from ear to ear, with her sexy ass!

"What's good wit'chu!" SixPacc and I responded as Scrap just nodded his head in greeting.

"Now which one?" he asked.

"Look at the girl sitting by Lia," I instructed.
He looked right at her before I could even finish my sentence.

He was quiet for a moment as he stared at her. I tried to read his expressions, but he was just blank, and then he mumbled under his breath. "Damn . . ."

That's all he could say.

Yeeeeah! And that's all I needed to hear! In my head, I was singing. *I don't have to pitch in for no food! I can just sit back and eat as much as I want!* "We goin' to Red Lobster! We goin' to Red Lobster!" I sung out.

As I was thinking about the free food I was about to get, I turned my attention back on him. He hadn't taken his eyes off her yet. He wanted her fa'sho!

"Well, let's go introduce ourselves," he said in a low voice as he kept his eyes on her. I agreed because I wanted to go holla at Freckles anyway, and SixPacc just looked at us and shrugged.

"Aight," he said, not really caring what we did.

We walked up the steps, and as we approached them, I squeezed through Skittles and sat next to Freckles. I looked at them both and smiled, while they laughed at my ass for squeezing in between them. Man, I'll do some thangs to both of their fine asses!

SixPacc found a spot on the step above Lia as he continued his assessment from earlier and began the flirt session all over again.

"Wassup, ladies?" Scrap greeted them before he turned his attention back to the girl. They all looked at him and greeted him back. He looked at Lia. "Wassup, Ms. Attitude? I see you came to the game." Lia chuckled.

"Wassup, Scrap?" she greeted, trying to be nice.

He finally looked down at the girl. He was quiet for a moment as they stared at each other and he appraised her, getting a better look, and then he smiled.

"Can I sit right here?" he asked. She scooted over, and he sat down. "How you doin' tonight?" he asked her.

"Fine," she responded, shyly.

"Did you enjoy the game?"

"Yeah, you played good tonight."

"You were watching me?" he asked, amused. She blushed.

"You had my attention," she said, smiling. He returned the smile.

"What's yo name, Ma?"

She was trying her hardest not to blush, but she couldn't help it. "Janeeva."

"Janeeva?" he repeated. "I'm Scrap." He held his hand out to shake hers.

She reached her hand out to touch his own, and he gently grabbed it, caressing his thumb across the top of her hand.

I could see her body tense up as he touched her. *I don't know how this nigga do it!*

"You're beautiful," he said, staring into her light brown eyes.

She dropped her head and tried to hide the big-ass smile that she was displaying. You could tell that she was a shy one.

"Thank you," she said in a faint voice.

They talked for about ten minutes. Well, Scrap did most of the talking while she answered a question or just listened. They didn't even really pay attention to anyone else.

What surprised me is seeing him give up his number. Normally, he gets the girl number and tried to avoid them calling him, but tonight, he switched the game up.

What was funnier was seeing some of the females sitting around her, trying to listen into their conversation and then snickering to their friend. I couldn't help but chuckle at it. Females love to hate on a bitch.

As for myself, I was disappointed, because instead of getting a kiss or my threesome that I had all planned out for Skittles, Freckles and I, these bitches acted like my plan was stupid as fuck!

I don't know why Skittles was *frontin'*! She knew this would have been the perfect opportunity to take Freckles' fine ass down! Always trying to fuck up a master plan!

I stopped tripping off them when I finally saw Quarterback coming up the steps. I figured he was looking for his sister.

When he spotted her, I knew that it was about to be some problems. As he walked up the steps, Dimples greeted him. "Hey, Quarterback. Came up here to collect lil sis?" Dimples crooned as she stuck her sucker in her mouth.

"Yep. Let's go. I'm tired," he responded. Janeeva rolled her eyes in irritation.

"Okay," she said, impatiently, like she wanted him to just walk to the car and she'd be right behind him. "You can go, Trevor . . . I'm right behind you," she said.

I was shocked that Scrap's dumb ass wasn't catching on. When he finally put two and two together, he laughed. "Quarterback? Yo brotha'? Are you serious?" he asked, still laughing. Janeeva nodded her head. I think she was scared that her brother was about to embarrass her.

"Man, Janeeva, I said now!" Quarterback demanded, frustrated.

"Stop talking to me like you're my daddy," she retorted.

"Man, bring yo ass on before I drag you by yo neck nigga! You were supposed to meet me at the car!" he retorted.

Everyone stopped what they were doing and looked at Quarterback. He looked frustrated and tired. Janeeva glared at him and got up. Before she could walk off, Scrap grabbed her hand, ignoring her brother.

Quarterback looked at him like he was crazy. SixPacc and I got ready to strike if he tried anything.

"Are you going to call me tonight?" he asked, with no hesitation.

It killed me how this nigga just didn't give a fuck! I think he was trying to test Quarterback's ass because he knew that he was in no mood to be fucked with right now. We already knew that he was tired as hell. He played hard tonight, trying to impress the coach.

However, I don't think that was the best excuse to use in this situation. Everybody could see that his attitude was displayed because of his sister. He was too overprotective of her. That wasn't hard to see. Janeeva smiled at Scrap.

"I'll try. I have homework to do."

"I do, too," he responded as he stood and stepped closer to her. "But that don't ever stop me from doing the shit that I do." She blushed again as she looked away. Quarterback grabbed Janeeva's arm and yanked her back.

"Ouch!" she yelled, looking at her brother dumbfounded. "What's wrong with you?" she snapped.

Quarterback glared at him as he stepped in front of Janeeva and then demanded her to start walking down the steps, not taking his eyes off him. She glared at him but didn't say anything. I knew that she wasn't the type to just disobey her brother or make a scene. So, she just did what she was told. Lia sighed and got up, too.

It wasn't like we could really do anything. That was her brother, and I figured that he hadn't adapted to the new look yet. Scrap glared back at Quarterback.

When he started walking down the steps, he turned around and smiled at us. Sneaky-ass nigga! I knew that he just did that shit to get under his skin. SixPacc and I laughed.

The funny part about this shit is that Quarterback is family! He's from the same set that we from. We don't really fuck with him like that though. Even though he's around age, he is around Scrap's older brother's the most. They have a lot of respect for him, and they said that he listens.

Scrap isn't the type of nigga to just be friendly with you if he doesn't fuck with you like that, and after the scene that just took place . . . I don't know how their relationship was going to turn out in the future.

Chapter 6 Unnecessary Stress

"Why the fuck did you embarrass me like that? What did I do to you?"

"You didn't do shit, but you not about to be running around this bitch chasing after no nigga," he responded.

I was appalled. I barely touched him! "What the fuck are you talking about? I never had a boyfriend in my life, Trevor, and the one night that I got a little bit of attention, you wanted to embarrass me in front of everybody! Why would you do that?"

My eyes watered from the anger that I was feeling. He sighed because he could hear it all in my voice. I didn't do anything wrong but talk to Scrap! And must I say that was the best moment of my life until Trevor ruined it!

"I just don't want you to get hurt," he admitted.

"I can take care of myself!" I retorted, still pissed off. He shook his head.

"Jay, you just don't get it. You don't know shit until you get involved, and I feel like you're about to try to involve yourself in something that you're not going to be able to handle." He explained.

"Why can't you just be happy that I'm happy with my new look?" I asked.

"I'm not saying that I'm not happy for you. I just don't want you to be happy for the wrong reasons." He caught me off guard with that comment.

I looked at him confused. "What do you mean?"

"I mean . . . you only sixteen . . . and you never had a boyfriend. I'on even think you kissed a nigga before . . ." I cut my eyes at him. "Niggas take advantage of young females. And you don't know who Scrap really is . . . I do. You don't even know how many girls that nigga talks to. I'm just saying, before you get into anything, you need to learn the rules of the game and pick someone else to talk to because that nigga is *out!*"

"What is your issue with him?" I asked, annoyed.

"Look, just stay away from him, please. He ain't worth it," he said, ignoring my question.

I dropped my eyes and let it go. Trevor was paranoid about this. He was so used to me keeping my distance that I knew, if I ever did get that far with Scrap, I would be stalked everywhere that I went, and I didn't want any other boy. I only wanted *him*. In my mind, it wasn't me and anyone else; it was just me and Scrap. That was the only reason for this change. He was the only one that I wanted to get to know.

However, Trevor's words were burning in my head. And the main person that wouldn't leave my head was Lovely. Would I be the only female that he talked to? Was Lovely his girlfriend? He said that she wasn't. What about girls on the side? I was anxious to find out, so right after my homework was done, I was going to call him.

I had forgotten all about Lia in the back seat. She was asleep by the time we got to her house. I figured that she wasn't really trying to hear us arguing. She's usually like that though. She is so used to Trevor and me about to rip each other's heads off, that it's nothing that fazes her.

After dropping her off, we went straight home. I went straight upstairs and did all my homework, and for some reason it seemed like it was taking me longer to do. It was hard for me to concentrate with Scrap on my mind. I wanted to know so much about him. As much as I wanted him, there was a lot of stuff that Trevor had left on my mind. If I did talk to him, would I be the only one? Of course, I couldn't answer that question. I never had a boyfriend before, so it was weird to me.

I wish my brother would have just kept his mouth shut. Damn! Now he got me thinking! I finished my homework, and it seemed like it took me forever. I couldn't believe that they gave us homework on the first day back to school. It wasn't hard at all, but I had my mind on other things and I couldn't think straight.

I looked at my clock that was sitting on my dresser beside me, and the time was going on eleven thirty. *Should I call him? It's way too late. Should I? I think I should just wait until tomorrow.* I couldn't take my mind off him, though. That was the whole thing; I wasn't going to get a good night's sleep until I spoke to him. Maybe I could just ask my questions tomorrow at school.

When I woke up in the morning, I was agitated. I couldn't sleep. I barely slept at all. I even got up a couple of minutes before my alarm went off. He had me on a straight mission. I wanted to find out as much as I could about him, and I wanted to hear it from him.

How would I put it, though? How would I say it? Be real. *This is Janeeva talking, the shy girl. What am I going to do? Stand in front of him and let him read a letter and then tell him to answer my question?* I had to rethink everything. I just met this boy, and I was already going crazy. No wonder females go through so much drama! I was going through drama mentally, trying to figure out a boy that I just met.

I did my morning routine like usual. Trevor was surprised that the bathroom wasn't occupied, and as I waited downstairs for him impatiently, I became curious about my appearance. I went to the guest bathroom that was next to the kitchen and looked in the mirror. I had on a black hoodie with some regular blue jeans. My hair was still pressed out straight. I closed the door and locked it as I went into more detail.

I pulled my sweatshirt up and revealed a tight black spaghetti strap shirt that hugged my torso. I couldn't let my parents or Trevor dramatic ass see it, so I was waiting until I got to school to take it off.

I tried to straighten it out and pull my pants down just a little bit. I wanted to look extra cute when I saw him. After I was satisfied, I smiled and went back into the kitchen.

My mom was running a little late again. I sat down and did my usual routine. Trevor walked in two minutes later. He sat down and stuffed his mouth with the toast that I put in the toaster for him. *What a wonderful sister I am, huh? Now bring yo ass on so that we can get to school!*

"So, how were you guys' first day back to school?" my dad asked, flipping through his newspaper. I looked at Trevor, and he looked at me with a smile on his face.

"Good," I said.

"Well, what was it like? Did you enjoy it?" my nosyass daddy just kept going with the questions. Trevor smiled, and so did I.

"Oh yes, I enjoyed it alright," I answered, in a muffled voice.

"That's good," he said, not really paying attention or listening to anything that I was saying.

Trevor rolled his eyes. I didn't know why he was smiling, but I guess he was waiting for my parents to find out about my latest look.

When my mother finally came into the kitchen, she hurried up and made her coffee and then grabbed a slice of bread.

She was running so late that she hadn't even noticed that my nappy-ass hair was pressed out. My dad just wanted to keep the newspaper in his face and ask questions that he thought had something to do with bonding.

"Let's go, Maimi!" she said, grabbing Maimi's backpack off the counter and handing it to her. "Bye, my beautiful family!" she crooned.

Maimi growled as she got up from the table and stomped out the door right behind my mom. Trevor looked at the time and dropped his toast.

"We gotta go, too!" he said as he got up from the table. I got up as well, happy that we were finally leaving. I wasn't trying to rush things, but I needed to talk to Scrap.

"Bye, Dad!" I crooned as I got up, grabbed my backpack and ran out the door. Trevor was right behind me.

When we got to school, I was more than anxious to find him. I looked everywhere for him, and he just wasn't anywhere around. I got tired of looking. It was too damn early in the morning, and I was getting a headache from the lack of sleep.

Even with the migraine getting worse, I couldn't help but notice the boys that were noticing me in my tight black spaghetti strap shirt and my plain blue jeans that fit me perfectly.

As I got into my first period class, I didn't see Scrap anywhere. My heart was racing as I predicted the worst. *I hope he's okay.*

I barely knew this boy and I was already worrying about him. I was afraid that he wasn't going to come to school today, or maybe he transferred because his mom didn't like the school.

Are you kidding me? It's the beginning of the school year! I'm just trippin'. I need to chill out! I looked up, and I saw Lovely walking over to me. She sat next to me. I looked at her for a moment as she texted away on her phone. When she realized that I was staring, she looked at me. She already knew what I was thinking.

"We have assigned seats now, which I don't know how the fuck that works out with these chairs being in a circle," she said.

"Oh . . ." I responded.

She looked at me for a moment. "I like your new look."

"Thank you."

She didn't say anything else. She just chuckled as she kept texting. She tried to hide her phone under her backpack out of Mrs. Joyce's sight.

While she remained distracted, I decided to lean over and be nosy. *"R u comin to school 2day?"* Two minutes later, someone was texting her back.

"*Yea*" That was all her text buddy responded. She placed her phone in her backpack and smiled hard. She looked at me.

"Girl, it's nothing like a sexy-ass gangsta' with a bigass pipe . . ." *A what*? I didn't understand what she meant by that at all.

I wasn't trying to be nosy, but I was curious. "Who were you talking to?" I asked.

"Brian Gaither," she crooned, not even paying attention to my ass being nosy.

I looked at her for a moment. "The boy they call Scrap?" I asked, choking on my words, taking her out of her trance. I was a little disappointed.

"Mhm! My future baby daddy . . ."

I turned away as Lovely sat straight up in her chair and gave the teacher her full attention again. I was heartbroken. I was hoping that they weren't what mostly everyone assumed. I felt so sad, and I barely even knew him.

My brother was right. What was I even trying to do here?

When passing period came, I walked through the halls just thinking. I was confused. I thought I had him, but maybe I was wrong.

As I walked into my chemistry class and sat down, I got my binder and the rest of my stuff out and waited for the teacher's instructions.

As I waited, I looked at all the students around me. Everyone was talking, sitting at the desk and playing around. Everyone was happy, and I just sat there looking so damn depressed that I felt a need to just talk to someone.

I threw my arms on my desk and buried my head in them. I was in my own little world, thinking for exactly a second and then I was startled.

"You didn't call me last night," a smooth masculine voice whispered into my ear as he leaned over my desk with his hands on it.

I looked up to see Scrap standing over me with a charming smirk on his face. His face was so close to my own when I looked up that I stopped breathing.

This boy was so damn gorgeous that I was entranced all over again by his beauty. He smelled so good . . . He was looking good. I was stuck, and I couldn't speak as I looked into his gorgeous green eyes.

"Um . . . I know . . ." I said as if I couldn't think of anything to say. "After my homework, I was just too tired. I'm sorry," I said innocently.

"Did you get a good night's sleep?" he asked, licking his lips and smiling at me.

"Um . . . not really," I admitted.

"And why is that?"

"I had a lot of things on my mind," I confessed.

"Oh, was it me on your mind?" he assumed. I flinched.

He just came out with it, and as he took me off guard, my words choked in the dead center of my throat. My mouth was open, but nothing came out.

Thank God my teacher walked in and told everyone to take their seats, because I was so embarrassed that I think I had accidently displayed the embarrassment on my face. He smiled at me, already knowing my answer, and then went to his seat.

Throughout the whole period, I couldn't pay attention. I was too distracted. I kept looking back at him, and every time that he looked up, I would turn around in my seat quickly.

The bell had finally rung, and everyone rushed out of the classroom. I really wasn't in any kind of hurry because I was trying to finish my last sentence in my packet.

When I was done, I packed my stuff up and got up from my seat. As I turned around, I saw Scrap sitting on the desk, just waiting there patiently, looking right at me with a smile on his face. I smiled.

"What are you still doing here?" I asked.
"Waitin' on you," he said. I blushed. He got up from the desk and walked closer to me.
"So, who was on yo mind last night?" he asked again.

I shied away, not being able to control the smile on my face. He wasn't letting this go. I turned from him, smiling from ear to ear, and started walking out of the classroom. He walked next to me through the halls.

"Why do you think it was you on my mind?" I asked.

"Oh! I wasn't?" he asked, putting his hand on his chest as his bottom grill shined with the smile he was displaying. "Damn! And for a moment, I thought that I was *winnin'*!"

I chuckled. "You were on my mind . . ." I admitted. "I guess I'm just trying to figure you out."

"What chu' tryin' to figure out?" he asked.

"Why me?" I asked, looking into his eyes. I saw the confusion on his face. "Out of all the pretty girls sitting up there with me, what made you want to talk to me?" I clarified.

He stopped and stared at me for a moment, trying to read me. "For one . . . *pretty* ain't got shit on you. You're *beautiful*," he said.

My heart clinched, and the hardest smile that could embarrass me at this moment surfaced as I threw my head down.

"Are you surprised that I decided to talk to you?" he asked. I shrugged. "I do want to get to know you betta' fa'sho."

"Me too," I responded.

"So, what do you like to do for fun?" he asked.

I shrugged as I thought about my normal routines. *I am no fun.* I chuckled to myself. "Honestly, all I do is sit up in the house all day, do homework, read a book or watch television." I didn't know what else to say.

"Damn! Yo peoples got you locked down or somethin'?" he asked, looking at me like I lived in a torture home.

"No, I've always been like that, I guess."
"That's cool . . . I guess . . ." he said, chuckling. I could tell that he knew that I was a little nerd or what my brother's best friend always called me, a little *square*.

"How come yo brotha' not that way?"

"Trevor has always been the opposite of me," I responded, shaking my head. He nodded his, agreeing. He stopped and turned to face me.

117

"So, when am I gon' get the chance to kick it wit'chu?" he asked. It seemed like he was a "get straight to the point" type of guy.

"Kick it with me?" I asked, trying to figure out in what way he meant it. "Kick it like what? What will we do?" I finished.

He stared at me for a moment, squinting his eyes in deep thought. "You know what? I said that wrong . . . When can I take you out?" he corrected. "We can go to the movies or somethin' . . ." he said softly and stepped closer to me. I chuckled. "What's so funny?" he asked.

"Nothing. You just seem like you have two different personalities."

He laughed as well. "Only when I see somethin' I want."

"And you want me?" I asked, smiling.

"If I didn't, do you think that I would be asking you out?"

I blushed. "But what about Lovely?" I asked out of nowhere.

The question honestly just slipped. He scrunched his eyes up again as he observed my face.

I could tell that he knew that he couldn't just deny the fact that they had something going on, so I figured he didn't bother lying about it.

"We have our own type of relationship . . . It's mostly business though. She's just a friend."

"What kind of business?" I asked interested.

He smiled at me. "You gotta' lot of questions, don't you?"

After that say and the look on his face, I knew that I was asking too many questions, so I went back to his. "So, when do you want to take me out?"

"Well, you seem to be a busy girl, so when can I?" he asked, sarcastically. We both laughed.

I couldn't believe what was happening to me right now. This boy was just so fine, and in a matter of twenty-four hours, he was standing in front of me asking me out on a date. My knees were weak from just listening to him talking to me. I was so entranced by him that I didn't know what to do or how to act.

"How about I call you tonight and we'll talk more about it?" I said, realizing that we were both about to be late for our next class.

"Are you really gon' call me?" he asked, smiling.
"Yes," I said nodding my head with this big Kool-Aidsmile on my face. "I promise," I swore.

"Aight then . . ." he said, as he started backing away. "I'll be waiting for that call," he finished as he turned around and walked off.

"Okay," I said under my breath as I watched him.

When I got home, I ran upstairs and did my homework. I didn't want to call him too early and make him think that I was desperate, so I waited until eight. I finally called him, and my chest tightened as the phone started ringing. I started to panic and almost decided to hang up before anyone answered. My heart was racing.

"HELLO!" a young boy screamed through the phone.

The tone in the young voice scared my ass because the volume was so loud, and I turned the phone down. I heard a bunch of people in the background. "HELLO!" he yelled again. "Bruce, who phone you on?" a deeper voice said as I heard him snatch the phone from the younger voice.

"Is somebody on the phone, nigga?" he asked as I heard him moving the phone around. "Who dis?" a calmer but much deeper voice said. I hesitated to speak.

"Uh . . . can I speak to Scrap?" I asked, a little taken aback.

"Oh, this BomBom phone," he said, as I heard him pulling the phone from his ear. "Yeah. Hold on," he said as he came back. "BOMBOM!" he yelled out.

"WHAT!" I heard Scrap yell in the background.

"COME GET YO PHONE NIGGA!" the deep voice yelled back.

"Aight!" They were all very loud in the background. I heard the phone being moved around, and then a smooth, deep, raspy voice spoke.

"Who dis?" Scrap greeted.

"Hey, it's Janeeva," I said, in my sweetest voice.

"Oh, what's good wit'chu, Ma? I was hoping you wouldn't stand me up like you did last night." We both laughed.

"Yeah, I'm sorry about that," I said, apologetically.

"I ain't trippin'. So, wassup? How's yo night goin?" he asked.

"It's fine," I responded.

"That's good . . . Aye, what you doin' after school tomorrow?" he asked.

"Um . . . Nothing . . . I don't think . . ."

"Well, you wanna come over and chill with me?" he asked.

"Oh . . . I . . ." I didn't want to say that I had to get permission from my parents because that would just be embarrassing, but I didn't know what to tell him.

He chuckled. "Let me guess. Yo peoples don't let you get out like that." He was practically reading my damn mind.

"No, it's not that . . . It's just—"

He cut me off before I was about to lie. "Yo brotha' trippin' about you talkin' to me, huh?" There was a silence through the phone as he asked me that question.

"Well . . . I think it's everything changing all together," I lied. It wasn't exactly a lie, but Trevor did say that I needed to choose another boy to talk to. "He's just used to me staying to myself," I finished.

"I feel it. So, what he tell you about me? I'm pretty sho he warned you?" he asked.

"*Warned me?*"

"Yeah . . ."

He and Trevor were both confusing me. Trevor did *warn* me, but I wanted to know why. What was so bad about Scrap to where my brother had to tell me that he doesn't care who I talk to as long as it's not him.

I tried to change the subject. "So, about that date . . . Are you free this weekend?" I asked.

"Yeah, I am. How about Friday after school?" he said.

"Yes, I can do Friday."

"So, what chu' wanna do?"

I didn't know. I was hoping that he would answer that question. "Um—"

He cut me off again before I tried to answer the question. "How about we start off with a movie and we'll get some food afterwards?" he suggested.

"Okay. Do I need to bring some money?" I asked.

I honestly didn't know how this worked. There was a quick silence on the phone, and then I heard him laugh.

"Don't worry 'bout that, Ma. I got 'chu," he said. I flinched.

"Are you sure?" I asked.

"It's just a movie and dinner. I'm no young broke-ass nigga. What type of niggas do you fuck with?" he asked, laughing.

None. Once again, I was embarrassed as hell! Then I became curious. "What do you do?" I was interested in hearing, but he just laughed it off and told me not to worry about it.

"BomBom!" I heard someone yell in the background.

124

"YEAH!" Scrap responded, taking the phone away from his mouth so that he wouldn't yell in my ear.

"We gotta go, so get off the phone and c'mon," I heard the same calm but deep-ass voice say.

"Aight," he responded.

"Who is that?" I asked, being nosy.

"My brotha'," he replied.

"It seems like you have a lot of nicknames," I stated. He laughed.

"Yeah, I do. But I gotta go, Ma. If you still up, then hit me layta tonight."

"What time?" I asked. I honestly wasn't ready to get off the phone with him.

"Probably around three."

"Three?" I asked.
Yeah, I'll be sleep. Well . . . I'll stay up for him.

"Yeah, I gotta go handle some shit real quick?"

"Okay."

I didn't want to ask him too much, so I just left it at that.

Once I got off the phone with him, I called Lia. After telling

her about the good news, I couldn't wait until this weekend.

Chapter 7 The Block!

Scrap

It was a slow-ass night. It was cold as fuck too. I had on a black hoodie with my black snapback on standing outside of my room at Motel 6. We had a couple of rooms in this ma'fucka right now, *trappin'*.

I looked down at my phone, and my nose flared as it started ringing. I was getting irritated. Mia's bitch ass was blowing my fucking phone up asking where the fuck I was when she should be worrying about my money.

I looked down to the parking lot at Cherokee and Lovely as they posted on my oldest brother Brandon's car with his two hoes. Cherokee left the group and walked up the steps to me.

When she got to me, she leaned against me as I leaned against the rails, still looking down at my brothers and their hoe bitches.

"It's a slow night, Daddy."

Cherokee is my little *Compton* bitch. She's Columbian and sexy as fuck. I gave her the name because she looks like a little Indian doll.

At first, I didn't know that she got down the way that she did until I start realizing that she would do anything to be with a nigga. I just had to make her feel loved and she was rockin'.

I knew that she wasn't too happy about me putting my new bitch Lovely on, but my bitch goes hard, and she's *badd* than a ma'fucka! She doesn't give a fuck about what type of night it is! She's going to be all over LA county bussin' that shit down to get her bag, Cuz!

I don't care what these niggas be talking about, even if you want my bitch's company, you better be paying her. Lovely with the *shit*! She brings back at least three racks a night, and that's her alone! That's probably why Cherokee don't like her ass that much. She knows Lovely is starting to become my favorite.

"I know, cuz! It's too slow!" I looked at my phone and went to my text messages to see what time her next trick was

128

coming. "You gotta date at eleven. This nigga keeps talkin' about you goin' to Inglewood," I said, and then I shook my head.

I texted him back and told him that he needed to come to her.

With this nigga being a regular, he knew better. His ass was in love with Cherokee, but she was also under my protection as well. So, this nigga was gon' bring his ass here, or I was cancelling the date.

"I don't mind going to Inglewood, babe," she said.

I looked at her like she was crazy. "And if somethin' happen and this nigga end up bein' on that weird shit, what you gon' do?" I snapped. "You strapped? Is a nigga gon' come and save yo ass? Because I'm not goin' to Inglewood. You not the only bitch I gotta manage," I said. She dropped her eyes as she stepped back from my hostility.

I looked down at Lovely as I waited for Cherokee's trick to respond. I want to make that bitch my main so bad, but Mia had been rockin', and she's a ridah too but she don't know how to shut the fuck up!

129

Lovely smarter than her. She makes sure that no matter what she does, she's not *hot*! She doesn't talk to nobody like that. She makes sure that she got everything to where, if she does get pulled over, it's nothing on her.

Mia ratchet ass want to fight every bitch that she feels like I'm gettin' too close to, then make a fuckin' scene in public!

I looked at my phone at the time, and it was going on ten thirty.

"Lovely!" I called out. She looked up at me and started walking up the steps to us. "Aye, Cherokee gotta date at eleven. I'm makin' the nigga come here. I'ma have to dip for a minute, so I need you to be here with her in case that nigga is on some weird shit," I told her.

I pulled out the Glock tucked in the back of my jeans and handed it to her. "Don't let nobody else in this fuckin' room unless it's my brothers," I told them both. They nodded their heads.

I trusted Lovely to put a bullet right in that nigga's head if he was on some weird shit. I knew that Cherokee wouldn't do it, and that's why I had to give the gun to her.

As I was about to turn away from them, I thought about something and smiled. That nigga fa'sho wasn't about to turn down Lovely.

"And if y'all can, y'all should double the fun up. Test y'all self out and go double or nothin'," I said.

They looked at each other. Cherokee didn't look so happy about it. I knew she didn't swing that way, but Lovely was all up for it. I think Cherokee was more worried about Lovely steppin' on her toes than about the threesome.

"It's all up to you, Ma," Lovely said with that seductive look in her eyes.

She made my dick hard, but this was strictly business right now.

Cherokee thought about it for a moment, sighed and nodded her head. "Well, let's go get cleaned up so that we can get this shit over with," Cherokee said as she sighed, walking into the room.

As Cherokee walked into the room, I grabbed Lovely by her arm, and she looked at me. I smiled and stepped closer to her so that I only had her attention.

"Make sho you clean up good so once I get back, I can take that shit down," I said as I brushed my fingers across her pussy.

"Yes, Daddy," she said as she kissed me on my neck and walked into the room.

When they went inside, I walked down the stairs to Brandon and the rest of the team that was posted in the parking lot. As I was walking over to them, my brother Bavari was pulling up on his motorcycle.

On the streets, they call Bavari "Guda." He was twentytwo. As he took his helmet off, one of the homies walked up to him and dapped him up.

Bavari had a natural mug. That nigga always looked mad. He had these fresh silk dreads in his head that he maintained and kept up. His dreads used to fall to the middle of his back, but he cut them shoulder length because he didn't like dealing with the shit. He would normally have one of his hoe

bitches braid them up to keep them out his way.

He also had more tattoos than any of us did. His whole

torso was tatted all the way up to his neck, and he had a couple

on his legs as well. Most of them he got in the pin. He wore the

same green eyes as me and Brandon, and he was a little lighter

than me too. He hopped off his bike and walked over to

everyone else as I did.

"Aye, loc! You gotta take my car to school tomorrow. I

need my bike," he told me.

I nodded my head. I really didn't care. I just preferred

the bike because I liked doing tricks on that ma'fucka.

Brandon just turned twenty-eight. On the streets, they

called him "Taz". He raised me, my brothers and my sister. His

hoes, Trinity and Diamond, walked over to where I was

standing.

They were older than my hoes. Trinity was thirty, and

Diamond was twenty-seven. They old asses be trying to school

my hoes sometimes, but I don't get in the way of them doing

so.

They've been rockin' with Brandon for about 8 years. I know Trinity fa'sho been rockin' for damn near a decade. The bitch used to babysit me and the twins when my brothers knew that they were going to be gone for too long.

"Wassup, Bom?" Trinity greeted me as she approached us.

"What's good."

"Slow night, huh?"

I shook my head. This night was slow as fuck, but I was trying not to get irritated with it being so slow.

Brandon looked at me and laughed. He knew me too well. He always told me that patience was a virtue, because I had none.

"Chill out, Bom. I gotta couple of things on line right now," he said. "Aye! Did you handle that shit with Huey?" he asked Bavari.

Bavari smacked his lips. "Man, I been handled that shit, cuz," he said.

"What about that nigga's crib?" Brandon continued.

"Stripped that ma'fucka down to the last. We cleaned that whole place out."

Brandon nodded his head. "Bet. That's what his bitchass get. *Putain de serpent*," he said, adding his last comment in

French. It meant "fucking snake."

Huey was one of the niggas that was slangin' our product. We found out a couple of weeks ago that he was cutting us short every time we collected from his ass.

That was honestly our fault for putting a nigga that trusted Huey too much in charge to collect from him. It was one of Brandon patnas that was collecting.

After Brandon started becoming suspicious about Huey stealing from us, he told his nigga to fall back and that he was going to start making those rounds.

Once he confirmed what we already knew, he beat the fuck out of his loc for not paying attention, and Bavari merked that nigga Huey. His loc should be thankful that Brandon didn't make Bavari merk his ass too, because he didn't like him anyway.

I looked over at my brother Brent. He was laughing and smoking a blunt with one of his homeboys.

Brent was the second oldest. On the streets they called him "Yaya." He was twenty-five. His eyes were different from the rest of ours. He had these creamy light brown eyes, like a copper brown. They lowkey reminded me of Janeeva and Quarterback's eyes. My twin brothers were the same as well.

Bavari walked over to Brent as they both started talking shit to the lil homies.

My brothers normally don't be outside like this. That's what they have workers for.

Tonight, was more of a *chill* night though. We were all still working, but it was still chill. So, they were out kickin' it with the team.

"Oh yeah, Trinity!" Brandon called out, looking at his hoe. "You good with chemistry, right?" he asked. I cut my eyes at him as I pressed my lips together. She smiled and nodded her head.

"Yeah, I am."

Brandon nodded his head and pointed at me. "This lil nigga right here gon' need help. He needs to pass that class with at least a B," he told her.

"I got 'chu, Bom. Just let me know when you ready," she said.

I cut my eyes at her for a moment and then pressed my lips together. I didn't respond. I was honestly trying to stay away from the bitch. We got our own secrets that I wasn't trying to deal with anymore.

"Naw, I'ma let you know, because that nigga ain't gon' tell you shit," Brandon said.

I smacked my lips. "Man, cuz!" I said, turning my head.

"Bom, I'on give a fuck about none of that shit wit'cho punk-ass attitude. You finishin' school, cuz! There's way more out there than this shit."

"Whateva', cuz," I said, walking off.

"Yeah, whateva' my ass, nigga," he retorted.

The rest of that night, I had a couple of my regulars show up, but besides that, it wasn't a night for me. I was praying that Cherokee and Lovely come up tonight.

The trick made it over here with his bitch ass, so they were in the room right now with him. *They better have at least three racks in their hand before they come out that room, or that nigga better be* zellin *or* cash appin' *me the rest of my money.*

Cherokee was charging the nigga fifteen hundred for her time because of all the shit that he was trying to do, but now that I got Lovely helping her, I was praying that they made that shit happen.

My phone started vibrating, and when I looked at the caller ID, Mia was calling me again. She was pissing me off.

"Bitch, why you keep blowin' up my phone, cuz!" I greeted, in anger.

"Because you not answering my calls, nigga! Where you at?" she yelled through the phone.

"Man don't question me. Where the fuck you at? Ain't you supposed to be on Figueroa with Plenty?" I retorted.

Figeuroa was the hoe stroll in LA. All the hoes be up and down that bitch.

"I'm done!" she yelled. "Where the fuck is Cherokee and Lovely at?" she demanded.

"Bitch, question me one more time," I told her, losing my patience.

"Whatever, Green Eyes! I'm trying to give this money to you! That's why I've been blowing yo phone up!"

"Man, just meet me at the crib!" I told her.

"Aight." I hung up the phone, and Brandon looked at me.

"Why you always gettin' at that bitch like that, cuz?" he asked.

"Because she's dumb!" I responded.

He shook his head. "You better be cool; you know it's something wrong with that bitch, and I see yo ass gettin' all into Lovely. She gon' cut that bitch's throat if she sees you gettin' too close to her," he joked.

I laughed. "That bitch don't have no say-so on what the fuck I do."

When we got back to the house, Mia was already there with Bavari's hoe, Plenty. She's been with her ass all day because it's been the only transportation that she had.

Plenty was thick as fuck! That's how she got her name. She was thick from her breasts down to her thighs. Lil bitch that he pulled down south, I think he met her in Atlanta.

"Here!" she yelled, walking up to me and throwing the stack of money at me. I instantly got mad!

"Bitch, did you just throw some fuckin' money at me, cuz?" I snapped, balling my fist up.

"Yep! You should have answered ya phone, nigga!" she told me.

Brandon came between us. "Man, both of y'all chill the fuck out!" he said. "Y'all do this shit every night and then go fuck! So, make it easier on yo'self and skip the bullshit," he told us.

"Man, fuck this bitch," I said, pulling my jeans up and walking past her.

"Nigga, fuck you! You probably been fuckin' on yo new bitch! How the fuck you gon' recruit a bitch without telling me? That's my job, nigga!"

I turned back around and stepped in her face. "Bitch, why the fuck do you feel like you runnin' shit? I gave that much to yo ass because I thought you was a down-ass bitch, but you startin' to make me want to slap the shit out of yo ass. You need to fall back, and don't worry about what the fuck I do with *my* bitches! You either rockin' or you not, bitch! Don't think you can't be replaced!" I said, as I gave her a malice look. I knew I hit her hard with that last comment.

"Replaced? You got me fucked up, nigga!" she retorted sticking her finger in my face.

Bavari and Brent grabbed me because they knew what was next. They started pushing me inside the house, while Brandon tried to calm Mia down. They closed the door as I paced the living room trying to calm down.

"Man, this bitch got me fucked up, cuz. She gotta go! I ain't dealing with her shit no moe'!"

"Y'all niggas fight like a married couple. You do need to let that bitch go, though. The money ain't worth it. Besides, you still make twice as much as she's bringin' in," Brent said.

I paced the living room as I thought about dismissing the bitch, but I knew it was going to be more problems.

"Gotta think about that shit first though, Bom. That bitch is yo fatal attraction," Bavari said, laughing. I didn't say anything. I just kept pacing.

Brandon finally came into the house, but Mia and Plenty weren't with him. He gave me this hard look. I could see it all on his face that he was mad as hell.

"Bom, let me holla at you, nigga." He walked into his room, and I followed behind him. "Close the door," he instructed.

I did what I was told. The moment that I shut the door, his face was inches away from my own, and I saw the fire in his eyes.

"What did I tell you before you got into this shit?" he growled. I didn't answer because I already knew what was coming next. "What the fuck did I tell you, nigga!" he yelled.

142

I shifted my head as I stayed in my place and sighed. "Don't mix pleasure with business," I responded.

"And you keep fuckin' these hoes!" he yelled again. His face turned red. Knowing Mia, she probably said something that got under his skin. "You fuckin' Lovely too?" he asked. I didn't respond. He shook his head already knowing my answer. "You fuckin' up, Bom! These bitches gon' end up gettin' you caught the fuck up! You not supposed to fuck yo hoe bitch!" he yelled again. I sighed. "This shit ends now!
Either you stop fuckin' them and put these bitches in they place or cut 'em loose! And go check yo *bitch*!" he yelled again, pointing to the door. Mia must still be outside. "Bitch got me fucked up, cuz!" he said as he swung the door back open and

left.

I went outside, and Mia was still talking her shit to Plenty. Plenty leaned against her car quietly as she let the bitch vent. Mia wasn't even aware of the fact that I was walking toward her, and right when she turned around, I snatched her ass up by her neck and pinned her against the car.

143

"Get the fuck off of me!" she yelled.

"I'ma tell you like this . . ." I said to her in a low but more deadly tone. She calmed down a little bit and listened. "You gon' stop disrespectin' me, Mia. I wasn't playing when I said yo ass can be replaced. Since you want to act like this, then we gon' keep this shit strictly business. Ain't no calling me to fuck, ain't '*no baby this, no baby that*' shit. It ain't none of that! If you don't got my money, then don't fuckin' call me!" I said as I shoved her out of my face. She looked at me with that menace look as she caught her balance and I saw the tears coming along.

"It's like that?" she cried.

"Yeah. Now get the fuck off my block!" I told her as I walked back into the house.

As I walked, my phone started ringing. I looked and Janeeva was calling me. I ignored her call. I wasn't in the mood to talk.

After school the next day, Bavari and I chilled outside of the house, while my twin brothers Bruce and Bavarion rode

144

their electric scooter, the UberScoot 1600w, and their two-seat commuter scooter around the neighborhood.

They were twelve years old, badass lil niggas.

Bavari was in his car on the driver side with the door open blasting his music, while I chilled on the porch with my shirt off, smoking a blunt. I was texting Janeeva as I nodded my head to the beat that was playing from his car.

I was with her most of the day at school, just talking and trying to get to know her a little more. I didn't know what the fuck it was about her that had me so curious, but she was fa'sho different than the type of females that I normally talked to. She was a mystery to me.

While I smoked my blunt and texted her, I texted my hoe bitches too. I was about to go with Bavari and drop some packages off and collect from them as well, but I was waiting for that call.

As I sat there chilling on the porch and smoking my blunt, I looked up and saw the twins riding on the two-seat commute scooter with Bavarion on the back and Bruce was driving it.

I stood at my feet as they both wore these wide eyes in panic. I stepped off the porch as they came up the driveway, and as Bavari noticed, he stepped out of his car as well.

We observed them both. He turned around, grabbed his phone from out of his car to pause the music blasting from his car speakers and then turned back to the twins. Bavarion's lip was busted, and he had a black eye.

"Where the fuck is your scooter at, cuz?" Bavari growled at Bavarion.

"These older kids jacked him!" Bruce said as he helped Bavarion off the scooter.

"Nigga, where the fuck was you?" Bavari yelled at Bruce.

"I went a different way around the neighborhood, and when I came back, his scooter was gone, and he was laid out on the sidewalk!" he retorted.

"They jumped me," Bavarion explained.

"Man, cuz! Get the fuck in the car!" Bavari yelled.

I ran to the passenger side, not even bothering to grab my shirt, and the twins hopped in the back seat. Bavari backed out of the driveway quickly and scraped off from the way that the twins came.

"You know what them niggas look like?" I asked, looking back at the twins.

As they described the boys that jacked them and told us that they were around my age, we scoped the neighborhood out for three high school kids with a scooter. As we turned on another block, Bavarion leaned to the front with his arm extended and pointed to a group of kids.

"There go two of 'em right there!" he yelled, pointing to this tall, scrawny nigga that had this blue Dodger fitted cap on that was turned to the back and these faded black skinny jeans.

He was the one on Bavarion's scooter. The other nigga had on some basketball shorts and a white fitted t-shirt.

Bavari sped up, and as he scraped up on the sidewalk and the niggas noticed, the one on the scooter took off and the other one ran in the opposite direction.

I hopped out of the car and chased the one that ran, while Bavari scraped off and chased the other one who had the twin's scooter.

147

This nigga had me jumping over fences and running through backyards and shit. I couldn't wait to beat his ass for making me run in these new Js. I chased him through the alley, and as I did so, the nigga that was on Bavarion's scooter was coming in the alley from the other direction with Bavari right on his heel.

"Fuck!" the nigga that I was chasing yelled. He stopped and tried to turn around. The one on the scooter hopped off it as it kept going, crashing into the brick wall.

I ran up on the nigga that I was chasing and punched him right in his jaw. We both started fighting.

I was fucking his ass up, and as he tried to swing on me again, I bent down, grabbed him by his legs and slammed his ass on the concrete. I grabbed him by his shirt and just kept punching him in his face until his ass was leaking with blood.

"Bitch ass got me chasing you in these fuckin' shoes!" I yelled as I stood up and kicked him in his stomach.

I didn't realize that the only reason the nigga on the scooter didn't help his homie was because Bavari was already walking up to us with his gun in his hand with the twins right behind him.

When I finally stopped beating his friend's ass, I meanmugged the nigga that just stood there, ready to square up with him next.

He looked between me and Bavari, and as he walked up, the nigga shook his head.

"Guda . . . wait! Wait!" Before he could say another word, Bavari took the hand he held the gun with and pistolwhipped him, making him drop to the ground.

"You niggas chose the wrong lil niggas today, cuz! Where the other nigga at that jumped my ma'fuckin' brother?" Bavari yelled out as he pressed the gun to his head. He kept his head down, looking at the concrete.

"Guda . . . please . . . I swear we didn't know that was y'all lil brotha'. If we would'uh known, we wouldn't have touched 'em!" he said with fear in his tone. We didn't know them, but they knew exactly who we were when they saw us.

"You should'uh thought about that before you jumped a lil ass kid, cuz!" Bavari growled as he pressed the gun to his head harder.

"Aye, cuz! I swear we didn't know he was a Gaither! We wouldn't have jumped 'em!" he pleaded.

"I'on give a fuck about none of that shit!" Bavari said as he bent down and pistol-whipped him again.

He yelled in fear as he threw his hands back up. "Guda, please! Don't kill me, cuz!" he yelled. I tried not to laugh.

I mean I already knew that they were soft as fuck, just from jumping and robbin' a little kid, but this shit right here! I already knew what Bavari was about to do.

I stepped back as I continued to smile, trying not to laugh. The twins were already taking off their shirts as Bavari looked at the nigga and stepped back as well.

"Ain't nobody 'bout to merk yo bitch ass. Nigga, yous'uh bitch! You ain't worth my bullets, cuz! Twins!" he called out. "Both of you! Run this nigga shit!" he ordered.

The twins ran up on the nigga as he tried to stand to his feet, and they started beating the shit out of him!

His homeboy that I had already beat up hesitated to help him, and I just said, "Fuck it." I started beating his ass again, just for thinking about it.

As the twins jumped the nigga and I beat the fuck out of his loc, Bavari stood there, waiting for us to finish.

All three of us stopped when they both were barely moving. The twins ran through the nigga's pockets as I did the same, taking what they had on them, including their phones, and we stepped back.

They beat his ass so bad that both of his eyes were closed shut with blood leaking from his mouth onto the concrete.

His homeboy fa'sho had a couple of broken ribs with a busted lip and a gash on the right side of his forehead.

The twins grabbed their shirts, and Bavarion ran to his scooter and rode it back to Bavari's car to throw it in the trunk.

I just kept smiling as I looked at the two of them laid out, walking backwards.

I turned around, hopping back in the car.

Bavari turned his music up, and I threw up the set as we smashed off, leaving their asses there.

You fuck with one of us, then you fuckin' with all of us.

Chapter 8 First Date

Scrap

It was Friday, and I was tired as fuck.

I had a date tonight with Janeeva. Who would have ever known how fine her ass was under all of them damn clothes? I remembered her fa'sho . . .

That first day in class when I was trying to help her with her books, when she looked at me . . . I'm not going to *front* like she didn't have me stuck for a moment. Her creamy light-brown eyes were beautiful.

If I would have known that she was so cool, I still would have talked to her before, but I honestly thought she was gay.

Her ass still be acting low-key weird. But it's cute in a way. I'm trying to figure out if that's just who she is or if it's a couple of things that she was still just clueless about. We've been talking over the phone all week.

Mia was still blowing my phone up. I've been avoiding her ass. Besides, Cherokee and Lovely been bringing in twice as much as her ass anyway. They made up for all of Mia's shit. Now that I know that they can do it, I'm thinking about letting Mia go so she can stop calling me.

As my mind got carried away from them, I start thinking about Janeeva again. I still can't get through to her. Like I said before, she's different, but I don't know how she's different. I just have this feeling. She got my attention fa'sho.

I came out of my deep thoughts as I stood over the sink in the boys' bathroom looking in the mirror.

I turned on the faucet, put my hands under it, and as my hands filled up with water, I threw it on my face. I rubbed the water down my neck to cool off. It was hot as hell.

At Wilson, the bathroom was usually my normal spot when I was slangin' my freshman year. I was making bands in that bitch! But I knew that I couldn't do that shit anymore and risk getting caught up again.

Jordan was no better than Wilson. They did a random ass search every other week too.

The K9s be all through this bitch. I didn't even know at first that it was so many *knocks* that went here.

The bathroom door opened, and one of my patnas walked in.

"Aye! Wassup, Scrap! I've been looking for yo ass all day fam!" he said as I dapped him up.

"Sup wit'chu?" I greeted him.

"Aye, you on right now?"

"Yeah, but you gotta wait until after school, cuz. I'on bring my shit up here," I told him.

"Damn, nigga . . . I was trying to cash you out, bruh!"

"If you need the shit right now, then I'll hit one of my brothers to holla at you, and you can meet up with them."

"Yup! Just hit me when you get the word," he said as he dapped me up again, and I walked out the bathroom.

Lately, I've been on some "no-sleep" type shit, on the block just grindin'. School days make it hard when I'm stuck in a fucking classroom all day. If my brother wasn't on my ass, then I wouldn't be here right now.

He wanted it to be different for me and my younger siblings because of how Brent and Bavari turned out. He really been on my ass about everything ever since I got locked up.

I missed half of my freshman year and sophomore year because of that shit.

Of course, I had to take classes when I was in that bitch, and then Brandon made me do the homeschool.

I couldn't make any more mistakes and end up back in juvie. It was too easy to get caught up over the smallest shit.

As I was walking into my chemistry class, I smirked as I saw Janeeva's little nerd ass sitting there waiting patiently for class to begin.

Before I walked to the back of the classroom where my seat was at, I walked past her and traced the back of my finger across her forearm as I looked down at her with this seductive look in my eyes and kept walking to the back.

She smiled so damn hard that I tried not to laugh. She looked back as I took my seat, and I smiled at her. She blushed as she turned back around.

Ms. Laney came in as she started her lecture, telling us to pull out our chemistry packet that we had to finish last night for homework.

I honestly didn't even do it. She wrote one of the formulas from our packet down on the board as she looked back at the class and asked who wanted to come up to solve it. Nobody volunteered.

I sat there, slouched down in my chair, minding my fuckin' business, and then the bitch looked at me.

"Mr. Gaither. You seem a little distracted this morning. Would you like to come and solve this problem?" she asked.

"Naw . . ." I responded, nonchalantly, as I remained slouched down in my chair.

"Did you do the homework at all last night, Mr. Gaither?" she asked as she pressed her lips together, annoyed.

"I didn't get it," I said, shrugging. "I knew that we were going to be going over it in class . . . so I waited."

She pressed her lips together and sighed. "Ms. Boldin! Would you like to help Mr. Gaither solve this formula on the board, please?" she asked as she held out the marker in her hand to Janeeva.

"Um . . . Okay," Janeeva responded, in the lowest voice, as she got up from her seat and grabbed the marker from her.

She solved the problem on the board as if it were nothing and then handed the marker back to Ms. Laney and took her seat.

Ms. Laney reviewed her work and then smiled at her. "Thank you, Janeeva."

"Mr. Gaither, I hope you're writing this down in your packet. Do you understand what she just did on the board?" she asked me.

"Does anybody in here understand what she just did on the board?" I retorted.

I didn't like her coming for me. The classroom laughed. She sighed.

"I would like it if you paid attention in my class so that we can make sure that you pass. Your brother is making sure that I keep him updated on your progress," I sighed. *This nigga be doing too much.* "It's okay if you need a *study buddy.* I'm quite sure Ms. Boldin wouldn't mind helping. She helped tutor a couple of students last year."

My annoyed looked turned into a sneakish ass smirk. "Sounds like you're threatening me with a good time, Ms. Laney," I said.

The class laughed again as Janeeva turned, smiled at me and then chuckled. I winked at her as I licked my lips, and she blushed. Ms. Laney pressed her lips together and sighed, annoyed with me.

"Alright, class! Let's get back focused! Mr. Gaither gave us our laughs for the morning," she said, giving me the "eye" in disappointment. I just smiled at her.

This bitch better stop playing with me.

Once passing period came, SixPacc was already outside of my chemistry class, waiting for me.

Janeeva walked past me, out the door as we both looked at each other, flirting with our eyes and shit.

SixPacc looked at us both, and as Janeeva noticed him, she flinched when she realized how hard he was smiling, because he was watching us silently flirt the whole time.

159

She smiled harder as she dropped her head, and she walked over to where Lia was standing by the lockers.

"So, you got her?" he asked, once she was out of hearing distance, not really surprised about it.

"Yeah, she's coo' . . ." I said as we walked down the hallway. "I'm not gon' lie though. I really want to fuck the shit out of her, bro, but it's somethin' about her that got me trippin' or somethin' . . . I don't know what the fuck it is," I admitted.

SixPacc laughed. "Yeah, when they look that good, it seems to do the trick, and curious?" he asked.

I nodded my head. "It's her whole lil mysterious, shy-ass attitude," I confessed.

SixPacc looked at me, suspiciously. "Sounds like you found somebody that actually caught yo interest aside from just giving up some pussy," he responded.

I stood there in deep thought listening to him, and then I shrugged. "I'ma figure her out," I said, with confidence.

He laughed. "I know you are, nigga." He knew me too well. We both laughed. "But let me catch up wit'chu later. I gotta get to class. My dad been trippin' lately over bullshit." I looked at him and shook my head. *His pop is always trippin'*.

"Aight then," I said, as he walked away.
I pulled my attention back on Janeeva, still standing in the hallway with Lia.

She looked over at me, and something was telling me that she was still standing there because she was waiting for me to come over to her, so I did. I approached her and smiled.

"So, am I the only one who felt like Ms. Laney was trying to come for me?" I asked, raising my eyebrows.

She laughed. "She was definitely coming for you," she said, nodding her head.

I dropped my head and shook it, laughing. "She was right about somethin' though . . ." I said, as I stepped closer to her. "I'on mind havin' a study buddy," I said, with this seductive look in my eyes.

She dropped her eyes as she smiled and then looked back up at me. As she fought not to smile too hard, she shrugged. "I don't mind either."

Lia looked between the both of us as she observed. "You know . . . you two make a cute-ass couple," she said, smiling ear to ear.

I laughed it off and looked back at Janeeva. "You ready for tonight?" I asked her, ignoring Lia's comment.

"Yes," she said, shyly.

"Aight then. What time you want me to pick you up?" I asked. She shrugged. "How about seven?" I asked her. I assumed that she had a curfew.

"Seven is good," she said, still smiling. Before I could say another word, we were interrupted.

"Hey, Green Eyes," a familiar voice said as I looked over my shoulders to see this white girl name Yitsel.

Green Eyes was a nickname that I got when I was in middle school.

One of the girls that I was talking to back then gave it to me, and everybody else that I went to junior high with just started calling me it.

I sighed and rolled my eyes as I threw my head down. *Shit! This bitch . . .* I turned around to face her so that I could dismiss her, but I think she misunderstood that as me trying to hug and greet her.

She wrapped her arms around my neck as she pressed her body against mine and tried to hug me. I instantly pulled away. She held on to me, and I finally was able to get her off me.

Yitsel is this annoying ass white bitch that I use to fuck around with. She was cool until her ass started becoming attached. I'm the last nigga that you want to get attached to. She was on my nuts so hard that I was ready to merk her ass for her to leave me alone!

She's one of them ghetto white bitches that can't get enough, and I knew she was on some "weird shit" right now.

Janeeva looked at me and then at the girl. She wasn't as shocked as I thought that she would be, but her mouth slightly hung open as she looked at us, confused. Lia glared at her and me. I shook my head.

"Man, Yitsel, what chu doin' right now, cuz?" I asked, and she knew what I meant.

She knew that I was avoiding her because we hadn't talked in months, so I was confused about why she was doing all this extra shit.

"I just wanted to come over and see how you been? I missed you," she said as she rubbed her finger down my chest. I moved her hand and looked at Janeeva. I could see the anger and the hurt lighting up in her eyes.

"Naw . . ." I said looking back at Yitsel, shaking my head. "It ain't good, cuh. You doin' too much right now." I was really trying not to make a scene and dismiss her as quietly as possible.

"What you mean?" she asked, appalled that I was getting at her the way that I was.

"Man, you know what I mean. I haven't talked to yo ass in months, and now all the sudden you're approaching me when you see I'm in the middle of somethin'," I retorted, referring to Janeeva and Lia.

I've never been the "explaining type of nigga." If it happens than it happens, but Janeeva made me want to explain myself to her. Yitsel looked at Lia and Janeeva as she observed them and then she smiled at Janeeva.

"I see you stepped yo game up," she said with a devilish smirk on her face. "What's yo name again? Jay Somethin'?" she asked.

"Why do you need to know her name?" I retorted, trying to dismiss her again and shifting my body in front of Janeeva. She was just being messy and, on some hating-ass shit.

"I'm just having a friendly conversation," she said, shrugging with that sneaky-ass grin still on her face.

I smacked my lips. "Man, get up outta here, cuz. You on some *fuck shit* and you know you on some *fuck shit* right now. I'on got time for it."

This bitch knew that I wasn't one of them niggas to play around with and just let certain shit slide. I knew what the fuck she was doing, and I didn't have time.

"Why you so concerned about what we got going on anyway? We don't know you like that," Lia spoke up.

"Last time I checked, I was talking to your friend and not you," Yitsel responded as she snapped her neck at Lia.

"Bitch!" Lia retorted, stepping up to her.

She was about done listening and not seeing any action taken place. I took a deep breath and threw my head back.

"Who the fuck is you calling a bitch, lil girl?" Yitsel retorted, standing probably a good two or three inches over Lia.

Yitsel was a senior this year, and she was about fiveeleven. She wasn't that much shorter than me and I'm six-two.

She needs to get her ass into some damn sports and shit so that she can stop having free time to fuck with me. She so damn annoying that she wouldn't be the bitch to take home to your parents or shit, to my brothers! They might enjoy her though, might even try to throw her ass on Figueroa.

"You *bitch*!" Janeeva spoke up out of nowhere.

My head snapped toward her, shocked. I never even heard her curse. Just the fact alone that she wasn't being no punk, low-key turned me on. I smiled at her, amused.

"Oh, so now I'm about to get jumped!" Yitsel said, scooting back.

Her friends that were across the way weren't even defending her. They just stood on the side and watched.

I guess they figured she brought this shit upon herself. Yeah, I knew that they knew what the fuck she was doing, too. I came between them and tried to break the shit up. It was unnecessary.

"Yo, fall back. This shit dumb as hell. It ain't even that serious," I said, trying to calm shit down.

"Naw, bro, what you and this bitch got goin' on? Because obviously she thinks y'all got something going on?" Lia said, looking dead into my eyes.

I smacked my lips. "Hol' up. Don't be trying to check me, Ms. Attitude," I said twisting my lip up at Lia. "And this bitch knows what she's doin'," I said, turning my attention back to Yitsel.

"Don't call me no bitch!" she snapped.

"Then get the fuck on! I don't even know why you came over here when you know you just being messy right now, cuz! It ain't nothin' going on between me and you, and this is exactly why I stopped fuckin' wit'chu," I said, losing my patience.

She stared at me for a moment. I could see in her eyes that she was ready to cry. She glared at me and walked away.

I sighed because I was really trying to prevent myself from going there with her. I knew I didn't have any patience, but I knew the bitch was on some other shit too. I felt bad at how I got at her, but it was necessary.

In that moment I looked at Janeeva, and she didn't say anything. She just looked at me with a blank face.

I was really reconsidering if this was a good idea or not.

I could already tell that she was sensitive, and I didn't know if she was going to be able to handle a nigga like me. I didn't want to hurt her.

But that was the shit that had me in these mixed-ass emotions. I just met this damn girl, and we already got drama. *I don't even know why the fuck I'm acting like I care so much. What the fuck is it about her?* The shit was low-key bothering me. She looked at me and turned her head. She shook it as she and Lia started to walk away. I grabbed her hand, and she sighed.

"Look, me and that girl talked a while back, and ever since then I've been ducking and dodging her. She just wanted to make you mad. It ain't nothin' goin' on between me and her."

"I know," she responded, rolling her eyes and turning away so that she could leave.

I sighed, pulled her back and made her look at me. "Look, I'm not about to just let you walk off. I'm feelin' you . . . We just now gettin' to know each other. We barely got anything started . . ."

I stared into her eyes, trying to read them. She gazed back. I saw them soften, and then she pressed her lips together. "Okay," she said, trying to break a smile.

"I'll make it up to you tonight," I said in a lower voice, stepping closer to her, trying to make her smile. She gave me a half smile.

"See you tonight," she said, walking away with Lia.

Janeeva

Later that night, after school, I was so excited about my date that it was hard for me to even do my homework. I couldn't concentrate. I was really hurt about the white girl earlier, but Scrap said that he would make it up to me. I believed him.

It was five-thirty. I pulled out my dress that Lia and I picked out some time this week. It was this cute skin-tight dress that had all different kinds of tropical colors in it with white studs going around the straps. The strap went around my neck though, which was a little uncomfortable, and when I tried it on, it felt like I had too much skin out. My shoulders and my back felt so exposed.

I tied my hair up and hopped in the shower. The moment I stepped in, I slipped and fell. I started to freak out as my hair was getting soaked through the scarf I had on. I was devastated.

"Fuck!" I cursed. It was instantly about to frizz back up into its natural state. I didn't know how to press my hair back out.

When I dried it out, I thought about just putting it back in a bun, but I didn't want to go back to that style too soon. There was a knock on the door, and before I could say, "Don't come in," my mother opened the door. When I caught her eyes, she looked at me astonished.

"Janeeva?" she asked. I tried to smile and nodded my head.

"What the hell?" she mumbled as I was wrapped in my towel with the makeup already on my face.

"Do you have on makeup, baby?" she asked. I nodded my head again.

I was scared as hell! My mom knew that I was stepping out tonight. She knew Lia was my only friend, so she just figured that I was going somewhere with her. She never really

171

cared if I made it home by ten. Now I was given away with the makeup on my face.

"You look beautiful!" she crooned. My mouth dropped. I was shocked. "What is all this for?" she asked.

I was stuck. I didn't know what to say. "I . . . I kind of have . . . a date tonight," I choked.

Her eyes widened, and she was quiet for a moment. "When did you get a boyfriend?" she asked.

I shook my head. "He's not my boyfriend," I said, studying her face. "But I really like him," I told her.

I was really shocked that she wasn't acting like Trevor and making up all the excuses on why I didn't need to be dating or why I shouldn't be putting on makeup. She was gleaming with satisfaction. She probably thought that I was gay, too.

"Why didn't you tell me, baby?" she asked.

"I guess I wasn't really sure what you would say or how you would react," I admitted, shrugging. I still had this dumbfounded look on my face from her own reaction.

"What?" she asked, smiling! "And you were going to let me miss you walking out this house on your first date?" she complained. I chuckled.

"I need to know where you're going and who you're with at all times anyway, lady!" she said, playfully. I laughed. "This is your first date, right?" I rolled my eyes.

"Yes," I said.

"Well, in the future! I need to know these things so that me and your father can know that whoever you're with or wherever you are going, you're safe . . . Okay?" she said. I nodded my head.

"When did you start putting on makeup? When did you start liking boys? Where the hell have I been?" she asked, still in shock and placing her hand on her hip. I laughed.

I knew that she wanted me to tell her everything, but I was so happy that she wasn't angry that I just wrapped my arms around her waist and hugged her. She hugged me back.

Even though I'm convinced that the only reason why she's so excited and approving of all this right now is because she really thought that I was gay, and I wasn't going to be able

173

to give her any grandbabies once I was old enough. I know it!
"Mom . . ."

"Yes."

"I got my hair wet, and I don't know what to do with it," I said, hoping that she could help me. She smiled.

My mother did my hair for me, but she didn't press it out like Lia did. At this point, I didn't even have enough time to press it out. So, she blow-dried my thick long hair straight, and it just puffed out while it fell over my shoulders. She gave me three cornrows on both sides of my head and made a hump in the middle while the back remained free, falling over my shoulders. She slicked down my baby hair and smiled after she finished.

I looked in the mirror and flinched as I smiled hard. I did not know that the women in my life were such great hairstylists.

This was a different Janeeva from her first change. I went from the gorgeous Indian doll to this gorgeous African princess. "*Wow*."

She let me wear her chandelier diamond earrings that felt so light on my earlobes, and when she saw my dress, she was even more ecstatic! She made me put on a light half jacket though to cover up my back and my shoulders. It was more comfortable for me anyway.

When the doorbell rang, I was so scared that I just looked at my mom, praying that she didn't run for the door. She laughed at my facial expression, reading it clearly, and she just threw her hand out saying, "You first!" I exhaled in relief and walked downstairs to the front door.

When I opened the door, Scrap was leaning against the rails, waiting for me. However, when he saw me, he didn't smile like he usually did.

His facial expression was blank as he appraised me from my feet on up. We didn't speak for a moment as he continued, and then he smiled. I realized that the blank expression was him being in "awe."

"You look beautiful," he spoke.
I blushed as butterflies swirled inside my stomach.

"Thank you," I responded.

He kept appraising me until my mother came to the door. He took his eyes off me and looked at her.

"Hello!" she greeted.

"How you doin' tonight, ma'am?" he responded.

"I'm fine, young man," she said as she came in front of me and grabbed his hand, shaking it. "And what is your name?" she asked.

Scrap looked at me and then back at my mom. I could tell that he wasn't used to meeting parents.

"Brian," he responded.

"Well, nice to meet you, Brian. I'm Janeeva's mother, Mrs. Boldin," she said, introducing herself.

"Nice to meet you, Mrs. Boldin," he responded, displaying his charming-ass smile.

"You are one handsome young man," she said as she stared into his green eyes.

"And you're as beautiful as your daughter," he responded. She smiled as she looked at me. *Yes, he's a charmer.*

"I wish your dad didn't work late so he can meet your new friend, too, but he won't be back until later tonight," she said in disappointment.

"It's fine!" I said, relieved. I walked out the door and looked at Scrap. "Are you ready?" I asked. He nodded his head.

"Have fun, baby, and it was nice meeting you, Brian! I expect her to be home by eleven, and Janeeva, send me his number just in case I ironically can't contact you!" she said, already doing too much and embarrassing me. "I'm expecting a text right now with his number! Oh, Brian! Do I need to get your license plate number or is she just going to be home by eleven?" she asked, playing too much. *Well . . . at least she gave me another hour. I'll take it.*

Scrap was smiling from ear to ear as he listened to my mom, tilting his head, looking at me as we walked to the car. My whole face was flushing in embarrassment.

He turned around as he walked backwards to the car and yelled back to her, "I got 'chu! She'll be home by eleven, no layta!" he said, smiling at her.

177

"Okaaaaaay! Have fuuuuun!" she crooned. He chuckled as he turned back around. He walked to the passenger door and opened it for me. I stepped in, and we left.

I was happy Trevor was out somewhere with Talawny, because that would have been another issue to worry about. My mother and Maimi were the only ones that were home, but I think Maimi was already sleeping.

My mom really liked him. I was scared that he wouldn't be as respectful as he was, but he was perfect. I was even more nervous because I had failed to mention that it was my first date.

As we drove, I looked at him and apologized for my mother's behavior. He shook his head and smiled at me.

"You good. That's what a mom is supposed to do. Be happy you got her, because not a lot of people get love like that from their parents," he said, still smiling as he chuckled a little bit.

He stopped at the gas station to fill up his tank and asked me if I wanted anything out of the store.

When he got out and went inside, I watched some of the kids on their bike, riding around the gas station, and there were a couple of men posted outside of the store talking to this homeless man. The boy on the bike rode over to the men, and a woman approached him.

She had on some baggy torn-up, dirty sweats with a torn red tank top on. Her hair was matted up on top of her head, and her lips were severely chapped.

I watched them as the boy turned to her and smoothly passed her something in his hand as she passed him some money.

My window was rolled down as I watched them, and as I went into deep thought, I was startled by one of the men that was posted in front of the store approaching the car.

"Wassup, lil baby? What's yo name?" I didn't respond. I just turned away and tried to ignore him so that he would leave me alone.

"Oh, like that!" he said as I gave him the cold shoulder.

"Wassup, cuh?" I heard Scrap say in a malice tone behind him as the guy turned around. He wore this deadly expression on his face as he pulled his jeans up and sized the man up.

"Oh shit . . ." the man said, smiling and laughing nervously.

"You Taz lil brotha' . . . My bad, lil nigga. I didn't know this was yo bitch." Scrap kept the deadly look on his face.

"I'm nobody's bitch!" I snapped.

They both looked at me. I saw a hint of a smile on Scrap's face. The guy grimaced and pressed his lips together as he stepped back.

"Damn, girl. Aight. Ma bad, cuz," he said, walking back over to his friends.

Scrap watched him for a moment and then looked at me as he smirked and walked back around to the driver's side. He pumped the gas and then got in the car. He looked at me, smiling.

"I'm not your bitch, and I don't appreciate being called one," I said the moment that he came back in. He didn't say anything; he just continued to smile.

180

"What? What's so funny?" I asked.

"You," he replied. "You just keep surprising me." I cut

my eyes at him, confused. "I know you ain't no bitch, Ma.

That's just how niggas on the streets talk. He didn't mean it

like that, but if you don't want to be called one, then you

won't." He started the car and then looked at me, biting his

bottom lip with the same smile. I couldn't help but smile back.

As we pulled up to the parking lot at the movie theater,

he was getting a call on his phone. He checked his caller ID

and then answered it.

"Yeah . . ." he greeted. He had his air pods in as he

listened, and we sat there for a moment in the car while he took

his call.

"How you fuckin' lose the key to the room, cuz?" he

snapped. "Where Lovely at?" he asked. I looked at him as he

said her name. "Aight. I'ma call you back," he told whoever

was on the phone.

"Is everything okay?" I asked.

He looked at me from the side of his eye and then

nodded his head. "Yeah. We about to go in. Just let me handle

this real quick." I nodded my head.

He called someone else and waited for them to answer.

"Aye, loc, where you at?" he asked. "You with Cliff right now? . . . I need you to get this room key and give it to Cherokee . . ." He listened for a moment and then smacked his lips. "They out of town right now. They won't be back until the mornin' . . . Nigga, I told you that I had somethin' to do tonight!"

I then heard a voice through the phone as he yelled, and Scrap did a silent chuckle. He sighed and put whoever was on the phone on speaker.

"Aye! Am I on speaker?" the masculine voice said as I listened to all the noise in the background as well. It sounded like there was just a whole bunch of other men around him.

"Yeah," Scrap responded.
"Heeeeeeeeey, Janeeeeeeeeva! What you doin', girl?" the masculine voice said as I smiled hard.

"Who is that?" I laughed.

"SixPacc," Scrap said, smiling.

"Heeeey," I responded.

Scrap took him off speaker and then repeated his question. He smacked his lips. "Aight, I'ma just come to y'all." He hung up the phone and looked at me. "I gotta go handle some shit real quick. Are you okay with that?"

I shrugged. "It doesn't matter to me." He nodded his head and started the car.

As we drove, I observed my surroundings. As he turned on a street, I saw a lot of homeless people in alleys, and the streets looked dirty and degraded.

When he pulled over, we were in front of a small house, and there was a group of boys standing outside. Some of them were laughing and playing around, and some were just posted on the steps, talking and smoking a blunt. He looked at them and then looked at me.

"Stay in the car. I'll be right back." I nodded my head.

When I looked back at the group of boys, I noticed Twinkie on the steps, and then I saw SixPacc coming outside.

As Scrap approached them, he dapped everyone up and then handed SixPacc a card. They talked for a moment, and then SixPacc start walking back to the car with Scrap, smiling.

My window was up, and when I realized that he was smiling at me through the tinted windows, I rolled it down.

"Wassup, Jay?" He greeted me as he bent down and leaned onto the car door.

"Hey!" I said as I smiled back.

"My nigga gettin' on yo nerves yet? It's okay to tell 'em you ready to go home," he joked. I chuckled.

"Shut yo ass up, loc!" Scrap laughed as he walked over to the driver's side and got back into the car.

So, what y'all about to get into? Just a boring-ass movie?" he asked.

I shrugged. "Yeah, I guess so," I responded.

"If we can even make the movie. Lil Ma got curfew," Scrap responded, looking at me, smiling.

"Awe, you got curfew?" SixPacc teased. My face flushed.

Scrap's phone started vibrating, and as he looked at the caller ID, he sighed. He answered the phone.

"Yeah," he greeted. "SixPacc 'bout'a drop the key off to her now . . . Naw, cuz . . . I'm busy right now," he said, shaking his head. "*What?*" he snapped. "What nigga? . . . Aight . . . Naw, I'm coming!" he yelled. He looked at me with these apologetic eyes and then at SixPacc.

"I gotta go handle some shit at the room. This nigga just robbed Cherokee."

"What?" SixPacc yelled.

I can't take you with me, Ma. But I promise you, I'll be right back," he said to me.

"Wait . . . *What?*" I snapped.

"Trust me . . ." he said, looking into my eyes. "Aye, cuz! I need her to stay here. Make sure them niggas not all up in her face. Take her to the back room, and stay in there with her," he instructed. SixPacc nodded his head as he opened the door for me.

I could not believe this shit was happening! The moment that I stepped out, he scraped off. Are you fucking kidding me! I looked at SixPacc with this dumbfounded look on my face, not understanding what the fuck just happened! He sighed.

"C'mon . . ."

As we walked up to the house, all eyes were on me. I stayed close to SixPacc with my eyes glued to the ground.

Wassup, Jay?" I heard Twinkie say as he looked between SixPacc and me, confused. SixPacc answered his confused look. "Cherokee ass just got robbed."

"Oh shit!"

SixPacc took me into the house, and as I walked behind him, one of the boys outside hovered over me as I walked through the doors.

"Wassup, baby? What's yo name?" he asked, smiling. I leaned into SixPacc, not responding nor making eye contact with the boy.

"Watch out, loc. She with Scrap," he told him. He nodded his head as he turned his Lakers fitted cap to the back and stepped back out on the front porch with everyone else.

SixPacc walked me to the back, and as he opened one of the doors, he walked in, and I followed behind. I looked around the room, and it was the cleanest part of the house. I looked up at the ceiling fan as it spun and then around the rest

of the room. It was empty. The only thing that was in there was a small black leather sofa and a flat screen TV mounted to the wall. I looked at SixPacc as he closed the door.

"Whose house is this?" I asked.

He looked at me as he pressed his lips together. "Just one of the spots the homies kick it at," he responded. I could tell that he was lying. "You can sit. You thirsty?" he asked.

"SixPacc, what the fuck is going on?" I asked. "This is not how I pictured my first date to be."

After the words slipped out of my mouth, my eyes got wide. I looked at him, and he looked back with these wide eyes as well.

"Fuck . . ." I said under my breath. I took a seat on the sofa as the room suffocated us with this awkward silence.

"This yo first date?" he asked, smiling. I closed my eyes as I took a deep breath and gave him a hard nod. "Damn . . . that nigga fuckin' up . . ." He took a seat next to me as he leaned forward and rested his elbows on his leg.

"Look . . . I know y'all still gettin' to know each otha', but he really is feelin' you. To be honest wit'chu, I think I only seen him take one other girl out on a date or attempt to. The rest of them were just . . . *there*." We both had a silent laugh. "He just has a complicated life, and if you gon' be in it, you gotta know that it's gon' be a lot of *this*. At least he's making sure you're safe . . ."

"What does he do? What are the complications?" I asked.

He sighed. "To be honest wit'chu, Ma . . . that ain't my place to speak on. You gotta talk to him about that."

I stared at him for a moment and then dropped my eyes and nodded my head. We chilled back as we waited for him.

SixPacc played some music from his phone and turned on the flatscreen TV. We watched *Wild 'n Out* with Nick Cannon most of the time. He would get a call every now and then and had to go outside to the front, but he would always come right back.

It was going on at nine thirty at night, and I was getting anxious. I had to get home soon.

As I looked at my phone again, the bedroom door was opening. I looked up and it was Scrap. SixPacc got up as Scrap dapped him up.

"Good lookin', loc," he said to him.

"Yo . . . Cherokee good?" SixPacc asked.

"Beat up and mad, but she good. I handled it."

SixPacc nodded his head. Scrap looked at me as he pressed his lips together and sighed.

"I'ma let y'all talk," SixPacc said, walking out.

Once the door closed, he spoke. "I'm sorry, Ma . . ." I dropped my eyes. "Word is, I really fucked up," he said, giving me a half smile. I just gave him a disappointed look and pressed my lips together as I crossed my arms.

He took his arm from behind his back and held out a red rose.

He sat next to me, and as he leaned into me, he held it up with these puppy eyes and the same smile.

As hard as I tried to still act mad, I couldn't help but chuckle at the puppy eyes. I grabbed the rose.

"So, this was your first date, huh?" he asked. I nodded my head. "I promise you that I'ma make it up to you."

"I've heard that one already." He nodded his head.

"I know . . . And I'ma keep sayin' it until I get it right," he said as he stared at me with those beautiful green eyes.

I was melting. I came out of my spell and pressed my lips together. "Scrap, what do you do? Who's Cherokee, and who lives in this house?" I asked.

He pressed his lips together. He knew that I was about to ask a million questions. "I do a lot of things . . . And this house . . . is just where we do business. Cherokee is too . . . business," he responded.

"Like Lovely?" I questioned. He nodded his head. "What is the business?" I repeated myself.

"If I told you, would you judge me?" he asked smiling, trying to put on that charm. Now I felt like he was fucking with me.

"Well, everyone is judged in some way. But whatever it is, I'm sure that I can handle it." I responded.

He stared at me for a moment with this blank expression. "Well, if we continue fuckin' with each otha', then you'll figure it out sooner than later, and I'll let you judge." I sighed. "Yo brotha' don't really share a lot with you about the shit that he does on the streets, does he?" he asked.

I shook my head. "Not everything. I know a little . . . but he tries to keep me away from it. Why? Am I not supposed to be here with you?" I asked.

He chuckled. "We from the same set, Ma."

My eyes got wide as I looked at him. I looked around again. "You're from Shottas?" I asked.

The only reason I even know the name is because Trevor's best friend said something about it before, and Trevor told him not to talk about it around me. He nodded his head.

"We all are . . ." Scrap said, nodding his head toward the door, referring his last comment to everyone who was out on the front porch, and then it all started making sense, and I panicked.

"Is this a fucking trap house?" I asked as I tried to get up.

He calmly put his hand on my leg and made me look at him. I stared at him for a moment with this strained look on my face as he gave me this calm one.

"As long as you're with me, nothing will happen to you. You're safe. I didn't want to bring you in here, but I had no choice. That's why I made bruh bring you to the back."

"You're a drug dealer . . ." I stated as I stared into his eyes.

"I'ma lot of things," he responded. "But like I said, if we continue fuckin' with each other, you'll find out sooner than later, and I'll let you judge. Right now . . . we just chillin."

I dropped my eyes and then looked around again. I took a deep breath and started asking more questions.

"So, what's up with the tension between you and my brother if you guys are practically like family? I thought people from the same hoods are supposed to stick together and what not?" I asked, rolling my eyes.

I really didn't get the whole gang-banging shit. What the hell did people get out of killing each other?

"He fucks with my older brothers more than he fucks with the rest of the team. I gotta give it to him though. He about his dough. He's always all business." I could hear a hint of sarcasm in his voice. "I understand gettin' the job done, but we a family, and yo brother is the type who only talks business when it comes to gettin' his money. My brothers got respect for that nigga though. He just hasn't really grown on me yet," he admitted. "I'm the type of nigga that needs to be able to trust you to be around me. But my brothers trust him . . . So, I just fall back."

I continued to think. The tension between them two in the stands at the scrimmage was on my mind hard right now. I didn't want to worry about that though. I just wanted to know more about him. The only thing that I wanted was to get to know him better.

Even though my first date went to shits, I still wanted his heart, but I also wanted to know the type of person that I was dealing with. I sighed and changed the subject.

"How many siblings do you have?" I asked.

"Three older brothers, two younger and a lil sister. The oldest raised us . . ."

I flinched. "Your older brother?" I asked. He nodded his head. "Where are your parents?"

He looked at me for a moment and sat up. "Not everyone has parents who give a fuck like yours do, Jay . . ."

"I . . . I'm sorry," I choked, feeling sympathy.

He shook his head. "You good . . . My brother is my parent. He did what he could for us so that we didn't get separated. My dad left us when I was five, and my mom is just a drunk. I think after a while she just started depending on us because my brother made sure that we were taken care of, like we started disabling her or somethin'. I'on know . . . She just gave up . . ." I now saw why he was so impressed with my mother. He looked at the time on his phone. "I got a good hour before you need to be home. What 'chu wanna do?" he asked. I looked at the time as well and shrugged as I sighed. "You hungry?"

I smiled and nodded my head. "Yeah, I am."

"So, what's yo favorite food?"

"Street tacooooooos!" I crooned.

He laughed. "Oh! I got 'chu on that!" he said, standing up, grabbing my hand and pulling me up from the couch. I laughed.

We left the house and went to get something to eat. We stopped at one of the taco trucks that was parked in a parking lot down the street from our school. When we pulled up, there were only a couple of people in line. He looked at me.

"We came right in time. It's not a lot of people right now. It's still early though. Everybody out runnin' the streets and gettin' turnt up," he said, smiling.

We got out of the car and waited in line as we talked some more. He ordered my food for me. He said that this taco truck had the best street tacos in Long Beach. I could tell that he came here a lot because the chef knew him.

"Wassup, BomBom! Where yo brothas?" the guy asked. He was Mexican with a deep accent.

"Sup, Louise!" Scrap greeted him back. "You know how my brothas are, cuz, always on the move."

"How's your lil sister? I haven't seen my lil homie in a minute! Y'all be havin' her trapped in that house! Can't go nowhere!"

Scrap laughed. "She's good. You know we all just started back school, so we just haven't had time," he replied.

"Yeah, I know how Taz is about y'all staying in school, so I get it. Yo! Be grateful for yo brotha'! It's not a lot of big brothas who will go out the way to make sure their younger siblings stay on track!"

Scrap nodded his head. "Yeah, I know, but aye! I'ma holla at you layta," he said as he looked at me.

"Oh shit! My bad, lil lady! Well, go ahead and enjoy the tacos! Y'all be safe tonight!"

"Fa'sho."

We walked away with our food and went and sat on the hood of the car.

As we ate, I grabbed my arms because it was a little chilly outside, and the half jacket was not helping.

He looked at me, stood from the hood of the car, took his jacket off and placed it around my shoulder. I showed a half smile as I tried not to smile too hard and told him, "Thank you.

You know . . . you really surprise me . . ."

"I'm still surprisin' you?" he asked as he continued devouring his taco.

"I guess I just didn't expect for you to be such a gentleman . . ."

"Why? Because I'ma whole ass gangsta' out here?" he asked.

I laughed. I shrugged as I smiled. "I guess so," I responded.

"I show respect to people who deserve my respect. I treat 'em how they treat themselves. You act like a bitch, then I'ma treat you like a bitch. If you act like a young queen, then that's how I'ma treat you," he said as he stood from the hood of the car and came in front of me, in between my legs.

He slightly leaned into me as his hands maneuvered to my waist and he caressed it. My whole body tensed up from his touch, and I was screaming on the inside. I almost choked on my damn food.

"So, if this is your first date . . . What else have you not done?" he asked me.

I knew what he was getting at, but I didn't know if I was ready to confess all of that to him. He wasn't even supposed to know that my square ass has never been on a date before.

I shrugged as I blushed. "Well . . ." I started off, hesitating, "I honestly never really was into boys like that until . . ." I stopped for a moment as I quickly looked at him and looked away, "until I saw you that day . . . when you helped me with my books," I confessed.

He flinched. He tried to read my eyes, and then he stepped back as he observed me and thought for a moment. "This whole change was for me?" he asked. I nodded my head.

He had a couple of different expressions show up on his face, and my heart started racing. I hoped that I wasn't scaring him off. I didn't understand what any of them meant as he continued to observe me.

"So, you changed your whole look . . . just so that I would notice you?" he asked.

"I know it sounds stupid," I said, rolling my eyes.

He shook his head. "I had already noticed you, Ma," he said, stepping back in between my legs. "Those eyes . . ." he finished in a softer tone as he ran his finger down my cheek and gazed into my eyes. Chills were shooting all through my body. "To be honest, I really just thought that you liked girls." We both laughed. "But it was somethin' about yo eyes that had me stuck for a moment, and it was all that I saw," he admitted. I had butterflies in my stomach. I tried to keep my cool.

He came in closer, our lips inches away from each other. He traced his lips around my own as my body was screaming with joy, and then he gently pressed them against mine as he kissed me and pulled me closer to him while he caressed the small of my back. I wrapped my arms around his neck as the heat between us became more intense.

When they parted, he stayed close with his lips still inches away from my own.

"Was that your first kiss?" he asked in a faint voice as we were both still in the heat of the moment. I nodded my head. I felt too light and in bliss to really answer. "First date . . . first kiss . . . I'm startin' to become yo first every*thang*, huh?" I chuckled.

"You are," I responded. He kissed me again.

The whole ride home, I couldn't help but sit in that seat smiling my ass off.

I couldn't believe that any of this was happening. I couldn't wait until I got home and called Lia.

Even though I didn't get to spend as much time as I really wanted to with Scrap, he ended my night perfectly.

When he pulled up to my house, he cut the car off and shifted his body toward me. I smiled at him but didn't move. He smiled back, and I blushed.

"I had a good time wit'chu tonight, Ma," he said.

"Me too."

I sat there for a moment, just staring at him, and then I thought of something. "How many girls do you talk to?" I asked boldly. He flinched and his eyebrows rose. I could tell that he was taken aback by my question, but he played it cool.

"Why do you think I talk to a lot of girls?" he asked.

"Stories," I responded.

He chuckled. "Don't believe everything you hear." I pressed my lips together because he didn't answer my question. It was an awkward silence for a moment and then he spoke. "What're you doin' tomorrow?" he asked.

Tomorrow is Saturday. I just study all weekend and lounge around the house, but for Scrap, it could wait.

"Nothing that I know of . . ."
"I'm having a lil kickback at my house tomorrow. It's nothin' big. We do it every Saturday unless it's somethin' else goin' on, but if you want to come kick it with me, you can."

"I'd like that. Thank you. I don't know how I'm getting there though."

"Just hit me." I nodded my head.

Before I got out the car, he reached over and kissed me again. He just had me smiling the whole night.

"Night," he said.

"Good night." I got out of the car, and he waited until I was all the way in the house before he drove off.

I couldn't believe this shit. My heart was racing. I wasn't going to be able to wait until tomorrow to spill the whole night to Lia. I had to call her now!

I raced upstairs to my room, jumped on my bed and immediately called her. I told her everything! She was so excited for me, and she agreed to go with me tomorrow to his little get-together. She said that she's been wanting to go because that's all her friends talk about when it comes to the weekends, going to kick it over Scrap's house.

Chapter 9 Kickback

Janeeva

When I woke up that morning, I felt too light to control myself.

All I could think about was Scrap, his lips and how last night was the best night ever! I looked over at my clock, and it was almost twelve in the afternoon. Damn! I missed the whole morning.

I'm usually just lounging around the house with Maimi or studying on Saturday's. I never really have plans anyway. My life is boring.

I got up, took a shower and slipped on some sweats and a tank top. I went downstairs, and Maimi was still in the living room watching cartoons. Trevor was already gone, either to work, the streets or with Talawny.

I walked into the kitchen, and my mom was sitting down at the table on a business call. She smiled at me, and I walked over and kissed her on her forehead.

I could tell in her eyes that she wanted to ask me about last night, but I knew her little business call was going to take forever, so I went back upstairs. When I got back into my room, I called Lia.

"So, did he pop yo cherry last night? I forgot to ask you," she greeted me.

I laughed. "Nope. Still intact," I said, playing along. We both laughed.

"You know Dimples called me about his little kickback too. Has he called you today?"

"No, I haven't heard from him. I'm honestly just now waking up."

"Shut up! You never sleep in this long! It's damn-near twelve o'clock!"

"I know. I was as shocked as you when I woke up. I missed all my studying time."

"Well, it's cool to have a break every once in a while."

I ignored her comment because I wasn't exactly thinking about how I didn't study this morning. "Should I call him and see if he could come get us?" I asked.

"Yeah, I was coming to your house anyway, so my mom is about to drop me off. I'll be there soon. Go ahead and call him."

"'Kay," I said, getting off the phone with her.

I called Scrap, and I felt butterflies in my stomach from hearing his sexy-ass voice. "Hey, it's Janeeva."

"I know who it is. What's good?" he asked.

"Well, Lia and I wanted to come to your little gettogether today, but I was wondering if we could get a ride?" I asked.

"*My lil get-together*?" he asked, mimicking me, chuckling. "It's nothing big. We just kickin' back and drinkin' and shit, but yeah, I will. Just give me a minute. I'm takin' care of sum'n right now."

"'Kay."

"Aight." He hung up.

About an hour later, Lia had finally made it to my house, and the first thing that she did was rush me upstairs to play dress-up again.

She flat ironed my hair back out and brought a couple of outfits for me to try on. She had me in some black leggings and a hot pink tank top. I felt so exposed, but I wasn't going to lie—I was looking sexy in her leggings. My makeup was on point too, and she had my lips poppin' like the fourth of July!

"Oooouh! Sexy mama!" she said, getting too excited.

I received a text from Scrap, letting me know that he was on his way. We chilled back waiting for him, and when he finally pulled up, we ran downstairs like some true kids. We tried to act calmly when we walked out the door though.

I hadn't been outside all day, and it was hot as hell! I wish I had chosen the shorts instead of the leggings. As we walked to the car, Lia let me hop in the front, and when we got in, Scrap had his seat back while he leaned against the car door.

He looked at me, and it looked like he hadn't gotten any rest. His eyes were low and red. He was still looking sexy as hell though and smelled good as hell too.

I was entranced by the diamonds in his mouth again. He had his top and bottom grill in today. Lia stuck her head between us from the back seat and looked at him.

"Damn, nigga, you high as fuck!" she said.

He looked at her and smiled, while the diamonds in his grill shined. "Sit back, Ms. Attitude," he said, licking his lips as he started the car back up and pulled off.

As we drove, Scrap glanced over at me and smirked. "You look nice."

"Thank you." I blushed.

"How's your day been goin'?" he asked.

"Okay, I woke up later than expected and it threw my entire day off, but besides that it was cool. I just been in the house all day," I said.

"Yo, Scrap, who all at yo house right now?" Lia asked.

"Shit, most of the team. Yo brotha' over there right now," he said looking at me.

My heart stopped, and I was low-key panicking. "*What?*" I asked as the fear crept up on me. I could tell that he wanted to laugh at my reaction, but he just smiled and held his peace.

"Yeah, he's over there kickin' it with my brothers."

"Lord, please let this be a peaceful day," Lia said, sighing.

"You good, Ma?" he asked me. I didn't answer.

Once we pulled up to his house, the first thing that I saw was a group of boys out on the front porch, yelling and playing around. I was scared to get out of the car.

Lia and Scrap hopped out before I did, and as Lia walked off to welcome herself to the familiar faces that she knew, Scrap stood by the car and waited for me.

Well, I thought that he was waiting for me, but I had to get out of the car for him to lock the doors. He at least allowed me to catch up with him so that I could walk next to him.

"Wow, so many people at your house," I said in a muffled voice.

"You good?" he asked, seeing the discomfort all on my face.

I think he knew that I was scared. When we walked up, I felt six pairs of eyes on me, and everyone got quiet.

"Hello," a boy with this smooth dark skin said as he appraised me.

He was cute as hell with the prettiest eyes. I looked at him, and he gave me that flirtatious-ass smile. I just smiled back and said, "Hi."

"Yo, Scrap, who's yo friend?" the boy asked.

"This Jay. Jay, these my niggas: Leon," he started off, nodding his head toward the boy with the smooth dark skin. "You know SixPacc and Twinkie already . . . That's Boogie," he said pointing at a younger boy who looked mean as hell, "and my nigga Tutu," he finished, introducing me to all of them.

Lia sat down on the porch and grabbed the Hennessy bottle from Twinkie. She looked at me and patted the space next to her. I walked over and took a seat.

"Y'all thirsty?" Scrap asked.

"Yep!" Lia said, holding the Hennessy bottle up.

He laughed. "So, you just gon' take my *drank* without even asking me, huh?" he asked, playfully.

"Yup!" she responded, smiling at him. He shook his head and smiled back. He looked at me.

"You want some Kool-Aid or somethin', Ma?" he asked.

"Please!" I said, dying in this heat.

He nodded his head and went into the house. When he went in, we all looked toward the driveway as we heard the garage opening.

A man stepped out of it with his shirt off. I knew that he was one of Scrap's brothers because of his green eyes. He had these fresh shoulder-length dreads in his head, and I couldn't believe how tatted up he was.

His whole torso including his neck was covered. I saw a couple of tattoos on his legs as well with his black Nike basketball shorts on.

He had this cocoa-butter skin, like Lia's, that was right on the borderline of being considered light-skin type of complexion.

"Y'all niggas ready to race?" he asked, looking over at the boys sitting on the porch, smiling.

They all chanted as a couple of them hopped off the porch and went into the garage.

Twinkie was the first one to run inside, and I started hearing an engine revving up. When he came out, he was on a green and white sport Coolster ATV as he drove down the driveway and onto the streets, chanting, and then three more different ones came out: a black Pentora 250cc ATV Quad 4, and there was another one just like it, but it was yellow. They also brought out the Razor Dirt Quad 500.

Scrap came back outside, and as he saw his friends riding around in the street, he smiled, handed me my Kool-Aid and looked over at his brother. "Aye, loc! Where the other bike?" he asked.

After his brother confirmed that it was in the garage, he stepped off the porch and went into the garage. He brought out a motorcycle that was like the blue and white one that I had seen him ride, but this one was black.

He looked at me with his helmet in hand and revved the engine. "You gon' ride with me, Ma?" he asked, smiling from ear to ear.

I shook my head, nervously. "I'm okay! I'll watch," I responded.

He shrugged and said, "Okay."

As he took off down the street and did a wheely, catching up with his friends, I looked back at his brother.

He stared at me for a moment and then went back into the garage and grabbed the motorcycle that I had seen Scrap on before.

He hopped on it as he put his helmet on and turned the music up. You could hear the boys down the street on the ATVs and motorcycles chanting.

He played "Question #1" by Nipsey Hustle featuring Snoop Dogg. As Scrap came back down the street and his brother exited out of the driveway, the music continued to play. *"What they call you where you from, nigga, looking at the legend I become nigga, I can't help but feel like I'm the one nigga! What they call you where you from, nigga!"*

They both threw up the set as the music played and started racing down the street.

I couldn't help but smile. They were *lit*!

So, this was what all the fuss was about when it came to kicking it at Scrap house.

"So, where my girls at?" Lia asked Boogie as he stayed back and sipped on the Hennessy bottle on the porch. He looked like he was no more than fourteen years old. He had to be a freshman or sophomore.

"Shit, they said that they were on the way! They were supposed to have been here," Boogie said, hitting the blunt as well.

Scrap came back up the driveway and parked the motorcycle, using his feet to put the clutch down. He hopped off and walked over to us. He looked at me. "So, you really not gon' ride with me?"

I hesitated as I looked at Lia.

"Her dad got into a really bad motorcycle accident over a decade ago, so she's scared," Lia said, rolling her eyes.

I cut my eyes at her, and she pressed her lips together. "They're just not safe . . . I'm enjoying watching you ride, though," I said.

"What I tell you last night when we were in the room about fuckin' with me?" he asked with a smirk.

I thought about it for a moment and then smiled. "As long as I'm with you, I'm safe."

"And what I tell you before you got out the car when I had to leave you with SixPacc?" he continued.

I couldn't help but smile and shake my head. "To trust you . . ." I responded.

He smiled harder and held his hand out. I took a deep breath as Lia was trying to push me off the porch, and I grabbed his hand.

He bit his bottom lip, walking backwards, smiling at me as he pulled me toward the bike.

He hopped back on and handed me the helmet. I took it, put it on and hopped on the back.

"Hold on tight."

I wrapped my arms around his waist and closed my eyes. As he took off down the driveway, I could already feel my adrenaline rushing.

He sped up as I held on tighter, and I heard his brother somewhere close with his music playing. I opened my eyes and looked around.

As I held on to him, I couldn't help but smile. The rush that I was feeling on this bike was a different feeling. I could hear "Homebody" by Lil Durk playing from his brother's motorcycle as we rode down the street and went on to another.

I was in straight bliss all over again, holding on to him as we rode. He sang along to the song as he rode next to his brother, and the rest of the boys were behind us.

As we came back around by the house, he and his brother pulled back into the driveway with the song still playing. I still had my arms wrapped around his waist tight when he stopped.

I saw him smiling as he turned his head, trying to look back at me, and then rubbed his hand on top of my own as he grabbed it so that he could help me off the bike.

When I got off, he still had a grip on my hand as he brought me to him while he was still sitting on it.

"You trust me now?" he asked.

I was smiling so hard that my cheeks started to hurt. "That was fun," I responded.

"Mm-hmm . . ." he said as he leaned in and kissed me.

He got off the bike, and we both walked back over to Lia on the porch. She was trying her absolute hardest not to fucking show her Kool-Aid-ass smile in excitement. I automatically blushed.

SixPacc and the rest of the boys parked the ATVs in the driveway, and as they came up, Twinkie pulled the blunt he

had in his ear out and lit it as Tutu grabbed the Hennessy
bottle.

"Yo, Jay, you want to hit this blunt?" Twinkie choked
as he took his couple of hits.

"No. I'm fine. Thank you." He flinched at my
politeness. He smiled at me and then looked over at SixPacc
like, "*Did you just hear this shit?*" He let it go, though, and just
said "Aight," and passed it to the next.

A car pulled up, and I smiled hard because I knew who
he was. As he walked up and noticed me on the porch, he
smiled as well.

"What's good, lil sis!" he crooned.

"Cliff!" I said, standing up and hugging him.

"What're you doing over here?" he asked, checking out
the whole little look I had going on. I could tell that he was
shocked. "Lil sis growing up, huh?" I blushed.

Cliff was my cousin Recia's little boo-thang. So, I knew
a lot about him before I even start attending Jordan High.

Every time I went over to her house, he used to just appear in the house of his own will.

Even though he went to school with all of us, I didn't know that he kicked it with Scrap like that. I remembered Scrap mentioning a "Cliff" last night, but I didn't know that it was the same person.

"Just a little change" was all I said.

"You better be cool over here. I just got off the phone with yo brotha'. He just ran to the store with big bruh. He gon' be back over here."

"You say it like my brother runs me?" I retorted.

He shrugged. "I'm just sayin'," he responded.

I sat back down on the steps, and Scrap came to sit next to me with a half-rolled blunt in his hand.

"Do you guys smoke back-to-back?" I asked as I watched another blunt still being passed around.

"Until we pass out," he responded, smiling at me.

"Wow," I said, smiling back.

Scrap and I talked most of the time as Lia chilled out and talked with the other boys. His brother walked back out of the house and looked at him.

"Aye, cuz! I'll be back! I gotta go get that fuckin' Barbie Dream House from Walmart for Breanne."

"Aight," Scrap responded.

He hopped in his car and drove off.

"Which brother is that?" I asked.

"Bavari. He's the third oldest." I nodded my head.

About thirty minutes later, Dimples and Freckles were walking up to the house. And even though I wasn't shocked to see her, I still had this weird feeling in my stomach when I saw Lovely walking with Skittles.

She stopped in her tracks for a moment when she saw me sitting so close to Scrap.

He looked up at her, gave her a nonchalant look and then looked back down at his blunt and kept on rolling.

She stood there for another half second until Twinkie tried to get her attention. She looked over at him as he started up a conversation with her. I really felt like he only did it to distract her.

"Wassup, team!" Freckles yelled.

"What's good with yo sexy ass!" Cliff responded, giving Freckles a hug.

Skittles had a black plastic bag in her hand, and I could see the Patron bottle and Casamigos sticking out of it.

They were really getting fucked up. Who the hell was buying liquor for their ass, because all of them were underage?

As the music continued to play from Scrap's brother's bike and everybody just chilled back and talked, smoked and drank, he was getting closer to me. I could tell that he was *feeling* himself because he kept rubbing my thighs through my leggings and whispering into my ear. He had me blushing the whole time.

I knew Lovely wasn't liking the fact that I had his full attention. She walked over to us, and without even looking at me, she asked Scrap if she could talk to him. He got up and walked off with her for a moment.

They were only a little distance across the yard, and it was the first time that I saw them have a conversation that looked like there was a lot of tension involved. He put his hand up to stop her from talking and she continued, so he just walked off on her. She stood there for a moment and then stumbled behind him.

When they came back to the group, Scrap acted like nothing ever happened and he went back to give me his full attention. Lovely didn't look so happy, and my heart fluttered when she glared at me.

Scrap looked over at her and then at me. "Don't even trip off her. She on some otha' shit right now," he said.

"Are you sure you guys have nothing going on?" I asked, suspiciously.

"Business," he responded.

He then reached in the front of his shorts, and he took me off guard when he pulled the gun that was tucked in his shorts out and put it on his lap. He said it was uncomfortable.

This should have been some to shock me, but I had seen Trevor with plenty of guns, so it didn't exactly startle me. He even asked me if I was uncomfortable, and I told him no. I couldn't stop staring at it though.

I started to get a bad feeling, and right when the feeling started to creep up on me, my eyes flickered to a police car cruising down the street.

My first instinct was to grab the gun on his lap and stick it in my purse. That was exactly how I reacted, but he was a little quicker than me, and he jumped from my reaction and grabbed my wrist tight.

He looked at me confused, and I knew exactly what he was thinking. *What the fuck are you doing?*

I flickered my eyes to the cop car rolling up, and as he followed to where I was looking, he dropped his hand, and I grabbed the gun, stuck it in my purse, got up and looked at Lia.

"Can you come with me to the bathroom please?" I asked her.

"Down the hall to yo left," Scrap instructed as he stayed seated but kept his eyes on the car. Lia got up as she realized what was up, too, and followed me to the bathroom.

Lovely's whole face was distraught when she realized what I was doing for him. She glared at me. Her eyes followed me all the way into the house.

Scrap

Fuck! The boys! And I was fucked up at this point.

I warned my niggas, and they instantly started hiding shit in the cracks of my porch.

Lovely came to my side, and I handed her the rest of the shit that I had on me. She smoothly tucked it in her bra.

Of course, this would be the spot that they *blurped*, but I figured that they were going to stop when I saw the bitch-ass cop in the passenger seat looked dead at me.

Officer Brook! Bitch-ass nigga was the same nigga who arrested me my freshman year. I talked so much shit to that nigga in the back of that cop car that day that he was furious! They all had me fucked up! The cop that was in the driver's seat was a black buff-looking-ass nigga.

They both hopped out, and Officer Brook said my name. "Mr. Gaither!" I rolled my eyes and just glared at him.

"Are you staying out of trouble?" he asked with a smirk on his face.

"I'm home. What chu think?" I retorted.

"You know your mouth isn't going to get you too far, son."

I pressed my lips together. I felt like this nigga was just waiting for me to fuck up again. "Out of no disrespect, but I'm not your son." He laughed it off.

After going back and forth with the nigga, he finally started to get pissed off that he wasn't getting to me like he did two years ago. I would have been in jail for a good minute, because that nigga had me ready to beat the shit out of him.

He searched me and got even more pissed off that I didn't have anything on me, thanks to Janeeva.

The whole time that he was searching me, I was just thinking about how she did that. We were still getting to know each other, and I still didn't have to say shit for her to know what was up! I swear I couldn't figure her out.

Quiet, shy, but ain't no punk. Smart, nerd-type bitch, but a bitch that just saved my ass from going back to juvie.

Lia and she were just posted up in the house, waiting. I couldn't wait until these bitch-ass niggas left.

Once he was finally done searching me, he told me again to "stay out of trouble," and then they left.

"Fuck, cuz! That was close!" SixPacc said. He looked at me, and I knew that he was thinking the same shit that I was. "That bitch is a beast for that shit, loc," he said,

nodding his head.

I heard Lovely breathe in deeply. I didn't say anything to her though. I was still a bit shocked on how Janeeva did that shit, and it wasn't even about her doing it, because it had been plenty of bitches that held my shit for me while I was getting searched. *Speaking of that!* I looked at Lovely, and she passed my shit back to me.

I walked into the house without saying anything to her and went straight to the bathroom. I knocked on the door, and Lia cracked it open.

"Are they gone?" she asked.

"Yeah," I said.

She opened the door all the way, and I walked in looking at Janeeva sitting on the edge of the tub. She was calm with her purse in her lap. I smiled.

"Let me holla at chu'," I said, reaching my hand out to help her up.

She got up. I told Lia to go ahead and go back outside, and I led Janeeva to my room. When we walked in, she looked around and then looked back at me with those creamy lightbrown eyes. I stood there trying to read them. She finally looked away shyly, and I spoke.

"You know what you did was some beast-type shit, right? How did you spot them niggas so soon?"

"I'm aware of my surroundings, I guess. A very paranoid person too," she admitted.

I shook my head. "You just saved me from going back to jail," I told her.

She blushed and then shrugged. "I had to do it for my brother a couple of times . . . so I kind of knew what was up."

"Thank you," I told her, sincerely.

"You're welcome," she said, blushing.

I wasn't going to act like I didn't want to fuck the shit out of her right now. I placed my index finger under her chin and gently lifted it up. I kissed her softly on her lips, and she leaned into me. I felt her body melting in my arms. I wrapped my arms tighter around her waist, and as she felt the heat between us, she pulled back. I smiled.

"I'm not gon' hurt you, Ma," I told her.

She didn't say anything. She just kept her eyes down and stood the little bit of distance we had from each other. I sighed, filled that space in and gently lifted her chin up so that she could look at me.

"I'm not gon' rush you nor make you do anything that you don't wanna do. Whenever you ready though," I said, kissing her lips, "just say the word," I told her.

She knew what I was talking about, and I could see her body tensing just from me telling her that whenever she was ready to get the shit fucked out of her to let me know.

I reached down and traced my lips around her neck and then placed soft kisses on different spots of her neck and shoulder. I knew all the right places to touch, and her whole body tensed up again as she grabbed onto the sides of my shirt. "Let's go back in the front," she whispered.

"C'mon," I whispered back, motioning my head to the front.

She had me horny as fuck, but I was starting to grow more respect for her. Even though I hadn't gotten to the question yet, based off what I found out about her last night, I knew that she was still a virgin.

Chapter 10 Out of the Loop

Janeeva

We went back and chilled on the front porch with everybody else. When we came back out, Freckles was on the back of one of the ATVs, holding on to Cliff as he raced down the street and she screamed in excitement.

My body felt like Jell-O as we watched them. I just sat there, zoned off thinking about Scrap's lips on my neck and shoulders and the sensation that it gave me. My private area was throbbing.

Of course, I had to tell Lia on the low what had just happened, and like the girl that she was, she screamed silently in joy. Everybody was too drunk and high to really pay attention to what we had going on, and I was relieved that they were. It was so embarrassing, and I knew if Scrap was paying attention, then he would have been bending over laughing at me.

As we posted and I sat next to Scrap on the steps, a car pulled up into his driveway. My heart stopped when I saw Trevor in the passenger seat. When he spotted me, I saw his whole happy little expression turn to malice.

Two boys that looked like they were around eleven or twelve and a little girl hopped out of the backseat. The two boys were too cute. When they got out, they were carrying two Foot Locker bags in each of their hands. The little girl had a bag from the Disney store in the mall.

The man on the driver side hopped out of the car, and I stared at him for a moment. It was something about his calm and collected attitude that made me notice. He looked older too. It was crazy because I knew exactly who he was. Well, I knew that he was one of Scrap's older brothers. His eyes were the give-away like Bavari's were.

He was lighter than Scrap and Bavari though. To be honest, Scrap would be considered border-line dark skinned with his smooth almond-brown complexion. His skin made his eyes stand out even more. He was just gorgeous all the way around but back to the older brother . . .

He was a true light bright. You could tell just by his demeanor that those yellow-boy jokes didn't fly with him though. He wore this sexy-ass mug on his face, and he was at least 6'4". He was tall and built. You could tell that he worked out.

He had a high-top mohawk with these short silky curly locks in his hair like Trevor's, and his swag would turn any bitch on instantly. He had tattoos covering his right forearm all the way up to his elbow and an iced-out champagne diamond dial Rolex on his right wrist with an iced-out 20k gold chain around his neck that had a gold cross hanging from it.

He wore a crisp-black fitted short-sleeved t-shirt that made his bold shoulders stand out with the khaki camouflage cargo shorts on that had the outdoor pockets. I was admiring the Nike Air 1 Jordans he had on his feet as well. They were white and black with camouflage only covering the back of the shoe.

He was intimidating and *flyy* as hell. I appraised him from his head down to his feet. I knew that I shouldn't be looking this hard, but I honestly couldn't help it. His brother was fine as hell too.

"Wassup, loc!" one of the twins yelled out coming up the steps. His hair was long like Scrap's, but his was everywhere. It just hung down over his shoulders, puffed out.

"What's good, lil nigga!" Leon said to the little boy.
"So, which one are you? Bavarion or Bruce?" he asked.
"Naw, nigga, I'm Bruce!" the other one said as he came up behind his brother.

He had on a black snapback that was turned to the back, and I could see under the hat that his long hair was braided back into cornrows.

They were identical, but you could tell the difference between the two, because one was slightly taller than the other and the fact that Bruce had his hair braided up helped as well. Lia and I were quietly laughing. It was crazy how young they were, but they were talking like they were grown-ass men.

They were both a little darker than Scrap as well, but their eyes weren't green like their older brothers'. They were light brown like my own. The little girl that hopped out of the car with them ran straight to Scrap with her Disney bag. He smiled and picked her up. I will admit that this wasn't the way that I pictured her.

Her skin was a smooth dark-chocolate, and she had these mahogany eyes that only appeared lighter in the sun. She was so small. She looked very fragile, and her hair was twisted up into all kinds of different ponytails all over her head in knockers and barrettes. Her hair was damn near down to her back. He kissed her on her cheek.

"BomBom, look!" she yelled. She opened the bag and took out a stuffed Moana Doll. He looked at it and smiled. "Whaaaat! Brandon finally got you yo Moana doll?" he asked. She nodded her head with all her little teeth showing. He looked up at Brandon.

"Aye, loc! Where Brent at?" he asked.

"I'on know. Why?" he responded as he went around dapping everyone up in the group. I could smell his Dylan Blue Versace cologne just from where I was sitting. I knew the scent because Trevor wore the same cologne.

"It's supposed to be some lil function over here. We were gon' slide, but I need Brent's car tonight," he told him.

Brandon laughed. "Nigga, you had his car all day. Keep fuckin' with his ass and he gon' take all yo privileges away."

Scrap smacked his lips. "Well, let me use yo shit?" he asked.

"I got business to take care of tonight, cuz. And what the fuck you need his car for? You got transportation," Brandon asked him.

Scrap looked at me and back at his brother. Brandon then looked at me, and I saw the understanding in his eyes. I didn't know what the fuck it meant though, and I was little upset that I was so lost. I was trying my hardest to read between the lines with all these eye-contact conversations going on. It was frustrating for me that I was out of the loop.

It started to become all clear to me when Lovely walked outside. She had a car, and she was something to Scrap but I wasn't quite sure what she was yet. However, I figured that the whole scene had something to do with her. She had to be the transportation.

"Call 'em and ask," Brandon told him.
He nodded his head. "Aye! Wassup with you and my chemistry teacher, cuz?" Scrap asked before Brandon went all the way into the house.

He smiled. "You mean Ms. Laney's fine ass?" he responded.

"Man, you got that bitch on my ass right now. What the fuck you tell her?"

"I told her to keep me updated on your progress in her class. If you fail this chemistry class, me and you gon' have a problem and you gon' be mad when yo ass taking classes during the summer to make sure you graduate!" he responded.

Scrap pressed his lips together as Brandon walked all the way in the house, and he flipped him off when he was out of sight. I smiled. He looked at me.

"What chu smiling fo'?" he asked.

"You gotta dope-ass big brother. Like the taco truck man said, be grateful you have an older sibling that cares enough," I told him. "And I can be your study buddy if you need me to be. I don't mind helping you," I finished.

He stared at me for a moment. I didn't know what he was thinking because his expression was blank, and then he gave me a half smile. "Aight . . ." he said in the softest tone as he continued to gaze into my eyes with his head slightly tilted. As Scrap and I were in our moment, speaking with our eyes, Trevor was approaching us.

We pulled our eyes away from each other and looked at him. Scrap, Lia, Twinkie, SixPacc and I were in dead silence, just staring at him.

Of course, Scrap had a smirk on his face. I don't know why he got a kick out of taunting my brother. We were all trying to figure out what was about to be his first move.

"Let me talk to you," Trevor said to me. I sighed and got up from the steps. We walked off a little down the street so no one else could hear what we were talking about, or they just wouldn't hear me getting cussed out.

"What the fuck are you doing here, Janeeva?" he asked in a malice tone.

"Just hanging out. I came with Lia," I lied—Lia came with me.

"Man, I'm not trying to control you or none of that shit, but be careful over here, and if I hear about you out here doing the most, I'm gon' beat the shit out of you, cuz. I can't even really express how I really want to flash on yo ass right now because I got business to take care of, but don't make me have to fuck you up!" he told me. I just nodded my head. I wasn't about to argue with him. "And stay off the fuckin' bikes! You know what happened to Dad, so stay off 'em!" he finished.

My eyes wandered around as he said it. I wasn't going to tell him that I was already on it. He didn't say another word, but I could tell on his face that he was mad as hell about me being here.

I didn't understand why he didn't want me over here, but I figured it was because of whatever animosity he had toward Scrap. He walked off into the house, and I went and sat back down next to Scrap. He looked at me.

"You good?" he asked. I nodded my head. "So, are you coming with me tonight, or big bruh shut that shit down?" he asked, smiling.

"No, I can come, as long as I make it home," I told him.

"Damn, and I was tryin' to kidnap you," he said playfully. I blushed.

The little girl sitting in his lap looked at me and then she looked up at him. "Bom, who is she?" she asked pointing to me with the prettiest smile.

"Her name's Janeeva," he told her.

"She pwetty," she responded.

"Well, introduce yo'self. Stop actin' shy," he said to her. She smiled at me and then buried her head into his shirt. He pulled her off. "Jay, this my lil sister Breanne. Breanne, this is Jay," he introduced. I reached my hand out to shake her little hand.

"Hi. You pwetty," she said to me.

I chuckled. "Thank you. You're beautiful, too," I told her.

She blushed. "I like her," she whispered to Scrap as if I couldn't hear her.

"Yeah, I do, too . . ." he said giving me that seductive look and smiling. He just wouldn't make me stop blushing. She ran into the house with the twins after a while, and it was getting dark.

"Lovely!" he called out.

She wasn't acting like she usually did. Her expression usually was calm and collected, but right now it seemed like she was having a very frustrating day. She was talking to Skittles when Scrap called her over. She looked at him, got up and walked over.

"Yeah," she said with an attitude in her tone.

"What time you meetin' up with ole' boy? I don't see it in this text message he sent me," he asked.

She looked at the time and sighed. "I gotta be heading out to him right now," she said, shaking her head.

He nodded his. "I'll be right back," he told me. I nodded my head. He walked Lovely to her car, and they talked by the car before she left.

Once again, the conversation looked serious but normal at the same time. I was really killing myself on trying to find out where Lovely stood in his life. Like really, what the fuck did he need to walk her to her car for?

As I watched them, Scrap grabbed his gun that he had taken back from me, tucked in his jeans, and passed it to her. He then held his hand out, and once again, she slipped him a stack of money. Right when I was about to look up at Lia and ask her if she saw that, I heard her.

"Oh shit!" she said. I looked at her, and her mouth was hung open. "Skittles!" she yelled.

Skittles walked over to her, and Lia pulled her to the side. I didn't know what the fuck was going on. When they finally walked back over, Skittles looked at me and then at Lia.

"Lia don't say shit," she said. Lia shook her head. Once Skittles walked away, I looked at Lia.

"What?" I asked.

"Just be careful with this nigga, Janeeva" was all that she said.

Okay, now I was tripping. "Well, what is it?" I asked.

"I'll tell you later," she told me.

I couldn't believe that the entire day went by so fast. I still wanted to know what Lia was tripping off, but she said that she would tell me later, so I took her word for it.

Scrap had called his brother Brent, and he said that he could take his car. Once it hit eight thirty, two more cars pulled up in front of Scrap's house. It seemed like the party was taking place here. A group of females hopped out of one, and more boys hopped out of the other. They all greeted each other. "Scrap, killa!" a light-skinned girl yelled out to him. She was a little chubby in the face and gorgeous as hell. She had on some denim shorts with a tube top on. Her hair was slicked back into a high ponytail with these big gold loops dangling from her earlobes.

"What's good, Ngozi!" Scrap said, getting up and hugging her.

"Ma' nigga!" she crooned. She went around and hugged everybody else and then looked at me. "Hi . . ." she said, smiling, trying to figure out who I was. I guess I was the only new face in the group. I waved at her and smiled.

"Yo, Gozi, this is Jay. Jay, this is my *lil hitta bitch*, Ngozi," he said. I shook her hand.

"So, whose girl are you?" she asked. I didn't know how to respond.

"She on her way to being mine," Scrap said to her in a low voice while he gave me that seductive look. I blushed.

"Is that right?" she responded.
"Yeah," he told her.

He told her the story from earlier, and I could tell, when he was, that she couldn't believe it either. She kept giving me the look that I didn't seem like the type to bust a move like that. She was as shocked as everyone else when it took place earlier.

"No offense, but you don't look like the type, mami."

"What's 'the type'?" I asked, confused. I could tell that she was trying to figure out a word to not offend me, and then she just said it.

"You look like a *lil square bitch.*" I stared at her for a moment, not knowing if I should take it personally or not, and then Scrap spoke.

"She didn't mean it like that. That's just the way she talks. She's just saying that—" I cut him off.

"That I look like a *scary-ass* bitch, straight out the church that would never be involved with gangsters and guns and drugs?" I said, smiling. They both just looked at me. Scrap smiled as he stared at me in shock.

"Well . . . yeah . . ." Ngozi responded. We both laughed, and he shook his head as he joined us.

"Are you rockin' with us tonight?" she asked. I shrugged.

"I guess so," I said with a polite smile.

"Bet," she said, smiling back.

Once everyone was ready to leave, they all scrambled into the three cars we had. We left.

I didn't realize that we were so deep until we pulled up to the McDonald's down the street from Scrap's house and there were two more cars full of people waiting for us so that they could follow us to the party as well. Tutu was the only one who knew where the party was taking place, so we all followed his car when we pulled out of the parking lot.

"You guys have a lot of friends," I stated. SixPacc and Twinkie rolled with us as well, but they were in the back seat arguing about something, so they weren't really paying attention to us.

"This family," Scrap responded. "They're all a part of the team."

"Gozi too?" I asked.

"My lil hitta!" he said. "Yeah. She be beastin'. My lil down-ass bitch! She gon' *go* for you fa'sho. Neva' gotta ask twice!" he told me, nodding his head.

"What do they call her?" I asked.

"Lil Hitta . . ." he said, smiling at me. I laughed.

Now I knew why he kept saying that she was his *lil hitta*. It was also her street name. I found out as we drove that she went to a continuation school and dropped out last year. She was already eighteen. I knew that she wasn't anything to him like Lovely and the other girl Cherokee were. I could tell that she was just a close friend of his.

We pulled up on the block where the party was taking place, and the streets were packed. We had to go back around and park in the next block. We got out of the car, and I stayed close to Lia. I was excited but was a little nervous of what people were going to think of me.

We all walked in as a group, and of course there were a lot of eyes on us as we walked up to the house because we were so deep. It was crazy. I felt good walking in with them though.

We came into the party, and I was astonished by how everyone was getting down. They were *turnt up*! My group instantly started throwing up their set and dancing when they walked in.

"Shottas up in this bitch, nigggggggggga!" Cliff yelled out as he started dancing.

"Shottaaaaaasssss!" Ngozi yelled out as she twisted her fingers and threw the set up.

"Stay close to me," Lia told me as we followed behind Scrap. The group split up, and everyone went their separate ways.

Lia and I followed Scrap, Twinkie and SixPacc. SixPacc took his shirt off and started dancing with the girls that were twerking, and Twinkie joined in. Scrap just stood in his place, laughing, and danced to the beat while he was working his friends up.

"Get that bitch, loc!" he said while SixPacc worked one of the girls in the middle of the living room floor. I heard Lia smack her lips as she pressed them together. I was silently laughing because I knew that she was a little jealous.

Once they got hot enough, they went to the backyard where everyone was smoking at. I could tell that Scrap was feeling himself. He took a seat in one of the empty chairs, and he pulled my hand for me to sit on his lap. My stomach fluttered, especially because everyone was watching.

"Yo this shit is lit, cuz!" Twinkie yelled out, turning his hat to the back, still dancing to the music.

SixPacc still had his shirt off, dancing too. "Lia, I don't know why you keep playing with me. You know you want some," SixPacc said as he wrapped his arms around her waist and started dancing on her. She rolled her eyes.

"Believe me, the bitch you had on the floor wants you more than I do," she responded, throwing his hands off her.

"Mmm . . . I think I hear a lil jealousy," he said.

"You just never stop, huh?" she asked.

"Not until I get the last word, Ma," he responded with a smirk on his face. I knew that she was turned on by his determination, but still she played the hard-to-get role on his ass.

She rolled her eyes and then turned her back to him. He laughed. He stepped right behind her and kissed her neck. She turned around quickly about to go off on him but was stopped by his face being no more than an inch away from her own. You would think as close as their lips were, he was about to poke them out and kiss her.

"You gon' give in sooner than later, Ms. Attitude. So, I'm not even trippin' about that cold shoulder," he said, turning his hat back to the front and taking another swig of the Hennessy he had brought in a water bottle. Scrap laughed, pulled out a blunt and lit it.

SixPacc stood there still dancing, and he looked around at all the other females outside, and as one caught his attention, he slapped Scrap's shoulder. Scrap looked up, and SixPacc pointed in the distance. I looked over as well, being nosy.

It was two fair brown girls. One had on a torn-up Tshirt that hung off her shoulders and only covered up her breasts with some leggings on. The other had long hair that was puffed out with some shorts on, and her top looked like it was just a bra.

"What the fuck is Cherokee doin' with her, cuz?" I heard Scrap growl in rage. I looked at him, and I saw the anger all in his face as he stared at the two girls across the yard. So, one of them was Cherokee, the girl that I had been hearing about.

When the girl with the torn-up shirt looked over at us, the first person that she saw was SixPacc, and when she noticed his presence, she scanned our group, and I knew she had found who she was looking for when her eyes caught Scrap.

She looked at me sitting on his lap, and she instantly turned her lips up and gave me the deadliest look. Scrap did a deep sigh, and then he slouched down in the chair more.

"I don't got time for this shit, cuz. If she starts testing me tonight, I swear Lil Hitta 'bout to bang the shit out that bitch, on crip!" he said, shaking his head and hitting the blunt as SixPacc passed it to him.

I looked at him confused. *Now who the fuck is she? First Lovely and Cherokee and now it's another bitch to worry about?*

It didn't seem like this one was one of his favorites, though. Scrap looked at me when he realized my confused expression, and instead of speaking and explaining to me who she was, his hand squeezed my waist, letting me know that it was okay. I didn't want an "okay," though. I was tired of being out of the loop. Lia stood there looking between the girl and Scrap.

She pressed her lips together and then wrapped her arms around her torso as she gave Scrap that evil eye. I knew that she knew something that I didn't know. *I don't know why she continues to give away all these expressions when she knows that I'm a very observant person and I will ask a million questions later.*

"Who is she?" I asked Scrap.

"Nobody," he responded.

I watched the girl on the low watch us for about ten more minutes. Whoever the fuck she was, she wasn't too happy. My attention was taken away from the girl when Ngozi joined us outside. It looked like she was having more fun than SixPacc and Twinkie.

"Yo, Hitta!" Scrap called out.
She looked at him. "Wassup, bruh?" she asked.

"If this bitch Mia starts trippin' tonight, I'ma need you to handle that, loc!"

She looked around for the girl that was known as Mia.

When she spotted her, she smiled. "You already know!" she told him. I really wanted to know who she was but didn't want to annoy Scrap with all my questions.

I scanned the crowd checking all the people out. This whole house was packed. I looked over and saw a group of boys walking outside into the backyard. They caught my eye because they were the oddballs. Why? They weren't from around here, and even my square ass knew that. I kept my mouth shut though.

I knew Scrap had spotted them first because his body tensed up. I looked at him and caught him eyeballing the boy that looked like the ringleader of the pack. He was cute, too.

His dark-brown skin stood out, and he had a thin mustache that was freshly lined up as his sideburns connected. He had a low-cut fade that was dyed a reddish brown. I would say he was standing at a good 6'3". His left eyebrow was pierced. And you could tell that he knew that he was the shit. His whole demeanor showed that. He reminded me of Brandon only because, once again, I was intimidated. I caught Lia checking him out, too.

"Aye, bruh, we 'bout to go back in!" SixPacc said to Scrap. Scrap nodded his head as he stopped staring at the boy and slouched back down in his seat.

I knew nobody saw how he reacted to him, so I kept it that way. When the boy looked my way, he smirked and tilted his head. He was checking me out. He leaned over a little bit to see whose lap I was sitting on, and when he noticed Scrap, he laughed. He walked over to us, and Scrap sat up when he saw him coming.

"Wassup, nigga?"

Scrap didn't show any kind of interest or excitement in seeing the boy like he did with the rest of his friends. He kept a straight face. "Wassup, Domion. What 'chu doin' on this

side?" he asked.

The boy looked around the crowd of people. "One of my niggas told me 'bout this shit, so I just slid through," he said. "You know me, nigga, doing what I do, trying to catch a little thot," he responded. The boy looked down at me and gave me a seductive look. Scrap noticed but remained calm in his seat. I think this Domion boy was really testing his patience.

"Wassup," the boy said to me.

"Hi," I responded, keeping it short as possible.

"I'm Domion," he introduced himself, sticking his hand out for me to shake. Scrap sat there and watched his every move. Before I could even shake his hand, Scrap interfered and shifted his leg away. He did it as if he was sitting all the way up to have Domion's full attention and then gave him the deadliest look.

"Janeeva, Domion. Domion, this is Janeeva," Scrap said, with a sterner tone, introducing us as he kept the malice look on his face.

I pressed my lips together in this awkward-ass moment and nodded my head. "Nice to meet you," I responded.

"You too . . ." he said licking his lips again.

I heard Scrap snicker. I didn't know exactly what it meant, but I think he knew this Domion person was testing him. I understood, though. I felt extremely uncomfortable the way that he was looking at me and even the way that he was talking to me.

It didn't exactly seem like they were enemies, but they weren't much of friends either. As Scrap continued to display the malice look on his face, Domion chuckled, threw his head down and looked up at Lia. He flinched as he acknowledged her presence.

"Damn, I didn't even see you," he said, stepping closer to her. She smiled. "Domion," he said, introducing himself again.

"Lia," she responded, shaking his hand.

"Nice to meet you, Lia." I caught the expression that came across Scrap's face when Domion introduced himself. Lia blushed.

"How old are you?" he asked her.

"Sixteen."

"Damn, you young."

"How old are you?" she asked.

"I'll be nineteen soon."

Scrap sat back and just listened to the whole conversation. He didn't even have to look at Domion nor Lia to peep anything. He already knew all this shit. I couldn't wait until Domion walked away and I could ask my ninety-nine questions. Lia's eyes lit up. She always had a thing for older boys, so this was already a turn on for her.

"You should give me yo number so we can talk more and get to know each other," he said. She smiled and nodded her head.

As they exchanged numbers, I looked behind me at Scrap, and he looked back up at me. I saw the anger on his face, and even though I didn't know exactly what was going on, I already had a bad feeling about Domion. Lia got his number, and he walked off. Once he walked off, I started with my questions.

"So, who is he?" I asked.

"This nigga that goes to Poly. He's a senior," he answered.

"What was up with all the tension between you two?"

He looked at me and smiled. "Already starting with your million questions, huh?" he asked.

My face turned red from embarrassment. Lia pulled a seat up with a big-ass smile on her face.

Scrap looked over at her. "I see you got a lil molester on yo hands, huh?" he joked.

She flipped him off, not even caring about his comment. "No, I got a mature man on my hands," she told him.

Scrap laughed. "His age don't have shit to do with his maturity," he retorted.

"If he's about to be nineteen, then what is he doing going to Poly?" I asked. Poly was on the other side of Long Beach, east side. They were Jordan High's rivals.

"He kept gettin' kicked out and droppin' out of school in LA. Gettin' into too much shit, and the coach at Poly wanted to be captain save a thug because he heard the nigga was beastin' in football, so he took him in," he told us.

"LA?" Lia asked.

"Yeah . . . He a blood." *That's what the tension was all about . . .*

"What is he doing out here right now? He on the wrong side. Shit, if it ain't school baby! He needs to stay away before he gets himself killed out here," Lia said as she laughed. Scrap shrugged. "I mean he fine and all, but damn! He on the wrong side!"

"So is the coach just using him?" I asked, skipping over Lia's question.

"I'on know. Word on the streets is that the coach treats him like his son. I guess he wanted to get him off the streets because he saw the potential in him, and he's close with his family, but you don't just turn a nigga like that into a square overnight. He for the streets fa'sho . . . Be careful with that nigga and don't trust him."

"Why you say that?"

"Just be careful," he said, shaking his head and looking away.

He wasn't too fond of Domion, and if Lia was going to be rocking with them, he didn't want her involved with him, but he knew that he couldn't just tell her that. It wasn't his place to speak. I knew Lia had a smart-ass comeback, too. "You know, I keep telling myself the same thing about you when it comes to my girl," Lia responded. "*Just be careful . . .*"

she said, mimicking Scrap's words. "Would you stop doing what you're doing for her?" she asked, with a sneakish grin on her face.

Lia had Scrap's full attention. He gave that look like he was aware of what she was talking about. I didn't, though, and I was starting to get even more pissed off—still out of the loop. He sighed when he realized that she knew whatever I didn't know.

"Look, man, I'm not gon' tell you shit that you don't want to hear. Just be careful, Loc," he said, going back to the subject with Domion. "I don't trust that nigga, and you shouldn't either. It doesn't have shit to do with me. And you never know . . . Yo girl might be worth it . . ." he finished.

"Well, I hope she is. That's my best friend, and I would hate to have to fuck you up over her." *Whoa! Where the fuck is this conversation going?*

Scrap laughed her comment off. He didn't even take her threat seriously. "Don't trip. She's safe fucking with me, and

I'll never force her to do anything that she doesn't want to do. But I'm still telling you to be careful with that nigga."

"I hope you're telling the truth, and thank you for trying to look out, but I can handle myself," she responded.

"Okay, why are you guys acting like I'm not right here listening to your whole conversation? What is it that I don't know but everyone else does?" I asked, looking between them.

"Yo friend just looking out for you, Ma. It ain't nothin' big," he said, ending the discussion. Lia stared at him for a moment and then nodded her head. They were pissing me off.

After we went back into the house, Scrap walked away for a moment and told us that he would be back. I stood there smiling and laughing at Lia as she tried to get me to dance with her. I was too shy to dance, and I kept telling her to stop because I didn't want any attention being thrown at me. Domion walked over, and I guess he figured, since I wouldn't dance with her, then he would. She was too excited when he came behind her.

When SixPacc noticed, I felt him glaring at the two of them, and even though I knew that he wasn't going to act like he was mad, I could see it on his face. He played it off well though and acted like it didn't matter. He just pushed up on the next girl.

Scrap

This bitch, Mia, was blowin' my phone up talkin' all kinds of shit, and why the fuck was Cherokee with her? *That bitch knows wassup!* I kept getting text messages after fucking text messages: *"Where you at?" "Who the bitch you with my nigga?!" "I need you to come talk to me now!"* . . . Man, this bitch was sending me all types of shit. I felt like I had a stalker! I had to find the bitch and tell her to stop blowing my fucking phone up, and I was about to give it to Cherokee's ass!

Last night when she got robbed, some of my niggas were already in the parking lot, keeping an eye on her for me. The bitch lost her room key, and that was why I had to drop mine off to SixPacc to go take it to her.

She and her trick were waiting in the car, and I guess he was pissed off that she had him waiting, so they got into a heated argument in the car, and Cuz started punching on her. He snatched her purse with all the money in it that she had made from that night and pushed her out of his car.

When my niggas saw her getting pushed out the car and screaming, they started bustin' at him, and he smashed off. The nigga didn't get too far though. I was easily able to find his ass just from the bullet holes in his car. They were shooting at the tires as well, so he had a flat too.

Once I found his car, I saw the flat tire and his door was wide open with the lights still on. He couldn't have gotten far. After that, I saw his dumb ass running through an alley on his phone. I was almost sure that he was trying to find someone to pick him up.

When he saw me smashing through the alley, he panicked as I chased him, and I started bustin' as I drove. I put three bullets in his back. Once he dropped, I scraped up on the side of him and grabbed Cherokee's purse. I made sure all the money she made that night was still inside and stripped the nigga for everything he had on him as well, including his iPhone after I took the chip out of it. I hopped back in the car, leaving his ass right there in that alley.

Once I got back to her, we got into it, because the bitch was mad that I wasn't around, talking about, "You were supposed to be here!", crying and shit. But if she wouldn't have lost her fucking room key in the first place, the shit wouldn't have happened. That was why I had my niggas watching her. And I stayed close for a reason.

I knew she was mad about last night, but she had me fucked up right now, and this wasn't the way to go about it! She knew better than to cross me.

I had to find Mia before the bitch found me and fucked my whole shit up with Janeeva too. When I finally did find her,

I pulled her to the side so we wouldn't be noticed. Cherokee wasn't with her at the time, but I was hoping that her ass popped back up, too.

"What the fuck is yo problem, cuz?" I growled.

"Nigga, you got me fucked up! Who the fuck is the bitch you with, Green Eyes? Huh!? The bitch sitting all in yo lap and shit like y'all just a happy ma'fuckin couple!" she said, pumping herself up.

I don't know why I keep going through this shit with her when she already knows wassup! She doesn't want to take this argument that far.

I kept my voice low as I cussed her ass out.

"Bitch! We're not together! All this extra shit that you doin' right now don't mean shit, cuz! Make a scene if you want to, Mia, and I'ma have Lil Hitta beat the shit out yo ass!" I spat.

"Nigga, ain't nobody scared of you nor any other bitch! So, you can squash that shit right now! How the fuck you think you gon' replace me, nigga? That's why you haven't been answering my calls, because you gave Lovely my spot bitch!" she said a little louder.

I instantly started getting mad because I knew who was giving her all this information. It's crazy what jealousy could do to a bitch. Right when I was thinking about bashing her fucking face in, Cherokee walked up. I glared at her.

"Like that, Cherokee? You just gon' turn on a nigga?"

She gave me this nonchalant look and shrugged like it didn't mean shit to her anymore. "You turned on us for yo fresh meat," she responded.

She needed a reason after last night, and she was blaming it on me, letting Lovely take Mia's spot. I only did it because Cherokee won't do the shit that Lovely would, and that's merkin' a nigga when she needed to. I was gon' make sure that Lil Hitta banged her ass first.

"Bitch—" I was stopped when I saw SixPacc and Janeeva come outside. I knew they were looking for me, but before I could give them both my last words and walk off, Janeeva spotted me. *Fuck!*

I couldn't make a scene, and I was happy Janeeva wasn't any hood-ass bitch, because I knew that she wasn't going to make a scene either. I did see the fire light up in her eyes, though.

Janeeva

Lia was still in the house dancing with Domion and I didn't want to fuck anything up with her, so SixPacc came with me to look for Scrap. We scanned the backyard with the crowd of people and still didn't see him.

"Where the fuck is this nigga at, Loc?" SixPacc asked, fixing his hat.

I shook my head, and as I focused my attention to a dark corner by the fence, I saw Scrap with the girl that I knew as Mia and the other female that she was with, Cherokee. I was furious! I didn't know how to react though, and I wasn't the one to make a scene. SixPacc looked at me and saw that my attention was focused on something in the distance, so he followed my gaze.

"You see him?" he asked.

"He's right there . . ." I said in a faint voice. I didn't know what to think or how to feel. He looked up, and when he spotted them, he sighed. "Yo, let's go back in. That nigga probably handlin' some business right now."

Okay, now they all had me fucked up! *He's handling business with this Mia bitch, too? What is this fucking business? Somebody needs to talk!* I didn't care about what SixPacc was talking about! I wasn't going anywhere but toward the "business" that Scrap was handling. Yeah, don't underestimate the shy bitch! I walked over to the spot Scrap, Mia and Cherokee were at.

As I walked over and Scrap acknowledged my presence, he decided to meet me halfway. SixPacc ass just followed me. As I approached him, he pulled off a smile.

"You good, Ma?" he asked. I didn't answer. I just looked at the girls, and as they walked up, I was mean mugged by them both. Scrap was instantly furious when he realized that they didn't keep their distance.

I could tell that he wasn't going to introduce us as he turned to Mia. I guessed that she was the biggest threat since all his emotions were going toward her.

"So, you not gon' introduce us? Well, I guess we'll introduce ourselves. I'm Mia," she said, snapping her neck at me.

"Jay," I responded, giving her the same malicious look that she was giving me.

"And this is my girl, Cherokee," she said, crossing her arms over her torso. Scrap glared at Cherokee, and I saw his fist ball up. Cherokee's greeting was the same malice look. I could tell that I wasn't liked by these girls too much. I just didn't know why.

"I have to go back and get Lia; we were just making

sure you were okay," I told him.

"It's good. Let's go . . . I'm coming in with y'all," he said, turning me around and throwing his arm over my shoulder. "Aight then, Cherokee. I'll catch up with you layta," he told her.

I didn't know what way he meant that, but he didn't sound so happy. It sounded more like a threat. She didn't say anything. She just stood there wearing the same malicious look on her face and her arms crossed over her torso.

"Don't worry about that girl . . ." I heard Mia say as we walked away.

The party was almost over, and Scrap was ready to go. We then saw Domion and his boys outside getting into it with another group of boys, and as things start getting rowdy, Cliff tried to go out to the back and see what was going on. Scrap grabbed his arm, pulling him back.

"Ain't none of our locs out there, cuz, and you know with Domion, niggas 'bout to start shootin'. What they got goin' on don't have shit to do with us. So, let's go," he told him as he turned around and grabbed me by my waist, pushing me to the front door, quickly.

Cliff warned the rest of our group, and they all started doing the same as we slipped through the crowd and headed out the door. The moment that we got outside, we heard gunshots coming from the backyard. Everybody ran, and the people who were still in the house all tried to get through the front door and run.

Scrap wasn't fazed at all. He just hurried and dragged me to the car calmly with his arm around my waist and Lia right beside me. SixPacc and Twinkie ran to the car as Scrap unlocked it, and we all hopped in and drove off.

My heart was pounding, and even though the gunshots scared the fuck out of me, I couldn't help but look at Scrap's calm but malice expression as he drove. He was in deep thought.

I could tell that he was not tripping off the fact that someone may have just gotten killed. I knew Mia and Cherokee were on his mind. We sat in dead silence as we drove. I didn't know what to think after my mind carried away from the house party being shot up.

I thought about Mia and Cherokee and how I had been out of the loop all day. That alone was pissing me off as I sat there on the way home, but I didn't know how to react or even what to say at this point.

He dropped Twinkie and SixPacc off on the way, and once we pulled up to my house, I opened the car door without saying a word and, before I could step a foot out, he grabbed my wrist.

"Let me holla at you real quick?" he asked. It sounded more like a demand, but I knew that he didn't mean it the way that he was saying it. I looked at him and then at Lia.

"Well, I need to talk to both of you guys because I don't like being out of the loop and that's what I've been feeling like all day!" I said. He let me go and sat back in his seat to listen. Lia sighed. I started with her first.

"What did Skittles tell you earlier?" I asked.

"I told you that I would tell you later," she responded, shaking her head.

"Well, it's later, and I want to know now! There's a lot of shit that I want to know. Like, why does Lovely follow you everywhere like a fucking pet?" I cursed. Scrap's eyebrows rose. I could tell that he was amused by my words right now. I kept going though. I needed to get it all out!

"Who the fuck are Cherokee and Mia to you? Or why does Lovely slip you money, or why is it '*just business*' with not only her but with the rest of them? Like really! Why the fuck are you guys keeping shit from me?" I blurted out.

It was all built up inside of me, and I had to let it out because I had never felt so out of place with the shit that was going on around me in my life! It was stressful not knowing. A serious headache at that!

Scrap sighed and remained calm. "Would you judge me if I tell you?" he asked me, smiling.

He was pissing me off even more because the last time that he said that if I remained fucking with him then I would find out sooner than later, but I wanted to know now!

"Scrap, just tell me!" I said, losing my patience.

He pressed his lips together. "They're my hoe bitches . . ." he responded.

His what? "Your what?" I asked.

"They're prostitutes, Janeeva!" Lia clarified, rolling her eyes.

I flinched, and my heart clinched tight. "You're a *pimp?*" I yelled.

He sat there in the driver's seat just chilled back with this nonchalant look on his face. "Yeah . . ."

I shook my head in disbelief. "So, this whole time that you were talking to me, you were trying to make me your prostitute, and Lia you weren't even going to say anything?" I yelled, looking back at her.

"Whoa! First off, I just found out today that he was pimpin' Lovely. I didn't know about them other two hoes. I assumed but didn't know, and I don't know what the fuck his intensions are with you," she confessed.

"And it damn sho' wasn't that!" he snapped, twisting his lip up.

"Then what was it?" I yelled.

"What the fuck you mean what was it? I was feelin' you!" he retorted, appalled that I was even feeling this way.

I sat there in the passenger seat thinking about everything, and it was just too much to handle at the time. I shook my head and opened the car door.

"I can't deal with this right now," I said getting out of the car. Lia got out, too, and we went into the house. He was being judged right now.

I couldn't stop pacing my room. How could this be that the boy that I've changed my whole appearance for is a seventeen-year-old pimp? I couldn't believe this shit, but it explained a lot of shit!

"Jay, chill the fuck out!" Lia said.

"You should have told me when Skittles told you!" I accused, pointing at her.

"I didn't want you to make a scene, and honestly it really looks like Scrap is feeling you, not just to pimp you out. That's why I waited."

"He's a fucking pimp, Lia! It doesn't matter! This is a remarkable story to tell my kids when I get older. Oh yeah, Mommy got her first kiss by a pimp!" I said sarcastically.

Lia laughed. "You're seriously making this more than what it is," she said, shaking her head.

"How?" I yelled.

"Just give him a chance first, Jay. You know you still like him. Everyone has their flaws . . ."

My pacing slowed down a little bit because I started

thinking about all the things that Scrap told me about his life. I

don't know how the hell it just popped up in my head, but it

did: his dad not being around, his brothers and his little sister,

his mom being a drunk, etc. I started to feel bad.

"I don't know, Lia. Weirdly, I do still like him."

"Shit, you better after I just gave you a whole

makeover!" she said playfully. I laughed. "I wouldn't judge

you for still liking him though. The boy's got swag, and bitches

are already hatin' on you for him even giving you the time of

day. On some real shit, I don't even think his hoes got shit on

you and they're bringing in his money, but he still chose you

first," she said. I thought about it. She was right. He had been

putting me before them all day. Lovely was furious!

"I don't want to get in the way of him and his

business," I mocked.

She smacked her lips. "Please, Jay! You saw his

brothers! That's who he was raised by, and I can tell off top that Brandon taught all of them how to get their money, if it's good or bad. I bet you these bitches is just a side job," she said.

"You think so?" I asked.

"Scrap grew up off this game! He was raised in it! I don't know a lot, but I know enough to know that him and his brothers were making money before these hoe bitches came along. Believe me!" she said. "He doesn't depend on a bitch!" I looked at her for a moment and then paced the floors again.

Chapter 11 Feeling You

Janeeva

Monday finally came. I was stressing all Sunday on what I wanted to do about Scrap. Of course, I still liked him. I just didn't like the things that he did, and I honestly felt like if I kept talking to him, then people would mistake me for something that I wasn't. I didn't want rumors going around about being *pimped out*.

I walked to school with Trevor and his best friend Xavier. There were a couple of other people walking with us as well, but the only ones that I knew were my brother and his best friend. I put on my earphones and listened to Bcyonce as we walked. I zoned off into my own little world thinking of Scrap, and when I looked up, one of the girls was looking at me, trying to get my attention. I took one of my earphones out. "Your name is Jay, right?" the girl asked. I looked at Trevor, and he looked back at me. He looked at me as if I was tripping, though, because I still didn't answer her question.

Why the fuck couldn't he give her my name while she's over here interrupting a great song and my deep thoughts about the boy that I dream, sleep and breathe?

"Yeah," I responded.

"Yeah, I've been hearing about you. You talk to Scrap now, huh?" she asked. I flinched.

It's crazy how fast rumors spread, and this was exactly what I was tripping off before. *First, I talk to him, and then next I'll be his hoe.* My brother gave me a malicious look. I knew that he didn't want to hear that I was talking to him.

"Um . . . kind of, I guess . . ." I said shrugging. She smiled and nodded her head.

"You talk to Scrap?" Xavier asked, raising his eyebrows. "When the fuck did this happen?" he asked a little too shocked for my liking. He knew me a little too well.

Well, I guess everyone in our family or close to our family did. I knew they were all wondering how the fuck I made this fast-ass transition and ended up getting every girl's dream the first day.

I didn't answer Xavier, so because I didn't answer him, he wrapped his arm around my neck and sped my pace up, away from the group. He knew that I wasn't about to talk about this in front of Trevor. He was already having personal issues with my change.

Trevor and Xavier have been best friends since sixth grade. I fight and go to him about all my problems as well. The only difference between him and Trevor is that he has been waiting for me to come out of my shell. He was like a big brother to me as well.

Trevor wanted me to stay there. He was happier knowing that I was still a virgin and was going to be something in life instead of worrying about a boy knocking me up and dropping out of school. Even though I knew better than he did that he didn't believe all that bullshit because he did way more than an average seventeen-year-old could. I honestly didn't know what his problem was, but I wasn't going to let it get to me now.

"So, wassup, sis? What's with the whole change?"

I shrugged. "I guess I just wanted to try something different, and you've been waiting for me to come out of my shell so what's the problem now?" I asked.

He shook his head. "I'm happy that you're exploring new things, but Scrap?" he asked. "I mean I don't know if you know about the nigga's reputation, and—man's code—I can't step on his toes, but just be careful."

I sighed. "I know a little bit . . ." I admitted.

"So how did you guys start talkin'?" he asked.

"He gave me his number after the scrimmage."

He flinched. "Scrap gave *his* number up?" He was shocked and impressed. "Well, just be careful," he repeated. "And try not to throw that shit in your brother's face. I know he's mostly trippin' on the fact that it's *Scrap* and not just you with this whole change you got goin' on."

"But why?" I asked. Somebody was about to explain the animosity they had toward each other.

"He's a part of the team, Jay. It's just not a life that Trevor wanted to share with you, and that's why he doesn't tell you that much about that part of his life, and on top of that . . . Scrap's family is *dangerous* . . . Do you know who his brothers are?" he asked. "I mean, that's my nigga, but you just need to be careful."

I dropped my eyes as I listened. "I don't understand. Why do I feel like there's more going on than what I already know?" I asked him.

Xavier looked at me, suspiciously. "What did he already tell you?" he asked.

I didn't know if I was supposed to be sharing his business with him or not. "It's not what he exactly told me, really. You know I'm very observant."

He sighed. "So, you know . . . about the hoe bitches," he answered.

I nodded my head. "And the trap house . . ." I said, in a lower voice, looking back at Trevor to make sure that he wasn't in hearing distance.

"That nigga took you to one of the trap houses?" Xavier growled in a lower voice as we walked up some more.

I shook my head, trying to explain. "He had to drop something off to his friend and one of the girls was robbed . . . He didn't want to leave me there, but he had to, so he made his friend take me to the back, away from everyone," I explained.

I knew that Xavier would keep this between me and him. There's a lot of things that I've done that Xavier knows about and it still has not come back to me from anyone. I trusted him. His nose flared as he listened to me.

"And that's why we need you to be careful," he responded in a deadly tone. "You don't know what you're getting yourself into fuckin' with him. But I know you still gon' do what you do. Just be careful," he repeated.

I shook my head. "Trevor has already exposed me to some of this shit though," I retorted. "I've tucked guns for him before," I finished.

"That's the lil shit. You have never been around him in action. He had no choice but to pass things to you those last couple of times y'all got stopped by the boys. If it was up to him, you wouldn't know shit about this life!"

I sighed and shook my head. I knew that it was going to be a lost cause trying to argue with Xavier, so I just dropped the subject. "Okay . . ." I responded. I didn't want to go back and forth with him. It was too fucking early in the morning.

We had finally made it to school. Xavier walked with me most of the way, while Trevor tried to get the dark-skinned chick's number before he met back up with Talawny.

She usually walked with us to school, but I guess she had to take her brother to the dentist or some shit like that. I honestly didn't give a fuck. I was happy that I didn't have to hear her annoying-ass voice the whole way here.

Once we entered the crowd of students, Trevor and Xavier left me, and I searched for Lia. However, it wasn't that hard to find her today. She stood against the wall in the hallway with Freckles and Dimples.

As I walked toward her, Scrap, Twinkie and SixPacc approached them and started to chat. I stopped, a little taken off guard, and right when I was about to turn around and just walk to my first class, Lia spotted me and called out my name. "Jay!" she yelled, waving her hand in the air like I already didn't see her ass. I sighed. I walked over, and I tried my hardest not to look at Scrap. However, it wasn't that easy.

He was just so fucking gorgeous and *fly* as hell! He was rocking his black and yellow Air Jordans with his Oteil denim jeans that slightly sagged off him, and a crisp fitted white tshirt. There was a gold chain that hung from his neck, and he wore his leather gold snapback to the front on his head.

He was just so fucking sexy from his head down to his feet. I knew that they were going to make him take his hat off, but Scrap was just the type of person that didn't care.

Maybe that's what I liked about him, though. He was just so carefree. He was who he was, and that wasn't going to change anything. I looked back down as I realized that he was staring at me as well.

"Wassup, Jay!" Twinkie greeted.

I looked at him, smiled and said, "Hi."

"What's good, Ma?" Scrap spoke. I couldn't help but look at him. He had this sexy-ass smirk on his face.

"Hi . . ." I responded.

Dimples', Freckles' and Lia's nosy asses just watched us, smiling from ear to ear.

"You gon' walk with me to class today?" he asked. He was acting like Saturday never happened. I thought about it.

"Um—" he cut me off.

"I'm not gon' bite chu. I just wanna holla at chu."
I looked at Lia, and she just smiled at me.

I didn't have any clue why she wasn't tripping off Scrap like she would usually over any boy. Even being the pimp that he was, she liked him. I sighed and nodded my head.

"Okay . . ."

I walked with him to our first period class while some

of the students stared. He really didn't give a fuck though.

"So, wassup? You left a glass slipper in my car

Saturday night," he teased.

I smiled. "So, what made you want to be a pimp?" I

asked, changing the subject and getting straight to the point.

He sighed, knowing that I was about to go right into my

millions of questions. "More money," he replied.

"You don't feel like you're taking advantage of the girls

that you're pimping?" I asked.

"I don't make them do anything that they don't want to

do. It's their choice. I just use it to my own advantage," he

answered, shrugging.

"So, what else do you do?" I asked.

He stopped and turned to look at me straight on. "You

know what I do," he responded. I stared into his eyes, trying to

read them, and then pressed my lips together as I looked away.

"You really are a very observant person. I was impressed when you were telling me all the shit that you were peepin' on Saturday."

I kind of figured that he was trying to change the subject as well. I shrugged. "I've had a lot of time to sit back and watch."

"That shit is a turn on," he said, smiling. I blushed.

"You still haven't answered my question," I told him, trying to stay on the subject. I didn't need any more surprises.

"You figured out the two things that I do already, but you barely can handle that . . ." he responded. I sighed and dropped my eyes. "I told you that if we continued fuckin' with each other, you'll find out eventually, but I can't just tell you the shit that I do, Janeeva. It's one of my hood's codes."

"I just need to know what I'm getting myself into . . ." I said in a lower voice.

He sighed and lifted my chin up so that I could look at him. "If you promise not to leave a glass slipper behind the next time, then maybe *one day*, we'll talk. Just never here . . ."

he told me. We kept walking. "Even with the lil shit that you

already know that your brother does, I'm pretty sure that you

know the other things that I do."

"You're not my brother . . . And I told you already that

he doesn't share any of this with me . . . He never wanted me

around it."

He pressed his lips together as he stared into my eyes,

now trying to read me.

"So, what are your intensions with me?" I asked.

"Honestly, I don't know. But it was never pimpin'

you," he said, giving me this sincere look. "It's something

about you that I can't pin-point my finger on, but whatever it

is, keeps me wanting to get to know you more, and I enjoy

your company," he confessed.

"I'm not like every other girl to you?" I asked.

"As far as I know, no, you're not."

I took a deep breath. "Do you have sex with them?" I asked.

He flinched at my blunt question. "With whom?"

"Your hoes."

"Why are you so worried about them?" he asked with this frustrated look on his face. I looked away and shrugged.

I slowly threw my head down, imagining the worst. I saw his hand raise, and he gently placed his finger under my chin and lifted it up again. "It's not something you have to worry about. Trust me," he said.

I didn't respond. I looked around at all the students that were walking to their classes. We were across from ours, but it was almost time for us to go in.

I spotted Lovely walking down the hall to our class, and as she noticed us standing across the way, she stopped.

I looked at Scrap. "Your prostitute just spotted us," I said, being a smart-ass.

He looked up at Lovely. "She can wait . . ."

He bent down and gave me the softest kiss that had my body melting. I was shocked! I looked over at Lovely, and I swear that if looks could kill, then I would have been dead.

I walked with Lia to lunch. It seemed like our whole group was kicking it with Scrap's group, so we joined the crowd. Of course, there were a couple of people staring at me, including Lovely. She was sitting down below Scrap with her legs crossed, while he sat at the table, laughing and joking around. I wasn't going to lie or fool myself, but the shit was honestly annoying as fuck and weird for her to cling on to him the way that she did.

"Wassup, sis!" Cliff greeted me as he picked me up and hugged me.

I laughed. "Hey!"

"Lia, Lia!" he crooned smiling and nudging Lia on her chin.

"Wassup, bruh," she said, giving him a hug.

"Are y'all coming with us to Knotts?" he asked. We looked at each other confused. Knotts Berry Farm was an amusement park.

"We didn't know shit about it," Lia said, shrugging. I looked over at Scrap as he looked back with this sexy-ass smirk on his face, staring into my eyes. "When y'all goin'?" Lia asked.

"Tomorrow," Cliff responded.

She flinched. "We all have school, so how is that taking place?"

"Naw, tomorrow we're taking lessons at Knotts," Cliff teased. I could tell by the look on her face that she wasn't too sure about it, but I had already made up my mind. I wasn't going.

"I don't know about that. I have a test in my math class tomorrow," Lia responded.

"Stop being a square and come rock with the team, cuz!" Cliff said. "Jay, you goin'?" he asked. I shook my head.

He laughed. "I'm not even worried about you because I know someone who can make you go!" he said, pointing at me. They laughed.

"Don't be getting at her like that!" Lia snapped, defending me.

"Shut up!" Cliff responded as he playfully wrapped his arm around her neck, and she laughed.

"Lia, c'mon, man! Rock with us for the day!" Dimples begged.

Lia smacked her lips and thought about it. "Okay. But don't be mad if my mama finds out and come up there shootin'!" she responded. They laughed and then cheered.

"We got one on board! Now one to go!" Cliff said. He looked at me and then at Scrap. "Aye, loc! Handle that . . ." he said pointing at me. My mouth dropped, and everyone in the group laughed. I felt steam rising from my head. Cliff wrapped his arm around me. "Get that look off yo face, loc! I was just playin'!" he said to me. I was too embarrassed to really care if he was playing or not.

"Jay, just come! It's only for a day!" Lia said, trying to make me give in.

I thought about it and looked over at Scrap as he sat in silence smiling at me. He was speaking to me through his eyes because Lovely was right below him. You could tell that she was already pissed off by Cliff's comment, and no one in this group was sparing her feelings. Just from reading Scrap's eyes, I knew that he wanted me to go. I couldn't resist.

"Okay," I said, giving in. They all cheered. Lovely just rolled her eyes.

I left the group to go to the bathroom, and once I was done, I washed my hands and fixed the smeared eyeliner on my eyelids. I was still practicing putting my makeup on perfectly. Lia was teaching me. The bathroom door opened, and Lovely walked in. I froze as I watched her. She walked to the sink beside me, and she took her mascara and lip gloss out of her purse. She then looked at me and gave me this evil sneaky-ass grin.

"I see you tryin' to hang with the big dawgs now," she said.

I cut my eyes at her. "Excuse me?"

"I want you to stay away from Scrap," she responded.

"Last time that I checked, he was his own person."

"I don't give a fuck what he is, bitch," she said, stepping closer in my face. "He's mine! Besides, you're nowhere near his level. He needs someone that can hang. Not no lil ass girl who's still trying to figure out who the fuck she is. So, stay the fuck away from him or deal with me," she threatened. She walked out of the bathroom and left me there with her threat. I didn't know how to feel or think.

I went back to the group, and I was feeling down. I tried my hardest not to look at Scrap. It wasn't that I feared Lovely. No, it wasn't that at all! I was just having mixed emotions, and

I didn't know how to handle them. Maybe she was right. I was still trying to figure out who I was.

After school, Lia decided to walk to the house with Trevor and me. However, I was stopped by Scrap. Trevor gave him a malice look. He didn't say anything though.

"Let me give you a ride home?" he asked. I looked at Trevor.

"Naw, she good," he interfered. Scrap looked at him and pressed his lips together.

"Lia is coming back to the house with me, so I think I'm going to walk with them . . . But I'll call you," I told him.

"Aight. Call me as soon as you get to the crib," he said a little lower so that Trevor wouldn't cock-block.

It amazed me how he just didn't give a fuck. He knew that my brother didn't approve of me talking to him, but he just simply didn't care. I smiled and started walking off with Trevor and Lia. When I got to the house, I called him.

"Wassup, beautiful?" he greeted.

"Hey," I said.

He got straight to the point. "My big homie is havin' this lil kickback goin' on tonight, and I was tryin' to see if you and Lia wanted to go?" he asked.

"On a Monday night?"

"Yeah."

"Where at?"

"Ladera Heights," he responded.

"*Ladera Heights?*" I asked.

Ladera Heights was southwest of Los Angeles. It was where all the African American upper middle-class families lived! I know most people are more familiar with Baldwin Hills than Ladera Heights, but it's damn near the same area. You could see all of Los Angeles from those hills.

I had been with my mother a couple of times, visiting my uncle, and I stayed for a couple of weeks to spend time with him as well. The view was amazing! He died when I was twelve. Just thinking about it now was bringing tears to my eyes.

"What big homie do you have living in Ladera Heights?" I asked.

"A wealthy one. Do you wanna go?" he asked again.

"I honestly don't know if I will be able to get out the house."

"Well, if you are, then just hit me," he responded.

"Okay." Once we hung up, I looked at Lia.

"Who the fuck is in Ladera Heights?" she asked, rolling her eyes.

I shrugged. "I guess one of his friends," I responded.

"Well, shit! Let's go!" she said, excited.

"Lia, how are we going to get out of the house?" I asked.

"Believe me, the way your parents sleep, it's too easy. I woke up in the middle of the night, went to get something to drink, dropped one of your glass cups and they were still knocked out on the couch. They damn sure not about to hear shit from their room!"

"You broke something and didn't tell anyone?" I asked.

"That's not the point, Janeeva!" she said. "Let's go! I mean damn! Have some fun! It's not like you're going to school tomorrow anyway!" she said smiling.

I took a deep breath and then started to smile. They were becoming a bad influence on me. "I feel so bad right now."

She laughed. "So, call him back and tell his ass to come get us!"

I nodded my head. I called Scrap back and told him that we would go.

Lia decided to make me look extra cute tonight since we were going to an expensive-ass neighborhood. She told me that we'll never know whom we'll meet. I rolled my eyes but allowed her to fix me up.

She was having too much fun. She gave me a manicure and a pedicure. And she did a cute little hairstyle on me. It was a high ponytail with loops all around my head and a couple of strands that she curled, falling in my face. She hooked me up.

My makeup was on point as well. She didn't want to overdo my outfit tonight, so she just had me slip on a cute, laced tank top with some tight black skinny jeans. The damn jeans were so tight, I felt like I couldn't breathe.

"Lia, you have got to be kidding me!" I said, trying to breathe.

"Beauty is pain. Pain is beauty," she responded, poetically, closing her eyes with her hand on her chest. *Fucking weirdo*. I was only talking shit in my head because I was frustrated with the jeans.

"And you just don't know how amazing you look in those jeans," she said, smiling from ear to ear.

"In those jeans!" I sung out as we laughed. Once tenthirty hit, Lia was getting a call on her phone.

"Hello?" she answered.

"Yo . . . we outside," I heard Scrap say through the phone. I looked at my phone and realized that I had two missed calls from him. I figured that was why he called Lia.

"Aight give us a minute," she told him. I was too excited and scared at the same time.

"Lia, I'm scared as fuck right now."

"You're good," she whispered.

We snuck downstairs quietly, trying to not make a sound. I was so scared that I kept forgetting to breathe. Once we were finally out of the front door, we ran to the car.

Twinkie was in the front seat, so we hopped in the back. I didn't realize that they were in the car laughing at us until I got all the way in.

"Passed y'all curfew?" SixPacc asked. Lia flipped him off.

Scrap drove off as we headed to the west side of LA.

Once we got into the neighborhood, I couldn't help but get a little emotional. I hadn't been on this side since I was twelve. I felt my eyes start to water as I looked out the window at the huge houses surrounding me.

"So, who lives over here?" Lia asked.

"The big homie, Ice," Scrap responded.

"And how the hell is he able to afford this shit?" she asked. Scrap smiled and looked at her through his rear-view mirror.

"He has his ways," he responded. I shook my head, laughing. *He never gives a full answer.*

Once we pulled up to the house, I was a little impressed. It was a nice one-story house. It was still big as hell, and it was right on the edge of the hill where the best view of the city was. When we all got out of the car, I couldn't help but just stand on the edge of that hill and smile while I looked down at the big city and all the lights. Scrap scared the shit out of me when he walked up behind me.

"I didn't mean to scare you," he said, smiling. "It's nice, huh?"

"It's beautiful," I said in a whisper.

"Not as beautiful as you," he responded in a low voice, wrapping his arms around my waist from behind me.

I felt this chill burst through me as his cheek touched my own. I could smell the cologne that saturated his body, and I just felt like I was in heaven. I turned to face him. I don't know why I felt like I had to look at him, but I had to stare at those gorgeous green eyes that he owned. He gazed back for a moment and then smiled.

"You ready to go in?" he asked. I nodded my head.

We walked up the seven long-ass steps to get to the front door. Scrap knocked, and we heard a lot of commotion going on inside. When someone finally came to open the door, he looked at Scrap and yelled, "Wassup, nigga!"

He gave him a man hug and welcomed us inside. He was a scrawny dark-skinned man with dreads in his head, touching the middle of his back. He wore no shirt with some basketball shorts on and some house shoes. He looked older than us! He carried a bottle of Remy in his hand too.

"Wassup, Lil Scrap? How you been, lil nigga?" he asked.

"Stayin' up, cuz," he responded, while we walked with him to the family room where all the ruckus was going on.

"I heard you back in school. You goin' to Jordan now?" he asked.

"Yup."

"How is it?"

Scrap shrugged. "It is what it is," he responded.

"I know you happy to be out that house though!" the man said, laughing.

"Nigga, you don't even know! Anything better than being in that fuckin' house or back in that small-ass cell, cuz!" he said laughing.

The man laughed, too. "I'm already knowin', loc!"

When we got to the family room, I saw more older people. The first one that I noticed was Brandon. He was sitting down watching the football game on a big flat screen TV. There was a girl leaning against him with her leg crossed over his and his arm around her shoulder. She was a cute lightskinned chick with small mini-micros in her hair, pulled up into a high ponytail. Everyone was dressed casually. They all still looked nice, but I felt like I was overdressed even though

Lia told me that I wasn't.

"Taz! Yo lil brotha' here, loc!" the man said, looking over at Brandon. Brandon looked up. He nodded his head at Scrap and waved at the rest of us. I looked over into the kitchen, and there were people taking shots back-to-back of Hennessy.

Scrap grabbed my hand and looked at me. "Yo, I want you to meet somebody real quick," he said to me.

We walked over to the kitchen and approached a caramel-looking man with light creamy brown eyes like my own, a fresh-cut fade with silky waves in his head and a lightskinned chick whose eyes were wide as she stared at Scrap and my entwined hands.

When the man realized it as well, his eyes got wide, too. Well, they weren't exactly wide because I could tell that he was high as hell, but I saw the shock on his face.

Scrap let my hand go and grabbed the bottle of Hennessy and one of the red two-ounce plastic shot cups, pouring himself a shot. He then looked at the man.

"Yo, Brent . . . this Janeeva and her friend Lia," he introduced us. He then looked at me. "This my brotha'. They call him Yaya on the streets though, and this his girl Nakeia," he introduced.

Brent nodded his head at us in greeting with a cheesyass smile on his face. Yeah, he was loaded! However, I started to get it. These were all of Scrap's brothers' friends. That was why they were so much older.

"What's good," he said, throwing his arm over Nakeia's shoulder.

Nakeia stuck her hand out to shake our own. "Nice to meet you guys. I go by Lady Yaya," she greeted.

I smiled. It was funny because it was so close to Lady Gaga. I knew she got teased about that by the team. I didn't say anything though.

"Aye, nigga! No more than a couple of shots tonight. You crash my car or even get my shit towed, I'm gon' beat the shit out of you, cuz!" Brent told Scrap, pointing at him with the glass of patrón in his hand.

Scrap smacked his lips. "Ain't nobody 'bout to crash yo shit!" he said, taking another shot of Hennessey.

SixPacc and Twinkie started to take shots as Lia joined them. I rejected it. Lia started to enjoy herself after the third shot. They played some music after the game was over, and everyone was starting to loosen up more and started dancing around the house.

There were fifteen people at the most here, but they were still getting down once the music started playing. It was really a wrap when the song "Big Bank" by YG came on.

I was enjoying myself as well, and I was enjoying seeing everyone drunk. Scrap and I were probably the only ones who weren't. I looked over at the sliding door that had a balcony connected to it, and I couldn't help but go out there and look at the sparkling city.

I stood there outside, while everyone else enjoyed themselves inside, and I felt emotions coming back. My chest started to flutter as I thought about my uncle.

This was the same scenery that I used to spend most of my time watching with him. He was my favorite, and I was his. He used to come down and spend every weekend with Trevor and me, buying us all types of things. He would give me these juicy kisses that would feel sticky on my cheek! It was so disgusting but so funny! I cherish every sticky-ass kiss that he had ever given me!

A month before he passed, he gave me this beautiful ring with little diamonds going around it. I didn't know it would be the last time that I saw him. I wore it every day. My mom thought it was best to put it in the safe until I got a little older because I took it off one day and lost it.

Of course, I found it, but I was devastated. So, she put it away for me for safekeeping, and anytime that I needed it just for a moment, she would let me have it. I missed him so much! This view was bringing back too many beautiful memories with him. I don't think I was ever going to get over the pain that I was feeling. A tear dropped from my eyes.

"You okay?" I heard a voice behind me.
I quickly wiped that tear and turned around to look at Scrap. I pulled off a smile. "Yeah, I'm fine. Just enjoying the view."

He walked over and stood on the side of me. "Is this your first time seeing a view like this?" he asked.

I shook my head as we both leaned against the rail and gazed out at the beautiful city. "No, it just brings back a lot of old memories."

"Like what?"

I shrugged, not really wanting to share. Another tear slipped from my eyes, and he looked at me.

"You sure you okay?" he asked.

I quickly wiped that tear, and as I did, more started to fall. I kept wiping until he gently grabbed both of my wrists and stepped closer to me. He placed both hands on my cheeks and wiped my tears with his thumbs.

"What's wrong?" he asked with concern.

I inhaled deeply and let it go. "My uncle lived in this neighborhood. He died when I was twelve." After I said it, I shook my head, not wanting him to think that I was weak. "It just brought back old memories . . ."

He smiled and turned me back to face the scenery as he stood behind me with his arm around my waist. I didn't have to say anything else.

"Well, he must have brought you back to this side to watch this scenery with me," he said, playfully.

I laughed. "And what's so special about you?" I asked.

"First of all, I'm a ma'fuckin' KING!" he responded. I laughed harder. He turned me back around to face him, and he got serious. "But all bullshit aside, I'm still trying to figure out what's so special about you too," he confessed. "It's something about you . . ." he said, shaking his head.

I smiled. "Well, I guess you'll figure it out sooner than later," I said, imitating him.

He chuckled. "I guess I will."

As I stared at him, I decided to finally ask the question that I had been trying to figure out since I met him. "What're you mixed with?"

He smirked at me and tilted his head. "I'm black."

I pressed my lips together and rolled my eyes. "And what?"

"Blue."

I cut my eyes at him and smiled. "Stop playing!" I whined, slapping his arm.

He chuckled. "My dad is creole. So, I gotta lil bit of ery'thang in me," he joked. "A lil bit of French, Spanish . . ."

I smiled. "Can you speak it?" I asked.

"What? Creole? I understand the basic French more than I do it being spoken in Creole. Even though the Creole language is French Based and just broken up into all these otha' languages, I only understand a lil of it. My pops' mom is this pale-ass white lady that speaks mostly French. So that's all my pops spoke when he was around. Brandon and Brent can speak it, too. Me and Bavari understand it more than we can speak it. We're not fluent . . ."

"That's still dope! So, your grandpa is the creole?" I asked.

He nodded his head. "Yeah . . . He dead now. None of us ever met him, but I've seen some photos in black and white, and my pops used to tell us stories that his mom told him . . . about how his skin was darker than all of ours with the same green eyes. I was young but for some reason that story stuck with me."

"Tiiight!" I said, smiling. He laughed. "I did actually hear through the grapevines that you were creole, so I tried to do a little bit of research to understand it better."

He smiled hard at me. "Is that right? You did that for me?"

I blushed, dropping my head, trying not to smile too hard, and then nodded. He shifted his body so that he could face me straight-on with this huge smile on his face.

"You really feelin' a nigga, huh?" I continued to blush without answering him. "Don't feel offended when I say this, but you low-key just made my dick hard, telling me that." We laughed. "I appreciate the effort, for real, especially because ma'fuckas just be runnin' they mouth, makin' shit up, not knowin' what they talkin' 'bout," he said, shaking his head. I observed him as he showed this annoyed look on his face.

"You don't like all the attention, do you?" I asked.

He pressed his lips together and sighed. "Naw, not really. It's mostly because half of these niggas think they can play with me like I'm not gon' clap back. They take all this mixed-breed shit to a different level, like I'ma sucka' or somethin', and then they learn who I am and want to be all in my face and shit . . . These females too . . ." he said, shaking his head.

"Well, if it makes you feel any better, you're nothing like the rumors that I've heard about you, as far as I know at least . . . You're different than what I expected . . ."

"What did you expect?"

"All I can say is that I didn't expect for you to be such a sweetheart. I was a little scared at first because I was expecting an asshole, a 'fuck boy' . . . Well, that's the phrase Lia uses."

He smiled and then chuckled. "If that's what you were scared of, then why you still agree to let me take you out?"

I hesitated for a moment before I answered. "I guess something just told me to find out for myself."

"I'on know what you heard. It may be true; it may not be. But I'm not yo average nigga, Jay. There *is* a lot that comes with me. And to keep it hunnid, you different than what I expected, too. Somethin' told me that you were though when I approached you in them stands . . ." He gazed into my eyes, trying to read them, and I shied away as the butterflies danced around in my stomach.

He stepped closer, gripping onto my waist and pulling me to him. He traced his lips up and down my neck while chills shot through my body.

My heart stopped for a moment as I felt the throb in between my thighs.

I pulled away from him, trying to get myself together, and he showed this smirk on his face as he watched me. When

I realized how amused he was that I was fighting the sensational feeling that he was giving me, I turned my back on him in embarrassment. *Why the fuck am I acting weird now?*

He came behind me and pressed his body against my own, smoothly wrapping his arm around my waist. "I'on know why you fightin' it . . ." he whispered into my ear. "I want you just as much as you want me," he finished, kissing my neck.

I was fucking melting and couldn't control the arousal bursting through me. As he continued to put these soft kisses on my neck and shoulder, I felt his hands entwining with my own as he continued to hold on to me from behind.

"Can I hear you speak it?" I asked in almost a whisper while still enjoying the feel of his lips.

"What you want me to say?" he asked in the softest tone, now tracing his lips up and down my neck.

"Anything . . . I just want to hear you speak it," I replied with my eyes closed.

He thought for a moment and then whispered in my ear.

"*Je veux t'embrasser.*"

This chill burst through me as he let go one of my hands and his own traveled in between my thighs. He caressed my clit through my jeans. I smoothly gripped his wrist and then turned to face him.

He was all smiles when I turned to him. I couldn't help but smile back. I let him go further than what I expected to, and he knew it. The shit felt so good that I really wanted more. I was too scared though.

"Looks like I'm making somebody feel moe' comfortable wit me?"

I blushed and then chuckled. "So, what did you say?" I asked.

"I wanna kiss you," he responded. "Those soft-ass lips . . ."

He bent down and massaged his tongue with my own. I was melting.

What was it about this boy that just had the fire burning within me? And it wasn't just his looks that kept me so entranced; it was everything about him . . . I couldn't get enough of him.

Our lips finally parted, and we just stared at each other for a moment as he caressed my waist, and then I shied away again, to get myself together. My legs felt like Jell-O.

As I tried to shake the feeling off, I looked inside at his brother, Brent, and his girl. They were tonguing each other down by the fireplace.

"So, I take it that Brent is the second oldest?" I asked. He nodded his head. "His eyes are different. Him and the twins . . ." I stated.

"Yeah. I guess it just skipped 'em," he responded, shrugging. "People still be sayin' lil shit about their eyes though. They have eyes like yours," he said, gazing into my own. I blushed. "You beautiful, though. Them niggas' ugly," he finished.

I laughed, shaking my head. "You're so silly." He laughed. I looked at Brent's girl. "His girl is beautiful."

"She a ridah too. That's Lil Hitta's older sister."

I flinched. "Really?"

"Yeah. They all with the shit," he said, nodding his head.

"Are they all a part of the team?"

"Yep."

"How many siblings does she have?" I asked.

"They got another sister, Tweety. She the youngest."

"So how did she end up with your brother?"

He laughed. "You and your billion questions."

I blushed from embarrassment. "Am I annoying yet?" He shook his head. "Naw, it's actually kind of cute."

"Cute, huh?" We laughed, and we stood there looking out at the city and enjoying each other's company.

Chapter 12 Protect

Janeeva

The next day, we went to Knotts Berry Farm. Of course, that was an extremely hard task. Lia and I had to leave with Trevor in the morning to function as if we were really going to school, and after we went our separate ways like always, we walked to the back of the school and hopped in the car with Scrap, SixPacc and Twinkie.

Once we got there, I didn't realize that Scrap had already paid for mine and Lia's tickets because we were so busy talking and playing around with Freckles and Dimples.

Twinkie passed the tickets to us so that we could get in, and Lia and I looked at each other. He smacked his lips. "You know that nigga bought y'all tickets!" he said, smiling. We laughed.

The day was the most fun I had in my life! I spent most of my time with Scrap! Every ride we got on, I sat next to him. He won me a huge Bugs Bunny stuffed animal in a game of

"Shoot the Can," and it continued until night.

After three o'clock, I already knew that I was busted when Trevor called me a couple of times and then called Lia's phone, but I was having so much fun that I figured that I would deal with him tonight. I didn't want to leave Scrap. I was shocked that Lovely didn't tag along with him. I was happy that she didn't, because I didn't have to worry about her.

When I got home, I got cussed out by Trevor, but he said that he didn't tell our parents. I never told Trevor that I was with Scrap all day, but I kind of figured that he knew.

Trevor

This shit with Janeeva was getting out of hand. I didn't even give a fuck that she ditched; it was the fact that she lied to me about the shit that had me pissed off.

I knew that she was with Scrap. I didn't even bother asking. I really didn't even want her involved with the nigga. I never wanted to share this life with her. I knew if she kept fucking with him, she was going to find out about the robbing, pimping and dealing. I didn't want her to see or get caught up in none of that shit.

What if one of his enemies caught him slippin' and decided to pop off and Janeeva was with him? I wouldn't forgive myself to let this shit between them carry on. She's just not that girl. She's never been.

I've only told her what she needed to hear about my life on the streets if anything were to ever happen to me. I never let her experience the shit, aside from when she had to hold my piece a couple of times. But still, I never put her in a position where I knew that her life could be in danger.

Scrap? I honestly don't know the nigga well enough to trust him with her. Taz, Yaya and Guda were the only ones that I trusted.

Guda is the one who put me on my freshman year. He was just getting out of high school, and one of his niggas tried to punk me but I never been no bitch, cuz!

When Guda realized how my little ass wasn't backing down from beating his Loc's ass, he was impressed. His loc had me fucked up! And I was small at that time too, barely fourteen years old. He wasn't with the whole *bullying a little-ass kid shit*, so he told his loc to square up with him.

Of course, he worked his shit, and right after that, he pulled me to the side to see where my head was mentally. When he realized the type of little nigga that I was and the fact that I was booksmart too, he pulled a stack of money out of his pocket, all hundreds, and then he asked me if I wanted to make some real money. I never went back after that!

Ever since then, I've been under him and his brother's, observing and learning. I remember when I got put on. Scrap was one of the niggas that jump me in.

Anytime I make a mistake, they correct me and tell me the best way to do it. They were family to me. Of course, I had my dad, but most of the shit that I learned in my life that was valuable information came from the streets.

My dad *is* the one who made me, and Janeeva learn how to fight, though, and that's why ma'fucka's be so shocked when Janeeva speaks up for herself.

Yeah, she's quiet but she'll work yo shit if you push her far enough. My dad made sure we knew how to fight but remained humble, and between him and my mom, they always made sure that our education came first.

Now back to Scrap . . . He was the only one that I never got the chance to chill with like that. I didn't know if he felt some type of way about me being so close to his brothers or not, but I just never got the chance to get to know the nigga!

I know every time that I turn around, though, his brothers are telling me how he got into some more shit. I want to call him a bad ass lil nigga, but we're the same age. Those

are always the words his brothers use.

I sat up in the garage with them smoking a blunt. I couldn't stop thinking about Janeeva. I stared at Scrap as he played on the Play Station they had set up with Tutu.

Taz was getting shit in line to pick up some packages, Yaya was making calls and Guda was talkin' to his hoe bitches, trying to book rooms and shit.

They were always on the clock. It was crazy what money could do to you, and I respected the fact that their family was so money motivated, and they stuck together. Imagine some young-ass niggas making more money than an average dope dealer.

The one thing that I respected about Taz is his loyalty. He's loyal to his family and did everything at a young age that he could for them to stay together. He ended up raising kids when he was still a kid himself, but he had no choice.

He taught his brothers the only way that he knew how to survive so that they could help him carry the weight. It may have not been the right way, but he had to do something to make sure that they were straight since his parents couldn't do it.

His dad ran out on them, and his mom was a drunk. He had to step up and be the man of the house. He's been raising five kids by himself ever since he was sixteen. Breanne came along later. She was the only one who had a different dad.

He told me that it wasn't the life that he wanted for his brothers, but they still had to eat, they still had to have a roof over their head, and he didn't want to lose them to the system. He had to do what he had to do as the man of the house so that they would remain a family.

I know he regrets most of it, though. I see it in his eyes. He hates that he brought his little brothers into this shit because it was the fastest way to make money, and at the time, being the young nigga that he was, it was a way out to him.

He hated his dad for leaving them, but he hated his mom more for giving up on them. I would catch him staring at Scrap, and I would see the pain in his eyes.

Taz told me that Scrap was the way that he was because of his father. He doesn't trust too many people, and the reason that he treats females the way that he does is because of his mother. His parents caused him to be the way that he is today. *"Fuck a bitch and trust no nigga."*

I've seen the way he's treated his hoes. I've seen him jump down Mia's throat and made her feel worthless. She may have not been the best example though because that's just a ratchet-ass bitch, but I've seen all this shit and I can't picture my little sister fucking with him. I couldn't do this shit anymore. It had to end.

"Scrap!" I called out to him.

He looked at me. "Wassup?" he said as he continued playing the game. I got up and walked over to him. When he saw me get up, he paused the game and looked at me.

"Whatever the fuck you and Janeeva got goin' on is over, cuz. You need to call her and tell her you can't fuck with her."

"Now why would I call her and tell her that? So much for gettin' your sister feelins hurt, huh?" This nigga was always testing me.

"As long as she not fuckin' with you! It's good." I could see the anger lighting up in his eyes. I knew he had a short fuse, but I didn't give a fuck.

He stood and stepped into my face. "So, what? You tellin' me I'm not good enough for her?"

"It ain't got shit to do with you not being good enough for her. I never brought her into this type of life, and I still don't plan on getting her caught up in this shit!"

He laughed. "Nigga, how the fuck did you end up gettin' into this shit?" he retorted with a smirk-ish-ass grin on his face. "Ma'fuckin "4.0" student, captain of the varsity football team on yo way to college and you robbin' and slangin' just like the rest of us! I'm pretty sho' you have parents who spoil the shit out of yo *pretty-boy* ass. I don't get it. How the fuck did you get into this shit?"

"We not on my ma'fuckin life right now, cuz!" I said getting pissed off. "All I want is for you to stay the fuck away from my sister! If it was Breanne—"

He pushed me. "Keep my fuckin' sister name out yo mouth, nigga!" he exploded.

I knew at this point he was already mad, so he was going to find a reason to fight me. I pushed his ass back. "And keep mines out yo life!" I yelled. I didn't realize that they were all watching us until I felt arms fly over my chest and Yaya grabbed Scrap!

"Both of y'all chill the fuck out, cuz!" Taz yelled, coming between us. Scrap pushed Yaya off him. He glared at me as he walked past me and left the garage.

Scrap

This bitch-made-ass nigga had me fucked up! Was he really telling me that I wasn't good enough for his sister? I paced my room trying to calm the fuck down so that I wouldn't go back in the garage and bang his bitch ass! I couldn't believe that the nigga was even bold enough to tell me to stop fuckin' with her.

As I paced, I started thinking about the real reason that I was mad as fuck! Was it because he was telling me that I ain't shit and that I was never gon' be shit, or was it because he told me to stop fuckin' with her?

I started to realize the true problem. I was feeling Janeeva, and it wasn't just on some looks type shit. I was really *feelin'* her.

She made me feel different when I was around her. No drama, no loud-ass bitch telling you her life story and trying to fuck you every five minutes! I haven't spazzed out on her or none of that shit. She hasn't given me a reason to. I love her curious-ass attitude. I love the way she innocently asks a million questions not knowing what's up. I love all that shit.

Being with her felt like no worries, no stress, no business. It was just me! I wasn't sure if I was sounding like a bitch or not, and I wanted to call her every type of bitch that I could for making me feel like this, but I knew it was the truth! I didn't even know how to treat her like a bitch. It was her innocence altogether that had me stuck.

I finally stopped pacing. The thought of her put my mind at ease, but the thought of her brother underestimating me fired my ass back up. It was mixed emotions. What the fuck was going on with me? I didn't catch feelins for no bitch! But she wasn't a bitch . . .

I flopped down on my bed and lay back as I tried to get my mind right. Someone knocked on my door and I told them to come in. Brandon walked in.

"*Qu'est-ce que c'était tout ça?*" he spoke in French, asking me what the shit was about with me and Quarterback. I shrugged. I didn't want to talk about it. He came and sat next to me.

"Look, I don't know what that shit was all about, BomBom, but if you know that you gon' hurt that girl, then stop now. I don't need any problems between you and Quarterback."

I laughed. "So, you agree with this nigga? What? You think I ain't shit, too? That's crazy comin' from my own brotha'," I said, shaking my head, getting pissed off all over again.

"I never said that. I just know you," he responded.

I didn't say anything. He took a deep breath, and there was an awkward silence between us.

"Bom, I'm sorry—" I cut my eyes at him, trying to figure out what the fuck he was sorry about. "This was never the life I wanted for you. I just didn't know any other way for us to survive. I didn't know how the fuck I was gon' take care of us," he said.

I dropped my eyes. I felt where he was coming from, and I knew that we didn't have a normal family. "Do you think I'm not good enough for her?" I asked.

"I don't know her . . . I've seen her . . . What's so special about her, anyway? I've never seen you react over no female like this?"

"If I tell you, you wouldn't believe me," I said, shaking my head.

"Are you gon' stop talkin' to her?" he asked.

I shrugged. "You know I really don't give a fuck 'bout what Quarterback gotta say, but he's right . . . I don't want to expose her to none of my bullshit."

He flinched. *"Lil Brian pense à quelqu'un d'autre que lui?"* he asked, sarcastically. *(Lil Brian thinking about somebody else besides himself?)*

I laughed. "Don't call me by that name," I responded.

"I gotta meet her, cuz!" he said, laughing. "I was already as shocked as Brent when he told me you were all *cupcaked* up at Ice's kickback, entwining hands and shit," he teased. I laughed. We continued to laugh and then I stopped . . .

I sat there for a moment in deep thought.

"Brandon . . ." I said looking down at the floor, still thinking. He looked at me. "What if all the shit that we've done over the years comes back on us? . . . What's goin' to happen . . .?"

He cut me off and shook his head. "I'ma take that *L* before any of y'all ever feel that type of weight. You hear me?" he said, wearing this hard look on his face as his eyes dug into my own. I saw the pain in them. I dropped my eyes again as I went back into deep thought. "I brought y'all into this shit. That's for me to deal with," he finished. Right when he was about to get up and leave, my phone started ringing. It was SixPacc.

"Yeah," I greeted.

"Yo! Turn on the news. Channel four. You gotta see this shit, loc!"

I told Brandon to hold on so that we could watch whatever SixPacc was talking about, and I dropped the remote when I saw Cherokee's picture blown up on the news.

"What the fuck?" I yelled. Brandon wore the same expression that I did: confusion.

We were just catching the end of it, but all I saw was a dozen candles lit in an alley in Compton with her picture. I was for sure going to set Cherokee's ass up and have Lil Hitta bang her ass, but I didn't have shit to do with her getting merked.

"What the fuck happened?" I growled through the phone as I stood from my bed.

"They said some shit about raped and killed; I caught it at the end, too," he said.

"You know anybody who would have had something to do with this?" I asked.

"Naw . . ." he responded.

I couldn't help myself. I would have never wished death upon the bitch, and in my hood, we don't play that rape shit!

So, whoever they were, they better hope that I didn't know them, because as far as anybody knew, Cherokee was still my bitch. Even though she was about to get her head banged in the fuckin' concrete, she was still my territory, and getting over on her was like getting over on me! Unless they knew that she wasn't my property anymore.

"Where the fuck was Mia at when all this shit happened?" I asked. You could never underestimate that bitch!

"Yo, loc! I don't know shit. Aight! Chill!"

I just couldn't believe this shit! Brandon couldn't believe it as much as me either though. He knew the whole shit that went down with Cherokee crossing me. I told him about that the whole night, but he knew me better than that. I was probably always going too far when I got mad, but some shit like that—*"Raped and killed!"*—he knew that wasn't me. Brent and Bavari came into the room with their phones in their hands.

"Nigga, what the fuck?" Brent yelled.

I shook my head, too shocked to really react to them. "I don't know, cuz . . ." I said.

Quarterback walked in and gave me a malice look. "And this is why . . ." he said to me as he stood there. Then he left.

Chapter 13 It's Not You . . .

Janeeva

The next day at school, I kept hearing about a girl being raped and killed in Compton. She was the talk of the day. I was still trying to figure out who the hell she was, but I guessed she went to Lynwood High, and she was a senior.

It also spread quickly that she was a prostitute. I didn't get it. Why are there so many young prostitutes these days? Like, was there really any such thing as pride or morals?

Lia caught up with me at lunch, and I guessed that she had all the information that she needed on the girl that was killed and raped in Compton because her eyes were wide as she tried to fix her lips to tell me whatever it was that she had to say.

"Jay . . ." she said.

"What's wrong?" I asked.

"Do you remember when we went to that party and there was a girl there, she was with a girl named Mia?"

I nodded my head. "Yeah . . . Cherokee, Scrap's hoe—" I stopped as I thought, and my eyes lit up

"Please tell me that's not the girl that was raped and killed in Compton," I said, closing my eyes as I took a deep breath. She nodded her head. I dropped mine and shook it.

"Not a lot of people even know that Scrap was pimping her out. Freckles told me that it was the same female at the party though."

I couldn't believe it. "Is Scrap okay?" I asked.

She was shocked by my response. "What do you mean is Scrap okay?"

"Well, I know this has to be hard for him," I said shrugging.

"Janeeva, people think that the reason she was killed was because she got set up with the wrong nigga while she was on the clock."

"So, what? You think Scrap had something to do with this?" I asked, appalled.

"He honestly doesn't seem like that type of person, but it was *his* bitch . . ." I was appalled that she was even accusing him or thinking he could do something like that. "Never mind, Jay. We'll talk about this shit later, and in a more private place."

We walked into the lunchroom and went to our new group with the boys. Our group started to hang out with Scrap's group, so it just started to be our spot.

When we approached them, I saw Scrap talking to Lovely outside of the group against the wall. It looked serious, and he seemed upset. Lovely looked frantic as well. I saw a couple of tears fall from her eyes as he spoke to her.

When he walked back over to the group, Lovely wasn't with him. She wasn't anywhere in sight. He looked angry. The expression on his face was piercing into my chest. I wanted to

make him feel better because I knew this was over Cherokee,
but I didn't know how.

"You good, loc?" Twinkie asked.

"Yeah," he responded.

He looked around at everyone in the group, and when
his eyes fell on me, he stared at me for a long moment and then
looked away. I looked at Lia as she looked back. I knew she
didn't know what to say about this situation, either.

Lunch was finally over. Lia and I walked to class. Most
of us had the same class together after lunch, so we decided to
walk with SixPacc, Twinkie and Scrap as we tried to catch up
with them. When we caught up to them, Scrap looked at me
and grabbed my hand to stop me. Lia and the rest of them
stopped as well. I looked at Lia.

"Go ahead. I'll catch up with you in a minute." She
nodded her head. SixPacc and Twinkie kept walking, too. I
looked at Scrap, and before he could say anything, I gave him
my condolences about his friend.

"I'm sorry about what happened to Cherokee," I told him.

He flinched. "Why are you apologizin'?" he asked.

"I just know that she was something to you," I said, shrugging.

"It's good," he told me. I took a deep breath as we stood there in an awkward silence.

"So, wassup? Did you need to talk to me?" I asked.

He sighed. "Look, Jay . . . I don't know if I should keep talkin' to you." My heart started to clinch tight as I realized what he was doing. "We're just two different people. I can't get you caught up in my shit," he told me.

"What do you mean? I mean . . ." I honestly didn't know what to say. "Did I do something wrong?" I asked.

He stared at me for a moment and then rubbed his hands down his face. "No, you didn't. . ." he said, sighing deeply. "It doesn't have shit to do with you, Ma."

He stopped right there. He didn't say anything else, no explanation, nothing. He just stood there waiting for me to say something.

I felt my insides melting. I thought everything was going well between us, but here I was listening to him give me this short unexplained breakup, and we weren't even together, but I felt so heartbroken.

I took a deep breath as I sucked in my tears. I honestly didn't know what I could have possibly done. Before I could find any words to say, he just walked away . . . leaving me there as my eyes followed him until he went inside of the classroom.

Scrap

Breaking it off with Janeeva wasn't as easy as I thought it would be. I felt more like shit seeing the expression on her face. I never wanted to hurt her.

I lay on my back in my bed, naked, looking up at the ceiling, while Lovely was below me, giving me head. I was trying to concentrate on getting this nut off, but I had too much

on my mind—mainly, Janeeva.

Ice had a meeting with us about Cherokee and if we

knew who would have had something to do with her getting

killed. All of us were clueless, but I told him that she wasn't

even my bitch anymore, so we wouldn't know.

Cherokee wouldn't have let anyone else pimp her out

either. Something was telling me that she wasn't on the clock

when this shit happened. That shit was heavy on my mind. Ice

wanted me to stay out of the way because not a lot of people

knew that I wasn't fucking with her anymore, so of course,

people would assume that I had a part in her death.

This shit was crazy to me. As Lovely deep-throated my

dick and came back up, she sucked on my head. I closed my

eyes, enjoying the feel of it.

I started thinking about how she was the only bitch that

I had left. For some reason, I wasn't even up for recruiting

anymore bitches. I was getting tired of Lovely's ass too.

These hoes were just extra money, and I see a little bit of Mia in her. I see how she acted around Janeeva. I was happy that she was quieter about the shit, but I don't know if that was a good thing or a bad thing. It was cool knowing what the fuck was on Mia's mind, but Lovely was sneaky.

She knew how to handle things or get rid of somebody on her own—then something popped in my head . . .

My eyes snapped open as I sat up and looked down, cutting my eyes at her. She looked up, confused.

"What's wrong, papi?" she asked as she smiled at me with her hand wrapped around my dick. I stared at her calm-ass expression as she tried to put my dick back in her mouth. She told me to lay back down.

I slowly lay back as I continued to think, staring at the ceiling. Naw . . . she couldn't have had anything to do with this shit.

As I lay there, trying to concentrate on this nut, I sighed and pushed her off me. I sat up and grabbed my briefs off the floor. As I started putting them back on, she looked at me confused.

"What the fuck is going on with you? When have you ever stopped me from sucking your dick?" she snapped, appalled.

I looked at her as I pressed my lips together and then shook my head. "I'm just not in the mood," I told her.

"You're not in the mood?" she asked with an attitude.

"What? Is this about Cherokee? Or your lil nerd bitch?" she snapped. I cut my eyes at her.

"Bitch, I'm just not in the fuckin' mood!" I retorted. "Go bust a date or somethin', cuz! Get the fuck on with that attitude!" I said slipping on my basketball shorts.

She was shocked on how I was getting at her, but she was annoying the fuck out of me right now. I ignored her while I waited for her to leave, and she continued to glare. She finally got the fuck up and started slipping her clothes back on. While she was slipping them back on, somebody was knocking on my bedroom door.

I got up and opened it. It was Quarterback. I twisted my face up, confused because I didn't know why he was knocking on my door. He looked at me for a moment, and then Lovely was trying to walk past us with her punk-ass attitude. I looked at her as she tried to slide past me and out the door.

"You better fix that fuckin' attitude, cuz!" I snapped at her.

She didn't respond, and she kept walking to the living room. I looked back at Quarterback as he pressed his lips together and gave me a disgusted look. I turned my lip up and glared at him.

"What'chu want, nigga?" I snapped.

He stared at me for another moment and then sighed. Whatever he was trying to say, it looked like he was rethinking if he even wanted to say it now. "I just wanted to tell you thank you . . ." I already knew what he was talking about. My eyes softened a little bit as I still had my lips twisted up, thinking about Janeeva.

"Is she good?" I asked.

"She's been moping and shit, but she'll get over it." I didn't answer. "Look, I just wanted to tell you I appreciate you breaking it off with her. It was no hard feelings, but I had to think about my sister first. It looks like you got over it quickly anyway," he said, referring the statement to Lovely.

I smacked my lips. "Whateva', cuz. I didn't do it for you. Now get the fuck from in front of my door," I retorted as I stepped back in my room and closed the door behind me.

I lay back down in my bed, looking back up at the ceiling, going back into my deep thoughts.

I broke it off with Janeeva for her sake. It was best that she kept her innocence, and I wasn't the reason that she was exposed to all the bullshit. I wanted to call her, but I knew that I couldn't.

Chapter 14 Gangsta' Party

Janeeva

I sat on the couch with my backpack and all my papers around me. I was trying to finish up my packet but was too distracted to finish. I couldn't get Scrap off my mind. What did I do? It had been a week since we talked, and I was missing him.

Trevor, Xavier and Talawny walked in the house being loud as hell! It was a Sunday. My parents and Maimi were at church, so it was just us at the house. They all walked into the living room, and Xavier popped me upside my head.

"Wassup, Big Head?" he said, flopping down next to me. I socked him in his arm, and he laughed. He looked around and shook his head. He picked up my notebook and was shocked when he saw all the weird-ass formulas on it. "What class is this?" he asked.

"It's my chemistry class," I said, snatching my notebook from him.

"Yeah, I'ma need you to tutor me. I'm happy you're staying up on yo A game, though!" he said watching me study. Trevor sat in the armchair, and Talawny took a seat on his lap.

"Where Lia at?" he asked.

"I think she's at the park. Isn't this the day you usually go up there, too? Don't you all go up there to play football and stuff?" I asked.

He nodded his head. "My coach doesn't want me playing any street ball. I can't get injured." I nodded my head.

"You goin' to the party the team throwing next weekend?" Xavier asked.

I saw Trevor cut his eyes at him, and I looked at Xavier. "What party?"

"Shottas is throwing a party at Scrap's house," he said.

"Gangsta' party, gangsta' partaaaay!" he sung out.

I laughed. "No, I didn't hear anything about it. I don't think it's best for me to go anyway," I said. I felt my chest tighten up as I thought about Scrap.

"You good? You've been moping all week. I thought you would get over this shit by now," Trevor said.

I looked at him. "Get over what?" I asked.

He looked at me for a moment and hesitated to answer. I didn't tell him about Scrap and me not talking anymore, so I was trying to figure out what he *thought* that I was trying to get over.

"Get over what, Trevor?" I asked, putting all my papers and notebook to the side so that I could stand.

He sighed. "I know about Scrap not talking to you anymore," he confessed.

"And how do you know that?" I asked.

He paused for a moment, and Xavier looked away. "I'm the one who told him to stop fucking with you," he admitted. I felt the steam rising from my head. "Jay, I'm just tryin' to protect you."

"Are you my dad?" I asked.

"What?" he responded, confused.

"Are you my fucking father?" I asked in a more malice tone. "You don't run my fucking life! So, stop acting like you're my dad! You had no fucking right! I'm not a kid!"

"It ain't about you being a fuckin' kid; it's about yo safety!"

"I don't give a fuck about what it is! I can't learn from my mistakes if you're always over me trying to run my fucking life! I make my decisions, not you!" I yelled.

He sat there scowling at me. I left the room and ran upstairs. I couldn't believe he did that! I couldn't believe that Scrap quit fucking with me because of him. It didn't sound like him. He loved taunting my brother. I paced the room and then picked up the phone so that I could call Lia and tell her what the fuck Trevor did!

I didn't speak to Trevor that whole week, and even though I knew the truth to why Scrap stopped talking to me, I couldn't get up the nerves to say anything to him. I just watched him from a distance. I caught him looking at me a couple of times but would look away whenever I tried to stare back. This shit was killing me, and it was all Trevor's fault.

I decided that I was going to that party this weekend. I was getting drunk, and Trevor was taking me! I didn't give a fuck about what he had to say about it.

Another week had gone, and it was finally Friday. Lia came to the house with me so that we could get ready. I told her that we were going, and Trevor was taking us. She was shocked when I said it.

I decided to play my cards right, though. Xavier, Cliff, Tutu and Boogie were chilling in Trevor's room waiting for him to get dressed. I knocked on the door, and Cliff opened it.

"Wassup, sis?" he greeted.

"Hey," I said, and then I looked at Trevor as he was getting out his fit for the night.

"I'm going to that party, and you're taking me," I told him straight out.

"Is that a demand?" he asked, nonchalantly, observing his shoes to see if they matched his outfit.

"Take it however you want to take it, but if you ever expect me to forgive you, then I'm going," I told him.

"Janeeva, do you really think that I give a fuck about you forgiving me? I gotta deal with you for the rest of my life. You can't stay mad forever," he said, putting the shoes he had in hand back in the closet and grabbing his fresh new Recs out. "And I was just about to come grab yo ass and ask you if you want to go, but since you're coming in here telling me what I'm going to do—"

I cut him off. "No, no! That's perfect! I'm glad we have an understanding!" I said, leaving the room before he could say another word.

I heard all of them laughing once I left, but I didn't care. I was too excited! I guess this was his way of making it up to me.

I went back in the room, and Lia looked at me waiting for Trevor's to answer. I nodded my head with the biggest Kool-Aid-smile on my face. She was excited, too. We got all dolled up, and once Trevor was ready, we left for the party.

There were so many people at Scrap's house. There were way more people than there were at the last party that I went to with him. It was crazy. There were a couple of older people here as well.

We all got out of the car. We tried to get through the crowd that was blocking the doorway and sitting on the porch with blue plastic cups in their hands and some of them were smoking a blunt and cigarettes.

I could hear the song "Take that Shit Off" playing, by Vinny West. Once we entered the house, we were shocked at how packed his house was inside. The music was so loud, the bass vibrated the whole house, and everybody was turnt!

The first person that we spotted was SixPacc. He had no shirt on, and his hat was turned to the back. I could tell that he was already drunk.

When he spotted us, the first thing he did was walk over to Lia and backed her onto the wall. I laughed. She couldn't help but laugh as well. He didn't say a word. She decided to dance with him since he did it so cleverly. Trevor and his crew went deeper into the crowd, while I stood there by SixPacc and Lia scanning the place.

"Shottas!" I heard a familiar voice yell, and when I turned, Scrap had his hand in the air with a bottle of Remy, dancing. He also had his shirt off, with his royal blue snapback turned to the back. My whole body trembled as I checked him out. I never saw him with his shirt off, but I was turned on by the sweat dripping down his tight abs.

I didn't know that he had a tattoo covering the left side of his chest either. From where I was standing, I saw a moneybag shooting out dollar signs that traced up his shoulder with a scripture, and he had Shottas shaded in as well.

As I went more into detail, I noticed a couple of hypertrophic scars that he had on his shoulder and the side of his stomach. The one on his stomach was pretty big. It traveled from his rib cage down to his waistline. It looked like the wound was deep when it happened.

One of his homeboys was recording from his phone. I was sure that he was on Snapchat, and as Vinny West continued to play, Scrap took out the navy blue durag that was tucked in his back pocket, twisted up his fingers and threw up the set while he looked into the camera, and the light shined on his fine ass with his top and bottom grill blinging while you heard Vinny West sing out, "*On that Gang, Gang, Gang, Gang, Gang, Gang, Gang! You better take that shit off!*" And as Vinny West repeated the same thing, the rest of the team joined in, looking into the camera, throwing up the set. "*On that Gang, Gang, Gang, Gang, Gang, Gang, Gang! You better break that shit off!"*

As he danced, a girl came in front of him and started to grind on him. He danced with her for a while as I watched. I was startled as I felt hands grab my waist, and someone pushed against me from behind. I looked back, and it was Tutu. I laughed.

"Come on, Jay! Dance with me! Don't be shy!" he said as I laughed. I decided to dance with him.

I wasn't sure if I knew what I was doing or not, but as I observed all the other girls, I figured I could handle a little bump and grind. I obviously was doing it well enough to where others were watching. Lia and SixPacc even stopped, and Lia was so excited that she made sure that everyone knew that I was her friend.

"Get his ass, Jay! That's my bitch!" she yelled.

I was so shocked that I felt no anxiety. I think that I was finally coming out of my shell or Trevor had me so pissed off that I wanted to show him that I could hang!

When I looked up, I realized that Scrap was watching me, too. He was surprised to see me, and he couldn't stop smiling as he watched me work Tutu.

I found myself trapped in the middle of the circle that had formed as everyone watched the shy girl dancing. As Scrap got with our rhythm, he decided to take me off Tutu's hands, and then our friends really got turnt up!

"Ayyyeee get it!" they chanted as he grabbed my hand, turned me around and started to work me. I couldn't help but laugh because I was so tired. They all started dancing around us as we both laughed, and he wrapped his arms around my waist.

I turned around to look at him, and he looked back at me with this seductive look in his green eyes. I saw the desire in them, and my heart skipped beats. He didn't let me go. He kept his hands on my hips as he gazed into my eyes and backed

me into the wall that Lia and SixPacc were leaning against.

They moved out of the way.

I could tell that he was a little drunk. He didn't say a

word to me. He just bent down and caressed his tongue with

my own, giving me the most feverish kiss that he had ever

given me.

He gripped my waist and pulled me into him

aggressively as he continued to kiss me. My whole body felt

like it was exploding! I pulled him further down to me, and our

tongues were so deep down in each other's throat that I swear

our lips could have been attached. The heat between us was so

heavy that I felt the throb in between my thighs again as I

melted in his arms.

His hands caressed the small of my back and traveled

down to my ass, and as I felt him gripping one of my cheeks in

the palm of his hands, I could feel his fingers in between my

thighs where I knew all the heat was releasing. I could feel his erection through his jeans as he continued to kiss me and press my body against his own.

"Whoooo!" Freckles said as she passed us. "Y'all niggas over here making love and shit!" Our lips parted as we laughed.

Scrap looked at Freckles. "Mind ya' bin'ess," he said. She laughed.

He locked eyes with me again as he went back to caressing the small of my back. He then bent down and whispered into my ear. "Come to my room with me." My heart clinched.

I knew what he wanted at this moment, and as scared as I was, my body was screaming for him! He traced his lips up and down my neck as he continued to whisper in my ear. "I wanna taste you . . ." Chills shot all through my body, and the sensation between my thighs started to explode within me.

The moment that he placed his hand in my own to take me to his room, I felt someone throw all their weight on me and start punching me in my face.

We fell to the ground, and I was still getting punched. I looked up, and it was Lovely. Lia instantly jumped in and socked the shit out of her, and that one punch knocked her off me. And as I tried to get up and help Lia, I felt arms embrace around my waist and sweep me off my feet.

"Wait, get off me! Lia!" I yelled, trying to get back to her.

I looked and saw Twinkie grabbing Lia off Lovely. Lia struggled to get from his grip.

"Lia, chill, cuz!" he yelled as he struggled to calm her down.

"That bitch got me fucked up! Get the fuck off me!" she yelled. "Run that shit, *bitch*!" she spat at Lovely.

The music went off, and everyone stood around watching. I tried to break my neck and look at the person who had my ass restrained. I was shocked to see that it was Brandon.

He looked down at me. "You good?" he asked.

"Yeah," I said as I looked back over at Lia. Lovely stumbled as she got up. Her dress was twisted, and her curly updo was now falling into a messy half ponytail.

"What the fuck is wrong with you, cuz?" Scrap exploded stepping into her face.

She stumbled over again and pointed at me as her words slurred. "That bitch is my problem!" she said.

I had no clue how many drinks she had, but I was shocked to see her like this. She was sloppy drunk, and it wasn't a good look on her. Her cool, calm and collected appearance was now a raging drunk showing her true colors.

"Bitch, I told yo ass to stay away from him!" she yelled, looking at me.

"You did *what*?" Scrap snapped.

"Yeah, and yoooooou! Ugh! I do everything for yo ass at every fucking command, and you choose this *bitch* over me!" she slurred, falling over.

"Bitch, you a hoe!" he said, stepping closer and speaking to her in a lower voice, but in a more malice tone. "Stay in yo fuckin' place!" he growled.

This was honestly the first time that I had seen him speak to any woman this way. I had never seen him this mad either. She tried to swing on him but missed. He grabbed her by her arms aggressively and gave her a hard look.

"Stop making a fuckin' scene, Lovely," he told her.

She pushed him off her. "Fuck you!" she said, stumbling over, trying to move everyone out of her way so that she could leave.

Scrap followed behind her. Once they were outside, mostly everyone in the house ran outside as well, and I heard Brandon smack his lips.

He let me go as he followed behind to get his brother.

As Lovely tried to get to her car, reaching in her purse for her keys, Scrap was right behind her.

"Man, bitch! I don't got time for this!" he snapped, right on her heels. Once she pulled her keys out, Scrap came up behind her and snatched them out of her hand. "Give me my keys!" she yelled.

"Naw, you can walk. You too fucked up." Everyone watched. I did as well.

My brother came to my side. I guess he heard that I got punched, and when he realized the scene that was taking place, he looked down at me, pressing his lips together.

I was feeling confused at that moment. I had mixed emotions watching him as he continued to argue with her. He put her keys in his pocket and then turned to walk away. She ran up behind him and tried to swing on him again, but Brent grabbed her before she could.

"Bitch, chill!" he yelled.

"Scrap, give me my keys!" she yelled again.

"Man, somebody take her ass home!" Scrap said, with irritation on his face.

"I'll take her home, but give me her keys," Skittles said, stepping up. Scrap reached into his pocket and dropped Lovely's keys in her hands. She sighed and grabbed Lovely, and Brent helped her put her in the car. Once Skittles drove off, Bavari looked at all the people standing outside.

"Aight, get back in the fuckin' house and turn my music back on, loc!" he yelled.

Everybody went back in, and I stood there staring at Scrap while Lia and my brother stood next to me. He looked at me, and I knew the look on his face. I knew what he was feeling that he should have stayed away.

Trevor was lost for words. He didn't know what to say to make this situation any better. Scrap walked past me and went back into the house. I tried to follow behind him, but this time, Lia and Trevor grabbed me.

"Janeeva, let it go!" she snapped. I could tell that she was still angry. She was fed up with this whole situation.

I wasn't just yet though. "No!" I yelled.

I was so tired of people telling me how to run my life and telling me what to do. I yanked my arm away and went back into the house where the party kept going like nothing happened. I looked around for Scrap, but he was nowhere in sight. When I spotted Brandon, I went straight to him. He looked at me.

"Where's your brother?" I asked.

He stared at me for a moment with an expression that I couldn't read, and then he sighed. "He's in his room," he said, shaking his head.

His attitude threw me off, but I tried to not let it bother me because my main concern was Scrap. I walked away and tried to remember which door belonged to him. When I finally remembered, I knocked on the door, and I heard him say,

"Come in." I opened the door, and when he saw me, he threw his head back on his pillow.

"Don't seem so happy to see me."

"I'm shocked that you even still here," he responded as he remained in his spot, lying back on his bed. I walked over to him and sat on the edge.

"My brother told me that he told you to stop talking to me." He looked at me and pressed his lips together. "When did you ever get a thrill out of listening to my brother?" I asked him.

He sat up. "I didn't do it for him," he said.

"Then what did you do it for?" I asked.

He looked at me for a long moment. "I'm surprised that Lovely didn't scare you away." *Always trying to change the subject.*

"I'm not scared of that bitch," I spat in anger.

He flinched and smiled at my choice of words. "Is that right?" he asked.

"Should I be?" I retorted.

He smiled harder. "Not at all."

"Why do you continue to deal with her anyway if she has this crazy-ass obsession with you?"

"That's my hoe, Janeeva," he said, shrugging with this frustrated look on his face.

"And what am I?" I asked.

He paused for a moment before he answered and then dropped his eyes as he thought. "You're just a friend . . ." *Ouch . . . that was a hard hit.* My heart clinched when he said it.

"That's it?" I asked. "So, you feel nothing at all for me?" I finished.

He didn't answer. He just continued to stare at me, trying to read my eyes.

After a moment of him not answering, I took a deep breath, trying to suck in my tears, and I closed my eyes as I pressed my lips together. There were so many different emotions surfacing.

He sighed and looked away from me. "We can't do this shit no moe', Jay." The words pierced into my chest like it was glass slicing through my skin.

"Do you think you'll ever stop doing this?" I asked him, hoping for the right answer. He still didn't answer me. He knew what I was talking about though—was he ever going to stop pimping females?

As I started to realize that my brother was right, it hurt more than anything else that I had been going through with him. What was my purpose for really coming in here? He stared at me a while longer waiting for me to say something since, he knew that I already knew his answer. I sighed as I sat there still trying to control my emotions.

I got up as he hesitated, and then he grabbed my hand. I looked at him with these desperate eyes, showing a hint of hope, and as he stared at me, trying to find the right words to say, he dropped his eyes and shook his head.

"You better off without me, Ma. We just live two different lives. Me and you will never work."

The tears were already falling down my cheeks as I wore this hard expression on my face, trying to hold myself up. I took a deep breath as I felt this lump in my chest. All I heard was bullshit. I pulled my hand away from him as I started walking to the door.

Before I left his room, I turned back to him. "My brother was right . . ." I told him and then closed his door as I walked back to the front.

When I walked back out, people were still dancing and laughing. I made my way out of the crowd. Trevor and Lia were still outside. She took one glance at me and knew that I was breaking.

My chest felt heavy, and looking at the concern on her face had my eyes streaming with tears because I already knew her next question.

"Are you okay?"
I wasn't. The first boy that I was ever interested in and wanted to spend all my fucking time with wasn't choosing me. I looked at Trevor. "Can we please go?" I choked as I tried to suck my tears back in.

I could see the anger in his eyes, but he knew that it was the last thing that I needed. I started to understand why he didn't want me talking to Scrap.

"Let's go," he responded.

When I got home, I lay in my bed and cried my eyes out while Lia rubbed my head and tried to soothe me.

I was proven wrong, and I never knew that being proven wrong about someone that I wanted so much would hurt so bad.

Chapter 15 Weight

Scrap

Today was the day that we got our test results back for our chemistry test. I knew already that I failed that bitch. I didn't even try.

As Ms. Laney walked around to each student's table, handing out papers back with our grades on it, she stopped at Janeeva's desk. "Great job, Janeeva!" she whispered as she placed her hand on her shoulder and gave her a warm smile. Janeeva smiled and looked at her paper.

She hadn't talked to me since the party.

I just wanted her to understand. I didn't want to hurt her. We just lived two different lives. She didn't get that though.

It was crazy the rumors that ma'fucka's were coming up with between me and her. And of course, I was the "*ain't shit nigga*" in every rumor that I had heard. I really didn't give a fuck about what everyone else thought though. I just wanted her to understand.

Once Ms. Laney got to me, she handed me my test. I flinched when I saw the grade. The bitch gave me a C. I cut my eyes at her with my mouth slightly hung open, confused.

"Not so bad, Brian. I will be reaching out to your brother and letting him know how you did. You're hanging in there," she said, smiling and walking away.

What the fuck? And then it all started making sense . . . *Bitch!*

After school was out, I went straight home.

When I got there, Brandon had his bedroom door wide open, rolling dice with Brent in his room. I stopped at his door as I scowled.

"Nigga, are you *fuckin'* my teacher, cuz?" I said in irritation.

He looked up at me and smiled. "You late . . ." he responded as he shook the dice in his hand and rolled them on the floor, snapping his fingers. "I've been blowin' *Ms. Laaaaaney* back out for the past week," he said, putting emphasis on her name. "*Avez-vous réussi votre test?*" he asked, speaking in French, smiling from ear to ear.

He asked me if I passed my test. *Bitch.*

Brent laughed.

"Nigga! *Dead* that shit right now, cuz! That shit weird as fuck!"

"*Non . . .*" he said, telling me, "No," holding his index finger up as he watched Brent roll the dice. "You fuckin' yo hoe bitches is weird as fuck! You stop fuckin' prostitutes, and I'll stop stickin' my dick in yo teacher," he said, looking at me with a more serious expression.

I scowled at him. "Man, whateva', cuz," I said as I started walking to my room.

I busted into my room, mad as fuck, and when I looked on my bed, there was a Jordan shoe box on it.

I opened the box, and it was the new Air Jordan 18s. They were suede black with metallic silver and royal blue around the soles. I stared at them for a moment and smiled.

He knew that I had been trying to get these ma'fucka's but couldn't find them anywhere because they were sold out online and in every store.

"You welcome, nigga!" Brandon yelled from his room. I laughed and shook my head.

Brandon

I lay in Ms. Laney's bed, naked as she rode me, and I bit down on my bottom lip because the shit felt good as fuck while I gripped on to her waist, guiding her on my dick.

Her first name was Kim. That was what I called her by.

She moaned as she threw her head back with her hands on my chest. I sat up, wrapped one arm around her waist as I flipped her over on the bed and lay on top of her, holding one of her legs up as I continued to push in and out of her, touching every corner of her walls.

She squealed as she dug her nails into the small of my back. I sped up as I pounded her walls and she held on to me. I could feel her about to cum as I was about to as well.

As we both started to nut, she gripped on to me tighter. We both relaxed when we finished as I lay on top of her.

After I caught my breath, I rolled over as she shifted her body and laid her head on my chest.

"You are probably the best sex that I've ever had," she said. I laughed. I looked at her and kissed her lips and then got up.

"You're leaving already?" she asked as I started slipping my clothes back on.

"You know I'ma busy man," I responded.

She rolled her eyes. "Yeah, yeah . . . You take care of a whole tribe." I smiled and threw my head down. "Have you ever thought about taking care of you?" she asked. "You're only twenty-eight, Brandon. You need to live your own life too before it's too late."

I do." She sighed. "*Aye! Je vous remercie* . . . Thank you for making sure my brother passed that test," I said, speaking in French and then translating.

"I love when you speak French to me," she said with this straight face, shaking her head. I laughed.

I barely notice that I do it. It's a habit. When I do realize it, I try to translate because I know nobody know what the fuck I'm talking about.

She then pressed her lips together as she went back on the subject with my brother.

"And I only did it because I see how much you care for him and how much you want him to do better, but he really needs to apply himself. I can't do that again . . . Brandon, he didn't even *try* . . . It's like he doesn't care at all if he passes this class or not."

I dropped my eyes as I thought and nodded my head. "I'll talk to him."

I have a student in my class that he became very fond of . . . I haven't seen them talking lately, but I was hoping that she would be able to help him. She's smart, tutored some of the students from last year. She's college-level for sure."

"What's her name?" I asked.

"Janeeva," she responded.

"Last name Boldin?" She nodded her head. The only reason I knew her last name was because I knew Quarterback's.

"You know her?" she asked.

I sighed. "I heard about her."

"Your brother really likes her, or did . . . I don't know. . . It's just from what I've seen in my class."

I stood there thinking for a moment, and then I changed the subject. "Can I ask for a favor?" "What is it?" she asked.

My sister got a beauty pageant coming up, and she wants my mom there . . . Can you help me find something nice for her to wear?"

She looked at me confused. "You want me to help you dress your mom?" she asked, looking at me like I was crazy. "Like . . . How? Why can't she dress herself?" she asked.

I pressed my lips together trying to explain. "I need her to look like . . ." I didn't know the right words. "Like you . . ." I said, trying to explain. "*Décente* . . . like a lady."

She looked at me for a moment and then went into deep thought. She looked back up and gave me a warm smile. "I would love to," she responded. I smiled.

She took me to a store in Cerritos to help me pick out a dress.

I really wasn't planning on fucking with her when we first met. I was only there to make sure that she kept me updated on BomBom, but I don't think that I had ever seen a teacher as *badd* as her. It was hard for me not to flirt with her. One thing just led to another, because she was feeling me too.

The shit had honestly been working out in BomBom's favor, but I knew I needed to start having Trinity tutor him.

Even though my bitch was a whole prostitute, she was smart as fuck. I had been fucking with her since I was seventeen. She was loyal, and I trusted her.

Anytime that I needed her to come through, she always did. She used to babysit BomBom and the twins for me when the rest of us went out of town, too.

She's been rockin' with me for over a decade. I knew she had other feelings for me, but I made it clear to her years ago that I don't mix pleasure with business. I don't fuck my hoe bitches. She was only a good ass patna' that I fucked with hard and made money with.

As Kim and I walked around the store, I had to call Lady Yaya to figure out what size my mom was since she was already at the house with Brent.

Once we got her size, she went through all the dresses and shoes that went with it. She let me choose from the dresses that she picked out.

We were trying to figure out which one would look better on her. I honestly couldn't choose. I didn't know shit about none of this. So, she held them up, one by one on herself, and asked which one I liked best on her. I smiled.

After I looked at a couple of them, we debated on the one that I liked and the one that she liked. I just bought them both and was going to let my mom choose which one she wanted to put on. The shit was getting too complicated. Women are complicated.

Once the day came for Breanne's beauty pageant, I had Lady Yaya and her sister Tweety get Breanne ready to go.

My brothers were going to be there because she really wanted them there, too, but the main person that she wanted to come to see her spin around in her dress and tiara was my mom.

I opened my mom's bedroom door with the two dresses in my hand and the shoes that I and Kim picked out.

She was sleeping with the cover over her head and a bottle of Patron damn-near gone on her nightstand. I smacked my lips, grabbed the bottle and threw it in the trash. I went into her bathroom and started her shower, came back and pulled the covers from over her head. She didn't move.

"Mama, get up!" I said, damn-near yelling at her. I shook her out of her slumber and told her to get up again. She tried to hit my hand and shoo me away.

"Breanne's pageant is today, and she wants you to be there. So, get up, cuz!" I snapped, getting irritated.

"I can't go," she said under the pillow that she placed over her head. My nose flared.

"Mama, get the fuck up, and stop playing with me," I snapped again.

She sat up with her hair all over the place and these baggy eyes. I could tell that she was still drunk. "I don't even have anything to wear," she retorted, shaking her head with her eyes still closed.

I threw the two dresses on her bed with the two boxes of shoes, and as she opened her eyes and looked at them, she sighed deeply. She flopped her head back on the pillow, and I threatened her.

"Please don't make me hold a fuckin' gun to yo head just to make you get the fuck up to support yo daughter."

She opened her eyes again and looked at me. I gave her the hardest look to show her how serious I was. She sighed again and sat up in her bed as she looked at the dresses. "Who helped you pick these out?" she mumbled.

"*Ce n'est pas* important. Just fuckin' choose one," I said, telling her that it wasn't important who helped me pick the shit out.

Over the years, I lost all respect for my mom. It was hard to look at her the same way after everything that I and my brothers had been through. The only reason I even allowed her to still stay in this house was because the twins and Breanne still needed their mother, and I was hoping that one day she would just be one and stop fucking drinking so much.

There was a knock on her bedroom door, and it was Trinity and Diamond.

Trinity was doing her hair for me, and Diamond was going to fix her face up a little bit to make her look more presentable. My mom flinched. I looked at her and then at them.

"Let me know if she gives you any problems, cuz. Y'all got like four hours before we have to be at the place." They nodded their heads. As they came all the way into the room, Trinity smiled at my mom.

"Hey, Sheree!" she said, setting her hair bag on the bed. My mom didn't respond.

She never really liked Trinity. I never knew why.

She would talk to Diamond every now and then, but it was something about Trinity that she just didn't like.

I honestly didn't give a fuck though. She knew that they were my hoe bitches, and she didn't have any room to judge. So, she stayed quiet and pressed her lips together.

I just repeated myself again before I left. "You got less than four hours." I walked out of the room.

I was already getting pissed off that I had to be on her ass about this shit, but I didn't understand why I was still getting mad about the same shit that I had been dealing with for twelve years. It was expected.

Maybe, I was still hoping one day that I would get my mom back, the mom that I used to know. I don't know . . .

It was time to go. Her beauty pageant was at a park in Inglewood. Brent drove her up there so that she wouldn't be late while I waited for my mom. The twins left with Bavari, and BomBom took Brent's bike.

Once the time was up, I knocked on her bedroom door to warn them that I was coming in and then opened it.

I stared at my mom sitting in the kitchen chair that was on the side of her bed while Trinity put the last curl in her hair, and she already had makeup on her face with the dress that I picked out.

I knew that she was going to pick the one that I chose.

My heart skipped beats as I kept the hard look on my face and just stared at her.

I hadn't seen her dress up or look like this in a while. She looked like the mama I used to know, the mama that I adored before alcohol and depression. She stared back at me with misery all over her face, and I just pressed my lips together and nodded my head.

"She looks good," I said to Trinity and Diamond. "Y'all did that, loc. Good lookin' . . ." They smiled.

"You know we got 'chu," Diamond said as she started packing her makeup bag up.

They both left as I continued to stare at my mom. I looked down at her feet, and the shoes that Kim chose were on the ground next to her.

"You like those better than the other ones?" I asked.

"Yeah, they're more comfortable," she responded. I nodded my head.

I checked my phone to look at the time and told her that it was time to go.

We headed out as I smashed through the lanes on the freeway before LA traffic hit.

If anybody knew how the fuck it was being stuck on the freeway in Los Angeles during traffic hour, then you knew that you would be there for hours. They had me fucked up today! I was gon' shoot the whole freeway up if I missed Breanne's beauty pageant.

We pulled up to the park as we entered the parking lot, and there were kids and families everywhere. It was a lot of little girls in their dresses and tiaras taking pictures with their moms or both of their parents. My mom and I looked around at everyone before we got out, and then I saw Brent, Bavari and the twins standing by a tree in the distance taking pictures with their phone of Breanne while she posed.

We got out of the car, and Brent walked Breanne over to the back of the stage where all the other contestants were.

My mom and I went to find a seat for all of us. Luckily, BomBom was already here. This nigga had the whole second role blocked off, waiting on us.

"Y'all took long as fuck, cuz!" he complained. I laughed.

As the show started, and the rest of my brothers took their seats, we watched all the little girls strutting up and down the stage, showing their poise and elegance. They performed their talents, kept switching out of clothes and shit and then, finally, Breanne hit the stage in her gymnastic attire. Me and my brothers cheered as we watched her do cartwheels and front flips all around the stage.

As my mom watched us, she laughed because we were cheering like Breanne was a whole-ass football player.

She looked at all her sons as we stood, cheering for our little sister, and she couldn't help but show a smile as she watched us.

She was impressed with Breanne and her talents as well. Shit, as much as I was paying for the classes, she better be on point with that shit!

"Let's go, Bre! WHOO! WHOO! WHOO! WHOO!" Bavari yelled out.

We were just doing the most trying to support her and letting her know that we were there. Because she was so focused on nailing every flip and turn, she didn't notice that my mom was here yet.

Once it was time for her to get all dolled up for the final contest, which was her dressing up in her dress and tiara and modeling up and down the stage, we all started cheering again.

When she came out and she noticed all of us in that second row, including my mom, her whole face lit up as her mouth dropped with excitement. She smiled hard at my mom as she sat there with her eyes tearing up and her hands pressed to her chest as she waved at her.

I stared at her as I watched the expressions on her face while she watched Breanne walk up and down the stage, and then finally, she looked at me with those same teary eyes. She placed her hand on top of mine and gripped it tight as she continued watching her. I smiled and watched the rest of the show with her.

"Oh shiiiiit! You saw her curtsy, cuh!" Brent crooned, pointing to Breanne and slapping BomBom's hand. I laughed.

We got a lot of looks from other parents. Some probably thought that we were ghetto as fuck, some were "probably" entertained, and some were probably just ready to throw our asses the fuck out! It honestly didn't matter to us, because none of them had the balls to say shit anyway.

Breanne won second place. I honestly felt like she deserved first place, but she wasn't trippin', so I wasn't either. She was satisfied with it.

After I got her from backstage, she ran full speed at my mom and hugged her tight as she talked her ear off and told her how happy she was that she came to see her perform.

That was all I wanted was to make her day.

One of the parents sitting close to us asked if we wanted her to take a picture with all of us in it, so we did. The day was cool, and it was the first time in a long time that we had been out with my mom. I was happy that I could make it happen.

Later that night, I sat at the trap house making calls and watching some of my workers cut up and weigh the rocks that they had just cooked.

Bavari walked in as I started separating and counting the stacks of money that we collected from the little homies. "Aye, loc! So, when I stripped Huey's crib, I wasn't paying attention to any of the extra shit like all the papers, documents and shit that he had in his nightstand. I only took the dough and all our products. I found this shit in the bag when I was clearing it out."

He threw some papers, stapled together on the table. I picked it up and looked through it. The shit had one of our patna's, that we do business with, name on it. As I read the papers and receipts, my nose flared.

"Call Brent and Strap up . . . We takin' a ride to Hollywood," I finished.

Vito was one of the big homies that we partnered with to help us slang our dope. He owned a club in Hollywood, and that was where we were going. We stopped in Ladera Heights to switch out the cars at Ice's house and then kept going.

We pulled up to an alley that connected to the back of the club, and as we got out, I knocked on the back door and one of the security guards cracked it open with his gun to his side, looking to see who it was. I tilted my head and smiled.

"Oh shit! Wassup, Taz!" he greeted, opening the door all the way to dap me up.

"Sup, cuz? Where ma' nigga Vito at?" I asked, smiling and playing the role.

"That nigga up in here, loc! Hold on; let me make sure it's good," he responded, closing the door so that he could let him know that we were here.

I looked at my brothers while we waited, speaking in French.

He came back to the door. He let us in and led us up the stairs to the office. I could hear Vito outside of the office, laughing and joking around. The security guard opened the door, and we walked in.

"Taz!" Vito yelled as he held his arms out, smiling from ear to ear. "Wassup, nigga!" he yelled.

I smiled and walked over to him as I dapped him up and gave him a manly hug. "Wassup, loc," I greeted.

He had an open bottle of Moët and a cigar sitting in an ashtray on his desk.

I could smell the liquor on him, so I knew that he was already drunk. My brothers scoped out the room as I did.

Two security guards, including the one who walked us in—all of them were strapped.

My brothers stood back as I took a seat in the chair on the other side of Vito.

Brent stood by the security guard that walked us in, and Bavari stood across from the two that were standing on both corners of the room behind Vito.

"So, wassup, lil homie! What do I owe the pleasures?" he asked as he sat back in his chair.

Vito was in his fifties. He ran the streets with my dad once upon a time, according to him. I smiled at him and shrugged. "We just down here kickin' it, so we thought we would slide through, because we know how yo hospitality be when we in the buildin'," I said.

"You already know, cuz!" he said, holding his arms out. He grabbed the bottle of Moët off the desk and placed it in front of me. "That's a two-thousand-dolla' bottle, loc! Enjoy!"

My nose flared, and I snickered. *"Vous entendez cette salope?"* *(Do you hear this bitch?)* I spoke in French looking at my brothers with the same cheesy-ass smile on my face. Bavari's nose flared, and Brent cut his eyes at Vito.

"So did you hear about Huey gettin' merked?" I asked him, getting straight to the point.

It was the two-thousand-dollar bottle of liquor that set me off. He slowly looked at me, and his whole mood switched. "Yeah, I did. Whoever did that shit is a cold piece. Sprayed his whole car up, I heard . . ." I nodded my head. "You know who had somethin' to do with that shit?" he asked.

A smile crept up on my face. "Oh! I had everything to do with that shit," I responded. He cut his eyes at me.

After I said that, everything happened at once.

Brent held his gun up to the security guard's head and squeezed the trigger.

The moment that the nigga's body dropped, Bavari pulled out both of his pistols and started bustin' on the security guards that were in the corners behind Vito.

The shit happened so fast that none of them had time to register what was happening, and they all got dropped at once.

I grabbed the bottle off the desk and smashed the bottom of it on the edge as it shattered, and I held the top of it as I damn-near jumped over that desk and pinned Vito to the chair and held it to his neck.

"Nigga, you gon' offer me a drink with the twothousand-dolla' bottle that I bought?" I growled as he stretched his neck away from the broken glass with these wide eyes.

"I'on know what you talkin' 'bout, Taz. That's all that weed you smokin' . . . You gotta slow down!" he said, *playin'* with me.

405

I punched him in his face and held the broken bottle back up. "It's all that weed I'm smokin', huh?" I said in a malicious tone. "Guda! Come light this nigga's cigar, cuz!" I called out to Bavari in rage.

As Bavari came over to light the cigar, Brent came behind Vito and wrapped his arms around his shoulders to hold him down.

He tried to fight as Brent restrained him but couldn't get loose. I tore his shirt open as the buttons ripped off and fell to the ground, and Bavari passed the lit cigar to me.

He squirmed around, trying to get away from Brent's grasp and I took the cigar, and I pressed the lit cherry on different spots of his chest as he squealed in pain.

"You wanna keep playin' with me, nigga!" I yelled as I pressed the lit cherry to the side of his cheek, and he squealed again, jumping up and down in the chair as Brent held him down.

I punched him again and then took the papers that

Bavari gave me earlier out, holding them up to his face.

As he looked at them with the sweat dripping down his forehead, he dropped his head and shook it. "Fuck you, cuz!" he cried.

"Oh, now you wanna talk, huh?" I growled. "So, you decide to partner with this nigga Huey and use the money that your bitch-ass niggas stole from me to invest in a whole other club? All these ma'fuckin receipts? The brand-new bar you built downstairs . . . What did you tell me that shit came from?" I asked, bending down, trying to make him look me in my eyes.

"Nigga, fuck you! You think you doin' shit on these streets, don't you? Got yo lil brothers runnin' around slangin' and killin' anybody in sight! That shit catches back up with you, Taz . . . This game neva last forever, cuz! If you gon' kill me then kill me! Just know that karma is a bitch! And yo time is comin', ma' nigga! You can't have that much blood on yo hands, and don't think the *reap 'uh* ain't gon' make you pay for that shit!" He laughed as tears fell down his eyes.

"Oh, so you want to turn this shit on me for yo thievin' ass crossin' *me*?" I growled again.

He shook his head. "Yo daddy always said that you were gon' be somethin else . . . powerful. His exact words were that you were gon' be d*angerous in a good way* . . . You were gon' bring people to their knees because you were so strongminded." He laughed. "Well . . . he was right . . . If only he was here to see what you've become, not in the good way like he thought though," he said. "Go ahead. Kill me . . . Do it!"

He was begging me to at this point. He knew that I was going to kill him either way, and he just wanted me to get it over with instead of torturing him.

"If only yo mama was here to deep throat my dick one mo'—" Before he could even finish taunting me so that I would kill him, I jammed the broken bottle in my hand into his neck as I twisted it both ways, digging it deeper into him with this malice look on my face as the blood splattered from his neck.

I watched him choke and die slowly as I did it.

My brothers didn't even flinch. They just watched as life was slowly creeping out of him. I stepped back, leaving the broken bottle in his neck.

"Deep throat on that, bitch," Bavari said.

"Go get the footage," I told Brent. He nodded his head and left the room.

While Brent was checking the cameras, Bavari and I stripped this nigga's whole office, pulling out the drawers, looking for stashes, anything.

He had a safe that we needed a code for built into his wall. If we had enough time, we would have broken the code, but it was time to go.

Brent finally came back, and as we started walking out with the shit that we took, he lit a match and threw it where I broke the Moët bottle. Vito's office instantly started catching on fire. We walked back down the stairs to the alley as the fire

spread, and we hopped in the car, smashing off.

Chapter 16 Anxiety

Janeeva

Halloween was in two days! Maimi put me on "Maimi duty," so I was walking from house to house with her yelling, "Trick or treat!" and collecting candy. I was excited about it though! Lia said that she would come with me, too.

The whole shit with Lovely continued on, even though Scrap and I were not talking anymore.

Well, it wasn't even about me and Lovely; it was about Lovely and Lia. I guess Lovely woke up the next morning after the party with a hangover and a black eye, so she wasn't letting that go. They get into it every day now.

Of course, Lovely was back to her calm and classy self but that never stopped her from making her sneaky-ass threats to Lia.

Lia was the wrong person to test though. Her mother was a straight-up gangster, and based on the way Lia was raised and taught, she wasn't letting that shit go until she got another fade with Lovely.

You couldn't even see Lovely's black eye. She did an excellent job with her makeup; she covered it with concealer and foundation very well.

Every time that they would get into it, Scrap would shake his head and tell Lovely to shut the fuck up. I think that he knew that it would be a lost cause with Lia because Lia wouldn't care if she got her ass beat or not; she would still fight him too.

Lia and I sat at the lunch table next to Scrap and his group laughing and talking.

We separated from them after the night of the party just for my sake. Freckles and Dimples would go back and forth to us and then them, but we were only the next table over.

As we talked, I noticed a boy whose skin tone was a warm ivory walking into Scrap's group, and even though I could only see the side of his face, I couldn't help but think that I knew him.

I knew that his face was new around here, but I couldn't help but stare. He was cute as hell! Well, from the side he was, and his fresh lineup with his deep silky waves flowing through his head made him even sexier. When he turned all the way around and I could finally examine his face, my mouth dropped—*Xavion!*

Xavion is Xavier's brother. I haven't seen him in two years though. He moved for a while with his dad. I was wondering why I didn't hear the news that he was home. Well, we never really got along anyway, but still, I figured Trevor would have said something to me.

The reason that we never got along is because he would always pick on me. He was a true shit talker, and he annoyed the fuck out of me because he would talk so much shit. He never looked as good as he was looking now though.

Scrap

I sat at my table with the team as we talked and enjoyed lunch. Xavion walked into our group and greeted everybody. I met the nigga the other night when Xavier and Quarterback came by the house. He just got back from Florida. It was surprising that we had a lot in common and that nigga loved talking shit!

He had me at *hello*! No homo! But he was cool, so I decided to introduce him to the rest of the team.

He dapped me up, and we all chilled as we talked shit to each other and laughed. He slapped my shoulder as he looked across from me and out of the group. "Yo! Who dat bitch right there?" he asked, smiling.

I tried to follow his gaze, and when I realized where he was looking, I looked back at him. "Which one?" I asked.

"The one with the long hair," he responded.

"Who? Jay?"

"That's her name? I need Lil Baby to turn all the way around so that I can see what she looks like because she already got me from the back." I smiled and looked at Twinkie and SixPacc. They laughed.

She's off limits, cuz, I thought to myself. "Yeah, she's a lil cutie," I said, playing it off.

"I need to go over there and introduce myself," he said, smiling.

SixPacc and Twinkie were shocked that I didn't say anything. I didn't react to them staring at me like I was crazy.

We weren't *anything* to each other so there was nothing that I could say.

I don't know . . . The feeling was weird as fuck. I was missing her, but I knew that I had to stay away from her, and that was why I felt like it wasn't relevant for me to tell the nigga that we used to talk.

415

I also didn't need any more drama from Lovely and Lia, so I just kept the shit to myself since Lovely was right under me.

I stared at Janeeva for a moment, thinking, and once she turned all the way around, I heard Xavion gasp. "What?" I asked.

"I know her!" he said, in shock. "No fuckin' way!" he yelled and then laughed! "Yo! I'll be right back!" he said walking out of the group.

I, Twinkie and SixPacc looked at each other, and then I looked back at Xavion.

I figured that he would know her since he was Xavier's brother, but I honestly didn't want him talking to her. I didn't have time to be breaking niggas' jaws over a female that wasn't even mine.

Janeeva

Xavion finally recognized me.

He walked over to me smiling from ear to ear. I couldn't help but smile back and roll my eyes.

Even though we didn't get along that much in the past, we still had a love-hate relationship, so it didn't hurt me to get up and give him a hug.

As he embraced his arms around me and bear-hugged me, he picked me up and swung me around. I chuckled.

"Ma'fuckin' La'shae Boldin!" he yelled.

He never called me by my first name. He always got a kick out of calling me by my middle name.

"Wassup, Xave?" I greeted.

He put me down and appraised me from head to toe. "How the fuck have you been?" he asked, still smiling hard as hell.

"How does it look like I've been?" I asked, throwing my arms out.

This was the boy who used to always call me a

"tomboy" and tell me that I was an ugly little duck! So yes, I was getting a thrill out of seeing his facial expressions as he admired my whole look.

"Shit, good than a ma'fucka'!" he said, licking his lips. I smiled. "When did all this happen?" he asked.

I shrugged. "It was a last-minute thing." I looked down at Lia as she sat there talking to Freckles, and she looked up at us. "Do you remember my best friend, Lia?" I asked.

He looked down at her. "It was hard to forget her." She smiled.

Xavion had a big-ass crush on Lia two years ago, but Lia wasn't fucking with him. She thought he was funny with all the shit that he talked, but she wasn't into yellow boys like that. She had a thing with darker men. She would go with milk chocolate as well, but she preferred dark chocolate. She got up and hugged him, and he sat down to catch up with us.

I felt good because he switched sides for a day. Fuck Scrap's group! Xavion was on our team today.

After school, Xavion walked home with Trevor, Xavier, me and Talawny. He walked and talked with me the whole way home.

We reminisced on how much of an asshole he was back then, and we played around as I would get pissed off thinking about all the times that he called me an ugly duck!

Every second we ended up fighting in the streets as we walked, and Trevor and Xavier laughed at us. Xavion knew as well that I wasn't a punk, and I wasn't afraid to fight.

However, he didn't try to beat my ass like Xavier and Trevor did. He was very touchy-feely. I think that he was feeling me on a whole different level.

He picked me up over his shoulder and started running down the street with me. I laughed so hard that I couldn't breathe.

I was scared as hell too because I thought that he was going to drop my ass. I did a good job hiding the fact that his strength was turning me on.

When he stopped and placed me on my feet, I stumbled over from my knees being so weak from the fright. They all laughed even harder.

Once we got to the house, they all went to the living room and chilled. I decided to go up to my room and finish some of my homework.

Trevor

"Bruh! What the fuck happened while I was gone?" Xavion asked.

"What chu mean?" I responded, confused.

"Why the fuck is yo lil sister looking good enough to eat right now, cuz? Like, I would be all up in that shit like aaaauh!" he said, with his mouth wide open, twisting his tongue around.

What the fuck? I chugged the pillow on the couch at him! Xavier laughed, and Talawny's jaw just hung open, listening to Xavion dumb ass. *This nigga hasn't changed at all.*

"I'on know what the fuck she's going through right now," I responded.

"Man, cuz, I'm telling you . . ." he said, sitting back in the armchair. "La'shae can get it!"

Talawny almost choked on her soda after he said it, and Xavier was on the ground laughing! I couldn't help but laugh too because he had always been like this, talking shit and provoking people. He knew how I felt about my sister.

"Awe . . . My ugly duck all grown up!" he finished.

"Don't get fucked up, nigga!" I said, laughing.

"Aight. If I ask permission to take La'shae out on a date, would you let me?" he asked.

"Shit, at least he asked. Scrap didn't give a fuck about none of that," Xavier said, shaking his head.

"Wait!" he said, stopping all of us. "Scrap fucked with La'shae?" Xavion asked.

I sighed and shrugged. "They talked for a lil bit," I responded.

Xavion started laughing. "Damn, loc, I low-key feel bad now. When I didn't recognize her, I was asking that nigga who the fuck she was, and once me and her start choppin' it up, I spent the rest of lunch with her and Lia. I was wondering why that nigga kept looking over at us," he said, laughing.

That shit honestly made me feel good. I didn't want Scrap fucking with her, and I was really done after that night at the party with his bitch. So, he deserved to see what that shit felt like for her.

He had been acting different though.

I didn't know what was going on with him, and for some reason the shit had been hard on my mind trying to figure it out. He just seemed a little different.

I knew Lovely was his favorite bitch. It wasn't hard to see. She was his only bitch now that Cherokee was gone, and he just didn't want to deal with Mia.

He was starting to seem distant from Lovely now, too. In my eyes, it looked like he was getting tired of her or just didn't want to deal with her at all. I didn't know if anyone else noticed it, but I did.

"Yeah, well, it is what it is, and no, you can't talk to my sister," I said.

"Man, fuck you! I'll go up there and ask her myself! I don't need permission from yo ass!" he said.

"Get ready to catch my fade then, loc!" I said.

"You already know it's nothin'!" he said, standing up.

I stood up too, and we started slap-boxing each other in the living room.

Xavion was like a little brother to me, so it wasn't that I didn't want him talking to Janeeva, but it just didn't seem right. He was family.

Janeeva

The next day at school, Xavion walked with me to my first period class.

At this point, I knew that he was feeling me. And with him, it was never hard to tell because he never hid shit. His ass was an open book.

"I'ma start calling you Chunky Booty," he said as he stared at my ass.

"You are such a pervert," I retorted, punching him in his arm.

He laughed. "Well, shit! I'm sure nobody knew that you had an ass under them big-ass clothes you used to wear!" I shrugged. "So, wassup with the change? What made you want to do it?" he asked as we stood in front of my first period class.

I didn't feel like sharing that information with him yet, so I just shrugged. "I just woke up one morning and decided that I wanted to try something new," I said, exaggerating a little bit.

He shook his head, knowing that I was full of shit. He then changed the subject. "So, what are you doing for Halloween tomorrow?" he asked.

"I'm on Maimi duty."

"Damn, well, make sure you get her home as soon as you can because you gon' be on Xave duty too."

"What?"

"You're spending the rest of Halloween with me, La'shae," he said, smiling.

"Are you telling me I am, or are you asking me?" I responded, smiling back.

"I'm telling you."

"We'll see how that works out, Xave." I rolled my eyes.

"Yeah, we'll see . . ." he said, stepping closer to me.

I stared into his eyes and felt little butterflies in my stomach.

As I blushed and looked away, Scrap was walking up to us. I stared at him as he approached us, and Xavion looked as well.

"Wassup, cuz," Xavion greeted as he dapped Scrap up.

"Wassup," he greeted back and then locked eyes with me.

He stared at me for a moment and walked past us into the classroom. I didn't realize that Xave was watching me until he spoke.

"I heard you and Scrap used to talk," he said.

I sighed. "Yeah, but it didn't last long."

He observed me for a moment with a smirk on his face and then sighed and changed the subject. "Well, be ready to spend the rest of yo night with me tomorrow, Chunky Booty!" he said as he walked away.

"Don't call me that, Xave!" I yelled out to him.

"Aight, Chunky Booty!" I smiled and shook my head.

Scrap

Halloween!

The only thing that meant was that the homies were about to be out slidin' on niggas! It was about to be licks hitting left to right!

I knew that I would have a lot of clienteles too. This was not about to be a slow night.

The team was about to be *lit*, too! This night was the easiest night to catch a nigga slippin', and the best part about it was that you got to dress up!

We sat over at Xavier's house drinking and smoking, getting ready for the night. We were all going our separate ways but meeting back up later.

"Aye, bruh! Where Chunky Booty at?" Xavion asked Quarterback as he hit the bottle. Quarterback pointed at him. "Nigga, keep talking about my sister like that, and I'm gon' do more than slap yo ass up, cuz!"

I laughed. "You call her Chunky Booty?" I asked, smiling.

He smacked his lips. "Nigga, you've seen that ass!"

I laughed harder. "You stupid, loc," I said, shaking my head.

"Naw, but for real, loc! Did she already take Maimi trick or treatin'?" he asked.

"She still out with her," he responded. "I just texted her. And, nigga, why the fuck do you want to know where Janeeva at?" Quarterback asked.

"Because she on 'Xave duty' after 'Maimi duty', but you don't need to worry about that! I'ma take good care of yo sister tonight," he said, smiling.

I cut my eyes at him. The nickname was funny. Even taunting Quarterback made me like him more. Him talking about this whole "Xave duty" shit and making sneaky-ass comments about it, I was ready to break his fuckin' jaw!

Quarterback sighed. "Last time I got into her business, I got the silent treatment for a fucking week, so I'ma shut the fuck up, but you better be cool, nigga, because I'll beat yo ass!"

he told him. I scowled at Quarterback for a moment, looked at SixPacc and Twinkie and shook my head.

Yeah, the shit was bothering me, because I wasn't good enough for Janeeva, but this nigga was? It was pissing me off how he wasn't getting the same treatment, but I didn't say shit.

"So, what're we doing about this car situation?" Tutu asked.

"We're waiting for Guda and Yaya to get back and then we headin' out," Xavier said.

I had Brent's car, and I already knew who was riding with me, but it was so many niggas and bitches at Xavier's house right now that it was hard trying to figure out how everybody was going to fit.

SixPacc's brother Leonard was with us, too. Lovely was out on the clock already, but she was meeting back up with me at the function so I could collect.

"Well, shit, let me take yo car so I can pick up Janeeva and Lia," Xavion said to Xavier.

Xavier thought about that shit for a moment and told him to wait until he figured out the car situation.

The party was on the east side. Natalie Davarez was throwing it. She threw the biggest Halloween parties every year, and every year she tried to have Shottas host it. She wasn't a part of the team, but she was rockin' with us a lot.

Natalie was a senior. She had a thing for Twinkie, and Twinkie fucked with her for a little bit. He got tired of her after a while and moved on to the next.

Brent and Bavari finally showed up to the house with Lady Yaya, Lil Hitta and their little sister, and then bad news came.

Brent told us that he wasn't rockin' with the lil niggas tonight. He was going to the club.

Bavari was rockin' with us, but he still had to go pick up some of his niggas too. I knew how Bavari was though. He didn't really like hanging out with the high school kids like that, so I knew that he was going to end up ditching us, too.

The only reason that he was going was because he knew how Natalie's parties were, and there were always bitches over the age of eighteen in that ma'fucka. I knew his whole plan. He was going to pull a little thot and then dip.

With all this said, this shit left me without a car! I couldn't complain though because it wasn't my shit! I could buy a car if I wanted to, but I kept choosing not to because it didn't make any sense when I was constantly in Lovely's and my brother's shit, and it looked too obvious with four cars sitting in front of our house.

Expensive-ass cars, too!

Brandon had a black Mercedes Maybach SUV and his motorcycle; Brent had a black Dodge Charger, and Bavari had a custom royal blue Mercedes-Benz with his motorcycle.

Brent had his motorcycle as well, but Lady Yaya had it most of the time, not to mention all the ATV's and electric scooters we had in the garage.

We were already hot! So now we had to figure out what the fuck we were going to do about the cars.

After we got the shit situated, I ended up in the car with Quarterback and Xavion. *How?*

SixPacc and I argued for about thirty minutes about who the fuck was riding with Bavari. I didn't want to ride with Xavier because I honestly didn't feel like being around Xavion at the time, so I said fuck it and hopped in the car with Quarterback. The nigga was laughing at me because he didn't know why I hopped in his car, and I told him to shut the fuck up.

And then out of nowhere, Xavion's ass hopped in the back seat. *What the fuck?*?I then found out that the only reason Xavion was hopping in the car with Quarterback was because he was the one picking up Janeeva and Lia. I guess it was a last-minute decision. So, I had to endure a fifteen-minute ride dealing with Xavion all up in Janeeva's face and shit.

However, I did get a thrill with knowing that SixPacc and Twinkie were going to be pissed off because the only reason I agreed to let them ride with Bavari was because I knew how my brother were, and they were making at least three unnecessary stops. *That's always what Bavari does, all that weed starting to get to his dumb ass.*

When we pulled up to the house, Quarterback called Janeeva and let her know we were outside. When the front door opened, and they walked out, my mouth slightly dropped, and my dick instantly started jumping.

"What the fuck!" Quarterback yelled.

She walked toward us as I saw her trying not to trip in the shiny powder-pink heels she had on.

She had on a tight pink and white Velcro miniskirt, a pink leather vest with a white crop top under it and a loose black tie falling from her neck and over her exposed stomach. She had on some geek type glasses that had a bow on the right

433

corner of them, and her hair was pressed out, falling over her shoulders.

Now how the fuck did she get past her mama with this shit on?

Lia was looking sexy as hell, too. She decided to play cop.

She had on some black boy shorts and a shiny-ass silver belt around her waist with the black police shirt that exposed her stomach as well and was tied in the front with the hat. She also had the fucking fake-ass billy club (baton), which I didn't believe was safe in her hands. I knew SixPacc was going to be melting when he saw her, but I was too focused on Janeeva to really pay attention to Lia.

My window was already down, and when she realized that it was me in the front seat, she stopped in her tracks.

I couldn't help but keep appraising her costume. It was all types of shit going through my head, and one of them had to do with her legs over my shoulders in my bed. Xavion opened the door and hopped out of the car.

"Goddamn!" he said as he walked over to her. She smiled, and he hugged her. "Yo, make sure you tell everybody you on 'Xave duty' tonight so that they know that you mine," he said licking his lips.

She shook her head and laughed. "You're so crazy, Xave," she said.

She looked back at me. I stared in her eyes for a moment trying to read them and then was distracted.

"Wassup, Scrap?" Lia said as she hopped in the back and stuck her head in the front, hitting my shoulder.

"What's good, Ms. Attitude?" I responded, turning my head toward her and smiling.

Janeeva and Xavion got in the car, and we took off.

When we pulled up to the house, there were a lot of people standing outside and walking inside. It was a full house.

You could hear the music down the street, and niggas were already showing off and doing side shows in the neighborhood.

I saw a couple of "Opps," and I knew it was going to be a couple of fights that broke out tonight. I had my gun on me, too. I didn't go anywhere without it aside from school because of the metal detectors, so they would want to be cool tonight.

As we parked and got out, I heard people yelling my name, left to right.

All the girls were dressed up in their little sexy-ass costumes! We walked up to the house and walked in with a couple of more people that were walking up with us.

When I walked all the way in the house, I threw up my set and yelled out, "Shottas!" which caused a chain reaction, and I found the rest of the team.

I heard at least three separate groups around the house yell the set out, too. The name was a loud-ass echo through the whole house. It was more of the hood here than I thought, and the first ones who found me were Twinkie and SixPacc. Of course, they knew it was me.

Xavion walked in with his arms around Janeeva's shoulder, and the minute he stepped in, he pulled her to the side and started talking that *sweet shit*.

I tried not to let it bother me though. I wasn't about to let her fuck up my night. So, I kept myself occupied.

I started drinking some more and kept dancing on every bitch in sight and just kickin' it with my niggas.

Lia was with us most of the time, too, because Xavion wasn't playing about that bullshit ass "Xave duty." He made sure that he had all of Janeeva's attention. I was starting to get annoyed with the nigga.

Natalie got on the mic as she gave a shoutout to Shottas! We all cheered and threw the set up as we kept dancing.

Of course, we had a couple of hatin'-ass niggas in here, glaring and shit and their bitch admiring on the low. The fact that they knew who I was, they weren't gon' do shit. They knew that I wouldn't come here and not be strapped, and we were too deep. *The whole hood jumpin' in, cuz!*

Xavion and Janeeva finally came into our group and started dancing. I tried my hardest not to even give her ass any type of attention, but she was purposely dancing around me so that I would look. I turned away from her and started dancing with Lia. Then my song came on, "Lil Baby" by Mustard and Ty Dolla Sign.

SixPacc took Lia off my hands as this thick lil chocolate thang came in front of me. She was dressed up as Wonder Woman.

She bent over and started grinding her ass on me. Lil Baby Ass was so fat and plump that I just watched her with my hands on my hips, smiling.

"Girl, I'll beat it up, beat it up right, I will . . . And I'll

go deeper than yo ex man did . . . She be like slow down zaddy,

Yeah, that thang tooooo biiiig . . . Oooh! She a pretty young

thang, and she ain't got no kids! Lil Babe! Lil Mama! Lil Babe!

Lil Mama!"

She bent down touching her toes as she made her

cheeks clap together.

"Daaa'yuuum!" Twinkie yelled as our whole group

watched her twerking on me.

I finally placed my hand on her hips after I smacked

her ass, ran my hand up the small of her back and then started

working her.

All my homies started cheering as they watched.

I could feel Janeeva scowling at the side of my face as I

kept dancing with the girl. Once Lil Ms. Wonder Woman got

tired, she turned around and asked for my number. I told her to

give me hers.

I don't give bitches my number anymore. If I decide

that I'm going to call them and not delete their number later, then they'll have it, but I've had to change my number too many times from weird-ass females blowing my phone up and leaving twenty text messages and shit, even the ones that barely knew me. And blocking their number didn't do shit but made them call me blocked!

Janeeva was the first that I actually gave my number to in a cool minute. It was something about her though. It was everything about her . . .

After the girl gave me her number, she lingered around our group, trying to make me pay her some more attention, and I just turned away from her and started dancing with Lil Hitta as her little sister Nina (Tweety) started dancing in front of her. Twinkie came in front of Tweety and sandwiched her.

After a while, we went to the backyard, and I lit up a blunt. I took a seat at one of the tables Natalie had set up and started talking to the homies while we smoked.

I got a text from Lovely, and she was here. I told her to come to the back, and when she did, she sat on my lap and whispered in my ear, "Four Gs," and slipped me the stack of money wrapped up in a rubber band.

I smiled. "You had a good night, huh?" I said as I wrapped my arms around her waist. I was proud of my bitch!

The lil bitch who gave me her number followed me outside, and she twisted her lip up when she saw Lovely sitting on my lap.

I looked at her nonchalantly and hit my blunt as I looked away and started talking to the homies again, putting the stack in my pocket.

As I felt another pair of eyes on me, I could see Janeeva in my peripheral, staring. I looked at her and she just gave me this frustrated look, and then she looked away.

I saw the pain all in her eyes, and it made me feel some type of way. I didn't like the feeling. Lovely looked over at her, because I guess she felt her staring, too, and she gave her a sneaky-ass grin as she checked out her costume.

"Playing the sexy geek role tonight, huh? That was pointless; why play something that you already know so well," she said.

"Damn . . ." Cliff said.

Janeeva didn't say anything; she just glared at her. "Man, be cool, cuz," I said. I wasn't up for the bullshit.

"And we see that you playin' the thotty-thot-thot role tonight!" Lia stepped up with her hands on her hips. "Oops!" she said, throwing her hand over her mouth. "That's an everyday role for you, huh? Lil bitch!" Everybody started laughing, and I just sat back and massaged my temples. *Here we go!*

"You know, it's funny how you're always protecting your lil pet," Lovely said.

I sat up and told her to shut the fuck up. "Yo, you goin' too far," I said in her ear.

"Bitch, what?" Lia snapped.

"Your pet, you take them under your wings. They usually become your best friend, train them and teach them to be more like you," she chuckled. "You two fit perfectly for that description," she said as there was an awkward silence around us.

Yeah, these niggas didn't know how personal the shit was about to be. I knew Lovely's mouth, so I knew off top what the funk was about to be like.

However, I didn't expect the next thing that happened. Before Lia could even hop on Lovely's head, Janeeva quickly stepped out of her heels, grabbed Lia, pulled her back and ran up on Lovely, giving it to her ass until she fell off my lap.

I saw it coming, but I never knew Janeeva was so quick. I tried to get up when I saw her coming, but Lovely's ass leaned back and pushed me back down in the seat.

Once Lovely was on the ground, she tried to fight back as she reached up and tried to grab Janeeva by her hair, but Janeeva's blows were too quick.

Everybody was so shocked that it took a while for anybody to react, because no one ever expected this from her. She was going harder than Lia went when she beat Lovely's ass at my house.

Finally, Quarterback came into the group, and when he saw his little sister giving it to her, he instantly reacted and pulled her off, which made everyone snap out of the whole scene.

"Get the fuck off of me!" she yelled, with tears streaming down her eyes. She fought to get from Trevor's grip, but he wouldn't let her go.

I looked at Lovely for a moment, and her face was red. She was also spitting blood out of her mouth.

When she looked at the blood in her hand, she glared at Janeeva, stood to her feet and tried to get her while she was restrained.

I grabbed her and swung her back. "Now that's what we don't do. That's a bitch move, cuz," I said as I gripped her arm and shoved her into SixPacc and Twinkie.

They grabbed her as she tried to rush her again. I was already irritated with her and wanted to slap the shit out of her for causing this shit to happen. But I wasn't worried about her right now. I was more worried about Janeeva.

I turned and looked at them, but it looked like something else was going on . . . something was going on with Janeeva.

"I can't breathe . . ." I heard Janeeva say under her breath as she gripped on to Quarterback's shirt, breathing heavily.

She was looking down with these wide eyes as tears were falling from them and I could tell that she was trying not to make a scene, but her breathing started to get heavier.

"Try to breathe in slowly, Jay . . ." Quarterback said to her in a muffled voice, trying not to make a scene as well as she struggled to catch her breath.

"My chest . . . It hurts. I can't breathe; I can't breathe!"

she panicked. She pressed her hands to her chest and bent over

as I watched the tears falling from her eyes and hitting the

ground.

One of the girls outside pulled a chair up for her so that

she could sit down, and Quarterback shook his head.

"She needs to stand up," he told her.

Lia bent down in front of Janeeva and made her look at

her. "Look at me, Jay!" she told her. "Tell me the three things

you hear?" she instructed.

She didn't answer right away. She just kept breathing

heavily, and then she closed her eyes, trying to take slow

breaths like Quarterback had instructed her to do.

"The music . . . someone laughing . . ." she said as she

listened to the people inside still dancing and laughing unaware

of what was going on outside. "Someone talking . . ." she cried

harder with her hands to her chest.

"Stand up straight!" Quarterback said, trying not to panic as well while he watched his sister not being able to calm herself down.

He tried to pull her up so that she could take slow deep breaths, and then he told her to move three parts of her body. She moved her fingers, and that was it. She stopped as she laid her head on his chest. He shook his head and made her stand straight up again.

"The three things you see?" Xavier asked, as he stood close to them with these concerned eyes.

Her breathing started to slow down once Xavier asked that last question. I watched her as I saw in her eyes that she was becoming aware of her surroundings.

She slowly looked up and around at everyone in the backyard. Her eyes grew wide as she realized everyone was watching her, and she quickly buried her face in Quarterback's chest.

It calmed whatever was going on with her down though. Quarterback sighed deeply as she cried from embarrassment.

"Let's get her out of here, cuz," Xavion said as he sighed deeply as well, shaking his head.

I knew that Xavier and Xavion had been around her before having one of these episodes just from the way that they reacted. They knew what to do, and they weren't shocked like everyone else was.

Xavion walked over to grab her shoes where she had taken them off. While he picked her shoes up from the ground, he looked at me.

Natalie asked if she needed to lay in her bed for a while, and Quarterback nodded his head.

"Can we get some water too?" he asked, still holding on to Janeeva.

She led them to her room.

I looked at Cliff, and he didn't look shocked either. He knew what was happening as well. As he stared back at me, I saw the disappointment in his eyes. I was too dumbfounded to really give a fuck though.

I could see on the rest of the homies' faces that they were still trying to figure out what just happened as well.

Xavion stepped up to me as I turned around, not sure about how the fuck I was supposed to react to this shit.

"Yo, Scrap, let me holla at you," he said to me.

"Not right now, cuz," I said.

I was not in the mood to hear anybody tell me about my bitch.

"Scrap!" Lovely yelled looking at me like I betrayed her.

This shit was driving me crazy. I ignored her, and she yelled my name again. Before she could say another word, I snapped. "Lovely, shut the fuck up!" I said as she stepped back from my aggression.

I stepped back as well as I saw what she was doing to me. This bitch was making me treat her how I treated Mia.

Xavion stepped back, too. I rubbed my hand down my face in frustration.

"This is the shit that I was talking about. You still choosin' that bitch over me!" she yelled.

"Bitch . . ." I said, in irritation.

I dug in my pocket and pulled out the stack of money she gave me in the rubber band and threw it at her. "There! I'm done with you, cuz!" I said.

I didn't have to look at anyone to feel the shock that was displayed on each one of their faces. I even felt the shock from Xavion.

"What the fuck you mean you're *done*?" she snapped.

"Bitch, I'm through with you! You ain't my bitch! You ain't shit to me, cuz! I'm done! Keep yo money! I make moe' in a day anyway!"

"So, it's true . . . You still want that bitch," she said in a lower voice as tears started dropping from her eyes.

I sighed in frustration. "It doesn't matter if I do or if I don't. Just know that she's worth more than yo ass," I said, straight-out.

I heard a couple of people gasp as I gave her these harsh words. She glared at me with tears streaming from her eyes and damn-near ran to her fucking car.

The whole team and a couple of people I didn't know just stared at me.

Xavion looked at me with his hands in his pockets, but I couldn't read his expressions. I couldn't tell if he was ready to square the fuck up or what. The way that I was feeling right now though, he can run that shit.

I was relieved that Bavari hadn't left yet. He watched the whole scene but didn't interfere because he wanted to see how I would do under pressure. I knew that was what he was doing. My brothers were always testing me, and they never stepped in the heat of the moment until it got too serious.

Before I left, I had to find Lia.

I walked to the back of Natalie's house, trying to figure out which room was hers, and when I saw her walking out of a room, I knew that I had found what I was looking for.

She looked at me and hesitated. "Hey, Scrap," she said, blocking me from the door.

I smacked my lips. "Yo just tell Lia to come out," I said looking at her. She sighed and called into the room for Lia.

Lia came out and glared at me. "What the fuck do you want?" she spat.

I shook my head. "I ain't here to do this back-and-forth shit with you."

"Shouldn't you be wiping the blood from yo bitch's face right now?"

I shook my head. "She ain't my bitch no moe."

She flinched and then snickered. "You dropped her that fast?" she spat.

"That's not what the fuck I came to talk about."

"Then what do you want?" she asked in a malice tone.

"Just tell Janeeva that I'm sorry for all of this shit."

She looked at me, waiting for me to finish. "Is that it?" she asked with an attitude.

I smacked my lips. "Man, can you please just do that!" I snapped back, getting irritated.

She didn't flinch. She stared at me for another moment and rolled her eyes. "Aight, I'll tell her," she said.

As she was about to walk back into the room, I hesitated and then stopped her. "Lia . . ." She looked at me. "What the fuck happened?" I asked with these concerned eyes and a softer tone.

She sighed. "She had an anxiety attack . . . She gets them every now and then," she said, dropping her eyes.

"What was the whole three-thing y'all were saying to her about?" I asked.

She pressed her lips together, cutting her eyes at me.

"It's called the *3-3-3 rule*. It's a mental trick to pull her mind back to the present. When she feels an anxiety attack coming along, we ask her the three things that she sees and hears. Then we tell her to move three parts of her body. It helps her calm down," she said. "Look I gotta go." She went back into the room as I stood there, trying to gather my thoughts and process all this shit. 🔲

Chapter 17 Be Mine

Scrap

The rest of the team ended up meeting us back at my house. They were all still trippin' off Janeeva and, to no surprise, me!

"Bom! Are you not aware of what the fuck you just did?" Leonard asked, standing in front of me, bent down as I chilled back on the couch trying to get my thoughts together.

"What the fuck are you talkin' about?"

"Nigga, you just dropped the only bitch that you had left for another female that's not bringing in no dough, that you not about to throw on the blade and I'm pretty sure ain't givin' up no pussy!" he said, throwing his hands up.

"Bruh, I'm not even gon' lie . . . I'm more shocked than he is," Twinkie said, shaking his head.

"You're feeling Janeeva on a whole different level, loc.

Yo actions show everything!" SixPacc said.

Bavari and Brandon sat there listening to them.

Leonard couldn't wait to get to the house and tell Brandon what went down tonight, and Brandon was as shocked as them when he heard that I dropped Lovely and threw the money she was slaving for all day back at her ass. He was more shocked that I didn't keep the money.

Four racks ain't shit to me though. Better believe that, tomorrow, I was going to be making twice that shit.

"I really gotta meet this girl . . . like a one on one and not in the middle of pulling her away from a fight," Brandon said laughing.

A moment passed, and then Xavier, Xavion and Quarterback were at the door.

They walked in, and Quarterback looked at me. I honestly didn't have shit to say to him, but I was sure that he had a lot to say to me; before he could start though, I had to ask.

"Is she good?"

He stared at me for a moment with this blank expression and then answered. "Yeah . . . just embarrassed."

"For what?" Cliff asked.

"She hasn't had an attack in a while, especially in front of people."

"That ain't nothing to be embarrassed about though," Cliff said. Quarterback shrugged.

Xavion took a seat on the table and looked at me.

I looked back at him and smacked my lips. "Nigga, you obviously been havin' somethin' you've been wantin' to get off yo chest all night, so wassup?" I snapped.

"He told me what happened between you and Lovely," Quarterback spoke. "You did that for my sister?" he asked.

I didn't respond, and then Xavion spoke.

"Look, cuh, I'on know if I'm bustin' her out or not, but whateva' the fuck y'all had . . . is deeper than both of y'all think. I see the way that she looks at you, too," he said. He was quiet for a moment and then he sighed. "I'ma fall back . . . And, nigga, you just gave up a stack of money for her ass! You beat me by a couple of miles!" We all laughed.

I looked at Quarterback, and he stared back at me; he smacked his lips and spoke.

"Look, man, I'm sorry about how I was getting at you before. I didn't mean it in the way that it was comin' out of my mouth. You a smart-ass nigga. You got all the tools to be whateva' you want. Ain't nobody perfect, not even me," he said, shrugging.

Xavier and Xavion got up to head out with Quarterback. They dapped my brothers up and started walking out.

Before they left though, Quarterback looked back at me. "I'on know if she wants to talk to you right now . . . So don't push the issue . . ."

I nodded my head. "Yo, Quarterback!" I yelled out before he left. He stuck his head back in the garage. "Not now, but I'ma need you to holla at me about these attacks that she be havin'," I said.

He stared at me for a moment, dropped his eyes and didn't answer. He just left.

Janeeva

I felt like my fucking world was ending! I was so embarrassed! How could I let that bitch get to me like that? I was happy that I beat the shit out of her ass though.

It wasn't the worst attack, but it had been a while and it was the worst that I had had in a long time. I was so embarrassed that I was still crying about the shit.

Lia sat up in my bed, texting away, while I lay next to her. Domion was texting her ass nonstop. I knew his ringtone.

"You okay, Jay?" she asked. I nodded my head. "Would it make you feel better if I say that you beat the shit out of Lovely and you made me proud?" she asked. I chuckled.

"You also had a lot of people surprised. They didn't know that you could fight, even though I told their ass befoe' to not let the shy shit fool 'em . . . No one ever listens to me," she said, shaking her head.

As bad as I was feeling, she made me silently laugh.

I shrugged, acting like I didn't really care. I wanted to stay mad. I thought about Scrap and started pissing myself off even more.

It was his bitch, and he didn't defend me or anything. He just let her keep going. I shook my head as tears fell down my cheeks, and I wiped them on my pillow.

Lia tapped me as she got a text. I turned around and grabbed her phone. It was Scrap.

He has officially been blocked from my phone, so he texted Lia.

"Yo tell Jay 2 call me when she can" . . .

I stared at the message for about two minutes. He hadn't talked to me in three weeks and I damn sure didn't want to talk to him right now, but it was something inside of me yearning to hear his voice.

"So . . ." Lia said, waiting for me to hand her phone back. "While you're thinking, can I text my boo back?" she asked.

I rolled my eyes and handed her phone back to her. She continued to text away as I lay there and fell asleep.

The next day at school, I was worried. I was worried about people snickering and pointing about the whole shit that took place last night.

I also feared that I would have another anxiety attack because I was so fucking scared!

I looked like a mess, too. I wasn't in the mood to dress up.

I wore black sweatpants and a pink blouse with my hair thrown up in a high messy bun. My hair was still pressed out so the bun didn't look too bad, but you could tell that I wasn't in the mood today.

Lia walked with me to my first period class, and to my surprise, I wasn't getting the treatment that I thought I would. People were coming up to me concerned. They were asking me if I was okay and what the fuck happened.

Lia smiled at me while I stood there hearing Freckles and Dimples talk to me and hug me because they felt bad about what happened last night. They made me feel a whole lot better, and I wasn't stressing as hard as I was before.

I tried to stay away from Scrap for the rest of the week.

He tried to talk to me a couple of times, but he didn't push the issue, and for some reason, Xavion was a little distant as well. He wasn't distant, but he wasn't flirting with me every five seconds.

Another week was gone, and the weekend was here. However, I wasn't up for doing anything. I stayed at home, babysitting Maimi. My parents were out of town again.

Lia didn't want to stay in the house, so she decided to go out with Freckles and Dimples. Trevor was gone as well, so it was just me and my bad-ass sister.

Maimi was getting on my last nerve! She was running around the house like she was the fucking Speed Devil. She was driving me crazy!

Once twelve o'clock finally hit, the little devil went to sleep. I was so relieved. I lay down on the couch with her and watched cartoons as she slept.

For some reason, I couldn't go to sleep, and it was already going on at two thirty in the morning.

My phone started ringing, and when I looked at the caller ID, it was Trevor.

"Yeah," I greeted.

"Aye, what you doin'?" he asked.

"Laying down on the couch with Maimi."

"Is she asleep?"

"Yeah, she wore herself out. This house is a mess."

"Well, go put her in her bed and straighten up the house for me please."

"Why?" I snapped. I already knew the answer. He was having company over.

"Because I'm having a couple of people slide through." I shook my head and sighed. "Aye, don't be huffing and puffing at me, nigga!"

"Whatever!" I said, hanging up.

I really wasn't in the mood to get up at two o'clock in the morning. I could go up to my room, but I was comfortable with where I was at, and the nigga was asking me to clean up! He had me fucked up right now, but I did what he asked me.

When I finally heard the door unlocking, I hurried up, grabbed Maimi and carried her heavy ass upstairs to her room. I was tripping because I heard more than a couple of people coming into the house.

When I walked back downstairs, I was startled because the first eyes that I caught were those green eyes that I knew so well . . . Scrap's.

Trevor turned the music on, and everybody chilled back talking and laughing. It was damn-near three in the fucking morning.

Xavier, Xavion, Talawny, SixPacc, Twinkie, Lia, Dimples, Cliff and Freckles were here as well.

When the rest noticed me, I was instantly embarrassed. I wasn't dressed for this shit! I had on some black boy shorts with a lime green tank top on, and my hair was thrown up in a high messy ponytail! Lia would be the first to laugh.

"Damn, Jay! Ya butt cheeks all out and shit!"

I threw my hands over my butt as I blushed and ran back upstairs. I heard them laughing.

I went upstairs, threw on some sweats and let my hair down. I wasn't doing any more than that. I went back downstairs and looked at everyone.

"What happened to yo ass tonight, sis?" Cliff asked as he danced.

"I just didn't feel like going out. So, where did you guys go?" I asked.

"It was just a lil kickback at Scrap's house," Cliff said, shrugging.

"So, what's this all about?" I asked, looking around at all of them in my living room.

"Shit, you didn't come out to kick it with us, so we thought we would bring the kickback yo way!" he said, grabbing my hand as he moved to the beat. I smiled. I wasn't going to lie—I felt special.

"She should have kept them damn sweats off though. I like the boy shorts better," Scrap said as he came behind me.

I turned around, giving him my attention, and then stepped away from him as I glared.

"So, we still playing this game, huh?" he asked, smiling. I didn't answer. I just shrugged. Cliff looked at both of us, smiled and started walking away. "Y'all niggas got issues," he said.

Trevor came over to me and threw his arm over my shoulder. "You missed all the fun tonight," he said.

I shrugged. "Just wasn't my night."

"Shit, after dealing with Maimi's ass, I'm pretty sure you wished you would have made it yo night!" he said, laughing. I flipped him off.

He looked at Scrap, and Scrap looked back smiling.

"I'ma let y'all talk . . ." I was shocked to hear him say that.

"Now you really can't deny me!" Scrap said.

"Why are you so cool with this now?" I asked, ignoring him and looking at Trevor.

"Don't worry about all that," he said, nudging me in my cheek and walking away.

I looked back at Scrap, and he smiled at me. He motioned his head to the backyard, and I followed him outside.

Once we got outside, he slid his hand in his pocket, and we just stared at each other. It was an awkward silence between the both of us, and then he took a deep breath and spoke.

"You still mad at me?" he asked.

"Should I not be?"

He shrugged with a smirk on his face and stepped closer to me. He gazed into my eyes, and the moment that mine locked with his, I was stuck . . . Those green eyes had entranced me, and I couldn't look away.

He smoothly slid his hand to the nape of my neck, and as I stretched it out and closed my eyes, chills shot through my body. I opened my eyes, coming back down to earth when I heard him chuckle.

"That's my girl," he said in the softest tone.

"What?" I asked.

"You don't look as tense as you were. You look relaxed right now . . . content," he said to me, taking one more step closer so that there was no more space between us. "That's all I needed to do? Touch you to get that difficult ass look off your face?" he asked, smiling.

I pushed him off me. "Fuck you, Brian," I said, trying to walk back into the house.

He grabbed my hand and pulled me back. "Can you stop acting like you don't miss me, too?" he said, pulling me back to him. He caressed his fingers on the small of my back.

I was trying so hard to resist. "Why did you bring me out here?" I asked him.

"I miss you."

"I'm pretty sure your bitch misses you more," I retorted.

"Ooouh low blow, huh?" he responded, smiling.

"Why is this so funny to you?" I asked.

"Because you're speaking up on a bitch that don't have shit to do with me or shit to do with you."

"Oh, so.now she doesn't have shit to do with you?"

He shook his head. "I had to let her go . . ."
"Why?" I asked.

He rolled his eyes. "Here we go with the million questions."

"Well, I feel like I deserve to know," I said in a more serious tone.

He smiled. "Is that right?" I nodded my head. "If I tell you, will you judge me?" he teased, smiling.

I stared at him for a moment, and then I couldn't help but laugh. *Here we go!*

For some reason, it felt good though. I felt like I was back at the beginning of the school year, drooling over him all over again.

"Yes, I will."

His eyes lit up as he smiled. I knew he was shocked. "I appreciate you being honest."

"So?" I asked.

He sighed. "When you had that attack . . . I felt like it was her fault . . ." I saw in his eyes that he was being sincere.

I looked away and shrugged. "That's it? So, you let her go because I had an anxiety attack?" I asked, rolling my eyes.

"What causes them?" he asked, changing the subject. He took me off guard with that question.

"How are you going to put a question on top of a question?" I snapped.

"The same way you do?" he retorted. We stared at each other for another moment.

"Okay, answer my question and I'll answer yours."

He shook his head and chuckled. He knew that he wasn't winning this one. I was tired of him always trying to avoid my questions. "Aight . . ." he said, gathering his thoughts. "Yeah, I let her go because of you. Now, I'm 'bout to

say something that better never leave this backyard or me and

you gon' have problems. But you low-key had me spooked . .

." he admitted. He gave me this concerned look. My heart

fluttered.

"You were scared?" I asked.
He nodded his head. "I wanted to help but didn't know

how," he confessed. I was looking at him in a whole different

way at that point. I couldn't help but smile. "Now yo turn."

It took me a minute to speak, but once I finally got the

guts to, I didn't know what to say first.

"I started to get them when I was in third grade . . . I got

bullied a lot . . . They would make fun of me, throw things at me

. . ."

The same tears that were soon to fall a couple of

minutes ago were now drowning my eyes. "One day, I was

getting picked on a little too hard. The things that the kids

threw were never anything major. It was either food, a pencil . .

. small shit.

"It was a group of boys that just kept fucking with me that day, throwing shit and calling me all types of names . . . I tried to walk away, but they wouldn't let me. They were pulling on my arms, pushing me, and there were so many of them around me that I didn't know what to do.
So, I just started swinging on the first one that I turned to. The boy was so shocked when I punched him in his jaw, and I ended up fighting him while his friends laughed, stood around and watched.

"When he realized that I wasn't backing down and was getting a couple of hits in, I guess it made him angrier?" I questioned myself, looking into Scrap's eyes with this confused look, still not understanding why that day ever happened to me.

"He decided to pick up this big-ass rock, and he chugged it at my head." I looked down as I separated my hair so that he could see the scar on the side of my head from that day.

After I showed him, I kept my head down thinking about it, and it started hitting me harder than I expected. "I was unconscious and in the hospital for two days," I told him, now looking back into his eyes. It was something about the look that I saw in his eyes that scared the fuck out of me. I saw the fire, the anger, and I felt like I knew what he was thinking about.

"So, what happened to the nigga?" he asked in a malice tone.

I shrugged. "My mom wouldn't tell me. I know that the rest were pulled out of that school, and I ended up going to another school as well. She just said that they will never hurt me again . . . But it is one of the reasons why I just kept to myself all these years, why I don't like the attention being on me. It's the reason Trevor is so overprotective of me," I told him. "I remember him coming in my room one night after a nightmare. He lay in my bed with me and said, 'I promise that I'll never let anyone hurt you again.' And he just held me until I cried myself back to sleep, and now every time that I feel overwhelmed or paranoid, just worked up altogether, an attack comes along . . . I feel like I can't breathe, like I'm suffocating, and I get this pain in my chest . . ."

Scrap shook his head. "I'm sorry . . ." he said, placing his hand on my hips.

I pulled off a smile and shook my head. "There's nothing to be sorry about."

"That should have never happened to you, Janeeva." We stared at each other for a moment. He then sighed and decided to change the subject. "So, I have a question?"

"Shoot."

"If I asked you to be my girl, would you say yes?" he asked.

I flinched, thrown off by his question. I didn't see that one coming. I stared at him for a moment as my heart fluttered and I felt butterflies in my stomach. I dropped my eyes as I thought about what it took to get here, and I took a deep breath.

Even though I felt fireworks exploding inside of me, I couldn't go through this again. So, I remained quiet as I looked away. He made me look at him as he slid both of his hands back to the nape of my neck and locked eyes with me.

"You know that I would never hurt you, right?" he asked.

I dropped my eyes as I smiled and nodded my head. "I know . . ." I responded.

"So, what's wrong?"

I couldn't speak, but like always, chills were shooting through my body as I stared into his green eyes. "Promise me that I won't have to worry about another girl," I said.

He looked at me for a quick second and rolled his eyes. "I promise that you won't have to worry about another bitch. Now tell me that you'll be Lady Scrap," he said, smiling.

I smiled as I reached up, wrapped my arms around his neck and pulled him down to kiss me. I gave him the most feverish kiss as he massaged his tongue with my own. He came

back up and laughed.

"I guess that's your way of telling me *yes*?" he asked.

"Yes, I'll be Lady Scrap," I told him.
He smiled as he bent down and kissed me again,

caressing the small of my back and gripping my ass. I laughed

as he bit his bottom lip, smiling with his hands still gripping

one of my ass cheeks. ᴼᴮᴶ

Chapter 18 Lady Scrap

Janeeva

Brandon was throwing a barbeque for the team. So, Lia and I caught a ride with Trevor to Scrap's house. It was cold outside, but there were no clouds. I didn't know why they were throwing a barbeque in November, but I learned that they found any reason to party, so I stopped questioning it.

Aside from that . . . I was nervous. I was officially Lady Scrap, and I couldn't help but wonder what things were going to be like now. I had *bagged* my first boyfriend. *Look at me coming up in the world.* I was too nervous about what was going to happen when everyone found out and how Scrap was going to treat me now.

Lia knew everything, and she was so excited that she couldn't stay still. All she kept saying was "Lady Scrap."

Trevor didn't know yet, but I knew that he was going to find

out today.

When we pulled up, I was shocked to see that they had

the damn ATVs out. There weren't a lot of people here like the

last party they threw. It was just the main friends that were

always around and a couple of older people that I knew were

Scrap's brothers' friends. Twinkie and SixPacc were riding

down the street on the ATVs. It was too cold for this shit. They

were both wearing hoodies, racing down the street.

Lia kept talking about Scrap and me, but she wasn't

helping with the fact that I was already nervous as hell. I didn't

know that so many rules came with being official. She was

scaring the fuck out of me because she had me feeling like I

didn't know what the fuck I signed up for.

The first thing that I heard getting out of the car was

Twinkie yelling, "Lady Scrap!" while him and SixPacc raced

past us on the ATVs. They cheered and laughed, racing down

the streets.

My brother looked at me and smiled. "Lady Scrap?" he asked. I blushed and couldn't help but smile. He chuckled. "So, when was you gon' tell me this?" he asked.

"The right fucking time," I said, cringing and walking up to the house.

We walked in and went to the backyard where everyone else was. They had a patio setup with the cover over it just in case it rained. The twins were throwing a football around as Cliff and Leonard joined them in the yard. Bavari was on the grill, flipping patties and ribs with his shirt off, dancing to the song "Ain't Hard Enough" by Nipsey Hussle and Mozzy. *I swear every time that I see him, he never has a shirt on, even with it being so damn cold!*

Brandon, Brent, Ngozi and Scrap were sitting at the table on the patio playing dominoes, while Nakeia sat on Brent's lap. I was honestly impressed with the setup. It wasn't dark yet so you couldn't see the outdoor LED string lights lighting up the whole patio yet, but they were stretching the whole perimeter. I knew once they turned them on, it was going to be nice.

Brent looked up at us, and when his eyes fell on me, he smiled, said something to Scrap and then Scrap looked over at me. He smiled too as he motioned his head for me to come to him. As Trevor and Lia watched, they couldn't stop smiling. Trevor shook his head, and Lia just laughed.

"Bruh! Why does this shit feel so weird?" Lia asked Trevor.

Trevor wrapped his arm around her. "It really does, though. Our lil girl is growing up!" he said with his fake-ass cry. They both laughed. My whole face flushed from embarrassment. They were doing too much.

I walked over to Scrap as he held his dominoes in his hand. He scooted his chair out so that I could sit on his lap, and I couldn't help but blush again. Once I sat down, he kissed me, and everyone around us crooned. My whole face turned red.

"Aye, we not about to be havin' this, cuz," Scrap said, laughing. They all laughed.

"Welcome to the team, Lady Scrap!" Ngozi said. I just smiled.

"Yeah, I'ma have to holla at you layta," Brandon said to me.

It alarmed me when he said it. "Did I do something wrong?" I asked.

He flinched. "Did you?" he asked, smiling. I shrugged.

"He's fuckin' with you," Scrap said. They laughed again.

"Naw, I've just been waitin' to have a one-on-one conversation with you, try to figure out what the fuck you did to my brother," Brandon said, smiling at me. Trevor pulled a seat up next to us and told them that he was getting in on the next game. He looked at Scrap as Scrap looked back.

"Wassup, bruh?" Trevor greeted.

Scrap smiled. "What's good, loc?"

"Now when I told you that you could talk to her, I didn't think you meant you were going to make the shit all the way official," he said, smiling.

"Is that a problem?" Scrap asked, raising one of his eyebrows with a smirk on his face.

"To be honest . . . I'm not even trippin', loc." Everyone looked at Trevor, and I saw the shock on their face.

"Well . . . that was a quick turn," Nakeia said. Trevor shrugged.

"Aye, Quarterback! When you gon' let me throw yo bitch on the *blade*, cuz! She eighteen yet?" Bavari yelled over to Trevor.

Trevor flipped him off with this big-ass smile on his face. "You know you can't turn a hoe into a housewife, right?" he asked.

"Shit these weird-ass niggas is doin' it these days," Brandon responded.

"How the fuck did we start talkin' about my bitch, loc?" Trevor said, throwing his hands up. They all laughed.

"We were talkin' about her ass earlier, and you know this nigga Guda *pressed* on puttin' her ass on Figueroa to see what she do," Brent responded.

"I'on even know why you with the lil *thot*, loc! If you weren't around, ya bitch would have devoured me the otha' day!" Bavari said as he flipped the ribs.

"You just answered yo own question! It's what that mouth do!" Trevor responded. *He's just fucking disgusting.* They all laughed again.

"So, Jay . . . *Quel âge as-tu?* How old are you?" Brandon asked me in French and then translated, changing the subject.

"Sixteen. I'll be seventeen in April," I told him.

"Oooouh . . . *Jeune!*" Brent responded in French. Scrap chuckled. I looked at him confused.

"He said you young," he clarified.

"Oh . . ." I said, looking back at Brent as he smiled at me.

"Aye, loc! When you turn eighteen?" Brandon asked Trevor.

"February," he responded.

"Damn! So y'all like Irish twins or somethin', right?" Ngozi asked.

"I guess you can say that" I said, shrugging. Trevor and I were only a year and a couple of months apart.

"Naw, Irish twins is twelve months or less. We're right there though," Trevor responded.

"Well, then why yo ugly ass be actin' like her daddy, cuz?" Bavari yelled from the grill. They all laughed.

"Nigga, can you just keep flippin' them ribs so we can eat while you all over here?" Trevor responded. Bavari laughed.

Even though I understood why Trevor was so overprotective of me, he sometimes did go overboard. Brandon asked me some more questions as Scrap remained quiet and let him. I saw he had more respect for his brothers than he did for anyone else.

"You know how to play dominoes?" Brent asked me.

"She's a pro," Trevor spoke up for me.

"Is that right?" Brandon responded.

"Well, then you gon' have to get in on this next game so I can give you a better welcome. Tap that ass real quick. Consider it brotherly love," he said, smiling. I smiled back.

As I sat there, I talked to them while they finished their current game. I was enjoying myself a little too much. I was so comfortable.

Scrap let me take his turn the next game, and they were all shocked that I was tapping their ass in dominoes! I needed fifteen more points until I was out of my third house and win, and Brandon needed twenty. The game was honestly becoming more about me and him than anybody else because we were the only ones close to winning. I hit twenty-five points, closing the game out, and won.

Brandon couldn't help but sit back in his chair and shake his head. "She really just beat me in dominoes, loc," he said, looking at Ngozi. Ngozi laughed. "I'll give you that." He pulled out a bill and threw it on the table. I looked at Brandon and then at Trevor.

"We were betting?" I asked. They laughed.

"Girl, you don't see all this money on the table?" Ngozi said.

I shrugged. "I thought it was for the last game and you guys were just going to start a new one without my broke ass in it!" I responded. They all guffawed.

"First of all! You ain't broke fuckin' with the team, and second, all this is yours *Lil Baby*! You earned that!" Brent said, pushing all the money toward me. My mouth dropped, and I smiled with all my white teeth showing, and Scrap watched me as he laughed.

"I'm rich!" I whispered in his ear in excitement. He laughed harder. Lia had already left us in the middle of the game. She had a date with Domion, so Freckles took her back home.

"Aye, nigga! We still racin'?" Bavari yelled over to us as SixPacc, and Twinkie came out to the patio.

"Yup!" Brent responded. The clouds were starting to form, and I honestly didn't know how long they had before it started raining. They didn't care about any of that.

"Yeah, I'm in on that one," Trevor said, getting up from the table.

I flinched. "Weren't you the one who was telling me to stay off 'em because they're dangerous?" I snapped, looking up at him.

"Weren't you the one who didn't listen?" he retorted. I puckered my lips up and looked away. *Who told on me?* I thought to myself. "Yeah, Guda told on yo ass!" he said, already reading my mind.

"On crip, I ain't no ma'fuckin snitch, cuz! I didn't know her lil ass wasn't supposed to be on it!" Bavari yelled over to us. We all laughed as I shrugged.

"Well, it was fun, and I want to ride again," I told him.

He smiled. "Leh go! We probably gotta good thirty minutes before it starts rainin' on our ass," he responded.

I bounced up and down on Scrap's lap in excitement. We all went to the front as Scrap and Trevor hopped on the two ATVs that SixPacc and Twinkie were just riding. Brent and Bavari hopped on their motorcycles as Nakeia hopped on the back with Brent and Ngozi hopped on the back with Bavari. I didn't know the other motorcycle in the garage that Scrap took me for a ride on was Brandon's. He pulled it out and started it up.

Scrap gave me this seductive look, waiting for me to hop on the back of the ATV with him. Before I got on, he reached his arm around my waist so that I could come closer to him, and then he whispered in my ear. "You still gon' let me taste you?" I stared at him for a moment, not knowing how to answer, and then my whole face turned red as I smiled hard. He bit his bottom lip and then licked them. "C'mon," he said, motioning his head for me to get on. I hopped on and wrapped my arms around his torso as I laid my head on his back. We took off with the rest of them as we all raced down the street on motorcycles and ATVs.

I smiled and cheered as I watched Brandon and my brother doing tricks once we turned on one of the backstreets. Scrap told me to hold on tight as he did a wheely with me on it and then sped up as he tried to race down the street with Brent. Of course, we were no match with Brent being on his motorcycle, but it was still funny. I screamed and laughed as I held on to him tighter. We rode around for about forty-five minutes before it started to sprinkle and then decided to go back to the house with everyone else.

Obviously, Brandon trusted SixPacc and Twinkie enough to leave the house unattended with the people that were there. The twins were there as well so maybe that was why. I knew that they were all close to them, because being who the Gaither boys were, they wouldn't have left if they didn't trust them.

We pulled back up in the driveway as we all laughed and joked about Scrap trying to race Brent. As we went back into the house, it started to pour down rain.

"Right on time!" Brandon said, smiling. As I walked to the kitchen right behind him, he turned and looked at me. "So, I heard you pretty smart?" he asked me as he grabbed the Remy bottle out of the deep freezer.

I shrugged. "I guess so," I responded.

"Ms. Laney told me you helped a couple of students last year. She speaks highly of you, said that you're college level."

I flinched. "Ms. Laney was talking to you about me?" I asked, taken aback.

He nodded his head.

Scrap walked up behind me and explained. "Yeah, he fuckin' our teacher, cuz. I keep tryin' to tell him that she the *op*! Bitch always comin' for me," he said, shaking his head.

"She tryin' to help yo punk ass!"

"No! She tryin' to help *yoooou*!" Scrap said with emphasis. "I'm not the one fuckin' her! Now when you drop that bitch, because we all know it's gon' happen, and she start taking that shit out on me! You gon' be mad when I get expelled again for spazzin' out on her ass!" he finished. Brandon pressed his lips together. My jaw just hung open. It was the "*fuckin' our teacher*" part for me!

"We not gon' get into this shit right now, cuz. But you better talk to yo girl about helping you pass this class before you have to deal with me!" he told him as he went back to the patio. I looked at Scrap as he had his lip twisted all up. I smiled. He looked down at me with this confused look.

"What chu smiling about?" he asked.

"About you passing this class. It's gonna happen," I said with confidence as I walked past him, and he grabbed my arm pulling me back, wrapping his own around me with his hands on my butt.

I laughed as he snuggled his face into my neck and gently bit it. I felt the throb in between my thighs, and once he lifted his head up, I stuck my tongue in his mouth.

After Scrap and I were done making out in the kitchen, we went and grabbed a plate with everyone else. Cliff finished cooking the ribs and patties on the grill for Bavari, and we all chilled back.

I knew that, once the outdoor LED string lights came on, it was going to be beautiful. It lit up the whole patio. They had a small leather couch outside next to the table as well. Scrap and I relaxed on the couch as I leaned against him and watched his drunk-ass brothers play spades and talk shit to each other. I was honestly kickin' it and talking to Scrap's brothers more than I was talking to him.

I sat on the couch with him, joking and laughing with them while Scrap just watched us. Even Trevor sat back watching us and smiling. I saw why he was so close to them now. As intimidating and mean as they looked, they were actually goofy and fun as hell.

After a while, I figured out that this was exactly what Scrap wanted. He wanted to see how I would get along with his brothers and that was why he just sat back and watched. He wanted his brothers to get to know me, and for some reason, I felt like they liked me more than I thought that they would.

As we played some music and enjoyed ourselves, a lady came out onto the patio, and she was stumbling over. I stared at her as she came out.

Brandon and Scrap looked her way and instantly got up. She was sloppy drunk. Her long sandy hair was stuck to her face from the sweat coming out of her pores, and she was falling over everything. She looked as if she might be just a shade lighter than Breanne. Her complexion was beautiful. She wasn't that smooth mahogany like Breanne, but she was close to it.

Scrap sighed as he and Brandon walked over to her before she could get all the way to us. Brent remained seated as he shook his head in disappointment, and Bavari just smacked his lips.

"Mama what're you doin'?" Scrap asked in a muffled voice. I could hear the anger all in his tone. She didn't answer him. She just leaned her head against his chest.

She looked at him and smiled. "Look at my baby . . . You just so handsome . . ." she slurred as her hand reached up and rested on Scrap's cheek.

He pulled away as he grabbed her hand off him. "Man, c'mon . . ." he said, trying to take her back into the house.

Brandon moved her hair out of her face, and when she looked up, I was shocked to see how gorgeous she really was. Her dark-brown almond eyes were beautiful, and I now saw where Breanne got them from. I could only imagine how gorgeous she was without all the alcohol taking over her.

Brandon took her back inside, and as Scrap walked back over to me, he caught Breanne hiding behind the door with this long face. He instantly went to her side, picked her up and she rested her head on his shoulder as he walked back over to me. When he sat down on the couch, he made her look at him.

"You okay?" he asked her.

Her pretty little eyes watered up. She didn't respond. She just rested her head on her brother's shoulder as she wrapped her arms around his neck. Scrap sighed and just held his sister as she lay in his arms.

Once she fell asleep, Bavari took her back in the house and put her in her bed. I honestly felt bad for all of them. They should never have had to grow up the way that they did. I placed my hand in his own as he came out of his deep thought.

He smiled at me, trying to lighten up the mood. "Did you have a good time today?" he asked.

I nodded my head. "I did. Your brothers are cool," I said.

He gave me a half smile and nodded his head.

"So, what do we do now? Lia is stressing me out! She's making it seem like I must be this goddess just to be with you. I didn't know that there were so many rules in being official."

He laughed. "What the fuck?" he asked as he continued to laugh. He then shook his head. "Naw . . . Just be the person you've been. I didn't make you my girl so that you can keep up with the rest of these bitches. And lil do you know, they tryin' to keep up with you," he said, smiling at me. "I told you before that you were different. I meant that. That's how you kept my attention. I don't want you to change the person that you are," he said to me. I was just in "*awe*" for a moment as I stared at him, and then I smiled. He kissed me as I leaned into him and kissed him back.

Once Trevor and I got home, I went straight to my room, flopped down on my bed and just day-dreamed away . . . I felt so light and so fucking good inside. I couldn't get enough of Brian Gaither! And at that exact moment, I started to lose it because I realized that he was finally *mine*! He was *mine*! I finally got the boy of my dreams. Me! He was mine! I smiled hard as I threw my pillow over my face and screamed in joy. This moment couldn't have gotten any better.

Chapter 19 This Shit Ain't Over!

Janeeva

I leaned against Scrap between his legs as he sat on the table in the lunchroom. Our normal group crowded around us, talking and laughing like they normally do. SixPacc stuck with his daily routine, trying to make Lia give in. They argued most of the time, but he kept a smile on his face while he argued with her. It pissed Lia off, which made the situation funnier.

"Luth, get yo ass out my face, nigga!" she said, pushing him off her as he rubbed his whole body against her.

He laughed. "Stop acting like you don't like that shit, cuz!" he said.

Scrap rubbed the small of my back as I leaned against him, and chills kept shooting through my body. I looked up at him, and he gently kissed my lips.

"Scrap, you turnin' into a *square*! And he swears he ain't in love!" Cliff said, shaking his head as he laughed.

Scrap looked at him. "Nigga, why you all up in my shit?" he retorted. Everybody laughed.

"Shut up and go back to *cupcakin'* with yo soft ass!" Cliff responded.

"Are y'all goin' to the fair?" Dimples asked.

"Yeah," Scrap responded.

I looked at him. "We are?"

"What? You don't wanna go?"

I shrugged. "I didn't even know about it. Do you guys have to do something every weekend?" I asked.

"Hell, yeah! *YOLO*!" Cliff said. *YOLO*? I questioned myself. I looked at Lia.

"You only live once," she clarified in a faint voice so that no one else could hear us. After I understood, I started thinking about how the hell they were even able to do most of the shit that they did. I was shocked that most of their parents don't be trippin.' I was too embarrassed to ask though because I either had a curfew or must sneak out to kick it.

"So, are you goin' with me, Lady Scrap?" Scrap asked.

I smiled. "Yes, I will," I said.

"So, Lia, check this out! You should let me take you to the fair since yo best friend goin' with my best friend," SixPacc interrupted, stepping back up to Lia.

"Nope, I gotta date already," she said, pushing him out the way.

"Well, tell that nigga that you goin' with me!" he said. She laughed and started walking out of the group. "Really? You just gon' walk away from a nigga?" he said, throwing his hands up. She didn't say anything; she just kept going.

"I don't know why you keep fuckin' with her, loc," Scrap said, shaking his head.

"Because I know she can't play hard-to-get forever," SixPacc responded as he smiled at us. "I know she wants me.

It's all in her eyes!"

I smiled and shook my head. He was just too funny. I honestly didn't understand though because he was a true *man whore*. Right after he would be done fucking with Lia, the next bitch will be stopping him in the hallway, and he'll make plans with the girl in front of me. I told him that he was wrong for it, and this was exactly how he responded. "It's nothing wrong about it at all, sis. She wants to play hard to get then let her play that childish shit, but I'm not going to put my life on hold for what she's going through. I told you already; she'll get tired eventually of rejecting me, but until then I'ma do me."

I walked with Lia to my next class. Scrap had to go handle something with his brothers, so he left school for the day. As we walked, someone bumped right into me, and all my books fell to the ground. As Lia helped me pick them up, I saw a pair of stilettos in front of me, and I looked up to see Lovely standing over me. I instantly stood to my feet and glared at her.

"It's crazy how pathetic bitches are. I warned you to stay away from him, lil girl . . ."

Before Lia could even jump and say anything, I stopped her. I was getting tired of this bitch, and you would think after she got her ass beat the last time, she would fall back, but the bitch just wouldn't give up. I'm not going to lie though—after I beat her ass, I was feeling like *super woman.*

"If you haven't noticed by now, he's *mine* . . . I win! So, all this extra shit that you're doing is pathetic. So, before you start calling somebody the name, look in the mirror, bitch!" I told her.

"Boom!" Lia said, leaning over me, smiling from ear to ear looking at Lovely.

She scowled at me and sized me up, then a sneaky-ass grin came across her face. "This shit ain't over, baby. Just know dat. You're fuckin' with the wrong *bitch.*" She walked away. Once she was out of sight, Lia looked at me in joy.

"I'm such a proud best friend right now!" she said. I couldn't help but laugh. We walked into class and went about our day. **Trevor**

The fair was here, and the team was rockin' tonight! Of course, most of us had our own dates. Talawny came with me. Yaya brought his girl. Taz just brought some random-ass bitch.

I honestly thought he was going to try to bring Ms. Laney, but I'm sure Scrap talked him out of it. That was the last thing that he wanted anybody to know, that his brother was fuckin' his teacher.

The girl he was with was fine as hell. It's just that nobody knew who the fuck she was! Taz was like that, though. I knew after a couple of failed relationships, since he had a whole family to take care of and that he was always busy, he didn't let females get too close to him. They never really lasted that long. The pressure was too much for them. The nigga was always sacrificing for his siblings.

SixPacc ended up taking a girl from our school, Camari. I laughed because I knew Lia was going to be upset, but she had nothing to really be mad about. I've known her for too many years to know when she's feeling somebody, and even though she's always rejecting the nigga, I know she wants him as much as he wants her. I respect lil sis though, because after everything that she has been through, it makes her a stronger person today and she isn't just a naïve ass little girl. She knows the game when she hears it.

I wish I could say the same for Janeeva. Even though I have finally accepted the fact that Scrap and she are going to be together, it's still scaring the shit out of me. My job is to protect her, but I don't know how to protect her from this. I'm praying that he doesn't fuck up. That's not exactly something that she will be prepared for, especially with him being her first boyfriend.

Back to the team, though! Tonight, was supposed to be a *chill* night, but Guda was still on the clock. This nigga brought his hoe bitches. I couldn't believe that shit.

"Nigga, can you just have one night and chill?" I asked, laughing.

"Hell, naw! These bitches' betta' have my money by the time the night is ova' - Lesson!" he said, throwing his index finger up. "You see all these ma'fuckas runnin' around here gettin' turnt! Nigga, you could be slangin' right now because most likely, most of 'em is trying to find out who got the tree, who got that yay! Where the fuck the rocks at, cuz!? Shit, most of these perverted-ass niggas is trying to find out who givin' up some pussy tonight! You can be making dough while you cupcakin' and shit wit'cho bitch! Best of both worlds, crip!" he said, throwing his hands up, smiling. I took in what he said, and he was right. I could be making some dough right now.

"Let's go get on the fairest wheel," Talawny said, wrapping her arms around my waist. I agreed because I knew her freaky ass had other shit on her mind once we got to the top.

Janeeva

I swear there was never a dull moment with Scrap and his friends. We walked around, hopping on rides and playing some of the games with SixPacc and Twinkie. I saw Scrap making a couple of transactions on the low as we walked.

SixPacc's date was cute. She was just loud! I think I saw Scrap slide her something when we got out the car, though, so that was probably why her ass was so turnt up. I could tell SixPacc was getting a little annoyed with her, but he kept his cool.

"Nigga, what the fuck did she buy from you?" he asked Scrap in a low voice.

Scrap smiled at him. "Just know you gon' have a long night with that bitch," Scrap told him. SixPacc threw his head back and took a deep breath. "You gon' get some pussy tonight fa'sho though," he said, laughing.

"Man, fuck you, cuz! You should've told her ass no!" SixPacc retorted.

"And upset a loyal customer? Naw, cuz!" Scrap said shaking his head. "You should've asked me about her before you brought her," he told him, still laughing.

I was waiting for Lia to show up. I called her, and she was already on her way up here with Domion. I didn't know if that was a good look or not, but she seemed happy with him so far, so I didn't say much about it. When she finally did show up, she was looking even more gorgeous than any other day, and I knew that it was to impress Domion. He was looking *fly* as well, but of course, it was an awkward moment.

His attitude toward certain things reminded me of Scrap—someone who just didn't give a fuck—but Domion was completely different from him. He made me feel uncomfortable.

I could tell on SixPacc's face that he didn't sit well with this shit, but he didn't say anything. He just smiled and threw his arm over Camari's shoulder. Lia gave both of them a malice look, and then a smile came across her face as well. I chuckled because I knew what she was thinking: *You think that you're about to make me jealous with this bitch? She has nothing on me.*

I knew her too well, but she didn't speak out loud. And Camari *didn't* have anything on her. She was a *knock* (a drug addict), so Lia was already winning.

We continued walking around, and eventually we all split up with our dates. Everyone was on their own hype tonight. As Scrap and I walked around the fair and played some of the games, we talked.

"So, does your father ever try to get in touch with you?" I asked.

He nodded his head. "He calls every now and then, but I never talk to him. Brandon usually ends up being the one who talks to him, but he keeps it short," he responded. "He tries to send us money thinking that it'll make up for the years he missed out on, but we're making our own dough, so the shit don't mean nothin'. After what he did to my mom, he's dead to me. We try to help her the best way that we can . . . She's been in rehab at least four times, but every time she comes home, she relapses. We not just gon' put her out on the streets because of Breanne and the twins. She don't understand how much they need her," he said.

"What about you?" I asked.

"What about me?" he responded, not understanding what I meant.

"How much do *you* need her?"

He looked at me for a moment and then dropped his eyes as he thought. "When she first started going into her depression and then start drinking heavy, I'm the one who spent most of the time with her because I was too young to be around the shit my brothers were doin'. I had to help take care of the twins and look after her while they were gone . . ." he said, looking me in my eyes with this painful look. "Janeeva, I was *five* when my mom started goin' through all this shit. As the years went on, she needed us more than we needed her. I stopped depending on her being here for us a long time ago . . ." he finished.

I dropped my eyes because he really didn't answer the question, but I didn't want to *trigger* him either. I sighed and tried to pull off a smile as I looked at him. "She'll get better for you guys eventually. Don't give up on her," I told him. He looked at me and smiled.

"What?" I asked.

"You're just always so optimistic about everything. You try to see the good in others when they really don't deserve it."

"Do you think that you don't deserve me seeing the good in you?" I asked him.

"If you knew all the shit that I've done, I don't think you would be asking me that question."

My heart pierced as I stared into his eyes for a moment, trying to read them. He wore this hard look on his face, and I couldn't read anything. It was like he had this whole guard up.

There was so much that I still didn't know, but I was so head over heels for him that I wasn't sure how much I cared either.

"Just don't give up on her . . ." I repeated. "I know that you're not going to tell me everything, and I don't even know if I want to know everything, but after finding out how my life has been for years and where I'm at now, you have to believe that change can happen."

He chuckled and then shook his head. "You and my mom are two different people. Don't compare yo'self to her. You'll never be what she is." I pressed my lips together and sighed. "Let's stop talkin' 'bout it . . ." I nodded my head as we kept walking. As we walked, I chuckled.

"You know, thinking about all the things that I've feared and conquered over the past couple of months is just crazy to me," I said, shaking my head.

"What chu mean?" he asked.
"What I mean is that I went from this girl stuck in this shell . . . afraid of everything that can possibly happen or repeat in my past . . . or being *triggered* and having an anxiety attack . . . Then you come along, and the moment that I saw you, I felt that shell crack, like I was finally ready to get out. I had to have you . . . And now, here we are . . . ." I said, smiling.

"You earned it, Ma. Now, what was yo fears over these last couple of months?" he asked.

"Being rejected by you," I responded.

"Well, you got what you wanted, and even when I tried to stay away from you, all I could think about is yo tight-ass waist," he traced his finger down my waist, "yo beautiful-ass eyes," he stared into my light brown eyes, "and those sexy-ass lips," he finished coming down to kiss me. Chills were shooting all through my body.

"Was that all you thought about?" I asked smiling.

He stared at me with a smirk on his face as he went into deep thought. "You keep me sane," he said.

I stared at him for a moment with my head tilted, trying to understand what he meant by that. "What do you mean?" I asked.

"Just being around you, the person you are . . . You forced me to pull anotha' nigga out of me that doesn't come around too often. I'm sure you've heard how I treat females. I think you saw the way I treated Lovely after a while, but like I explained to you before, I treat them how they treat themselves. And with you . . . I don't feel like I have to have a guard up. I don't feel like I'm always fighting my own demons around you. You just keep me sane . . . at peace," he repeated shrugging, trying to understand it himself. "With all the shit that you've heard about me, you still looked past the hood nigga that you already knew that I was. After all the shit that I've put you through with my bitches, and you still looked past it . . ." he continued. "That's honestly why my brothers like you so much. You bring out a completely different nigga when you're around," he confessed.

My sensitive ass damn near had tears in my eyes. My heart was fluttering. "I have to go to the restroom," I said, trying to get myself together.

He looked around and thought about where a bathroom could be. We continued walking until we found one, and when we finally came across one, it was all the way in the back of the fair and it was dark. I'm not going to lie; I don't know how we ended up all the way back here looking for a bathroom in this big-ass park. I was a little scared. It was dark back here. I looked at him.

"You good, Ma. I'll be right here," he told me. I nodded my head and went inside.

At first, I didn't have to use the restroom, but I suddenly had a bladder that was about to explode. This bathroom was disgusting as hell, but I had to suck my pride in before I pissed on myself. I went into one of the stalls, took a squat and let it loose. Once I was done, I washed my hands and fixed my makeup.

I was feeling like a completely different person. At first, I just wanted him. I just wanted him to be mine. I never thought about *changing* him. I never in my right mind imagined that I would be the one that brought him peace. I couldn't help but feel good about myself.

Before I could think any further, I felt a blow to my head, and as I fell, my head hit the sink next to the one that I was using. I felt another blow and then multiple ones. I couldn't look up or see who was hitting me because all those hard blows that were being thrown were at my head, and then someone kicked me. I tried to fight back, but there were too many of them.

"Stupid ass cunt!" I heard someone yell as I tried to rise from the nasty-ass bathroom floor but was kicked in my side. "You should have listened, bitch!" I heard a feminine voice say. They stopped, and the moment that I heard the voice, I tried to look up because I knew it well, especially with the deep-ass accent she was carrying—Lovely.

They beat my ass so bad that her face was blurry as fuck. I saw two other girls standing over me as I tried to rise from the floor again, and they pushed me back down.

"Where the fuck is you goin', bitch?" one of them spat. The other grabbed me by my hair and pulled me to my feet while pulling me out of the bathroom and to the back of the building. As I stumbled, holding on to the girl's wrist as she had a tight painful grip on my hair, I heard Lovely speaking in Spanish to one of them.

Once we got to the back, my heart stopped when I realized that three men were on top of Scrap beating the shit out of him.

"No!" I said, as tears started to run down my face. "Stop! Please!" I begged as I tried to run toward him but was pulled back from the tight grip the girl had in my hair.

Scrap continued to try to fight them back, but there were too many of them, and they kept throwing blows until he was too weak to fight anymore.

Once he stopped fighting, the men backed off and laughed. The girl that was holding me by my hair pulled me toward Scrap and pushed me to the ground beside him. Scrap struggled to sit up as he tried to block me from them. He caught his breath and spoke.

"She ain't got shit to do with this, cuz. Let her go and we can finish this shit," he said, looking at Lovely. Lovely stomped over to us, bent down and slapped the shit out of Scrap.

"Stop!" I yelled, trying to throw my arms over him.

"Shut the fuck up, bitch! She has everything to do with it!" Lovely yelled. "I told you to stay the fuck away, lil girl.

Everything was going just the way I wanted it to until yo bitchass came along!"

"So, you're doing all of this because a nigga *chose up?*" Scrap spoke. One of the men stepped up, pulled out a gun and cocked it back as he bent down and held the gun to Scrap's temple. My heart dropped, and I broke down. I couldn't stop crying, and I didn't know what to do. I was frantic.

"Please . . ." I choked. "Please don't shoot him," I said in the smallest voice that I could find.

Scrap didn't even flinch from the gun being held to his head. He stayed where he was at, but he didn't flinch. "So, this is how we end, huh?" he said to Lovely. "Who the fuck are these niggas anyway?" he spat.

"My cousin. Real killas! Unlike you," she said.

Scrap snickered as he stayed calm with the gun still to his temple. "Is that what you call them?" he asked with a smirk on his face. "I would have squeezed the trigga . . .'" he taunted.

I didn't understand. "Scrap, shut up!" I yelled.

He placed his hand on my leg to calm me. "Let her go, Lovely, and just deal with me."

"No!" she responded. "She's the whole reason for this! I thought Cherokee was a problem, but this bitch was a bigger threat," she said shaking her head.

He cut his eyes at her. "What the fuck do you mean that you thought Cherokee was a problem?" he growled.

She smiled. "It sucks how you could be so blind from yo bitch's death. You shouldn't have given up on her so quickly. That bitch was a wreck after you threatened her at that party. She felt like it was the ultimate betrayal to you. The bitch loved you more than you thought, Scrap, but she knew that I was your favorite, and she knew Mia was the top bitch in the pack. However, I didn't have to worry about Mia too much because I already saw that she wasn't going to last. Anyways," she continued, "Cherokee wanted me to help her get some more clients, including the ones that I took from her, so she could make it up to you. Real shit! The bitch was talking about getting six racks in one night and giving all of it to you so that you wouldn't hate her anymore and you would welcome her back with open arms. She just knew you would give in, and I did, too. I wasn't having that. I was enjoying being your only bitch a little too much because I had finally gotten your full attention. So, I set her up with my cousin . . ." she said, introducing the man that was holding the gun up to Scrap's head. "Primo, this is Scrap. Scrap, meet my cousin Primo," she said. Scrap looked at the nigga from the corner of his eyes but didn't say anything. Primo just smiled. "Cherokee met up with Primo, and she did what she had to do to make some of that money. He made up this lie about his wife and how she had to go through the back door to the alley to leave or his wife was going to shoot the place up. Right when she opened that back door, she took one look at me and I put a bullet in her head," she said, smiling.

This bitch was truly mental, and I know that I said that I had never feared Lovely, but at this moment alone, she scared the fuck out of me! I never knew that a bitch could be this crazy and obsessed. She was obsessed with Scrap.

Scrap threw his head down and shook it. "I fuckin' knew you had something to do with that shit . . ." he said, feeling guilt. I didn't say anything. I was too shocked and too scared to speak.

You would think that this crazy shit would only happen in movies but no . . . There was a murderer standing before me, and I cried harder because I just knew that I was next. I had never known one that had confessed to my knowledge, and now that I did, I was losing my shit!

"Yes, Daddy! I had everything to do with that setup, and it was perfect! No one would have ever expected it from a bitch because she was 'supposedly' *raped and killed*. The evidence is there . . ." she said sarcastically as she laughed. "Everything was going perfect, and then you . . ." she said looking at me.

Scrap tried to push me behind him as my hands gripped tight to his shirt. "Let her go, Lovely," he said in a malice tone.

"No. I'm going to merk both of you and let it be that. You talked all that shit about a bitch crossing you, and you turned around and did the same shit you preached. You're worthless, and she's about to get it because she's hard-headed," she said.

Before another word could be spoken, I heard multiple guns cocking back behind Lovely. She quickly turned around, as did the rest of them, and I saw my brother, Scrap's brothers, Nakeia and Ngozi. Ngozi and Nakeia aimed their guns at the two girls that jumped me. They were all strapped and ready to shoot the first person that moved.

"Wassup, bitch!" Brent said as he aimed his gun at Lovely's head with a smirk on his face.

"So yooooou killed Cherokee . . ." Bavari crooned, stepping up slowly as he kept his gun aimed at Primo while his eyes flickered back and forth between the two of them.

Brandon and Trevor had their guns aimed at the two other men that jumped Scrap.

Primo still had the gun to Scrap's head, and Scrap sat there as calm as ever with his hand around my waist ready to make the next move. She didn't answer.

"What? Now you can't speak, bitch?" Bavari asked, smiling at her.

"Now you know this shit can get real ugly, so let them go," Brandon said as the rest of them stayed in their position with their guns aimed.

Lovely laughed. "Big brothers to the rescue!" she crooned. She looked at Brent and licked her lips. "You know, Yaya . . . I always wanted to taste you! You've always made my pussy wet with those pretty-ass brown eyes and that sexyass smile. Too bad it gotta end like this," she said.

Brent didn't flinch; he knew the game when he heard it. He just kept his gun aimed at her head. However, Nakeia's head snapped toward Lovely as she gave her the deadliest look you could ever receive from a female, and the moment that she looked away at Lovely, her friend grabbed Nakeia's wrist and punched her in her face. Ngozi's head snapped toward her sister, and then the other girl tackled her.

The moment that Primo had gotten distracted from the chaos, Bavari took his chance as he pulled the trigger and started *bustin'*, while Nakeia and Ngozi started fighting the two girls. Primo's body dropped to the ground in front of us, and I screamed.

After that it was all a chain reaction. The other two men that were with Primo and Lovely started to shoot, and it was just a whole war zone as they ducked for cover and hid behind the building where the bathroom stalls were. Bullets were flying from both directions while everyone was finding anything to shield themselves with.

Scrap had already thrown his body over my own as he pinned me down to the ground, and I threw my hands over my ears from the sound of the gunshots ringing in them. I shut my eyes tight as I cried. I was so scared that I couldn't help but scream as he shielded me from the gunshots that were being fired.

I could feel someone standing over us, bent down, as the gunshots continued, and as I opened my eyes and looked up in the middle of holding on to Scrap for dear life, I saw Brandon as he kept shooting until finally the other two men dropped to the ground.

The shit happened so fast that I just lay there shaking and crying . . . The gunshots stopped, and as I stayed down with my head buried into Scrap's chest, I slowly lifted my head with these wide eyes, trying to slow my breathing down. I looked around with tears in my eyes for my brother, and when I finally spotted him, he was looking back at me, ready to run to me.

I looked over at Lovely, and she was wounded. Her arm was drenched with blood while she tried to press her hand down on it to stop the bleeding. Her breathing was heavy as she bent over trying to walk toward where her gun fell out of her hand. Brandon was still standing over us as he wore this hard deadly expression on his face.

We all turned our heads when we heard the wrestling still going on with Nakeia and Ngozi. He stepped back from us and turned to them, while Trevor ran toward us.

Brent shifted his attention back to Ngozi and Nakeia as well. Trevor swept me up from the ground as I wrapped my arm around his neck, relieved to feel him.

"Get her out of here," Brandon ordered Trevor as he gave him a nod, and he ran with me still in his arms. He ran further to the back of the fair, and we came to the end of this fence. He put me down as he tried to take a breath and looked at me with his heavy breathing.

"Aight, we gotta climb this fence. I'ma help you as much as I can, but we gotta hurry up. Police gon' be here soon. Okay?" he instructed.

527

I looked at the fence. My vision seemed blurry, but it was probably because of the blows to my head. I took a deep breath and nodded my head.

I start climbing as Trevor did the same, trying to push me up as quickly as possible to get to the other side of the fence. As I had finally gotten to the top, I was startled by two cars scraping up in front of us. Twinkie and SixPacc hopped out of the car as they ran over to the fence to help me down.

"Just let go!" SixPacc said as he held his arms out to catch me.

I let go, and he caught me just in time so that I wouldn't break my fall. Trevor jumped down right after me and then helped me into one of the cars that had pulled up.

Leonard was in the front tapping his fingers on the wheel as he kept looking at the clock. "We gotta go, cuz," he said, shaking his head as he sat there anxious in his seat.

"Naw! Taz said wait!" Trevor said, aggressively. "We not leavin' them!"

Leonard sighed and shook his head as we waited for the rest of them.

Scrap

I sat there on the ground after I knew Janeeva was safe, trying to stand up as I held on to my side. These niggas beat my ass! And Lovely knew if it wasn't three of them, this shit would have played out differently.

Brent had his gun aimed back at Lovely before she could get to her own, and she had stopped in her tracks as she glared at him from her peripheral. Brandon walked up to her with the same hard mug as he grabbed her by her hair, pulling her away from the gun and then shoving her to the ground.

"Stupid-ass bitch!" Lil Hitta yelled as she repeatedly beat one of the girls in her face with the back of the gun. The other girl that had attacked Lady Yaya was lifeless on the ground with her eyes wide open, painting the grass with the blood flowing from her neck.

Lady Yaya had pulled out her pocketknife while they were fighting and jabbed it right into that bitch's neck. She finally stood to her feet as she tried to catch her breath, and Lil Hitta continued to beat the other girl with the back of the pistol. She finally stopped. The girl was unconscious with her face smeared with blood.

"Nakeia . . ." Brent said, making sure that Lady Yaya was okay as he kept his eyes on Lovely.

"I'm good," she responded.

Once he knew that she was okay, he spoke again. "Merk that bitch and let's go," he said to Brandon.

Lil Hitta stood to her feet with the same malice look on her face and walked toward Brandon and Lovely. She stood right on the side of Brandon waiting for his command. Brandon looked Lovely in her eyes for a long moment, giving her the same deadly look. She knew this shit was over, and she glared back preparing herself for what was next. He looked at Lil Hitta and stepped back.

"Do it for Cherokee, cuz," he ordered.

Lil Hitta instantly jumped on Lovely and started beating the shit out of her. Lovely couldn't do much because her arm was wounded, but even if she could, she knew that she was no match for Lil Hitta. She was beating her ass so bad that I knew that she wasn't going to stop until the bitch was no longer breathing. We all watched, waiting for her to finish, and in the middle of her beating her ass, we heard an unfamiliar voice.

"Oh shit!" we all turned our heads to find a security guard coming around the building and witnessing the whole scene. Bavari turned toward the security guard, aimed his gun and shot him twice in his chest and his head. Now it was really time for us to leave.

"Let's go!" Brandon ordered as Bavari came on the side of me to help me run, and we all left. We got to the far back of the park where there was a fence, and I could see the two cars waiting for us on the other side.

Even though I was in pain, I still smoothly climbed over the fence with a little help from my brothers, and the rest of them hopped over. As I ran to the cars, my brothers hopped in the first car, and Leonard had his window down looking at us in anticipation.

"Where she at?" I yelled.

"In the back!" he responded.

We heard sirens as the police was getting closer, and Lil Hitta and I hurried up and hopped in the back with Janeeva and Trevor, piling ourselves in, as Leonard scraped off with the first car before we could barely get the door closed.

As I sat in the back, I looked dead at Janeeva. She looked drained and beaten up. As I observed her, I saw that there was blood running down her forehead. I reached over and moved her hair out of her face.

"Oh shit, Jay!" Lil Hitta said under her breath.

Quarterback quickly tore the bottom of his shirt and pressed it to her forehead. She was in shock, with these wide eyes, as she was trying to process everything that happened. Tears rolled down her face as she sat in the car, zoned off with this heavy breathing. I didn't know if she was having an anxiety attack or not because she was so quiet.

I looked at Quarterback, and as he observed her hard breathing, he instantly started doing the *3-3-3 rule* with her. She responded to a couple of questions, slowly calming down, pressing her hand to her chest. I sighed and shook my head as I watched her. I was honestly feeling bad that I got her in the middle of this.

"Jay . . . look at me," I said as I gently touched her face and turned her head toward me. Her eyes finally met with my own as I stared at her apologetically. Tears continued to roll down her face, and I just brought her into my chest and let her get it out.

I honestly didn't know what else to do. This shit was new for me. This was my everyday life and I wouldn't even care if she was someone else, but for some reason, I knew I fucked her up with this and it was fucking me up knowing it.

We pulled up to the house, and as the doors opened, she didn't move. I sat while she rested her head on my chest, drifting off to sleep. I pulled her up and made her look at me again.

"Don't go to sleep," I told her. She looked into my eyes as I tried to keep her up.

The normal thing to do would be to get her to the hospital, but we couldn't do that. Quarterback continued pressing the shirt against her head while he looked at me, letting me know that we needed to get her in the house. I knew that she could see the guilt all over my face. I stared at her for another moment.

"I'm sorry . . ." I whispered.

She didn't respond. I could tell that she was still in shock. I helped her out of the car, and then we quickly went inside. We motioned her to the couch, and she lay down. Quarterback pressed the shirt back to her forehead, and then Brandon started giving orders.

"Aye, loc! Go get that first-aid kit in the garage," he ordered Leonard. "Lil Hitta! I need you to go grab a wet towel and warm it up," he said.

Lady Yaya pulled Janeeva's hair up in a loose ponytail as Brandon made me sit on the arm of the couch so that he could check my ribs. I knew that they weren't broken, but the shit hurt like hell.

Once Lil Hitta came back with the hot towel, Lady Yaya started to clean up the gash on Janeeva's head and bandaging her up with the supplies that were in the first-aid kit. I sat there on the arm of the couch, staring at Janeeva, while my brother examined my ribs.

"Does this hurt?" Brandon asked as he placed pressure on different spots of my side.

"Man, I said I'm good, cuz!" I responded.

"I can't believe this bitch was the one who took out Cherokee," Leonard said.

"How did y'all know that I needed y'all?" I asked.
"Boogie had already peeped Lovely and her lil mob, so he followed them, and when he spotted y'all, he already knew what was up, so he called us," Bavari answered.

There was a bang at the door. Brandon instantly pulled out his gun and looked through the peephole. He squinted for a second and then cocked his gun back. He opened the door, and I heard Lia's voice. He glared at her for a second and then stepped out to look around and see if anyone else was with her. He stepped back in and nodded his head for her to come in. Lia ran in, and the moment she spotted Janeeva, she ran over to the couch and hugged her.

"Please tell me you're okay?" she begged, damn near in tears.

"I'm fine . . ." Janeeva responded.

Brandon closed the door and grabbed the remote to turn on the TV to the news. The whole scene that took place was damn near on several channels. "Two men and one teenage girl dead and two teenage girls and one man in critical condition." They continued . . . "One of the young teens that was shot and severely beaten was carrying a handgun that matched the same gun that officers described killed seventeen-year-old Keota Crong where she was found raped and killed in an alley in Compton. However, police are trying to figure out if Keota was just in the wrong place at the wrong time or if her death was a setup," the news lady said as all of our eyes were glued to the screen.

"This shit is crazy, cuz," SixPacc said under his breath.

"Karma is a bitch though," Bavari responded as he sat on top of the coffee table and watched.

They then started talking about the security guard that they found. He was dead, but we already knew that. I dropped my eyes. Even though he probably didn't deserve to die, he had already seen all our faces and Bavari had to kill him.

He was our *main* shooter. That nigga had an aim that was so vicious, he damn-near never missed. It was like this shit was a *game* to him, and I knew that was why Brandon made sure that Bavari took the nigga who had the gun to my head. I was their main concern.

"This that shit that I was talking about," Quarterback said as he shook his head. I brought my attention to him.

"Quarterback, chill!" Lil Hitta told him as she sighed. She knew the nigga was about to start talking that shit that I honestly didn't have time for right now either.

"Trevor, please don't start," Janeeva begged.

He just shook his head. "Every single time I'm about to be over the shit some more shit happen, ma nigga," he said, looking at me.

"I ain't tryin' to hear that shit right now, cuz," I told him.

"Naw, nigga, you gon' hear it!" he said, standing up from the edge of the couch. I stood, too, pulling my jeans up and sizing him up.

"No!" Lady Yaya said looking between the two of us. "Y'all need to chill the fuck out, and Quarterback, I need you to fuckin' relax! We been through enough tonight!" she yelled.

"This nigga almost got my sister killed! You see on the news how many people died tonight?" he yelled, pointing to the flat screen TV mounted to the wall.

My nose flared; I held my ground ready to take off on his ass. I didn't give a fuck about what he was talking about right now. The nigga was too bold with me, and I was ready to break his whole fuckin' jaw.

He didn't want to do this shit here. I didn't care how close he was to my brothers. Janeeva tried to sit up, and Lady Yaya placed her hand on her chest to lay her back down. She moved her hand. She tried to stand, and you could tell from the way that she tilted over that she was light-headed.

I instantly calmed down and grabbed her. "You need to lay back down," I told her.

"I want you guys to stop fighting," she responded.
"Man, don't worry about this. Worry about yourself right now," I retorted. She rested her head on my chest, and I made her stand up straight. "You can't go to sleep," I said, looking her in her eyes.

"Why?" she whined.

"Because you may have a concussion," Bavari said as he walked past us and grabbed Quarterback. "Let me holla at you, bruh," he told him. I gave Quarterback a deadly look as Janeeva held on to me, and Bavari took him into the garage. I looked back at Janeeva, and we both sat down on the couch.

I couldn't stop staring at her. I didn't know what she was thinking, and once again, I was still in the middle of deciding if I should be with her or not.

This life—my life—it just wasn't for her. She wasn't built for this shit. Even though I was ready to square up with her brother, he was right. And still, after everything that happened tonight, she was still trying to hold on to me and stay close. I didn't understand her. You would think she would be running away right now and never wanting to see a nigga again. She was different, and I just couldn't figure her out.

Janeeva

I sat there on that couch, trying to stay up and to keep Scrap close. I wanted to continue to cry, but I couldn't help but want to comfort him too. Like, is this really the shit that he goes through daily? Is this really his life, dealing with crazy hoe bitches, being held at gunpoint and watching people get killed right in front of him?

Even with my silence, I had a million questions running through my head. For the first time in my life, I had witnessed a murder—a couple of them, and the more that I thought about how I was feeling right now, I couldn't even imagine the shit that he had already been through and the things that he had seen. I felt like he needed more comfort than I did. I also didn't want him to feel bad and deciding that he shouldn't be with me anymore. I went through that already, and I didn't want to go through it again.

He continued to observe me as I leaned against him. I felt multiple eyes on us as we sat there, and I had a feeling that I knew what everyone was thinking.

They were not used to him showing this much affection toward anyone. He stayed there beside me, trying to keep me up. Everyone lingered around waiting for a word or more news as Nakeia kept coming back with ice and ointment for my gash. I really didn't care about anything though. I just wanted Scrap to stay by me.

Trevor and Bavari came back in from the garage, and Trevor was on the phone. It was my mom. She was worried because she saw what happened at the fair on the news. Trevor was going back and forth with her because she wanted him to bring me home. He told her that I was being well taken care of and that his friend's mother was a nurse as well.

Of course, he had to tell her about the gash on my head because there was no way of hiding it. That was why he ended up arguing with her about bringing me home. I talked to her to let her know that I was okay, and she just told me to let Trevor know to bring me home as soon as possible. Once I hung up with her, Trevor looked at Scrap.

"I'm trying my hardest to be cool with this shit," he told him, shaking his head. Scrap didn't say anything; he just glared at him. "We gon' have to stay here tonight, loc. I can't take her home like this," he told Brandon. Brandon nodded his head. "But she stays in here," Trevor said, looking back at Scrap.

Scrap smacked his lips. "I ain't worried about that shit," he responded.

Trevor nodded his head. "Just making sure we have an understanding since we don't on nothin' else," he said.

"Man, I'm gettin' tired of you gettin' at me, cuz! If you wanna *go*, nigga, then run that shit!" Scrap snapped, squaring up with my brother again. He was fed up at this point. Leonard and SixPacc instantly stepped between them.

"Niiiigggas! Chill! Relax! Be happy that y'all still breathin', because yo ass could be dead over a bitch right now, loc!" Leonard spoke, pushing Scrap back. Scrap didn't say anything. He just looked over Leonard's shoulder, glaring at Trevor. "Just worry about yo girl right now, cuz!" he finished.

Scrap's nose flared as he glared at Trevor for another moment and then shook his head. "I need a fuckin' blunt," he said.

"Then roll that shit up," Twinkie responded, and that was exactly what he did.

He sat below me and rolled a blunt up. He went on to his porch to smoke with Twinkie and SixPacc as Lia stayed with me a little longer.

"I didn't know that bitch was that crazy," Lia said.

I shook my head. "I swear, Lia . . . I was scared for my life and his life. I was sure that we were both dead," I told her.

She shook her head. "Well, I'm happy that you're okay.

You scared the fuck out of me!" she said.

I took a deep breath and exhaled, trying to get the gunshots and the dead bodies out of my head. "Where's Domion?" I asked her.

"The moment the cops pulled up and I realized none of you were around, I started calling you guys and nobody answered. I hit Boogie and he wouldn't really tell me anything, but I knew something was wrong when he said that you got hurt. So, I lied and just told Domion that I had an emergency and took an Uber over here. I knew I couldn't have him drop me off. Brandon would have been pissed!" she said, speaking in a low voice, shaking her head.

I honestly didn't know what she saw in Domion and how it was even going to work out. The nigga was a blood, and Lia's whole family were crips. Her mom was one of the most known gangsters in Long Beach as well. Her dad was killed when she was four years old so she didn't really know him, but he was known on the streets, too, and this was why I was confused on what she really saw in Domion and how this shit could go left quickly.

"I heard you were trying to be *Captain Save a Hoe* tonight," she joked as Scrap came back into the house. I slapped her on her shoulder, and she laughed. Scrap did as well. "Thank you . . . Trevor may not understand, but I see the change in you. And even though I know you may not want to hear it because Scrap likes being an asshole," she said sarcastically as she teased him. He smiled. "But you *are* different toward her, so, thank you for protecting her," she said, sincerely. He just nodded his head.

Trevor took Lia home, and when they left, Scrap looked at me.

I smiled. "You really did protect me," I said as I replayed the scene in my head and what I was telling Lia. It was just now hitting me that he really did care. Even beaten up and bruised, he was still trying to protect me.

"I don't know why you thought that I wouldn't," he said, nonchalantly rolling his eyes.

I shook my head. "You surprise me every day," I said.

He gave me a half smile. "Don't be taking all this *lovey-dovey-cupcake* shit to anotha' level because I'm still a gangsta," he told me smiling, trying to make me laugh.

I chuckled. "Just kiss me," I told him. He moved in and caressed my tongue with his own. When he stopped, he chuckled. "What?" I asked.

"Since I'm *Mr. Super-Hero* and shit, when we gon' get past this kissing stage? You know I'm still tryin' to taste it, right?" he said, trying to lighten up the mood.

I laughed because I knew his ass was just high as hell at this point. "We'll see," I told him.

"Yeah, we will! You keep forgettin' that you already mine! Lady Scrap, remember . . . *Nourris-moi!*"

"What?"

"Feed me."

I laughed and then slapped my hand on my forehead because it hurt even more when I laughed. I grunted.

"You aight?" he asked with concern, showing all over his face.

I sighed and nodded my head. "Can I go to sleep now?" I asked. Hours had already passed. I couldn't hold on any longer.

He nodded his head. "I'll keep checking on you," he promised. I closed my eyes and felt myself already drifting off to sleep.

That morning when I woke up, I was shocked to see where I was. I knew the room well, and as I tried to sit all the way up, I realized that I was the only one in the room. The door was wide open, and I could hear small voices talking down the hallway.

I was in Scrap's room, and I was lying in his bed. I smiled for a moment as I took in my surroundings, and then I felt the most painful headache I ever had. I slapped my hand on my head and felt the bandages that Nakeia had wrapped me in.

Last night was real. Lovely's crazy ass tried to kill me! I heard heavy footsteps coming down the hallway, and then Scrap appeared with a glass of water and a bottle of Tylenol.

"You're up," he said, smiling as he sat on the edge of the bed, handed me the water, poured two pills in his hand and handed that to me as well.

"How did I get in here?" I asked.

"We had a full house last night so yo brother allowed me to bring you in here as long as I kept the door open," he said, laughing.

"You carried me in here?" I asked.

"Yeah."

I smiled. "My first time spending the night with you and sleeping in the same bed, and I don't remember any of it." I shook my head.

He laughed. "It would have been better if Quarterback wasn't coming in here every five seconds, peeping us out."

I threw my hands over my face and shook my head in embarrassment. "No way!"

He nodded his head. "You lucky you told me that story on why he acts like that, because I would have been spazzed out on his weird ass," he said, smiling.

I laughed. "I wasn't snoring, was I?"

He laughed. "Naw."

"So, have y'all heard anything else about Lovely and everything that happened last night?"

"Naw, not yet."

I stared at him for a moment in dead silence. I was hesitating to ask my next question. "How is Bavari? You know . . . about the security guard that they were talking about on the news?" I asked.

He squinted his eyes at me. "Why you ask about Bavari?" he questioned, suspiciously.

I dropped my eyes. "When they were talking about it on the news, I saw you guys look at him."

His eyes softened, and he just did a quiet laugh to himself. "You kill me on how observant you are." There was a quick silence between us as he just stared at me for a moment and then he answered my question. "He good . . ." I knew it was hard for him to answer that question, but it felt good that he was finally trusting me.

"He isn't panicking or worrying or even feeling bad?" I asked. Scrap shook his head.

I shook mine as well, not understanding how they could take something so big and act like it was so small. I couldn't help myself. I felt a million questions coming along again.

"This life that you guys live, does it ever cause pain? Do you guys ever feel anything that y'all do?" I asked.

He stared at me for a moment and took a deep breath. "Of course, we do, but being in this shit, our main priority is protecting our loved ones and ourselves. We gotta be mindful of our surroundings, and we can never show weakness. The moment we do is the moment a nigga will use that shit to their advantage . . . We've been doing this, but it's not because we want to. It's because we have to survive. Yo brother was right. . . I shouldn't have brought you into this shit."

"You better not be breaking up with me, dude," I retorted, shaking my head.

He chuckled. "Naw, I'm not. I thought about it . . ." he admitted. My heart clinched as I waited for him to finish. "But I'm leaving this up to you now. I thought last night would have scared you off, but you still wanted me to be by you. That shit shocked the fuck out of me. I'm not gon' push you away again . . . Whenever you don't want to be a part of this shit no moe, just give me the word."

I sat there for a moment and thought. Yes, last night did *spook* me, and it was REAL! Who would have ever thought that Lovely was that fucking crazy? The bitch was *ill* than a mothafucka! I thought shit like that only happened in movies, but this was REAL!

And Scrap! He still had his whole life ahead of him. But he was raised into this game, and I knew that it was going to be hard to convince him to step out of it. I knew all of this because of the simple fact that the pistol to his head did not faze him. He was even taunting the man when his life could have ended at any moment. This was what he was used to.

I didn't know what it was. How could you be faced with so much shit at such a young age? Did he want to die? Was he truly just used to getting a gun pulled out on him? Or did life not scare him?

Whatever it was, I was too curious to find out, and I still saw him as this gorgeous-ass warrior angel that I just couldn't get enough of. There were a lot of things about him that I wasn't ready to walk away from.

Maybe I was just this naïve-ass little girl, but whatever I was, I just wasn't scared enough to walk away from him. I wanted more of him.

So, in my mind, at this moment, I wasn't going anywhere, and I was going to try to keep him for as long as I could have him. I was cherishing every second with him, because he was too good to be true to me.

So far, he was my first everything, and I was not ready to let go. I knew that I was in for some shit! Good, bad, even heartbreaking . . . but I wasn't ready to walk away.

I pray that he remains my fantasies and deepest desire and remains all that I've dreamed, because I didn't want anyone else. He was all that I wanted.

I stared into his green eyes and responded to his comment. "I think I can hang . . ."

He smiled. "Is that right?"

I nodded my head. "You'll protect me," I teased.

He laughed. "I will. Just remain who you are and don't switch up on me," he responded, with a slight smirk on his face.

"I won't."

He leaned in, softly placing his hand on the back of my neck and pulling me to him. He massaged his tongue with my own and then lay back on the bed, pulling me to him. I laid my head on his chest and started drifting back to sleep.

I loved everything about him, the good and the bad . . . What could be worse than what we already went through to make me walk away?

Big Brian

I sat in the chair at my kitchen table in my small apartment with a picture of me and my boys in front of me from twelve years ago. My cigar was lit in the ashtray next to me with a bottle of whiskey sitting on the table as well. Ice sat across from me, taking shots.

"So, what's the word on what happened to Vito?" I asked him.

He sucked his teeth. "Same shit with Huey it sounds like. They were in the shit together," he responded.

"And my boys took care of it," I finished.

He nodded his head. "You know they don't let shit like that slide. Them lil niggas are some real-life beasts when it comes to a nigga crossin' them."

I took a deep breath as I listened to him. "That's why you put them at the front of the line, right?" I questioned with this malice look on my face.

He looked me in my eyes for a moment and pressed his lips together. "I wasn't tryin' to make them into killas, *ill*. But them niggas was hungry and was willin' to do anything to get to the top. Don't put that shit on me. I took them under my wings when you left them," he responded.

"You know why I left!" I snapped.

"It still ain't no ma'fuckin' excuse, cuz! You don't know what them lil niggas been through after you left! You see how Taz responded to you! That's why you here now, right?" he barked back. "They did what they had to do to survive, and the only reason I'm here is because you've always been 'big bruh' to me! When I needed you the most, you came through! But the shit with yo own sons! I'm not gon' suga' coat shit with you like I fuckin' understand, because I don't! I don't give a fuck what happened between you and they mama! They didn't have shit to do with that!" he snapped.

I dropped my head as I stared at the picture. I shook it. "They had everything to do with it. It's not their fault, but they're in the middle of it . . ." I changed the subject, trying to take my mind off the past. "Wassup with these *Lil Hyenas* I keep hearing about on the streets? How are they affiliated with Shottas?"

He had a silent laugh. "Affiliated? Them lil niggas *are* Shottas," he corrected with emphasis.

"Lil Scrap runs that lil crew. Taz and Yaya put him in charge of them."

"Who are they?"

A sneakish-ass grin crept up on his face as he leaned forward so that I had his full attention. "They the young reapuhs . . . These are the lil niggas that ain't got shit to lose. No family, no nothin'. Crazy ass lil niggas that's choppin heads off for that dough. When shit starts gettin' shakie in the streets, yo boys pay them to handle it. Them lil ma'fuckas are lethal, and they only answer to the baby, and the baby reports back to his brothers."

A chill crept up on me as I listened to him and poured another shot.

As I sat there in silence, I thought about what had they become. I didn't raise them like this . . . But I left . . .

I shook my head and took a deep breath, changing the subject again. "I heard Dino still lookin' for me," I stated.

He chuckled. "That old-ass buff lookin'-ass nigga is a bitch! Yeah, he's still lookin' for you. Tellin' the same fuckin' story about how you played him before you disappeared! Taz been at war with that nigga for years now, takin' over his blocks, havin' shootouts with his whole hood! We dun had a couple of soldiers drop over they beef!"

"The fuck they beefin' for?"

"Territory . . . Them blocks that Gunna Mob tried to claim is where all the heat be. Taz had the Lil Hyenas run through them ma'fucka's and got shit crackin', takin' over! They got us so rocky with them Gunna Mob niggas that you can't even walk outside without that Banga on yo hip. It calmed down a lil bit, but once that nigga Dino find out that you been back in town, I know shit bout to start clappin'."

"And I clap back so I ain't even worried about that. I'm not leavin' until I make shit right with my boys." He nodded his head. "Last question . . ." I said, looking him in his eyes. "The lil girl that BomBom has been seeing?"

"Lady Scrap," he responded. I flinched. He nodded his head. "Yeah, he made lil ma official. You ain't the only one shocked."

"Does he know who that lil girl is?" I asked, feeling my heart clinch.

He shook his head and pressed his lips together. "Now how the fuck he gon' know that when they don't even know why you left?"

I was stuck with these wide eyes, and my mouth hung open trying to process it all.

To Be Continued . . .

"Now You See Me"

Book 2